Acknowledgement~

As implied in the title there are mar·
and so the critical advice of Fie
Rosemary Burch has been invaluable ⎯⌐e
masculine critiques of Adrian Timothy ⌐ion Gill
yet again typed from my dictation, Bai advised me on
legal niceties and Maarten van Kempen ᵤ ⌐ateau Fayolle Luzac
ensured my wine references were accurate. In addition I am indebted
to the late John Parker for insights from his particular view of the
world and to my wife Gwyneth for her patience.

Monday May 5th 2008. The London Clinic for Women and Children

It is not always easy to identify the moment when a flow of good fortune dries up and is replaced by a torrent of bad luck. Had he been able to get his head above the torrent and look back upon events, Lucien McCulloch would probably have chosen 8am on Monday 5th May 2008 .

It was a sunny morning after a rainy night, the streets still mirrored with puddles as he walked up Harley Street to the London Clinic for Women and Children. Seven thirty, a good hour to start the day, a straight forward day. Or at least as straight forward as it ever is for an obstetrician, a gynaecological surgeon, a senior member of his profession. He sprang purposefully up the stone steps of the entrance and paused as the perfectly polished glass doors slid gently apart.

"Good morning, Professor" said the receptionist.

"Good morning Professor McCulloch" said the nurse in the corridor.

"Good morning Professor" said the porter in the lift.

He emerged on the 5th floor of the clinic, a floor completely occupied by operating theatres neatly sequenced along the roof line of the clinic, their big glass windows invisible from the street and not spoiling the fine Portland stone facade of the building. On the wall opposite the lift a row of four clipboards, on one the first sheet announced:

Theatre 2, 8am - Mrs Noorah al Quadhafah - Room 541
Operation: Caesarian Section
Surgeon: Professor L McCulloch –
Anaesthetist: Dr. Gwyn Davies.

Lucian McCulloch slipped into the changing room and donned his blue theatre pyjamas, declined a cup of coffee and went through the door on the other side into the clean area of the theatre suite.

"Good morning Professor" the nurses chimed,

1

"Good morning Sister, good morning all, lovely day, all set up?"

"Yes sir, she is in the anaesthetic room" said the theatre technician.

Moments later the doors of the operating theatre were pushed apart announcing the opening scene of the familiar drama. The anaesthetist, Gwyn Davies, stood holding both doors open with his outstretched arms; Samson and the pillars of the temple. Sister, two nurses, a technician and incongruously a paediatrician stood arranged across the room on the opposite side of the operating table.

"Are you ready?" asked the anaesthetist, rhetorically "Patient is ready, baby is ready"

Behind the anaesthetist in the bright halogen glow of the anaesthetic room a woman lay neatly on the centre of the trolley, two drips and an oxygen mask. The swelling of her abdomen confirming the fact of her pregnancy.

Lucien McCulloch went to the stainless steel trough in the Scrub Up Room and began to scrub, carefully lathering his hands with a pink Chlorhexidine soap from the wall dispenser. Gwyn Davies, the anaesthetist came to the doorway,

"How's the blood pressure?" asked Lucien McCulloch

"Perfect …. As you would expect from one of my impeccable anaesthetics" Gwyn Davies replied, as Welsh as he could be. "Don't forget she's got an epidural in and minimal sedation so though to your inexpert eyes she may seem asleep, in fact, she might hear what you say - particularly if you call me a cocky Welsh bastard again as you did last week!"

All this with a big smile and then, lowering his voice, "And by the way Lucien why the hell did you take this woman in again? Don't you remember what happened last time? Eighteen months ago when she came for her last Caesar? Her husband threatened to kill me!"

Lucien looked up unsurprised.

"No" he said "If the operation went badly he would have killed you!" Lucien smiled at him consolingly, "And all went well, you are still alive and just to cheer you up it was me that had the e-mail yesterday saying 'If any harm comes to my wife or new son during the operation, I can assure you that things will go badly for you!' Not strictly a threat to kill but considering its provenance it could be!"

Lucien rinsed his hands in the warm water being careful to keep them up so any residual bacteria would drain back to his elbows. He took a sterile green towel and carefully dried his hands, starting at the fingertips and working down to the elbows.

"How is she anyway?" he asked Gwyn Davies who was still hovering at the doorway, occasionally glancing over his shoulder to check all was well in the operating theatre.

"Oh, she's fine, so it's over to you. It is nice to be dealing with a pre-eclamptic who is being delivered before things get out of hand. But I'm worried you know," Gwyn went on "I mean things could go wrong through no fault of mine and that man would be after me" The more agitated he became the more Welsh his normally well concealed accent became. Lucien smiled at him,

"I really don't think you need to worry. Anyway it is me that got the e-mail this time not you"

"Oh, you're OK, he wouldn't dare make trouble for a chap like you, senior obs and gynae man, on the college council, head of department at a top teaching hospital, famous round the world for your work on fertility, had your hand up the fannies of the wives of all the rich and influential blokes in the land, delivered their snotty little kids. Oh no boyo you're safe".

There he stopped, he tried never to say "boyo" but he had done it, reverted to his origins, he'd best shut-up. He went into the theatre and sat down at the patients head. Lucien held his arms up and let the nurse tie his gown, then went through into the operating theatre,

The theatre sister had already swabbed the patient's abdomen with iodine solution and now she and Lucien began carefully to apply the green towels, one covering the patient's upper third but raised at the head end to obscure the patients view of the operation whilst leaving the head clear for the anaesthetist, another the lower third stuck to the abdominal wall immediately above the pubic hair.

"Urine output OK?" Lucien asked the anaesthetist as if reminded by the sight of the catheter from the bladder emerging between the patient's thighs,

"Fine"

Then the two side towels leaving only the fulsome swell of the pregnant belly rising above the green surroundings.

"This lady" said Lucien addressing himself to the anxious looking student nurse hovering just behind the gowned up theatre sister "This lady is having a Caesarean Section to deliver her fourth child. It is not at term yet, it is only thirty-four weeks not forty, but mother has pre-eclampsia which is under control at present - you know what pre-eclampsia is?"

"Yes, Professor" replied the student nurse looking relieved to have been asked something she knew, "It is like when the blood pressure gets very high towards the end of pregnancy and like difficult to control".

"Well done," said Lucien encouragingly, "also proteinuria and sometimes problems with the liver and blood clotting. This lady has had pre-eclampsia with each of her pregnancies and each time a bit worse then before which is unusual, it usually gets milder with each pregnancy but it's unpredictable so as this is a particularly precious baby we don't want to put it at risk by letting it go to term"

"Why is this one particularly precious, aren't all babies precious?"

"Yes, but this is a boy"

"Oh!" said the student nurse uncertain what to make of this seemingly inappropriate observation.

"And the patient would like to be sterilised when the baby is safely out so as to avoid the dangers of further pregnancies".

"How are you going to do that?"

The Theatre sister flashed the nurse a disapprovingly look, the student was supposed to be observing not chattering to the surgeon. Lucien did not mind, he always enjoyed teaching inquisitive students and more often than not these days it was the student nurses who had the most questions rather than the medical students.

"We will simply put two ligatures around each fallopian tube close to the uterus and remove a small section of the tube between them. That is about 90% guaranteed to prevent further pregnancies"?

As he was speaking Lucien had silently held his hand out for the scalpel and with complete certainty made a gentle curving incision across the lower abdomen just above the one from the previous caesarean.

"Retractor please, scissors, diathermy, artery clip, and again, two Langenbecks please, would you please retract there sister, thank you" glancing over his half- moon spectacles at the theatre sister.

Very quickly the russet coloured uterus had been exposed.

"Now" said Lucien talking as much to himself as anyone else, "We want to make an incision across the lower part of the womb, not too big, just the right size to deliver this little chap through - ready Sarah?" he said to the paediatrician waiting to receive the baby.

"Yep".

Lucien cut across the muscle of the womb, surprisingly thin at this stage of pregnancy.

"Gentle suction there please sister" as a gush of amniotic fluid poured out and then magically black curly hair and then the head of a baby appeared in the incision. Then the closed and wrinkled eyelids, then a snubbed nose, then an open mouth, then tiny hands grasping at the air. "Suck out please" said Lucien easing the baby out of the opened womb. "Cord clip please, two clamps for the cord, scissors and bingo here you are Sarah" wrapping the baby in a towel and passing him to the paediatrician who had barely put him into the warm blankets of the incubator before the first reassuring wail of protest; angry at the world from the very first. The student nurse for whom this was a first exposure to the drama clapped and jumped up and down. Everybody smiled, Lucien clamped and tied the two fallopian tubes.

"There you are Gwyn, tubes ties so no further death threats we trust; you can let her wake up now and we will show her the baby - and make sure she sees his willy so she knows it is a boy" he said with a chuckle.

"Mohammed I believe he is to be called, Mohammed ibn Gamal al Ghanem.. Now let's put everything back together again."

A mere twenty minutes had elapsed since the patient had entered the operating theatre. It took another thirty minutes effectively to close the opening in the womb, accurately to put together the layers of the abdominal wall and then, most importantly, to close the skin incision so neatly that within a week the wound would resemble just another fold in Noorah al Quadhafah's abdomen, now much flatter but still revealing the plumpness that her position in life required.

As he finished Gwyn Davies put his finger to his lips gesturing to Lucien that the patient's sedation was wearing off and that she was now fully awake, then patting the patient's cheek gently he said

"Wakey, wakey Noorah, time at admire your handsome baby boy."

A smile of relief spread over her face. Lucian took her hand.

"We'll get you into Recovery and you can have young Mohammed beside you on the bed for a while"

"*Alhamdulillah!* Thank you, *shukran*, did you do the other operation?" she asked.

"I did"

"Thank you, thank you, please tell nobody like we agreed"

"Yes, I'll remember. I am going to contact your husband now about the birth, but I will mention nothing else"

Lucien was relieved that all he had to do was send Gamal Ghanem an e-mail. He always felt disconcerted when the father was in the operating theatre during caesarean sections but enjoyed sharing their excitement if they had not fainted and been ushered out! He liked phoning the fathers who weren't able or willing to be present but in Gamal Ghanem he drew the line, the man was odious, unnecessarily aggressive, a thug in a suit. An e-mail would be perfect.

E-mail from Lucien McCulloch to Gamal Ghanem: "*I am happy to be able to tell you that your son, Mohammed, was born at 8.20am this morning. Mother and baby are well*".

Monday morning May 5th . Tripoli, Libya

In Tripoli, 1500 miles to the south of Harley Street, Gamal al Ghanem. Minister of Trade and Commerce, Member of the General Peoples Committee of the Great Socialist People's Libyan Arab Jamaharia, close ally of President Muammar Gaddafi, stood at the window of his office looking out across the scrawny palm trees lining the Shat al Fatih to the almost empty harbour and the glittering waters of the Mediterranean beyond. He was not thinking of his wife so far away in London or the dangers of her pregnancy, instead he was reflecting on the sparseness of the ships; he could see only one unloading at the jetty. He was irritated by how little had been achieved in getting Libya back to the status a normal Mediterranean country, possible in theory since the slow improvement in relations with Europe. The objective of more commence was after all his to achieve. As head of the Ministry of Trade and Commence, there were many trade deals to be done and thereby much profit to be made for himself. Not for nothing had he become the head of this ministry. His family connections, the powerful relatives of his wife, his polished manners, impeccable English and a diploma from The London School of Economics made him the best, indeed in straightened times, the only candidate worth having. There were plenty of opportunities, all he had to do was get the deals arranged and trade would flow…. and he had to stay alive. He remembered the old saying "You must stroke the head you cannot cut off" and there were many heads he needed to stroke for he had made many enemies along the way, sometimes he thought the only person he could trust was his older brother Zahir, but Zahir he knew was as ambitious and ruthless as he was himself so it was only family that bound them and Gamal's was wary never to be in a position where Zahir's interests conflicted with his own. He lit another cigarette. And his wife? She was as responsible as anyone for his position. Fortunately, she was about to do the right thing at last and about now would be delivered of a son. The first of several he hoped. At thirty-five she was not too old for that. He was fond of his daughters of course, but they were not sons. To have more sons perhaps he ought to have sex with her more often. He had not married her for love or for sex but it was not

7

an unpleasant thought. She was comfortable, receptive and as far as he could judge loving but not at all like Maria, reminding himself with quickening pleasure of her small lissome body squatting above him, her long black hair sticking to the sweat on her back, her nipples hard under his hands. She may be just one of his Philippina maids but well worth the extra 100 Dinars a week he paid her; and with none of the complications that might arise from screwing a Libyan woman. He had enough problems already from fellow Libyans without adding to them. Thoughts of his Philippina maid hand got him going; he went out of his office and Alesha, his secretary, looked up from behind her glasses.

"I'm going home for a few hours" he said.

"But what about your meeting?"

"Rearrange it" he said curtly "Tell Ali to bring the car to the door."

"There is an e-mail for you from London."

"It can wait."

Monday May 5th, London

After Lucian had sent the e-mail to Tripoli and seen Noorah al Quadhafah and her baby safely onto the ward he phoned his daughter. It was a sunny morning, he had an hour free, could he come and see her? Lucien did not have far to go, just the familiar amble down the sunny side of Harley Street, dodge the shoppers meandering along Oxford Street and cross into South Molton Street. Lucy McCulloch managed a shop in that appendage to Bond Street, selling art jewellery. Expensive, sometime quirky, single items by big names - not the sort of place where you just drop by for something to match a new dress; more likely that you would have been contacted by Lucy provocatively to inform you that the newest creation by whoever was now in the shop, only a single example and would you be interested? Of course you would so it was you not someone else seen by the cognoscenti in the latest creation.

Lucy's shop was one of the line of small and very exclusive shops that line South Molton Street, a very different ambience from the department stores of Oxford Street just a few paces away. Lucien pressed the discrete button beside the door and was let in. Lucy, all smiles, kissed him on both cheeks French-style. She looks radiant thought Lucien, as always almost incomprehensibly overjoyed to see his daughter. Jeans, chic high heeled shoes and a full sleeved silk blouse covering those ill-advised tattoos on her arms. Her hair once spikey and disordered, now cut short but impeccably and expensively shaped into a boyish bob. To Lucien, Lucy was, as ever, a vision of salvation: the proof that beyond the miserable phase of drugs, tattoos, inappropriate partners, violence and despair lay a happy and worthwhile life. Lucy's renaissance began when her brother was killed. It all seemed so very recent but in real time it was five years ago. Lucien had eventually emerged from that darkness to cherish even more the two women in his life, his daughter Lucy and his wife Diana.

"Show me what's new in the shop" he said to Lucy "Not that I can afford any of it but I enjoy looking". He liked to share the warmth of Lucy's enthusiasm as she unlocked the little glass cabinets on pedestals and took out beautifully crafted necklaces, pendants, huge and impractical rings and finally a pair of ear-rings fashioned from red feathers. "They look very fragile, won't last long" said Lucien. Lucy smiled.

"That's sometimes the point - the people the wearer wants to impress will know that they are expensive and unique and their transience implies that the wearer is more responsive to their beauty than to any long term value."

"Sounds like a good sales pitch" said Lucien wondering whether to offer to buy Lucy one of the trinkets but none had a price on it and he remembered the old adage that if you needed to ask the price you could not afford it. Anyway Lucy looked great in her own choice of jewellery.

"Will your mother and I see you this weekend?" asked Lucien always eager to enjoy a meal with Lucy and her mother together.

"Not sure yet, I will let you know. Anyway I believe Mum is planning to go to Saint Jean for a week."

"I did not know that" said Lucien.

Diana, his wife, was recently, he reflected, very keen on flitting off to their house in France at short notice. Her job as a part time teacher allowed it. He wished he had as much freedom but his over-full diary rarely permitted it. Either he was spending a week examining would be consultants for the MRCOG, or was at a conference somewhere, or he was on-call for his own hospital, or simply unable to wriggle out of a council meeting at the College or one of the endless committees that he had been persuaded to chair. He envied Diana her freedom though in the last few years it had seemed more like restlessness than freedom. She affected to envy his life at the top of his profession but she was not very convincing in that. And now on the same treadmill he needed to be back at the hospital for his outpatient clinic at 1.30 pm (prompt). It was supposed to have no more than 10 old and 15 new patients booked, but he knew that as ever there would be more; he would get caught up in their stories and anxieties and as usual it would over-run and he would be home late.

There was never a problem finding a taxi in Bond Street, they hung around hoping for a big tipping celeb just out of Cartier or Asprey's.

"The Royal United Hospital, please."

The taxi driver knew well enough where to go to find the NHS' new model hospital built on the site of the old military hospital beside the Tate Gallery. The sun was still shining as he arrived, reflecting off the river and lighting up the bright spring foliage on the plane trees along the Embankment. "Beautiful" thought Lucien. The sun in London always gets noticed, in France it was simply an habitual companion. The sun showed up the new hospital at its best; a six storey building built of glass and soft russet coloured brick to incorporate and flatter the old Military Hospital buildings. None of the architectural arrogance of exposed pipework or glass lifts clutching at the exterior, just good proportions and a careful attention to the details. Inside though it was still a hospital indistinguishable from any other, full of bustling staff in brightly coloured uniforms mingling with anxious patients struggling to find their way about this incongruous and unfamiliar health machine. Lucien went up to the fourth floor in one of the huge lifts filled with half a dozen people and a bemused patient in a bed explaining to all around that she could perfectly well walk but had be told that she had to go to and from the X-ray department in her bed. Lucien patted her arm and reassured her that it was probably no reflection on her health, simply compliance with some printed set of rules.

"Morning Prof." perked Dolly the receptionist in the Department of Women's Health as Lucien strode in.

"Good morning ladies" as he strode towards the office door, ever open, to signify his accessibility to the staff, or that's what the person at the management course had averred. Pam his PA was on the phone at her desk strategically placed to ensure that accessibility was a carefully regulated commodity. As he approached she held up her hand as traffic policeman would whilst continuing to talk on the phone.

"Could you hold on a moment please" she put her hand over the mouthpiece and looked up at Lucien, "It's the Daily Mail, they want to talk to you about the paper in the BMJ. Do you want to take it or are you unavailable ?"

"OK, I'll take it - they'll keep calling back if I don't."

He went into his office and picked up the extension.

"Hello Lucien McCulloch here, can I help?"

11

"I hope so" said a strident voice at the other end.

"Marjorie Paskin here, Daily Mail. I want to talk to you about the article in this week's British Medical Journal, the one on fertility."

"Yes, of course" said Lucien "You appreciate it was written by two of my colleagues not by me?"

"But your name is on the paper, you're the senior author and the head of the department?"

"I am, yes."

There was an aggressive, confrontational note to her voice which warned Lucien that it might have been better to avoid the call. He sighed. He was used to journalists trying to make a story out of the blandest of information. The paper in the BMJ merely charted the relentless diminution in fertility that affected women progressively after the age of thirty.

"Don't you think it was a bit crass to say that women over thirty should abandon their careers to stay at home and have children?"

"That is not what was said in the paper."

"It's what it implies."

"I really don't think so" said Lucien trying not to show his irritation "the paper merely chartered the fall in fertility that occurs year on year after the age of thirty and tried to put it in a social context. We stressed the importance of women understanding the if they delay childbearing to further their careers they might not subsequently be able to become pregnant."

"But why did you not point out that IVF or egg saving would still allow pregnancy?"

"If you had read the paper you would see that we did make that point but noted that even then a woman's chance of successful pregnancy falls progressively and significantly each year from the age of thirty regardless of what fertility aids she uses."

"Maybe so but the whole tone of your article is anti-feminist and unhelpful; you male gynaecologists are all the same just misogynists at heart."

Lucien was getting riled but trying not to show it.

"I am not sure whether you noticed but the other two authors were women, consultant obstetricians, it was they who wrote the text of the paper."

"Well they should be ashamed of themselves, it makes for an even more important story if women gynaecologists are also women haters."

"Don't be ridiculous" retorted Lucien now openly riled.

"No, Mr. McCulloch it is you that is going to look ridiculous" retorted the journalist and she hung up.

"Oh Hell!" though Lucien and rang through to Pam. "Would you get in touch with Lesley Keefe and Terri Mason please and set up a meeting for the three of us. I know they are busy today but may be they could come at 6 o'clock and tell them it is important."

Another problem, another late finish, he thought and phoned home to say he would be late. As usual, the ten unanswered trills and then his own voice coming back at him from the answering machine. He left a message.

Tuesday May 6th. Royal United Hospital, London,

The next morning Lucien did not seek out a copy of the Daily Mail. The previous evening he had reassured himself that his two colleagues who had written the paper were well aware of the attitude of the journalist who'd phoned.

"Oh, that will be FeMail" said Lesley Keefe to Terri Mason "they love gynae stories" and having heard that they were comfortable with what they had written he put the matter out of his mind.

Halfway through his morning clinic the phone on his desk rang.

"Excuse me" he said to the patient who was half way through her history "I am very sorry this is not supposed to happen."

"Is that Professor McCulloch? This is Samantha, Director of PR, I need to talk to you now about what is in the Daily Mail."

"I'm afraid I am with a patient in the middle of a clinic."

"Get someone else to do it."

"That's not appropriate" said Lucien "I can see you at about midday between the clinic and my operating list."

"OK, come to my office" and she hung up.

Lucien had not met Samantha Grey the new Director of Public Relations, she had been brought in by the new CEO when he was appointed. The previous PR director was unceremoniously sacked, 'out-placed', to make way for her. Her predecessor was a charming, well-spoken middle-aged woman who faultlessly oiled the relationships between the media and the hospital. Her diary seemed to contain the phone numbers and e-mail addresses of every health correspondent in the land but having once met the new CEO she raised no objections to leaving .

By one o'clock Lucien had finished his clinic.

"No lunch again" he muttered to himself "good for the figure" as he trod the thickly carpeted, newly decorated, corridors to the Director of Public Relations' office. The door was ajar so he went in. She was on the phone but on seeing him waved him out imperiously to stand in the corridor like a naughty schoolchild.

"You can come in now" she announced a few minutes later.

"What the hell is going on in your department that the Daily Mail can run this story?"

"May I sit down" said Lucien bemused the sight of this harpy in giant red framed tinted specs, high heels and a skirt so short that it barely reached mid-thigh.

"This article in The Mail is about how misogynous and anti-feminist obstetricians and gynaecologists are, particularly at this hospital! What the hell is going on?"

Lucien tried to explain that the journalist appeared to have conjured an emotive article about women's doctors from an innocuous article about fertility.

"Have you read the article in the BMJ?" enquired Lucien.

"Of course not" she retorted "that's not my job, my job is to ensure that this hospital is seen in the best possible light - why was the article written by three male consultants, you and this Leslie and this Terry? Haven't we any women in these posts?"

Lucien tried not to smile.

"Lesley, LESLEY and Terri, TERRI, Teresa are women and they wrote the article."

"Well they should know better. I have discussed it with the CEO. In future I want to see all articles from your department before they are submitted for publication in case they need altering."

Lucien looked at her calmly and was silent for a moment.

"I don't think that would be possible. Articles, as you call them, papers as we call them are almost invariably based on scientific research and/or clinical observation; the only connection they have with this institution is that they are written by people who work here. It would be completely outwith normal practice even to consider allowing the PR Department to edit them."

"We shall see about that" she retorted "the CEO is adamant that this hospital needs to be portrayed in a positive way as a successful, cutting edge leader and will do whatever it takes to achieve that."

"I doubt if there would be an objection to you seeing papers after they have been accepted, but before publication. If you impose that rule on the whole hospital that will be a thousand or so for you to deal with each year. I will send you one that we had accepted yesterday. I am sure you will enjoy reading it, its title is *"IL-15 and IFN regulatory modulation of uterine NK cell subsets in murine pregnancy"*. And with that smiling graciously, but inside seething with anger, he left.

No sooner was Lucien back in his office than the phone rang again.

"It's Samantha Grey, PR" announced Pam wearily.

"And I need a new CV from you" said Samantha Grey, she clearly wasn't one for preliminary courtesies.

"I think you'll find you have one on file."

"Yep, I have been looking at it, it's too long and too staid; we need something a bit crisper and more positive. Did they not teach you how to do it on one of the management courses you were sent on? By this evening please in case I need it to help me with this Daily Mail business."

He had barely put the phone down because the ever efficient Pam was at the door holding a file.

"Your current CV" she said "fourteen pages, Samantha Grey wants one side only, if you just dictate one I'll make sure she gets it today."

Lucien took up a pencil and wrote :

CURRICULUM VITAE
LUCIEN JAMES McCULLOCH.   CBE, MA, MB, BChir, PhD, FRCOG

DOB:6.12.1945
Nationality :British
Civil Status: Married, two children (one deceased)
> *Education: Wellington College, - St Catherine's College, Cambridge. - St. Mary's Hospital Medical School,*
> *Current Position: Consultant Obstetrician and Gynaecologist and Professor of Fertility Research at The Royal United Hospital, Millbank, London SW1. Appointed: June 1982.*

Other Roles:
> *Council Member, Royal College of Obstetricians and Gynaecologists*
> *Joint Editor British Journal of Obstetrics and Gynaecology*
> *Examiner: MRCOG Part II*
> *Chairman: National Enquiry into School Age Pregnancy*

Crisp at least, one side only. But he noted how little a CV actually said about Lucien McCulloch the man. The effect on him of his father dying in the jungles of Malaysia when he, Lucien, was just ten and away at boarding school; the speed with which his distant French mother found another man to support her; the constant house moves; how he came to rely on the ordered life of a boarding school pupil to give structure to his life.

His CV said something about what he had done but nothing about what he would like to have done - join the Army, become an artist, play rugby for England or come to that for France. It mentioned one child "deceased" though he was not quite sure why he put that in - part of the habit of never forgetting. Never forgetting his handsome son who did indeed join the Army, not the RAMC like the grandfather, but the fighting army. Never forgetting his death at the age of thirty blown apart by a road side bomb in Iraq. "*The family have been informed*". Never forgetting the newspaper photo of a smiling, dust flecked, suntanned faced under a lopsided helmet. "*Major Robin McCulloch is the most senior officer to die in the current conflict*". A Major but still a boy really, just beginning life, lost for what? Given up to advance the misinformed imaginings of George W. Bush and the sycophancy of Blair - all for nothing though he loved his life and Lucien knew that even if Robin had known years in advance of that deadly package hidden in a culvert by a dusty desert road, he would not have had his life differently. So it was left to Lucien to feel the guilt simmering in the background of his own life, the knowledge that Robin was somehow fulfilling his own dream of an army life. A life of daring and excitement that had evaded Lucien.

Saturday May 10th. Dulwich, Lunch with Lucy

Often when Lucy came to Dulwich for lunch she would bring a friend to protect against the conversation becoming about the past and Robin, but this week with Diana away it was just her in a polka-dot dress promptly at the door at midday with flowers and a bottle of good Chablis. Even though it was only the two of them they observed the formalities that since childhood had made family meals so important. Lucien sat at the head of the table and Lucy to his right at the side. They were in the kitchen, it was always the kitchen with its reminders of childhood and Lucy's cork-board on the wall by the 'fridge where she kept the postcards from friends. Also the picture of Robin in battledress and the one of her with him as children and the one of Lucien and Diana on holiday in France and usually a picture of her current boyfriend with the name on it so he'd be recognized if her came to the door asking for her. There was no boyfriend picture at present. Lucy was also the source of the fridge magnets with their little nuggets of wisdom; *"Mother knows best", "Wine. How posh people get shitfaced", "You never lose by loving, you always lose by holding back."*

"I've done salmon en croute for you assuming you're still a pescatarian" announced Lucien from the oven.

"You're sweet daddy, I'd love that but next time we can have meat if you and Mum would prefer. Being a pescatarian was a just a stage between vegetarianism and eating normally. I'm glad to be back eating proper food; I used to hate the way French waiters treated me when I said I was a vegetarian. You'll remember that time when I asked for the vegetarian option and the waiter simply came back with some tongs and took the meat off my plate and put it on Robin's? I'm sorry Mummy's not here, being with the two of you together is very important to me and I don't see you enough, Mum always seems to be out in the daytime these days if I phone."

"She likes to keep busy."

"You're still alright together are you?"

"Of course we are, but even after forty years we still need to retain our own lives. If we're not together all the time it doesn't mean there's a problem."

"I wish I had a relationship as good as yours." Lucy paused "Can I ask you something personal Dad? It's not something I could ask you if Mum was here."

"How personal?"

"Why did you marry Mum?"

"Because I loved her."

"That's too simplistic, can't you be more specific?"

"Why are you asking?"

"Well I've believed I've been love with various blokes over the years all of whom turned out to be shits. A bit of guidance as to what to look for next time would help. You've been married to Mum for over forty years, you must know why you've stayed together or it is just a habit!"

"No, but what keeps people together after forty years is different from what got them together at the start. Now it's shared memories, trust, being comfortable together."

"And when you first met what was it then? Was it sex? I think that's what I liked most in blokes but it always turned sour and I'd hitch up with another one just to forget the one before. It went wrong so often that I even wondered if in fact I was gay and didn't realize it."

"Poor Lucy. For us it wasn't just sexual attraction; there was that of course, but there was much more and it's difficult to say exactly what. I guess there's always an incomprehensible part – magic, like music – if you're a musical ignoramus like me you can still be bowled over by a bit of music and not know why."

"Not the sex then?"

"No Lucy, not the sex!"

"OK Dad, come on. If it's not just sex appeal I'm to look out for how am I going to tell when the right bloke arrives. Obviously he needs to be handsome, clean , smart, funny but what else should I look for? I'm not really any good at running the business of my life."

"I really can't tell you except that when he does you'll simply want to be together all the time and I can't say why that is, pheromones, perhaps. If it's right you'll feel somehow incomplete when you're apart."

"Is that all there is to love?"

"I don't know, I suppose it is; it's difficult to describe without using 'squidgyisms' ."

"Squidgyisms?"

"You know, the sort of stuff they put in romantic novels, Mills & Boon, Barbara Cartland, loopy, love-struck stuff."

"C'mon Dad, try!"

"Oh really Lucy, OK, *wholeness*. With the right person there's a sense of wholeness, completeness – how's that?"

"You haven't ever thought this through before have you Dad?" said Lucy reaching across the table to tweak her father's ear lobe.

"No, I've not felt the need."

"What you've described sounds a bit staid, just comfortable companionship, what about the passion?"

"Lucy this is where we started. You said it was passion, by which I assume you mean sexual passion, irrational, mad, which got you the wrong men. Passion can be dangerous." By which point the topic seemed to have run its course and he got up to make some coffee for them.

"I am going to church on Sunday" said Lucy brightly, aware of the need for a different topic.

"You're what?"

"I'm going to church on Sunday"

"Why ?"

"Just want to, might be fun."

"I'm not sure it's about fun."

"Okay, then maybe it will make me a better person, will you come with me?"

"Well when I was younger I might have but since Robin was killed I think I've probably lost any modicum of faith that I might ever have had. I don't think now I really believe in any of that stuff, certainly not enough to lead me into church."

"But you must have some sort of belief Dad?"

"I have yes, just not in God as the power behind everything, controlling everything."

"You've got to believe in something?"

"Yes, I believe in order, the rules, the importance of sticking to the rules even if you don't feel like it and I prefer a proper set of rules which I suppose is Christian ethics and the social do's and don'ts that come from them. They don't cause harm and they don't hurt anyone."

"You do Dad, you hurt people, you operate on them"

"That doesn't count."

"But there must have been times you wanted to break the rules."

"Yes I did as a teenager, as a young man that's expected. Anyway someone has to break the rules otherwise they'll fall into disuse. But the older I got the more guilty I'd feel if I did break them."

"So sticking to the rules is just you being selfish" Lucy added mischievously "it's just a way of stopping yourself feeling bad. Since you don't believe in God you don't believe in sticking to the rules so as to be rewarded by life after death or believe that by breaking them you'll be punished by going to Hell, that sort of thing?"

"This conversation is becoming a little too theological for me" said Lucien.

Lucy wasn't giving up that easily.

"Okay, tell me when you've wanted to break the rules, give me some for instances then, that's not theological."

"Well to be honest sometimes when I see a beautiful woman or an empty straight road that has technically got a speed limit."

"The woman?"

"No I never did before you ask."

"The straight road?"

"Okay, yes, just a bit occasionally."

"So you do break the rules!"

"Yes, I suppose so; but not so it would hurt anyone."

"Unless a child ran into the road! The trouble is Dad is that you've led too safe a life, never pushed yourself or been pushed close to the edge."

"What do you mean?"

"Experiences, Dad, big ones, dangerous ones."

"Such as?"

"Being attacked, being raped, hallucinating your own death on drugs, sleeping in the gutter, going hungry for days, being skint and lost in a strange city."

"I'm not sure they're the memories I'd cherish, they're not improving."

"Go on you must have done something outrageous or illegal sometime."

Lucien thought about it. His life as a student had had some exotic moments but none he was keen to discuss with his daughter.

"I got drunk and vomited into a grand piano once" he admitted.

"Cool Dad, not very gross but a good start, what else?"

Lucien remembered the aftermath of the trip that had involved downing a pint in every pub in King's Street, Cambridge. The headache, the nausea, the bill, the difficult interview with his tutor – no, bad behaviour wasn't his thing. It was more trouble that it was worth; as to it being improving, making him a better person he wasn't sure that he bought that concept either.

"Church tomorrow, maybe, so what are you up to this evening?"

"Clubbing Dad, same as ever on a Saturday night."

"I thought you gave all that up with the bad ways it got you into."

"I gave up the lifestyle Dad, not the music. I'm going to 'Fabric' in Smithfield, same place as I used to go. It was cool then but now it's full of pilled up kids and tourists. I'm going 'cos Laurent Garnier is DJ-ing tonight. Deep House, Detroit Techno, that sort of stuff." Lucien looked totally baffled "You don't know what I'm talking about do you Dad! I'd take you but I don't think you'd enjoy it. Anyway I'm going with my new fella and he couldn't cope if I were to appear with a Dad in tow!"

December 31St 1969. London. - Diana

Given the bad outcomes she'd experienced Lucy had no reason to think that a good start to a relationship might predict happiness so Lucien wondered why she'd been so intent on discovering what had first attracted him to Diana. In fact it was the violent end to a New Year's Eve party that had brought them together 42 years earlier. Lucien was then a senior house officer at St. Mary's and Diana was a teacher in a primary school; they had never met but were both invited to a noisy New Year's Eve party in a house near the Portobello Road; a stuccoed three storey Georgian house with Christmas lights still blinking on a tree in the front garden; nowadays chic and expensive but in 1968 quite decrepit though attractive to a bohemian mix of dropouts and young professionals. 'Bring a bottle and you'll be welcome, bring two and you'll be twice as welcome.' Inside the tables were strewn with the familiar, now despised, tipples of the time, Blue Nun, Black Castle, Hirondelle, Matteus Rosé. Butts of cigarettes and joints floated in spilt wine; slabs of cheese quarried into craggy hunks lay amongst torn roundels of French bread.

Lucien arrived without a partner. Diana was already there, a tall slim blonde in a mini-skirt, hair heaped up as a chignon giving her an extra four inches of height making her strikingly visible in the smoky crush. She'd come with her boyfriend, Declan, whose curly red mop and ruddy cheeks identified him as blatantly Irish. In a purple polo neck sweater and lurid green velvet trousers he looked, as someone unkindly remarked, like a souvenir you'd buy in Dublin airport. He liked the Irish tag and affected a lilting Kerry accent even though he'd be born in Battersea. Like Diana he was a primary school teacher but described himself as an author and poet; he considered himself in the true line from James Joyce and that included the drinking. Diana sometimes wondered why she was with him given her proper, home-counties upbringing with a horse in the paddock and a private school education. For a start he was a good three inches shorter than her even without her chignon, but she enjoyed his difference and he was funny. "The quickest way to get a girl into bed" Declan would declaim "is to make her laugh." It had worked on Diana and had kept on working for six months.

On this night as midnight approached Diana went from crowded room to crowded room looking for him. Not finding him she went upstairs scrabbling past couples sitting on the stairs. The bed in the first room upstairs was piled high with coats and scarves, the door of the second bedroom was half closed, pushing it open she found Declan sitting on the edge of the bed with his trousers round his ankles. Facing him squatting on his lap – impaled – was a rotund girl with purple hair and tattoos, her skirt and knickers on the floor, her breasts popping out from beneath the bra which, still fastened, had been pushed up. Declan was grasping her buttocks as she bounced up and down her hands on his shoulders, her cigarette almost igniting his hair.

"Declan what are you doing?" shouted Diana as if it wasn't obvious.

"Bringing in the New Year with a bang" retorted Declan his voice slurred.

"Do you want to join us?" quipped the girl taking a long drag from her cigarette whilst continuing to bounce.

Downstairs the host was calling everyone together, it was midnight. Diana stumbled down the stairs and went into the loo to conceal her tears and anger. She emerged five minutes later as the ragged strains of Auld Lang Syne died away and was standing in the hallway as Declan and the girl came down the stairs.

"You bastard" Diana shouted at him "That's it, I never want to see you again."

"Please yourself" said Declan pushing past her to rejoin the throng.

"And you can stop all this literary pretence you oaf. You can't write, you're rubbish in bed and your poetry's crap."

At which Declan turned, lurched towards her and punched her in the face. Diana screamed and Lucien who'd come to see what the shouting was about, grasped Declan from behind pinioning his arms.

"Let me go you fucker" shouted Declan freeing himself and turning to face Lucien "I'll do you too" and drew back his fist to hit him but Lucien with the longer reach and the school boxing medal at home, punched him hard in the solar plexus. Declan went down roaring, clutching himself. Everybody began shouting and some other men in the room started fighting between themselves for no particular reason.

Lucien stepped over Declan into the hall where Diana stood clutching her face.

"Are you OK?" he said putting an arm round her.

"Yes; I want to go home."

Behind them the hubbub of drunkenness and fighting was increasing.

"Me too" said Lucien "have your got a coat?"

"No, I came in a taxi."

"OK let's get out of here, I'll take you home, where do you live?"

Wrapping his jacket around Diana he helped her down the steps and hailed a cab. In the taxi he examined her face exploring it gently with his fingertips.

"Your eye looks OK and I don't think he's broken your zygoma but you're going to have an impressive black eye tomorrow."

Diana said "Are you a doctor?"

"A very junior one" admitted Lucien.

"Never mind – I'm a lucky girl."

When they reached Diana's flat she begged him to come in – she was shaking now and hugging herself as if to keep warm – she went into the bedroom and lay down. Lucien wasn't sure what to do next and sat on a chair near the door.

"Please would you lie down here with me, I feel frightened."

Lucien took his shoes off and lay next to her with his arm around her shoulders. She pulled the bedspread up over them and moved so her head was resting on his chest.

"Thank you."

Lucien lay awake for a long time wondering if the mad Irishman would come wanting to smash his way in. He wondered why he should suddenly feel so protective of this woman whom he'd never met, why he felt so irrationally content to be lying with her in a crook of his arm. Eventually he fell asleep.

The next day he took her to the hospital to be checked by his colleague in the Eye Department, that evening he took her out to dinner in her eye-patch, the next day her put her on the train to go back to convalesce with her parents in Dorset. Her father, a bulky red cheeked man in tweeds, was a Vet in practice just outside Dorchester; a "large animal practice" he was at pains to say; large animal vets being a cut above the cat, dog and hamster vets found in cities. Diana's mother, a practical, pride of the Parish sort of woman was sympathetic about the black eye and the wounded pride

"It's just the sort of thing I warned you about Diana. If you go and live in London these things are bound to happen sooner or later." She was however pleased that Diana seemed already to have a Doctor in view as her new boyfriend. Diana's mother harboured predictable prejudices about suitors and the thought that a doctor might be just as likely to get drunk and punch her daughter as any red headed Irishman would never have occurred to her.

A week later on an icy January day Lucien met Diana at Waterloo Station; she was wearing a fur jacket with a shawl collar and forever thereafter he would remember embracing her, one cheek against hers inhaling the unrecognized perfume of her neck, his other cheek caressed by the fur. After that they spent every spare hour together that could be arranged. They talked about the books they'd read, films they'd seen, places they'd visited. They went to concerts and art exhibitions but both were anxious that in conversation about what they'd done they might display some prejudice that would offend the other and put their new-found relationship at risk for they both, sensed that it felt different, more important, from any they'd had before. Each time they met they wondered whether it was as good as it felt, whether at any moment it might go wrong. Neither of them was sexually naïve but both sensed that much was at stake and so it was not until a month later that they first made love, cautiously and considerately in the same bed as they'd spent New Year's Eve. Lucien was so tense that he came far too soon; Diana, embarrassed for him, was more intent on reassurance than her own pleasure so they sat in bed together like an old married couple reading. In the middle of the night however, their inhibitions dulled by sleep they found each other and succeeded, as they observed over breakfast, "magnificently."

Diana lived in a flat that her parents had bought for her, their pretence being that it was acquired solely as an investment. It was a top floor flat in a tall Victorian terraced mansion in Kensington Gardens Square just north of the Bayswater Road. The flat was at the top of the house accessed by its own narrow stairway at the rear of the floor below; a stairway made secret by a cream painted door concealed in the panelling. The front windows of the flat had a view across the tops of the trees in the square on a level with the rooks and a squirrel's dray and high enough to receive the warming light of the setting sun. From the little hallway of the flat a ladder attached to the wall led up to a roof terrace just large enough for a café table and chairs, some potted plants and a bay tree planted in a dustbin. It's just a short walk from Kensington Gardens Square to St Mary's Hospital in Paddington but Lucien continued to share a flat with three other young doctors on the north side, the wrong side, of the rail tracks that lead into Paddington Station; a flat in a converted council block with an unappealing view of the elevated section of Westway where traffic entering central London slows to a disgruntled crawl.

The incentives to spend more and more time with Diana and at her flat were persuasive but he was careful not to impose himself and only stayed on Saturday nights and sometimes in the week if they had gone to bed in the early evening to make love; "enjoying their After Eights" they called it. After a few months of this, as Lucien made ready to leave one evening Diana said "Lucien this is silly, why don't you move in here, I'd like you to," but added that they would need first to visit her parents to get permission. At which Sunday lunch in their house at the end of a narrow Hampshire lane, after the roast beef had been cleared from the table and the plates put on the floor for the dogs to clean up, Diana's father put his elbows on the table and leaned across to Lucien.

"Look here Lucien, if my daughter wants you to live with her that's OK by us but why don't you just be done with it and get married eh? She's a good girl and a passable cook. I know she's a bit skinny but she's got a good set of hips on her, shouldn't have any trouble whelping!"

"Daddy! Really that's most unfair on Lucien."

"Not unfair at all" replied a bemused Lucien "but perhaps it would be better if Diana and I took it a bit more steadily, see how we get on together first."

"Please yourselves but we'll be doing the wedding so you'd better make sure it fits in with the foaling season down here or I might not be available to give her away."

Lucien already knew that he wanted to marry Diana but he didn't want a proposal to come too soon after this push from her parents so he waited until July 1st, exactly 6 months after they had met; though by then it had become obvious and inevitable.

Diana was an only child. Beyond the joshing and the veterinary allusions to her as a lamb, a foal, a calf she was uncritically adored by her father, an adoration that his brusqueness over lunch that day was designed to conceal. How could he cheerfully relinquish his daughter to another man, but in loving her how could he protest? Anyway Diana's mother had insisted that Lucien would be the perfect match.

It was easier for Diana. Her father was not being relinquished; he was and always would remain The Man in her life, the man pushing her pram on whom she imprinted, the man steadying her on her first pony, the man who'd taken a spotty teenage boyfriend by the jacket and thrown him out of the house for saying, when drunk after lunch, that Diana was " a nice bit of skirt who'd do him for now."

"Well Now just ended so bugger off and don't you dare go anywhere near my daughter ever again" her father had shouted after the boy's departing Lambretta. God how she loved her father for that.

And as the years went by she loved Lucien too but he was in reality, deep in her subconscious, just a boyfriend that she'd married and had children with. If a psychologist had taxed her she would have said that Lucien was in a different category from her father not simply a lower rung on one hierarchy. But even as her father aged and faded, the obscenities of Parkinson's Disease blunting to imperceptibility his gestures of love toward Diana – even then he remained the one true man in her life, ever present, ever enfolding which subliminally told her that it didn't matter what she did he'd always be there to love and forgive her.

1963- Cambridge. Felicity.

Why did he marry Diana? He wished he'd been able to give Lucy a tidy, persuasive answer and he hadn't except to say that it wasn't for sex. Actually that had sounded wrong; sex was partly the attraction obviously, Diana was beautiful and amorous. No it was just that for once he had been attracted by something other than looks or sexiness. Perhaps also he was ready for something else, something more mature, more lasting.

Like all men his teenage years had been dogged by the desperate need to copulate. At school it had come to no more than stroking the pictures of pinups taped to the back of his locker door and, of course, committing, like all the others, what the chaplain called "the monstrous sin of onanism." Once they'd found out from the big dictionary in the house library what he meant it became a source of jollity rather than remorse – the old perv. In the holidays at his mother's insistence he went to dance classes to learn the waltz, the quick-step and the cha-cha-cha, none of which led to anything more than hand holding and tight lipped kisses on the door step. By the time Lucien went up to Cambridge, his still unsatisfied sexual drive had been softened by layers of fluffy, expectations of Romance; that's Romance in the rose tinted sense of endless loving companionship. Life as an under-graduate in Cambridge was the perfect seedbed for those expectations. Expectations quickly shared with a girl called Felicity who by accident or design settled into the seat next to him at the first lecture of the first academic year. For an eighteen year old boy familiar only with the cloistered life of a boy's boarding school, the closeness of a pretty girl with long, lustrous hair, a flounced, floral skirt and a figure hugging cardigan offering her hand and agreeing to join him for coffee after the lecture was nothing short of miraculous. Felicity was the only child of a teacher and a nurse, she was wide eyed with the excitement of living away from her parent's home in Salisbury, but she didn't quite have enough self-confidence to do that on her own and knew that a nice boyfriend could share and perhaps dilute the stresses of a new environment. So within a week Felicity and Lucien were, in the parlance of the time, 'going steady', always together in lectures, to be seen walking hand in hand along The Backs or snuggled up together in the corner of the pub drinking schooners of sherry – then the fashionable drink. Their ever inquisitive class mates categorized them as 'in love' but realistically they were not. They were in love with youth, with the pleasures of undergraduate life, the walks through the meadows to Grantchester, lying on the grass listening to madrigals sung on the river on warm summer nights. They were in love with love. Sex beyond the kissing and nuzzling was something outside the frame of this picture of a student idyll. On the narrow bed of his college room, slightly drunk from too much sherry exploratory fumbles followed the same unsatisfying pattern; the sexual free for all of the sixties had not filtered through the closed curtains to undo their middle-class anxieties and courtesies. Felicity was programmed to protect her virginity, Lucien to respect her reticence so however strong their urges the 'heavy petting' never came to more than that. Their passions never got beyond the early pages of the manual in sexual technique that he'd brought in Heffer's bookshop hoping it might be their litany. The painfully turgid organ A. shown in the illustration on page fifteen never came to assuage itself in the moist and receptive cavity shown at B.

Overall for all the outward signs of lovey-ness Felicity remained more committed to her studies that to her relationship with Lucien and however much she said she'd loved/liked/admired/was friends with him preservation of her virginity remained the central and daunting feature of their relationship. In the third year of their time at Cambridge Lucien decided the relationship had run its course and fond as he was of her it was time to move on. It wasn't simply the aching failure to consummate their relationship it was the realization that whilst they had a good friendship, in truth that was all there was to it. At first he'd believed he was in love but now realized that it was simply the idea of love and it's trappings that had him in its thrall. They had simply become entrapped in this silken web they had spun.

Breaking up was awful, several weeks of goodbyes reneged upon "Is there someone else?" she'd ask.

"No-one" he'd honestly reply clutching her to him and wiping her tears away with the tip of his finger. "No-one, it's just that we won't be together for the rest of our lives and we both need to spend time with other people. We'll still be friends and maybe in the future, who knows, we'll get together again." He wasn't to know it of course but the same words were being uttered by boys and girls all over the world breaking up with their girl-friends and trying to soften the blow.

When Lucien and Felicity were undergraduates there were ten male students for every female so when he parted from Felicity other males who had been circling were quick to pounce. Felicity chose the tallest, the most handsome and the richest, a self-satisfied Etonian called Christopher who took her to smart places, bought champagne, overwhelmed her modesty with smooth talk and within a few weeks had, as he proudly told his drinking friends, "popped her cherry". Never ones to overlook a piece of gossip her classmates were quickly in the know and the embarrassed Reader in Physiology had to start one lecturer by rubbing from the blackboard the announcement "Felicity fucks!" Felicity herself was not there to be upset by this for she'd started skipping lectures and then tutorials and then she disappeared, gave up, went home. Lucien felt guilty. Lucien felt guilt far too easily, he felt guilty because, he reasoned, that maybe Felicity had blamed her break up from Lucien on her own sexual reluctance and had given it up quickly with the next man so as to be, as she perceived it, more like other girls. Lucien had no need to blame himself, Felicity's fall was simply because Christopher was practiced and persuasive and unscrupulous. Lucien needed none of these when shortly before the end of his final term the girlfriend of a friend asked Lucien to go with her to a party as his friend would not. Half way through the evening, in the dark corner of a cellar bar she told him she much preferred him to his friend and promptly took him back to her flat where without preliminaries, anxiety, shame or respite they shared the joys of sex until the sun came up on a new life. "Jesus" he said quietly to himself "all that angst blown away in an instant."

After a long summer of sex in the campsites of southern Europe Lucien returned to London to start his clinical studies at St. Mary's and the girl went back to Cambridge where she quickly found someone else to replace Lucien in her bed.

Lucien remained on good terms with Felicity after they separated, but after she dropped out of her course he had no more contact with her and depended on the unreliable speculation of classmates. He had her address in Salisbury and sent her cards for the first two Christmases but getting none in return, he stopped sending them. More than thirty years went by before he heard from her and then it was simply an e-mail sent to his hospital address: *"Hello Lucien. It's Felicity, you may remember me from Cambridge. I Googled you and found this address. I'm OK but I'd love to chat sometime and hear your news. I was sorry to hear about your son. Love F"* and a phone number. Lucien wasn't sure whether he wanted to phone. Felicity was part of his past and he was instinctively wary of looping back to revisit it. He had no worries that he might suddenly fall for Felicity again though he supposed that was a risk even if a remote one, just as it was a risk that belatedly she'd take him to task over their parting; but a mix of curiosity and courtesy got the better of him and a week later he phoned her from his office. Her voice was immediately recognizable, unchanged. She congratulated him on his achievements – said she regretted leaving Cambridge in her final year and not going on to become a doctor.

"I suppose you know why I dropped out?"

"I'd heard the gossip."

"What did it say?"

"That you'd got pregnant and decided to keep the baby; it was Christopher's I suppose."

"It couldn't have been yours could it Lucien! What a pig's ear we made of all that! If it had been yours you'd have stuck with me, not Christopher though he'd had what he wanted by then." Lucien didn't want to revisit all that. The bitterness of girls who discover too late that the stag with the largest antlers, the loudest roar and the biggest prick is not invariably a better partner than the quieter, more considerate one they turned down.

"Why didn't you go back after the baby was born? Didn't you want to?"

"Desperately, but I couldn't. David, my baby, was born very handicapped so I had to care for him full time even though I was back at home."

"I'm so sorry, how he is now?" There was a pause.

"He died six months ago, that's why I phoned really, I read about your son being killed and thought I might be able to help - you know- share."

"Oh Christ!" thought Lucien "What now?"

"That's very sweet of you" he said after a pause "but we're a strong family, that's my wife Diana, my daughter Lucy and me – I think we will get through it OK. But who's looking after you, are you still with your parents. God I'm sorry I forgot to ask, are you married?"

"No not married, it wouldn't have been fair on anyone to have taken us both on. I'm still at home with Mum. Dad left, then Mum had a stroke, so I'm destined for life as a carer – I'm quite good at it. Practice I suppose, but you don't want to hear all this. Look it was nice talking to you Lucien but you're probably busy. If you feel like meeting for lunch sometime just call, any time, Bye...."

And with that she was gone and he'd been pushed back into their past and couldn't help himself wondering how different things might have been for her. She sounded sad and tired. He wanted to help but he knew it could only lead to complications. Diana quite rightly would wonder what was going on and perhaps Felicity would indeed try to re-start their relationship; if she did, how would he know how his pity was to be distilled, might it be mistaken for love by one or both of them? No it was best to stay away. But he kept Felicity's number.

Friday May 16th –Meeting with the new CEO

It was barely a week after the Femail incident that a meeting of the Women's Services Directorate was called by the new CEO, an unusual step as it was normally thought sufficient for the top team in the directorate to meet once a week and additionally for Lucien, the Clinical Director, the manager he worked with and the Head of Nursing and Midwifery simply to attend a monthly meeting with the hospital's executive to report and to be told how things were going generally within the organization, to be told about new, so-called, initiatives and warned of financial shocks that might be on the way. It was a system where all parties pretty much respected each other and understood each other's roles. It worked well and the hospital had weathered the regular and usually unnecessary NHS reorganizations. However if rumour was to be believed the new CEO, Winston Arkwright, wanted changes, he wanted changes in everything though it was not clear why, but he was going from directorate to directorate having 'review meetings'; meetings that a colleague had told Lucien reminded him of those grainy newsreels of Mussolini shouting at the crowds from a balcony. Now it was the turn of Lucien's directorate 'Women's Services'.

The meeting was held in one of the cramped, mindlessly bland meeting rooms in the Administrative Wing. Lucien and his two colleagues sat on one side of the Formica table, the CEO on the other flanked by his Finance Director, the Director of Nursing, the Medical Director and Samantha the Director of Public Relations. What the hell was she doing here? With the exception of Henry Lightwood, the Medical Director, all the others had been brought by Winston Arkwright from his previous post.   Some agenda papers were arranged around the table face down like exam papers. Lucien noted that the CEO and his hench-people had cups of coffee but on Lucien's side of the table there was none and none was offered. Lucien was familiar enough with the ploys available in meetings to be instantly wary of how this meeting might proceed. No prior view of the agenda, no coffee, confrontational seating arrangements, it all added up.

"Good afternoon, I'm Lucien McCulloch Director of Women's Services" said Lucien "Shall I introduce my colleagues as we have not met three of you before."

"No need" said Winston Arkwright curtly "We'll get straight down to business."

"Before we start may I ask why the Director of Public Relations is here – hardly a normal part of a clinical planning meeting?"

"No you may not." Which told Lucien everything he needed to know – either the meeting was designed to lead to a laudatory press release or Samantha was simply there because the CEO wanted her company... his mistress perhaps, or so it was rumoured.

"I am aware that your Directorate satisfies all current requirements, has a good reputation and importantly is well within its budget but what I intend to achieve in this hospital is results better than government targets, better than anyone else's and at lower cost. Something the Minister can be proud of, something he can hold up to the media to show what a good job the NHS is doing particular in this their flagship hospital." He was standing up now his hands on the table leaning forwards "I tasked Henry Lightwood our Medical Director and Elizabeth Dickman our Head Nurse with identifying specific areas where these exceptional results will be delivered. They are listed on the paper in front of you."

The paper which had been provided listed five items:

- *A thirty percent reduction in the number of births by caesarean section.*
- *A doubling of the number of home births.*
- *Reduction by one third in the number of births and outpatient visits involving an obstetrician.*
- *Halving the time spent in hospital after delivery.*
- *All gynaecological surgical operations to occur within four weeks of the outpatient visit.*

"Our aim" said Winston Arkwright before anyone had a chance to speak "is to have better results in these five areas than any other hospital in the country, Samantha is poised to issue a press release to say that is about to happen. All my team now need to do is work with you to ensure these targets are met."

Lucien let his papers slip onto the floor and bending down to retrieve them he could see that under the table Samantha's hand was stroking Winston Arkwright's upper thigh, his upper inner thigh.

"We will, of course, look at this very carefully" responded Lucien sitting back into his chair, "we will need to do that with our clinicians and the midwifery team before any announcements are made to the press. They might otherwise prove embarrassing if something is promised that can't be achieved. I think you should know that there are factors specific to this hospital and the part of London that we serve that may make your targets unachievable."

Winston Arkwright was on his feet again

"Look I don't just want a recitation of your excuses, you bloody clinicians are all the same resisting change at any cost and saying it's all in the interests of the patients. I'll give you a month to sort this out and at the next meeting I want something constructive, OK. Right, meeting over."

Lucien noted with clinical sharpness the range of emotion on the Executive Team. Angry CEO, anxious Medical Director, patronizing smile from the Chief Nurse and just smugness from Samantha the Head of Public Relations.

"And the Medical Director will be keeping an eye on your Department to make sure there's no backsliding." Henry Lightwood smirked at Lucien triumphantly. "I want to see you in my office please Samantha" said the CEO as he left the room.

"I bet you do!" thought Lucien.

The full name of the new Chief Executive of The Royal United Hospital was Arthur Winston Arkwright but as he crawled up the corporate ladder he had left the Arthur behind, preferring the resonance of "Winston". Winston Arkwright was of middling height but seemed smaller. His hair, suspiciously free of grey for a forty-five year old, was carefully cut and lacquered into place to conceal his early baldness. He always wore a suit and a shirt with a cut-away Prince of Wales collar. His favourite shirts were those with broad blue stripes but with collar and cuffs in plain white, a habit of dressing acquired in the City of London for he'd not spent his whole life working in the NHS. He was now CEO of the RUH because he'd seemed the best of the small bunch of 'high fliers' served up by the head hunters. The unwritten request had been that they find someone who'd spend the bulk of their careers outside the NHS, someone from 'business'; the unspoken assumption being that such people would know better than anyone from inside how to run a large NHS organisation. Winston Arkwright's CV was quite impressive though only he knew that several of the items on it were either miscasting of the truth or out and out fabrications. As far as he was concerned nothing was to stand in his way to the goal of a salary of £300,000 or more and if a knighthood was also the reward for putting up with the inconveniences of the NHS then so much the better.

In his one previous NHS job he had exhibited an unquestioning adherence to government dictats, a superficial ability to charm and a streak of ruthlessness when it came to dominating the agenda that was just what was required to get him this new job. His domineering behaviour had for him the pleasurable corollary of allowing him to dictate to the professionals in the hospitals he'd overseen for what he really hated about the NHS was the doctors; he detested them mainly because he couldn't fire them and they tended to be better educated than him. Lucien knew that the new CEO disliked him though he was at a loss to understand this obvious antipathy; the man hardly knew him. An outsider, however, having inspected their life histories and watched them would have understood immediately what it was. It was Lucien's calm self-confidence, his education, the fact that most staff deferred to him in a respectful but friendly way, the reality that he represented an entrenched professional group and lastly his good looks and full head of hair. The new CEO resented not just Lucien but equally the other consultants and ranted at the near impossibility of achieving anything that they disapproved of. They were always playing their ace card "Oh, if you do that patients will be harmed or die!" Winston Arkwright assumed that this was never true though he hadn't sufficient knowledge to check. He was once heard to say to another manager during coffee at an 'away day' "actually I hate fucking lot of them and if I achieve nothing else in this job I am going to take them all down a peg". The dislike of Lucien and his colleagues was compounded by knowing that most times only they could persuade consultants to change and therefore he needed some of them on his side within the management set-up. That said there was no way he was going to work through a toff like Lucien!

At that time it was a requirement that all hospitals should have at least one Clinician and one nurse on the Executive. Usually The Medical Director and the Director of Nursing who in better times had been called 'Matron'. The Director of Nursing had long ceased to be the large and reassuring stickler for the details of uniform and care, regularly quizzing patients about the quality of nursing on the ward. Now she was just another senior manager, in this case lean, trousered and concerned primarily with nursing protocols, training and the obsessional completion of 'care plans', 'dependency assessments' and data returns. It was widely believed that her laudable intention that every nurse should be university graduate was in reality to supplement a feminist, 'nursist' agenda to do with hospital hierarchies rather than improved care. Winston Arkwright appreciated her stance and together with the Director of Finance and Samantha of Public Relations had brought her with him from the previous hospital which he'd overseen. The one now gratefully celebrating his departure to a London Teaching Hospital! The only home grown member of the core Executive team was Henry Lightwood a Pathologist bored by a life staring down a microscope and desperate for status. The son of a travelling Insurance salesman masquerading as a 'financial adviser' he'd exceeded all his parents' hopes by becoming a doctor and then by marrying a rich woman. Latterly he'd joined a Club where he could proprietorially entertain people to lunch and be recognized by the waiters and   now he'd joined the people at the Hospital's top table where he   was determined to be like them. He'd even begun to ape Winston Arkwright's mannerisms, standing up when making a point in committee and demanding rather than asking. His demand now was that Lucien and his team should assemble at 10am the following Wednesday to hear the detail of the CEOs plan. If clinics and operating lists had to be cancelled to free up the staff then just do it!

Wednesday 21St May. RUH, Directorate Meeting.

When Lucien had first entered his new office on the 4th floor of the recently opened RUH building on Millbank he was delighted. The office was on the corner of the building and looked two ways; across the river to the green and white ziggurat of the MI6 building – Lucien liked the boldness of its design. The other window looked along Millbank to the Tate gallery, Tate Britain as it now was. He had a clear view of the wide steps leading up to the portico, its classical design just as handsome as the MI6 building. How fortunate and privileged, though in fact it was simply a quirk of bureaucracy that allocated it to him on the basis of its number; room 437. This morning though as he stood looking out of the window it felt more like a prison designed to tantalise him. He could see couples sitting together on the steps of the Tate, a skateboarder, children buying ice cream from a van at the kerb. On the river a fire boat from the fire brigade HQ on the opposite side of the river was testing its pumps; in the sunshine a sprinkle of diamond drops disturbed a cormorant from his perch on a buoy. Lucien felt trapped and wished he could be out there in the summer weather instead of preparing to meet the senior doctors, midwives, and nurses from his directorate to decide what they might do about the CEO's demands. Lucien had been expecting to chair that meeting but now it seemed that Henry Lightwood the Medical Director would be in charge.

This plate glass cell felt as if it were the Pandora's Box of all his disaffections. He was dispirited not just by the demoralising effect of the new managerialism, it was more personal than that. He no longer got the same lift from caring for patients. There was a hideous sameness about the conversations with them, he was aware that his genuine desire to reassure, to explain, to encourage was slowly descending into platitudes. How many women had he reassured about their difficulties conceiving? Thousands. How many pregnancies had he helped women through? Thousands. And if the human pleasures were diminishing so were the intellectual ones. Research in his department now needed sparks from bright young men and women to get started and their vigour to get it completed. His only role was as the masthead 'senior author', the person who occasionally had to point out that a piece of planned research was not as original as it was being claimed. And worst of all being head of an academic department had become a burden, a frustration as he tried to keep the flow of money coming from bodies that were only interested in the number of publications and whether the journal in which they appeared had a high enough 'impact factor'. They didn't care about the quality of care or how well students were taught. Oh yes, he'd run his course all right, gone stale. Not unusual he knew that. Some surgeons lost their bottle, became too anxious about complications and couldn't go on. Cancer doctors "burned out". People found other roles from themselves on committees that met in far off cities or as examiners overseas or on lecture tours. Anything to try and perk up their flagging enthusiasm for being a doctor. The general public didn't know this, they just took your quietness for wisdom or concern. How fortunate to have Pam to push him to where he didn't wish to go. At which, on cue, she came into the office oblivious to the world outside.

"It's ten o'clock Professor, time for the meeting." Lucien shrugged as if to dispel his darkening mood. Pam handed him a clean white coat. Lucien, aware of most of the tricks that managers use in meetings, knew that wearing a white coat was one of the ploys he could use and so subliminal was its guarantees that even managers often deferred to it.

The directorate seminar room was an uninspiring windowless room, its polystyrene ceiling tiles already dirty, the walls ornamented only with posters for conferences long past and a cork board too small for the notices on it. On the back of each plastic chair a receptacle for the papers of the person in the chair behind, like church pews. The room was packed with his senior staff. Behind a table across the end of the room sat the Medical Director, the Director of Nursing and two other people that Lucien didn't recognise. Behind them, on the white board, the CEO's five targets had been written out. At the end of the table almost by the door a chair had been left for Lucien.

Henry Lightwood stood up. He too was wearing a white coat. "Cheeky" though Lucien "for a man who doesn't do any clinical work – and never did."

"Good morning everyone, thank you for coming to hear about this exciting new venture for the directorate." There were a couple of barely suppressed sniggers from the audience. "I am, as you know, the Medical Director; you will also know the Director of Nursing and I expect you will have come across your head boy Professor McCulloch." He paused expecting a laugh – none came. "Now I'd like you to meet our two colleagues from Dominant Consulting Inc. Perhaps they'd like to introduce themselves."

The first, a young man whose sole distinguishing features were very white teeth and a crew cut, stood up. He wore a white t-shirt, a black linen jacket and jeans. The uniform for his profession as it turned out.

"Hi, my name in Anton Dmochowski, I'm a senior analyst and associate vice-president in Dominant Consulting Inc. We are based in the US where we have a large portfolio of re-profiling projects in health delivery. We have been brought on board by your CEO to assist here. In preparation we have drilled down into the spread-sheeted data from this group and normalised it vis-a-vis comparator units stateside to scope the project. I have been looking at the clinician issues and my colleague here, Marita Gonzalez, has been considering nursing and midwife options ojectivewise. We are absolutely confident that four of the five targets you have been given are within an envelope of achievability given high quality buy in by you folks. Perhaps you would like to say a word Marita?"

"Thanks Anton it sure is a privilege to be here in London and it's been an honor to help. In summary we have concluded that all the midwifery targets can be met by changing midwifery practice. To do that we need a paradigm shift to move work out of the ward setting into the community and away from the option of caesarean section to natural home delivery as part of a broad commitment to holistic care. For this to work we have to leverage your core competences as midwives. This will have the advantage of facilitating a deliverable proactive reduction of obstetricians and nurse levels. We need to do that because negative staff level trends are mission critical for the right financial outturn figures. Back to you Anton."

41

"Just a moment" interjected Lucien "Before we deal with the other one of the targets let's just be clear about what you proposed so far. You're suggesting training up the midwifes to do work currently done by obstetricians and also getting them to spend more time out on the district doing home deliveries?"

"Yeah, upskilling."

"And meanwhile you'll fire some of the obstetricians and the ward nurses to save money. Quite apart from work-load issues for the midwives you seem to have ignored factors that would make your changes unworkable. Are you not aware of the nature of our practice here? Difficult pregnancies are referred from all over London and the Home Counties as are pregnancies complicated by concurrent medical problems. Have you not enquired about our local catchment population? Were you not told that almost 30% of the pregnancies we deal with in our local district are to single mothers often living alone? In the part of our catchment south of the river, teenage pregnancy rates are four times the national average, drug use five times higher, life expectancy eight years shorter and so on. Did you know any of this? We have difficulty delivering high quality care as it is and reducing staff and expecting it to be done out in the community is fraught with risk!" There were murmurs of assent from the audience that clearly annoyed Henry Lightwood.

"But we'll of course re-appraise all of that later when you've show us your data" continued Lucien trying not to let his frustration show. "And the fifth demand from the CEO that you think might be unobtainable – was that the maximum four week wait to surgery?" Anton Dmochowski, was on his feet again unfazed.

"Thank you Professor. Yes we believe that too is achievable but not yet. Not until operating theatre and anaesthetic departments have been incentivised for change and aligned with this department's reformatting going forwards."

Lucien felt that reply was futile and would be futile even if he spoke the same language so he just sat down gesturing to the audience to have their say. Apart from a couple of junior managers and two of the midwives there was no support, barely even comprehension. However one of the new young obstetricians stood up, Harvey Bauermann, a slim well-dressed fellow with steel rim glasses and hair combed back and Brilliantined in the 1950's style.

He intrigued Lucien because he was different. Not much clinical experience but a lot of research on his CV. Lucien had not voted for him at the selection committee and nothing since then had changed his view. The man seemed driven, unsympathetic to the patients, obsessed with technology. He dressed like an undertaker.

"Perhaps we should not be so hasty in rejecting these changes." Said Harvey Bauermann. "Having babies is a natural process and moving to acknowledge this and let women get on with it at home is perhaps the better way... even if they are single mothers on their own." He said flashing a supercilious smile at Lucien .

"Just as they do in Africa. Is that what you are aiming for." It was Lesley Keefe who joined in and then others.

Harvey Bauermann looked over the heads of the audience to Henry Lightwood shrugging as if to imply that only he and Lightwood truly understood. The meeting dragged on for an hour, the members of the department airing their frustrations and disbelief while Henry Lightwood, the Chief Nurse and the two Americans said almost nothing falling back of patronising half-smiles as their response.

Back in his office Lucien's mood was blacker than when he set out and worsened after a parade of staff had been at his door asking what he was going to do about all this.

"You're our Clinical Director, our leader, can't you stop this nonsense?" Lucien knew that the answer was probably "No, I can't." They were all trapped in a system where messages were sent down but few of those sent back up the line were heard however carefully reasoned and if they were heard were probably ignored. Lucien had discovered long before how illusory his power was when it came to matters of management. When Peter Griffiths the Chief Executive of Sainsbury's famously stated that "If Florence Nightingale were carrying her lamp through the NHS today she would be searching for the people in charge" in a report which a decade earlier began the slow managerialisation of the NHS, Lucien had just been appointed a consultant and the debate on how the NHS should be managed was invisibly low on his list of interests. The changes did not leave doctors out of the plans and in due course hospital specialties became divided into clinical directorates each with an identified budget and a doctor or occasionally a nurse as the head of the directorate. The theory was that if doctors and nurses, the prodigal big spenders, were put in charge of the budget it could be controlled. Lucien was neither especially perceptive nor alone in noting that responsibility for controlling the budget sat uncomfortably with a much larger responsibility for providing the best available care for each patient. He'd stayed out of the director's chair for as long as possible and it was barely two years earlier that he had eventually been persuaded that he was his 'turn' and as the most senior person it was his responsibility to take it on. And anyway with his CBE and connections in The Department of Health and The College surely he would be able to achieve whatever the department needed. Ah the optimism; the assumptions that everything would be done for the best!

He stood at the window wishing he was sitting on the steps of The Tate with no more care in the world that finishing an ice cream before it melted. The bitterness of his frustration was born of the knowledge that short of unseating the new CEO and his henchmen he was powerless to resist the damage that the CEO's ignorance was about to inflict not just on his unit but also, as best he could judge from his colleagues, on the whole fragile edifice of the hospital. He felt for the first time the anger of true powerlessness. He didn't feel it with his patients. If a cancer could not be cured or an infertile woman made fertile then that needed to be accepted – not this. Thank God that in two days' time he would be up and away from this for a week. It was his annual visit to Libya, to the Tripoli Medical Centre. The three hour flight would give him time to sort through all the figures and the plans and prejudices that were blowing around the CEOs demands and he might see a way to frame proposals that would preserve the quality of care whilst satisfying the CEO. He was not optimistic. Anyway after Libya he had a week's holiday to look forward to.

Friday 23rd - Sunday 25th May. Libya

From 35,000 feet Lucien could see the whole outline of Corsica and then Sardinia as his BA flight to Tripoli glided gracefully across the clear blue sky above an azure sea. He gratefully accepted another glass of Chablis from the Business Class steward for he knew that once in Tripoli alcohol was not allowed, at least in public places. Libya was far from being his favourite foreign destination, but he had been going once a year for over ten years even when the politics of Muammar Gaddafi made it difficult. His visits were to give a couple of lecturers, advise on some problem patients and generally keep open the links with their senior doctors in his specialty. Doctors generally try to stay outside politics, not to be partisan about who is treated and crucially maintain the effectiveness of the global fraternity of medicine. His host, as ever, was Professor Mohammed El-Hammedi, now head of Women's Services at the Tripoli Medical Centre but many years ago Lucien's senior registrar and trainee. By remaining good friends they had kept open the lifeline between Tripoli medicine and London medicine for nearly twenty years.

The neatly outlined coast of Tunisia floated slowly into view, all browns and ochres with occasional smudges of cultivated green. Then the invisible border with Libya, the slow banking turn and an effortless landing at Ben Ghashir, Tripoli's airport. Lucien was always bemused by the smallness of the major airports in other capitals compared with the organised chaos of Heathrow and Gatwick.

Mohammed El-Hammedi met him just inside the door of the terminal building; unmistakable in the crowd, six foot tall with a frizz of white hair and a tie-less cotton shirt worn loose in deference to his well fattened belly. His height, shape and sharply pointed beard gave him an air of importance with which the milling throng of sharp suited, sun glassed Libyans could not compete.

"I am glad to see you my very good friend, I hope you had a happy flight" and he guided him imperiously through Passport Control and Customs with barely a pause. His white Mercedes was waiting at the curb immediately outside the exit cutting out the need to deal with the heat, the shouting porters and the insistent taxi touts.

"Pleasant isn't it to cut out all the difficult parts of travel" said Mohammed El-Hammedi "it has been a privilege I have much enjoyed since they made me Minister of Health. Look they even allow me a very smart card."

He took out a visiting card from the breast pocket of his shirt and pressed it into Lucien's hand. The card was thick and shiny, one side in Arabic the other in English and headed "Great Socialist Peoples Libyan Arab Jamaharia, General Peoples Committee" printed in the ubiquitous green of the revolution. Libya was, thought Lucien, a design consultant's dream everything coloured was in the same matching green, the visiting card, the shop fronts, the flags, the shutters of the old colonial buildings, the huge posters of the great leader that lined the road into the city from the airport.

"Our patient Noorah al Quadhafah is well following her Caesar, but unfortunately her baby Mohammed is not – he is in the clinic here with acute neonatal leukemia and the oncologist tells me he is unlikely to survive."

"How sad. How's his father taking it?"

"Badly. His usual nasty self, trying to find someone to blame. I'm glad I'm not the child's oncologist!"

They arrived at the hotel, the usual awful government sponsored one with echoing concrete halls and a grey drabness that nothing could conceal.

"I know it's not the quality you expect Lucien but I hope you will at least, be reasonably comfortable. You must be tired now. I'll send a car to you in the morning" said El-Hammedi "we can talk more then and look at some patients together."

The hotel with its barely eatable food, absence of alcohol and a rattling air conditioning unit which had covered everything in his room with a fine layer of sand was not a place in which to relax, so Lucien took a walk along to Green Square and around the lake, the al Saraya al Hamra. It was a warm evening and families with children were strolling about and sitting in groups under the shade of the citadels' walls. Lucien was uneasy, the news about little Mohammed the long demanded son of Noorah al Quadhafah and her violent husband, brought back to him the dilemma of her sterilisation at the

46

time of the caesarean section operation. She had been adamant that he tell no-one else outside the hospital but she had at least signed the formal consent needed for the operation to go ahead. In deference to her wishes Lucien had not mentioned the sterilisation in his medical report that had accompanied her back to Tripoli. If the child died Gamal Ghanem would expect Noorah to produce another son for him to cement his connection to the Gaddafi dynasty. If he discovered that she had been sterilised there would be trouble for sure.

The next morning the white Mercedes was waiting outside the hotel as he came down the steps; the obsequious driver with the big smile and small moustache leapt out to open the rear door for him. As they shared no language smiles were the only communication. The driver smiled at him in the mirror and nodded, Lucien smiled back and nodded.

At the hospital in a cramped, hot room Lucien oversaw a seminar on early miscarriage with ten of the Libyan trainees, all of whom spoke English and all of whom wanted to leave Libya and train in the UK or elsewhere, an option denied to them while Gaddafi's espousal of terrorism abroad made all Libyans suspect and exchanges almost impossible.

At coffee Professor El-Hammedi joined them.

"*As-salaam alaykum.*"

"*Wa'alaykum salaam*" they all intoned in response.

He took Lucien's arm and turned him to one side.

"I am sorry to tell you that baby Mohammed al Ghanem died in the night."

"I'm so sorry" said Lucien "There is something I need to tell you about his mother" at which point and before he could say anything more two of the students came over and the professor was taken off to see something, mouthing "see you for lunch, my office" as he left.

In Arab countries office size is very important; there must be a large ante-room and the office itself must be large and uncluttered. There must be a prominent portrait of the ruler, Muammar Gaddafi in this case, on the wall and a saying from the Koran on a plaque somewhere. The desk must be huge, usually in Lucien's experience at least 6ft by 3ft and adorned with a few onyx and golden objects. On the far side of the room there is always low obeisant seating around a table at which coffee or chai can be taken whilst courtesies are exchanged for a while before the actual business of the meeting is reached. Between Professor El-Hammedi and Lucien such courtesies were not needed, instead they sat companionably together with the Pepsi Colas and sandwiches that would be their lunch.

"About Noorah al Quadhafah" said Lucien as soon as they sat down; he had to tell Mohammed El-Hammedi about the sterilisation but Mohammed put his fingers to his lips then waved it from side to side to forbid the topic.

"Let us have lunch then we can walk outside for some exercise."

Mohammed El-Hammadi wolfed down his sandwiches and then sat eating nuts by the handful washed down with Pepsi.

"Come my friend we need to take exercise."

Outside the day was at its brightest, the air at its stillest but the regularly watered grass beneath the ordered rows of palms beside the hospital was cool. An Indian gardener was sprinkling the flower beds from a yellow hose.

"We must assume that everything said in that office is listened to or recorded and I sensed unease in you my friend, so perhaps what you want to tell me should just be between the two of us."

Lucien told him about the sterilisation, apologizing and explaining why it had been excluded from letters and reports. Mohammed waved the apologies away.

"No, no I understand – you did the right thing but that leaves us with a problem of course as Gamal Ghanem is going to expect her to bear him at least one more boy if his links to the Gaddafi tribe are to be made permanent. But now you have a lecture to give. I will phone Noorah in the morning and see how she is."

The following morning the white Mercedes and its inanely smiling driver delivered him to the main entrance of the hospital in time for the 08.30 ward round. Lucien knew the routine well and also many of the medical staff so they were making good progress around the patients when Mohammed El-Hammedi appeared on the ward looking agitated and anxious.

"I'm afraid I will need to take Professor McCulloch away now – please take over the ward round Dr. Bashir" signalling to one of the trainees.

He grasped Lucien's sleeve and guided him briskly out of the ward, down the marbled stairs and out into the sun.

"*We* have a problem" he said "*You* have a bigger problem. Come and sit in my car, switch on the engine and the air conditioning and I will get your things from my office."

He led him to a large Lexus 4x4 parked in the shade of a bamboo canopy.

"Lock the doors. I will back in five minutes."

In less than five minutes he was back, sweating copiously bearing Lucien's jacket and briefcase. Without speaking he drove out of the hospital and joined the traffic heading west on the Second Ring Road.

"You have a very big problem my friend" he said grimly "I spoke to Noorah this morning and she is very distressed. She had a big fight with her husband last night – he told her he expected her to have another boy and she unfortunately told him she couldn't and confessed to the sterilisation. Her husband beat her up a bit but said it was nothing to what he would do to you, indeed he said he would kill you."

"Oh dear!" said Lucien limply "can he do that?"

"Of course he can."

"But you're and important person, a Minister, can't you remonstrate with him? What about the police?"

Mohammed took both hands off the wheel and threw them up in exasperation or in prayer.

"No Lucien, there is nothing I can do I'm only a doctor, the necessary means of violence are not available to me and as for the police don't bother."

"The embassy?"

"My dear Lucien you are too trusting, you have the expectations of an Edwardian Englishman, you assume that everything is orderly and if not the Imperial power will fix it; you assume that most people behave properly but believe me my friend the sort of people we are talking about, Ghanem and his henchmen, don't behave properly. Have you ever heard of Abu-Salim Prison?"

"No, why?"

"Well our man Gamal Ghanem was in charge of that at one point in his rise to the top; it is where he got his reputation as a pitiless and a violent man."

"What happened at Abu-Salim?"

"Everything bad you could imagine torture, rape, starvation, murder, over a thousand people or more died there. No-one will ever know the truth of what happened. We only know the numbers because a worker in the kitchen was told to wash the blood from the watches of the dead so they could be sold and he kept a secret record of the watches he washed. Perhaps it is good that we don't know the details but Gamal Ghanem was in charge and if he wants to kill you my friend whilst you are here in Libya no-one will stop him."

To say that Lucien was not used to this sort of danger understates the world of propriety, law and respect that he normally inhabited.

"I'd better leave then" concluded Lucien lamely.

"That will not be easy, Gamal Ghanem probably knows you are here because he knows you were due to visit and he will already have his people looking for you. He will certainly have had you put on the Deny Exit list at the airport."

"What shall I do?"

"Do not return to the hospital or your hotel. I have a friend who owes me many favours, he will help but I cannot take you to him or be seen near his office. We will go now to the Corinthia Hotel where all the VIPs stay, we will have a cup of coffee together and I will leave. I will give you a piece of paper on which I will write an address. It is the commercial section of the British Embassy. Give it to any taxi driver outside the Corinthia and he will take you there. It's only a few hundred metres down the Al Kurnish Road but nobody walks. When you get there ask for Charles O'Dwyer."

At The Corinthia they sat in the wide, marbled atrium sipping coffee and looking out at the innocent, sparkling sea with little yachts dotting its surface. In the lobby were Americans, Germans, Italians and other normal people from normal countries coming and going at ease. It was like any other 5-star hotel anywhere in the world and its familiarity felt safe if incongruous in the circumstances.

"Don't stay here too long and don't tell anyone your name" said Mohammed as he stood to leave and embraced Lucien "Goodbye I hope we shall meet again" and he was gone, his huge bulk sweeping through the great glass doors into the sunshine.

Lucien waited ten long minutes and then walked out to the taxi rank. The commercial section of the embassy was twenty floors up in a tower block at the Burj al Fatih complex; the area beneath was largely deserted, the wind blowing rubbish along empty pavements. Emerging at the twenty-fourth floor he was greeted by a young woman at the reception desk; she wore a white blouse, had red lipstick, an Alice band and was as upper class English as it was possible to be. It was almost as if he had stepped out of the lift and into a different universe. When Lucien asked for Charles O'Dwyer she ushered him through a door labelled "Commercial Liaison Secretary." Mr. O'Dwyer was young, fit and straight forward. Apart from shaking Lucien's hand he made no attempt at chit-chat.

"I hear you are in a spot of bother with the notorious Mr. Ghanem."

"Apparently he wants to kill me."

"If that's all he did to you, you would be a lucky man! Mohammed El-Hammedi has told me briefly what's going on."

"You know Mohammed?"

"Let's just say we are acquaintances. We need to get you out of Libya today. We can do that but it will take a few hours to fix and in the meanwhile you will need to stay here. There is not much to do but there are a few magazines and some boring government reports in the Waiting Room. Janet at the front desk will get you food and drink if you need it. Please don't make any phone calls - they are easily traced. I will need your passport and your hotel key. I'll have your mobile too please."

Two hours, three cups of coffee and a cheese sandwich later Lucien was back in Charles O'Dwyer's office.

"Can I have your wallet please."

Puzzled, Lucien handed it over. O'Dwyer removed the credit cards, the visiting cards, the membership cards, indeed everything with Lucien's name on it and replaced them with a clutch of new cards. He handed it back with the phone and a passport. The passport was not Lucien's.

"For the next twenty-four hours you are Lawrence Aston, this is your passport, the picture inside it is of you. There is a Libyan entry

51

visa in it, the credit cards tally and there is a new Libyana SIM card in your phone. It is not perfect as a temporary identity, but it is not Lucien McCulloch and it will have to do to get you through exit procedures at the airport. They keep a "deny exit" book at Passport Control and Lucien McCulloch is probably in it by now. Lawrence Aston isn't. You are booked onto this evening's BA flight as Lawrence Aston; steerage I'm afraid, HMG doesn't pay for business class. You will need a legend, a personal history in case anyone asks, nothing special but something you can talk to if necessary. A hospital manager or health planner advising on the public health services in Libya, something like that. It is best not to be identified as a doctor, it won't cut any ice and you'll just get asked for bigger bribes! They don't have photos in the Deny Exit book so it's okay for you to look the same. When you get to the UK go through Immigration on the Aston passport then destroy it. We will get yours back to you in due course plus your credit cards, SIM card and luggage. Do you understand all that?"

O'Dwyer must have been at least thirty years younger than Lucien, the same age as his junior registrars, but his self-assurance and the bizarreness of the encounter had Lucien passively nodding assent at every turn.

"You're not really the Commercial Secretary are you Mr. O'Dwyer?" said Lucien trying to regain the upper hand.

"Of course I am" said O'Dwyer flashing him a huge grin. "Didn't you read the sign on the door?"

"Well thanks anyway for making all these arrangements, but isn't all of this a bit complicated?"

"Do you just want to risk it?"

"No of course not, isn't there any safer way out of Libya."

"Possibly, yes, but much slower. You could take the boat to Malta or head for Tunis, but the border at Ras Ajdir is busy and there is a heavy police and army presence there. Going east across Libya to Benghazi and into Egypt would leave you too long in Libya for your own safety. Your best bet is the airport – now! I'll drive you back to the Corinthia. Get a taxi to the airport from there. No-one will ask any questions there are too many people making that journey for you to be out of the ordinary."

In spite of the heedless speed of the taxi along the thirty kilometres of straight and dusty highway to the airport, Lucien had plenty of time to reflect on his situation. He was becoming increasingly anxious, sweating in the heat, sweating with anxiety, his suit now so crumpled he looked exactly the part of the harassed first time visitor as he checked in.

"Good afternoon Mr. Aston." At least the BA desk was courteous.

"Er, Umm, yes, er, good afternoon," his sweating increased, his shirt was now soaking wet and sticking to him. He now had to face up to Passport Control.

At the kiosk his passport was taken from him by a burly, sullen man in olive fatigues and a beret, wearing colonel's pips on green epaulettes. The man is a lookalike for Saddam Hussein. The man looks intently at the passport flipping through it page by page, he puts it on the desk and picks up a battered file, old pages, new pages, names crossed out, names added on post-it notes. "This must by the Deny Exit file" thought Lucien and in a panic noticed that some pages had photos. His new passport is in the name of Aston, the man should not have to delve far into the file to check the A's. The Saddam look-a-like has opened it in the middle, but then slowly turns back to the A's, the first page. He doesn't find anyone there called Aston. He flips the file shut, hands the passport back to Lucien and without a smile or a frown or a comment, turns to the next person in the queue. At the next desk a junior plants an exit stamp over the grandiose full page entry visa and hands him the passport and a ticket that looks like a pink raffle ticket. Lucien moves on to the gate into the departure area where another man in uniform takes the raffle ticket and nods him through.

The hour in the Departure Lounge passes agonisingly slowly, it's hot, crowded, smelly and there is no bar. There is a shop selling a few tatty tourist trinkets; wooden camels and posters of the great leader, nothing worth taking back for Diana or Lucy, they'll have to do with a BA perfume again but at least with luck they will be getting him back alive he thinks shrinking back into his seat in the furthest corner of the lounge. At last the flight is called. Oh, the joy of passing onto the BA plane. Never did the meaningless greeting from the stewardess at the top of the steps feel more heartfelt. No vehicle arrives in a rush beside the plane, no-one comes up the steps at the last moment to drag him off, the plane taxies out and lifts off.

Lucien's mouth is dry, his heart still racing, he beckons the stewardess.

"Might I have a drink, please."

"We will be around with those later, Sir" she tartly replies.

And in what seems just an instant in relation to his time at Tripoli airport they are back at Gatwick. He phones Diana to explain what has happened and that he is home three days early. There is no reply from his home number so he phones her mobile. She sounds flustered.

"I'll be home in an hour" she says.

"Me too" says Lucien suddenly realising with a rush of gratitude that he is safe.

Only the next day was Lucien able to think rationally about his Libyan experience; his fear, his abject acquiesce to instructions, his absurdly florid relief at arriving back in the UK unharmed when perhaps – looking at it objectively – there was no evidence that he was under threat at all. These were categories of experience he had never been exposed to before. He was glad that he and Diana had ten days in France to look forward to. St Jean des Crapauds was somewhere where very little happened – and that for him, particularly just now, was a good reason to cherish it. After that however he had the meeting with the CEO to prepare for, he doubted that the CEO would accept any blunting of the proposals and so he would have to decide what his own stance should be. Resistance or Acquiescence? Fight or Flight, both needed the same hormone, adrenaline. So not much to choose between them.

June 2008. St Jean des Crapauds

The sensation was always the same. As the white cliffs of Dover slowly shrank away to the north, the gulls hovering and wheeling about the stern of the ferry, Lucien and Diana would both feel the same release. The tentacles of responsibility and stress did not seem long enough to stretch out beyond the mouth of Dover harbour; the foaming wake of the ferry somehow cleansing. His patients, her pupils, the bills, the phone calls at night, the pages of pointless e-mails, the hassle and bustle of London life was immediately so distant that it could not reach out and pull them back. Once onto the roads of France even the chaos of the Paris Peripherique seemed benign for they always had before them the certain calm of the house in St. Jean, deep in La France Profonde. So as they travelled south there were none of those concerns about whether they would arrive at a hotel too late, where they'd eat, what would the children think of it. They knew the destination was their familiar haven which as the years went by became more important, more sacred, the journey a pilgrimage.

St Jean des Crapauds. It was the name that twenty-six years earlier had attracted Lucien and Diana off the main road from Bergerac to Duras in the first day of a summer weekend break. Crapauds are toads and the surmise that the particular St. Jean for whom this village was named may have spent a reclusive and penitential life communing with toads at the bottom of a well proven more or less correct. The village though was everything that was required to satisfy their romantic view of a French country village, an open square in the centre shaded by tall plane trees, a Romanesque church with a clock on its bell tower, a café with a striped awning and half a dozen tables in the sun, a baker, a Mairie flying the Tricoleur and down a curving lane a little river and a mill. All around the village vineyards; none with the gloss and glamour of the Medoc or Saint Emilion but handsome work-a-day domaines of the Bergeracois. St. Jean des Crapauds even boasted a chateau of its own that, unusually among the thousands of "chateaux" in south west France, actually looked the part. An elegant, 18th century building with grand gates, a driveway lined by old cedars leading to the house itself finely built of honey coloured stone with a slate roof and peaked towers at each corner. Chateaux Montbelle.

Lucien and Diana sat outside the café, the Café des Vignerons, the only customers; Lucien with a beer, Diana with a glass of Montravel local dry white wine which, never one to be too readily in thrall to anything, she declared to be a little too flinty. That was however all they could find wrong with St Jean des Crapauds and when the patron emerged from the bar and presuming they were staying for lunch laid the table, one knife, one fork, one spoon each, one basket of bread, one carafe of red wine and then served a slice of game terrine followed by a plate of *porc au caramel* of unmatchable sweetness and richness, they knew this had to be the village. A decision as overwhelming as it was irrational. On this memorable day Lucien was thirty-six and Diana thirty-two, their children back at home with granny for a weekend just ten and twelve. Lucien and Diana held hands across the table and plighted their troth to St Jean des Crapauds.

Their visit to France was part holiday, part search for a holiday house, though they never really admitted the second purpose to each other let alone anyone else least they failed to come upon a home they wanted; they didn't want this interpreted as a failure. Anyway there was plenty of time. Lucien had just completed his training and been appointed as a consultant obstetrician and gynaecologist in London, his training had been long and hard and as is the nature of obstetrics babies bawl to be let out of the womb at night just as often as by day, so an unwelcome proportion of his 80-hour working week was made up of night calls. Diana had the different burdens of teaching in a south London state primary school, of being a mother and a supportive wife to a perpetually exhausted husband. London was their workplace, the theatres, galleries, concerts halls even cinemas merely happened to co-exist with them in the same city. There was never time to enjoy them. So somewhere else, somewhere not London, not tainted with the stress of work was what they yearned for. In the past holidays had been spent in campsites, Gites, hotels, canal boats but this never satisfied their need to feel settled elsewhere. They had looked for a country cottage in England but even the meanest was unaffordable. Fortuitously, however, if that does not sound too selfish or unsympathetic, Lucien's maternal grandfather had died in 1982 leaving a legacy. It was an unusual one, one which in French law was difficult to arrange. Lucien's grandfather, grandpere André Delmain had never forgiven his daughter, Lucien's mother Sandrine, for abandoning France for a foreigner and, as he saw it, the perpetual greyness and drizzle of England. So his legacy of 750,000 Francs carried with it the stipulation that the money must be spent in France of any purpose that "afforded an understanding and continuing enjoyment of France, its culture and its land to Lucien McCulloch and any legitimate children". French law is always concerned about degrees of legitimacy when it comes to inheritance.

Lucien and Diana had not decided how this money might be spent. Educating Lucy and Robin in France? They didn't want that. Funding expensive French holiday for all the family each year? That seemed particularly prodigal. Buying a piece of France, a property, was however much more in line with grandpere's wishes and could guarantee a connection in perpetuity. So without wanting to rush the process it was this generosity of grandpere that had led them to the Dordogne. The danger, they both realised, of money in the bank was that they might make a precipitous decision about a house. It was too easy to fall in love out here. This then was their second year of not looking!

"Do you know of any houses for sale in this commune?" Lucien asked Jean Luc the patron of the café as he paid the bill.

The patron looked immediately wary for in many communes incomers of any nationality, and to this were added Parisians, were not welcome, but Lucien's impeccable French and Diana's good looks and questing smile must have persuaded him, or else the chance to test the sincerity of one of his regular customers, Bernard Desvignes, whose grumbles as he lent against the bar were always that his house was too big for him, too draughty, too infested with mice and woodworm and what he and his wife really wanted was a little house in Arcachon within sight of the sea and, he would add, "nowhere near any damned vineyards". But he never made the trip to Bergerac to the Immobilier to put it on the market. "Too busy." Perhaps this would test the dream and in one way or the other might spare Jean-Luc the interminable grumpiness. There is nothing worse than to be trapped behind the bar of an almost empty café polishing glasses or wiping tables in the hope of escape.

"There is one possibility" said Jean-Luc "I will phone the owner and see if he is at home."

He was and just ten minutes later having walked up the narrow lane that led out of the square beside the boulangerie, they were at the door of a large house covered in Virginia creeper. Attached to the house was an old tower and attached to the gate a name plate "Le Vieux Tour". The owner, a small man in baggy black trousers held up by braces limped to the gate to let them in, sat them at the big kitchen table, poured them glasses of wine and told them that it was a very special house in which he had lived most of his life but that it was not for sale. However, would they like to look around? It was a grand house fallen on hard times, the huge oak beams had survived unfazed by the passage of many centuries but the stone window and door surrounds were chipped and eroded, the floors uneven and some of the larger and grander rooms had been crudely divided by thin partition walls covered in rosebud wallpaper. The kitchen and bathroom needed radical rejuvenation. Outside the owner gestured to an oak copse that filled in from the back of the house to the top of the hill, he admired proprietarily the distant views from the front of the house to the south west across a patchwork of erratically shaped little vineyards marked off by low stone walls. These stretched down the hillside to a valley where the mill was just visible, its mill pool glinting between the tree trunks; the stream ran on into a couple of little *etangs*, lakes, bordered with poplars and willows, the margins thick with yellow irises.

When they returned to the kitchen the owner asked if they wanted to buy the house.

"But we understood you were not selling."

"Depends on the price I'm offered" replied the owner slyly, 750,000 Francs might do it."

"That's a lot of money, way outside our budget."

"How about 700,000?"

"How about 600,000?"

"OK that would do. I'll phone the notaire and you'll go to see him tomorrow for the deposit? It's Maitre Sorel in Bergerac, Rue Victor Hugo."

Diana had said nothing, she had just squeezed Lucien's hand under the table to indicate assent. Lucien reached across the table and shook Bernard Desvignes' horny hand firmly.

"We look forward to seeing you again as soon as we have settled the formalities with notaire."

"No need" said Desvignes gruffly and showed them to the door.

"Phew!" said Lucien once they were back in the lane "are we mad?"

"No darling, absolutely not. Houses speak and this one said very strongly 'buy me!' We have looked at lots of houses and none of them has said that, so let's just do it."

At the notaire's the next morning they completed a sheaf of forms and arranged for the trust fund to pay the 10% deposit.

"What do you plan to do with the vineyards" asked Maitre Sorel "Same as at present?"

"What vineyards?"

"The ten hectares in front of the house, Monsieur Desvignes handed over their care to a neighbouring producteur over ten years ago. He receives 10,000 francs and six cases of wine each year as payment. It's all legal, you can take the vineyards back any time you want."

"How nice! But we're in no position to take them on ourselves, we know nothing about vines and wine making and anyway we live in London. Let's just leave it as it is for now" said Lucien, astonished by the revelation.

Outside in the street Diana did a little twirling dance down the pavement.

"Our very own vineyard and we didn't even know, how exciting; we can retire, grow wine, get pissed all day and die of liver disease just like the locals! Seriously though, I love it, love it, love it."

And off to lunch they went hand in hand.

Three months later Le Vieux Tour was theirs together with the oak copse and the vineyards and almost all the furniture: oak tables, upholstered chairs and huge wardrobes of chestnut wood. It had turned out that Mr. Desvignes had even less affection for the furniture than for the house.

When they brought the house in 1983 they were the only owners in the commune who were not French, the tide of Brits and Dutch which for the last forty years has engulfed the Dordogne had passed by St Jean, primarily because so few houses were given up. Now in 2008 there were eight foreign families amongst the two hundred and thirty residents recorded at the Mairie. The McCulloch family in the Le Vieux Tour; Terry and Molly Tuffnall next to the garage which he ran, Hans Van Boeken and Elsa at the mill, Harold and Geraldine Makepiece in the converted barn at the end of the lane that ran past the Le Vieux Tour. A Trevor and Pat lived in the old farm off the main road, Anna Ponsonby, Hector Ponsonby's widow, in the Chateau Montbelle. The other two families were recent and neither invitations nor chance encounters nor even gossip had revealed the family details or what category they fell into; the disaffected hoping that France would somehow be different, retirees hoping their money would last longer here, or impoverished holiday home owners expecting to turn a quick profit after a year of summer bricolage, DIY. Overall, there were not enough to form a colony nor any wish to do so.

Lucien and Diana were happy with that. They had no wish to spend their time solely with compatriots as do so many Brits in France.

They got up late, lingered over their breakfast croissants, dawdled around markets, pottered about in the garden, sat in the sun outside the Café des Vignerons with a carafe of local wine, tested new restaurants and then as the golden evening light flooded across the hillsides sat quietly reading and listening to music. They had long since abandoned all sense of obligation about "going places". When asked what they did on holiday they'd stopped being embarrassed to reply: "Nothing, nothing in particular."

When Lucien returned from France he was refreshed but depressed. The gap between his life there with Diana and his life at the hospital locked into everyone else's disillusionment was so sharp that he found himself turning daily to thoughts of retirement.

"Perhaps it's time to retire, what do you think about that Mrs. McCulloch?" he asked Diana at breakfast.

"What! and commit us to being together for twenty-four hours of every day?" she replied simulating horror. "What would we do?"

"Living, going places, cooking, making love. That sounds okay to me. Maybe even find time to meet friends and make new ones. We could spend much more time in St. Jean. You'd like that."

Diana pursed her lips "I think it's a bit premature to be making decisions like that Lucien...you're only thinking about it because we've just had a sunny week in France and you've got this business with Arkwright to sort out. We'll talk about it another day perhaps."

In the week that followed he had five meetings with staff in his directorate trying to work though the anger and complaint towards a coherent response to the CEO's proposals. Everyone seemed to think Lucien could magic a winning proposal out of the very few changes that his staff would accept. He was non-plussed by how readily they committed their future to him. How appealing not to feel responsible for one's own future, how liberating. By the day of the review meeting with the CEO Lucien had prepared a response of sorts, carefully argued and supported with data which was referenced. It even had an option appraisal in it just as he'd been taught on management courses. The option appraisal of course contained the "Change Nothing" option though they'd not dared to put that as their preference even though the evidence showed it was the correct one. The department was, after all, highly rated nationally and by the patients. All the stats were better than the national averages and they kept within their budget. The problem was, as he'd deduced years earlier, that doctors are wary of change whereas managers live for change. His document was printed out, bound up and sent to the CEO's office to be circulated forty-eight hours before the meeting.

Friday June 20th. Second Meeting with the CEO

Eight-fifty AM. Lucien and his team were waiting for the lift in the administrative block to take them up for their meeting with the CEO. The lift came down and out of the mirrored interior stepped none other than their colleague Harvey Bauermann looking very self-satisfied in his best undertaker's suit and white shirt.

"Good morning team" he said as he brushed passed them.

"Harvey looks pleased" said the Head of Midwifery. Lucien was now very alert and wary but said nothing.

When they reached the CEO's meeting room Lucien noticed that the coffee cups were already empty.

"Excuse me just a moment." He went back into the corridor where he phoned Pam his PA on his mobile.

"Pam this meeting with the CEO is scheduled for nine, is that right?"

"Yes Prof."

"Would you do me a favour. Check with Mr. Bauermann's secretary to see if he had a meeting with the CEO this morning." She was back within a minute

"Yes Prof. At eight-thirty; she doesn't know what it was about."

Lucien went back into the meeting. No Samantha this morning he noted, just the CEO, Head Nurse, Henry Lightwood and Constance Jefferson-Jones the Director of HR. Winston Arkwright was, as usual, standing up on his side of the meeting table as they entered but today he was sporting a beatific smile, his arms spread wide as if welcoming a sinner into the church.

"Good morning Professor and team, nice to see you all again. This is crunch day of course for your directorate – we've read your very detailed proposals and I'm sure you're keen to hear our view," he paused "Well I can tell you our considered opinion. It's crap!" his mood had changed in an instant "It's simply an attempt to perpetuate the status quo. It doesn't identify any of the headline changes and savings we want. It hasn't identified how many nurses and doctors you are going to shed, how many beds we can close. Why could you not do that? We gave you every assistance in the form of outside consultants and they have reassured us that the targets are achievable so this report of yours is just foot dragging. It's not good enough. Tell me why."

Lucien had foreseen this and with a helpless sense of resignation acknowledged to himself that trying to reason with the man would be futile.

"Had your team looked carefully at our arguments you would see that apart from shortening the delay from consultation to operation, none of the other proposals could be achieved to the level you wanted without seriously damaging the quality of patient care both in terms of outcomes and adherence to basic tenets of compassion."

"That's just your opinion."

"It's our opinion as a team based on our knowledge and experience and on published data."

"But it's fundamentally just opinion and that's not good enough – and for that I hold you, Professor McCulloch, responsible. You've clearly not managed to get traction on to our ideas and I don't sense any buy-in to our innovation strategy. That's a failure of leadership. You're too old McCulloch, too attached to the old way of doing things and you're fired."

The Chief Midwife and Teresa Mason both started to speak but Lucien put his hand up calmly to stop them. He didn't want them also subjected to the CEO's caprice.

"I am older than you Arkwright and I'm not being arrogant if I point out that I have a lot more experience of women's health than you do... or your executive colleagues... or your expensive American consultants. I'd also venture to suggest that each member of my team could claim the same and reasonably say they had a lot more concern for our patient's welfare than you appear to have. If we fall short on that we've not just our consciences but our professional regulators, The GMC and The GNC to answer to. It seems you answer morally to no-one and sadly there is no professional body to oversee your behaviour."

This had clearly goaded Arkwright who'd picked a teaspoon from the table and was bending it back and forth. Soon it, like his composure, would break. Lucien was beginning to enjoy himself.

"The clinical directorship is a voluntary post and as I'm clearly not living up to your curious expectations you are very welcome to my resignation."

"No McCulloch, I said you were fired not just from the directorship, I've already appointed Harvey Bauermann to replace you, but from your post as a consultant as well. So you need not look so relaxed because it means I'll be separating you from your livelihood." The HR Director started to interrupt him but thought better of it and fell silent. "Well McCulloch what to you make of that?"

Lucien stood up slowly, standing across the table from Winston Arkwright his palms on the table mirroring the CEO.

"Well I'm sorry to disappoint you Arkwright, your 'separating me from my livelihood' as you put it but without any of the normal preliminaries is probably illegal and certainly worth challenging as I'm sure your Director of HR was about to tell you, but that won't be necessary because she can also confirm that I'm actually not an employee of yours. I'm appointed and paid by the University so your Alan Sugar impersonation was rather wasted" at which he gathered up his papers and left the room followed by the rest of his team.

Constance Jefferson-Jones, the HR Director, followed them and caught up with Lucien by the lift. A huge Jamaican woman with a radiant and reassuring smile she was the enemy of no-one. She was not one of Arkwright's imports from his previous job and she well understood not just the convolutions of employment law but also the hospital's history and culture.

"Professor – what would you like me to do? Will you be appealing or formally complaining? Do we need to discuss your career trajectory. I can find time this morning if that would help." Lucien put his arm around her then removed it.

"Sorry. That probably counts as harassment. You're very sweet Connie but I'm happy, in fact overjoyed, that I'm no longer the director. I don't need to make any formal complaints I'm sure our CEO will eventually be consumed by his own bad behaviour without any help from me. As to my 'career trajectory' as you call it, don't worry it's steady and downward and heading for, I hope, a soft landing outside The NHS."

When he got back to his office he found Harvey Bauermann standing over Pam.

"Mr. Bauermann says he's the new clinical director so he will be taking over your office Prof. Is that true?"

"Yes it is and no he won't. This floor is part of the University Department of Obstetrics and Gynaecology of which I remain the head, which is different from the Clinical Directorship – Mr. Bauermann has a lot to learn." Then turning to Harvey Bauermann he gave a little Viennese bow. "Welcome to the Clinical Directorship Harvey or should I say you're welcome to the clinical directorship Harvey!"

That evening Lucien tired and still angry went to bed early but could not sleep properly, tossing and turning. He opened his eyes to find Diana in bed but sitting up, her spectacles on the end of her nose, reading. Still lying flat and half asleep Lucien wriggled over to her side of the bed and nestled his head against her breast, his hand on the warm softness of her belly.

"Hello" she said, "can't you sleep? Are you still cross about that awful little man Arkwright?"

Lucien struggled back to full wakefulness and sat up.

"Arkwright. Yes I suppose so."

"It's probably the first time in your life you've not come out on top!"

"Maybe, but I'm pleased to be out of the clinical director job though you're right I am annoyed."

"Well darling you'll need to adjust to these upsets. All those pinnacles you've scaled along the way; consultant, professor, Head of Department, College Council, you'll have to come off them one by one now you're approaching retirement age. Resenting that's a self -inflicted problem you high achieving men have. It's not a problem for us girls. We graduate, have kids, kids leave home, nothing left to lose after that, just resign ourselves to being the supporting act for our husbands." This was said with more than a tinge of bitterness, which Lucien failed to notice.

"Thanks, you've done it brilliantly. I wouldn't have achieved anything without your help. And when I've given it all up I'll still have you, that's all I need . You know that don't you?" He snuggled closer to her and kissed her ear. Diana put down her book, took off her glasses and moved across until their hips and shoulders were touching.

"When you're no longer the boss of everything you're going to have to find a new way of living Lucien- less striving. It would be nicer for both of us."

Lucien put his hands behind his head and leaned back "Actually I'm looking forward to it. I hate to see colleagues who won't let go, who can't stop reflecting on their past achievements, can't move on. They get peevish and reactionary, write letters to The Daily Telegraph. That's not for me. I intend just to let it all wind down gently, hand over to others and step gracefully off the treadmill into your arms!"

Monday June 23rd. Dulwich.

Having no operations scheduled and, as a result of the recent spat with the Chief Executive, no management meeting to attend, Lucien was at home on this Monday morning when the post arrived. He hardly bothered with the mail normally for it was advertisements, magazines and bills, junk; but this morning as he bent to clear the doormat he noted a stiff white envelope that bore the words "General Medical Council" on the top left corner. The letter inside was brief to the point of rudeness given the contents;

Dear Mr. McCulloch

This letter is formal notification that the General Medical Council is in receipt of a complaint from... *Mr. Gamal Ghanem*
in relation to... *the surgical sterilization of his wife Noorah al Quadhafah without proper consent.*
When we have obtained documentation in relation to this complaint the matter will be considered by two case assessors and a judgment made as to whether this complaint should go forward to a full hearing by the Fitness to Practice Panel.
Your employers... *The Royal United Hospitals* and... *The London Clinic for Women and Children*, have been notified and asked for any documentation that might assist the assessors.
You may, yourself, submit relevant documentation should you wish.
If you are a member of a professional defence organisation you are advised to contact them.

Yours etc.

Lucien's response was irritation, then anger, then resignation tinged with anxiety. The allegation was easy to refute; there was a signed consent form in the hospital notes and the law and the RCOG guidance on sterilisation clearly stated that a partner's consent was not required. Lucien knew that in Muslim countries the husband's consent would have been mandatory, indeed in many situations it would be the husband's not the wife's signature which would be on the consent form. Lucien was absolutely certain that Gamal Ghanem would not have given consent even knowing the hazards that a future pregnancy would entail for his wife. That's why he was not asked, and at his wife's request not told.

Lucien paid the Medical Defence Union £15,000 a year to insure himself against the consequences of litigation in private practice. Obstetrics was one of the most expensive specialties to insure; uncomfortable bedfellow with the plastic surgeons for whom litigation was more common but the outcomes cheaper – their litigation never involved a damaged baby needing a lifetime of care. Fortunately he had never had to ask for MDU advice before about anything so catastrophic or even about something so straightforward as this complaint to the GMC.

The adviser at the MDU listened carefully, concluded that he too felt the complaint was easily resisted but that the MDU would need to instruct a solicitor to deal with it. The solicitor would contact him.

Diana had already left for work but he'd tell her about it later and see what she thought, though given her feisty feminism he was sure her sympathies would be with Noorah al Quadhafah, which over supper was exactly Diana's view.

"Rather a lame move from this Gamal Ghanem isn't it?" she smiled "normally he just wants to kill you! He's probably hoping you will die a slow death from professional disgrace and painfully expensive litigation." She seemed to think that was rather funny.

Two days later a letter came from Hutchinson & Semple the MDU's solicitors asking Lucien for a formal statement. The letter was signed by a Lily Harper-Smith, solicitor.

Lucien knowing the existence of a signed consent form and knowing there was no legal requirement for a spouse's consent, managed to get the salient facts onto one side of A4 the same day and tried to put the business out of his mind. Miss Harper-Smith could get the consent form from the hospital notes.

For a week he heard nothing further about the matter, then he received a letter asking him to contact Lily Harper-Smith the solicitor.

"We have a problem" she said when he phoned her "there is no consent form in the LCWC notes – it appears to have been removed.

The hospital denies that this could have happened once the patient had left the hospital and the notes filed. They say it must have happened on the ward."

Lucien thought for a moment

"I suppose Noorah al Quadhafah herself could have removed it to conceal the fact that she had consented to sterilisation."

"Possible, of course but you should be aware that it might be proposed that you yourself had removed the form."

"Or anyone else could have!"

Lucien felt a stab of anger that this seemingly straight forward matter was becoming more convoluted.

"Has a statement from Mrs al Quadhafah been seen yet?" he asked

"No, nothing; though I have asked the civil servant dealing with this to chase it up."

"A civil servant?"

"Yes, the middle man for handling this complaint appears to be someone in Whitehall."

"Isn't that rather irregular?"

"I'm told it's because of difficulties in dealing directly with Libya – they no longer have an embassy or consulate here."

"Which department in Whitehall?"

"The man did not say, he just said HMG were assisting a foreign complainant. I presume he is from the FCO."

"Is this common?"

"I've never encountered it before but it makes things a lot easier for us, so I have no problem with it. Incidentally, I should also mention that if no proof of consent can be found it opens the possibility of you being charged with assault."

The next day Lucien was at the Clinic and sought out the medical records officer; she was adamant that the consent form could not have been removed after the patient was discharged and no request for the notes had been made since discharge. The patient must have removed the form herself. Why did it matter? Lucien explained.

"Loss of the original shouldn't be a problem" she said "The existence of a consent form for sterilisation would be documented in the nursing record and the theatre records. If you come back in half an hour I'll have them here."

Sure enough the existence of consent for sterilisation was indeed documented separately in several part of the hospital record apart from the notes.

"Thank God for all the form filling – I promise never to the rude about it again – may I have photocopies."

Lucien phoned Lily Harper-Smith to tell her.

"Good, that saves me a heap of work; I'll draft a letter now to The GMC saying there is no case to answer and I'll copy it to the man in the Foreign Office."

And sure enough The GMC wrote a few days later reassuring Lucien that no further action would be taken. That should have been the end of the matter. Case closed.

Friday July 18th. London W1.

It was mid-afternoon almost three weeks later and Lucien had just finished seeing his patients at the London Clinic for Women and Children. Pleased to have found all of them comfortable and happy he had come down to the Lobby looking forward to setting off for a quiet weekend at home. The receptionist hailed him as he was about to leave." The Chief Executive wants a word Professor. He's in his office."

The Chief Executive of the LCWC was culturally very different from Winston Arkwright at the RUH; ex-army, previously a brigadier in the Guards. Urbane, very tall and impeccably tailored. He came to the door to meet Lucien and saw him seated before returning to his side of the desk. His office had none of the trappings of modern management, no computer , no wall charts, no box files, no teetering in-trays just good quality antique furniture, a few framed and signed pictures of Royalty and discreetly in the corner a picture of the Brigadier in battledress leaning nonchalantly against a tank in the desert somewhere. The door to his secretary's office was ajar, the Brigadier quietly closed it.

"I was sorry to hear about this trouble with the consent for Mrs al Quadafah's operation, sounded as if it might have been the Clinic who mislaid her form. I was sure it could not have been; our security is , as you know, impeccable."

"No, not the Clinic's fault and in fact the Clinic's good record keeping has allowed the matter to be resolved."

"I'm glad, we wouldn't want the Clinic's good name besmirched would we. Are there any other difficulties outstanding?"

"None that I know of."

"I hope not, the Police were asking for you earlier this afternoon but would not say why. They want to talk to you. They will be here shortly so perhaps you'd wait in my secretary's office for them. Would you'd give me a call later if there is anything that might involve the Clinic." And with that he ushered Lucien into the secretary's office not allowing any opportunity for questions.

"Do you know anything about this Police thing Justine?" Lucien asked the Secretary.

"Of course not Professor; would you like a cup of tea whilst you wait?"

"No Thanks." Actually he did but didn't want to be put into a supplicant's role sitting on a hard chair with a cup of tea in his hand when the police came. He did not have to wait long before a crop haired man in an ill-fitting suit accompanied by a uniformed WPC were shown in. They made no attempt to shake hands.

"Are you Lucien James McCulloch and can you confirm that you practice at this hospital?" Lucien nodded. "I am Detective Chief Inspector Brownleigh and my colleague here is WPC Sheila Sprague. We are here to arrest you for offences of indecent assault on two women whom we believe to be or have been patients of yours. We need you to accompany us to Marylebone Police Station where you will be charged with those offences."

"This is ridiculous, there must be a mistake. I have no idea what you are claiming but if it's about my patients I would need their notes..."

"Unfortunately we cannot allow that, they will be seized in due course but we cannot allow you access to them now. Also I must warn you that anything you might say will be taken down and can be used in evidence."

"May I phone a solicitor ?"

"You may." DCI Brownleigh's expression showed clearly that he would prefer it if Lucien didn't phone a solicitor. His view was that they were uniformly Busybodies, pains in the arse, slowed everything down and seriously reduced the chance of a quick confession. Lucien checked in his diary for Lily Harper-Smith's number and called her; he explained what was happening and that it seemed to be to do with patients so presumably covered by the MDU.

"Where are they taking you?"

" Marylebone Police station."

"I'll have to check with the MDU but assume I'll be there. If they want to tell you what it's all about that's OK but say nothing until I get there."

72

Marylebone Police Station is in Seymour Street just a few blocks west of Harley Street and a few steps north of Oxford Street. Like so many roads in this part of London it is mostly made up of fine Georgian, cream coloured, stuccoed houses, each with four levels of well-proportioned tall windows. Marylebone Police Station wedged between them seems a perverse attempt to cancel out any elegance, to stress the horizontal, to be bland, to be uninviting. So bland in fact that until Lucien got out of the police car at the door was unaware that there was a Police Station there. Although Lucien was now in his 60s he had not been into a Police Station since he'd handed in a purse he'd found in the street; and that was when he was 14. Nothing about this building was welcoming, the ramp up to the entrance, the black stone cladding , the narrow horizontal windows, it all added to his anxiety about why he'd be brought here silently by two police officers. Inside he was taken before the Custody Sergeant at the desk who read him his rights, DCI Brownleigh then led him into an Interview room on the ground floor. It seemed designed to increase any sense of anxiety or hopelessness that the interviewee brought in with them. Vinyl floor, Formica table, plastic chairs, fluorescent strip lighting and that single transverse slot of a window high on the wall. Lucien had seen the format a hundred times on television but never imagined himself in the same landscape sitting across a table from a surly detective, the WPC standing in the corner of the room.

DCI Brownleigh opened the slim, buff file in front of him, confirmed Lucien's full name, date of birth, address and the rest then turned to two typewritten sheets. Both were clearly in English with the bottom of each page embellished with streaks of Arabic writing overlain by rubber stamped crests.

"These two documents have been passed to us by the Crown Prosecution Service for action. Each is a statement by a female patient of yours from Libya, witnessed by a judge. Each states that during a routine visit to you in your Consulting Room at the London Clinic for Women and Children you, and I quote 'fondled the breasts, stroked the belly and inserted your fingers into the vagina for the purpose of your own pleasure'. The CPS has concluded that this constitutes a Sexual Assault under Section 3 of the Sexual Offences Act 2003. Additionally they have concluded that the evidence satisfies the evidential test in that it allows a reasonable prospect of conviction. Personally I find it a little strange that both these statements are almost identically worded and perhaps written by the same person but my view is of no consequence because we have a clear direction from the CPS to charge you. Your solicitor is not here yet so you don't need to say anything until she arrives though I can see from your expression you'd like to! You will just need to wait quietly here with WPC Sprague. While you wait for your solicitor you can read through the two statements."

Even without the notes Lucien remembered the two patients that had apparently made the statements, they had both been referred to him from Tripoli by his friend Professor al Hammedi about a year previously. One was a young woman complaining of infertility who had quickly been diagnosed as having polycystic ovaries, the other a middle aged woman with fibroids but not bad enough to need an operation. Both had seen him just twice and, not requiring surgery, had been referred back to Tripoli. There had been no suggestion at the time that there was a problem. As he was reading WPC Sprague had moved a couple of steps closer to the table and was standing just to one side, arms folded. Looking up from the statements Lucien had an unappealing view of two fat legs emerging from below the blue serge skirt of her uniform. Her black tights were laddered and her rubber soled shoes dirty.

"Well Mr. McCulloch, what do you think of what those women have to say eh?" her voice was harsh and aggressive. "And you know something Mister Ever So Posh McCulloch, I really hate you professional perverts; using your status to get your way with women. You doctors and the schoolmasters who touch up 14 year old girls and priests who bugger altar boys, you're all the same, just scum. If I had my way they'd bang you up for 20 years, minimum."

Lucien felt a cold mix of anger, affront, and fear welling up; he wanted to tell this fat harridan with her laddered tights and her dyed hair to go back to police college or wherever and learn the basic principles of truth, impartiality and the presumption of innocence but he had enough self-control just to look away and dig his nails into his palms. Christ! what a relief, Lily Harper Smith was at the door, crisp white blouse, smart black jacket, a briefcase in her hand; what a contrast. DCI Brownleigh was with her. She sat down next to Lucien and read through the two statements.

"Did you do anything other than simply examine these women in the course of a routine consultation?"

"Of course not. These women were patients and the routine examination, as for all other women, involves palpating the abdomen and doing a vaginal examination to feel the uterus and the ovaries. If they are from overseas and have not been under what we would consider normal regular care it also includes a general examination, including the breasts, done separately. And there will have been a nurse there as chaperone, there always is"

"That makes it worse" interjected the WPC. DCI Brownleigh shot her a glance to silence her.

"You have heard what my client has said Mr. Brownleigh. As an experienced Officer you must realize that even if these statements are to be believed the allegations depend entirely on the women's subjective view of what was done."

"Of course but you know how it is now, if someone says they were abused, harassed, touched up, whatever, then they were."

"That may be but I think I can safely say that of course my client refutes these allegations. In my view they are monstrous, how on earth can you charge him!"

"I'm sorry to disappoint you but the statements are there and I have to charge him. We are not expecting to keep him in custody and he may leave on bail pending a hearing. Now I need formally to charge you Mr. McCulloch so follow me and we will go back to the desk." Lucien looked at Lily Harper Smith.

"Can they do this, it's all a fabrication, surely that's obvious?"

"I'm afraid they can and having done so you will need to appear before a magistrate on Monday morning, also the GMC will automatically be informed but we can talk about that afterwards."

As they left the room WPC Sprague leaned forwards to Lucien: "Gotcha!"

Back in the street Lucien felt faint and sat down on the steps of the police station, he felt his pulse distractedly, about 100, regular, poor volume.

"Are you OK?" asked Lily Harper-Smith "you probably need some fresh air and a drink, come on, I'll come with you."

Next to this pretty girl in her smart clothes and high heeled shoes Lucien suddenly felt very old, he held out his hand to let her help him up and they walked slowly back along Wigmore Street to the Cock and Lion pub by which time Lucien had recovered enough to get Lily Harper-Smith a large glass of Pinot Grigio and himself a double scotch . Lily waited until he'd had the first "God, I needed that" swig.

"Do you know what will happen when the GMC get the paperwork?" she said.

"I suppose that in the interests of public safety they will suspend me from clinical practice. That's what they usually do in circumstances like this isn't it? They don't have any choice."

"Correct, I'm afraid you'll just have to accept that. In the meantime I'll see what more I can find out. If you come across anyone publically or in print suggesting you are guilty or in any way impugning your professional competence let me know."

They finished their drinks. In the street Lucien squeezed Lily's hand in gratitude and then headed off towards the LCWC to tell the Brigadier what had happened.

Monday July 21st. London

If he'd expected the Brigadier to be supportive or even sympathetic then he was mistaken for he had at the moment of being charged at Marylebone Police Station slipped, regardless of his innocence, from being a respected public figure, an asset, to being a presumed criminal, a doctor being investigated by the GMC and from the point of view of the Clinic a reputational liability. Within half an hour or re-entering the Brigadier's office Lucien found that his admitting privileges had been cancelled, his access to the Clinic, his consulting rooms and his secretary denied. If the press asked questions they would be told that any alleged incident occurred in Professor McCulloch's own consulting room and was not the responsibility of the Clinic.

"I'm afraid Professor that the Clinic is a business with a reputation to maintain and shareholders to be kept happy." But the brigadier did at least shake him by the hand as he showed him out of the office. In his world wounded soldiers were sent promptly to the rear, the wounds regretted but not allowed to disrupt the flow of battle.

Lucien's descent was hastened by his appearance the following Monday morning at the Magistrate's court. Waiting outside with the drunks, the musicians and the petty thieves, his only consolation was that Lily Harper-Smith was there with him. He had hoped that Diana might be there to support him but as he stood in the dock to confirm his name and hear the charges read out again he was glad she was not.

Lily Harper-Smith told the Magistrate that her client would be pleading not guilty and the case was adjourned. A Mr. Fletcher-Pratt appearing for the Crown Prosecution Service was asked how long an adjournment was needed. "Four weeks". Lily Harper-Smith was asked if she had any observations. "Not at this stage" and that was that. Feeling soiled and diminished Lucien left the court and took a taxi to the RUH where he went straight to the Medical Director's office. Over the few months since the awful Winston Arkwright had arrived Dr. Henry Lightwood, the Medical Director, had quickly become, like his new master, a stickler for risk control, blame and obfuscation. Lucien told him what had happened and that the GMC would shortly suspend him.

"Then you'd better clear your desk and go this afternoon" said Henry Lightwood "I'm sorry but you and I know the CEO will not want you anywhere near the hospital; your PA will have to sort out the clinics. Between you and me the CEO will be delighted to see the back of you. Let us know if you get off won't you."

"If I get off! You're a shit Henry. How long have we known each other? Twenty years? Now the best you can offer is to tell me to let you know if I 'get off' as if it just depended on me finding a suitably wily lawyer. Don't tell me you think I was guilty of all this!"

"I don't know Lucien, you know what they say 'everybody has a public life, a private life and a secret life' who knows what your secret life involved."

"Or yours!"

And with that Lucien left the carpeted empire of the Executive and headed for the spartan surroundings of his office to "clear his desk". As he passed Henry Lightwood's secretary in the outer office he said

"Goodbye Harriet, regularly remind Dr. Lightwood that he is a little shit will you!"

"Of course professor, a pleasure! Look after yourself, I expect we will see you again soon."

Lucien reflected that although they had an entirely civil professional relationship he disliked Henry Lightwood, particularly since Lightwood had been made medical director a few years earlier. The unspoken animosity was reciprocated, possibly the fact that Lucien had variously called him a quisling, collaborator, a lackey, or on one occasion a sycophantic bastard, had not helped things. It was clear that Henry bore a grudge and like the CEO he must have been delighted to be rid of Lucien. In fact Henry Lightwood resented Lucien McCulloch for a more subliminal set of reasons. Grammar school versus public school, self-doubt versus self-confidence, laboratory pathologist versus bedside clinician; any would have sufficed.

Tuesday July 22nd. Life suspended

It is hardly surprising that when Lucien arrived home the evening before he'd felt drained, abused, exhausted. Diana was not there – a parent's evening to be coped with at school. Lucien tried to stay awake but was asleep long before her return. In the night he awoke and in doing so woke Diana.

"So how was it yesterday?" she asked "I was worried about you, I know it's four o'clock in the morning but would you like a cup of tea?"

When she returned he was awake enough to give an account, brief but depressing. Excluded from his NHS hospital, his private practice, potentially in prison and struck off the medical register he was no longer the heroic husband he knew she would prefer.

"I think it's the sense of injustice that weighs more heavily than worry about what might happen."

Diana moved across the bed closer to him and stroked his face.

"Dear Lucien, everything will be OK. Everyone who knows you understands that all this must be a fabrication and will soon be seen as nonsense. Why don't you just enjoy the fact that you're still being paid but don't have to go to work. For years the alarm's been set at six-thirty so just turn it off.... let's have a cuddle then we'll go back to sleep."

Lucien woke to the sound of the doorbell. It was 8am.

"I suppose that's the bloody postman" he said shrugging on his dressing gown as he went downstairs; but as he opened the door he was dazzled by a blaze of flashlights.

"What the hell is this?"

"We want to talk to you about your arrest for sexual assault Professor McCulloch, have you anything you want to tell us? We're from The Sun."

"No I haven't, would you please go away."

"We'll publish anyway, it just won't have your side of the story."

The photographer's flash fired off again several times before Lucien was able to push the door shut. He peeped around the curtain, they were still in his front garden. They knew from experience that given enough time and harassment he might change his mind. Diana had appeared beside him her hair an explosion of uncombed, blonde tresses, her dressing gown clutched around her. She flung the door open.

"Would you please go away!"

"Are you his wife? What's it like to be married to a sexual predator?"

"Let's have a picture, darling" shouted the photographer.

Diana retreated indoors shaking and slammed the door, then opened it a crack.

"Go away or I'll call the police."

"Waste of time love, there're on our side."

It was a sunny day outside but Lucien and Diana sat in the kitchen with the curtains closed shocked by the crudeness of this assault on their privacy.

"I'll phone the solicitor to see if she can do anything"

Then the phone rang. This time it was The Daily Telegraph, more courteous but no less demanding. Lucien hung up. He wanted to give his side of the story, shout about the injustice, reject the presumption of guilt that everyone he dealt with had slipped into so readily but he knew he'd need talk to Lily before doing that. Someone had got into the back garden now and was tapping on the kitchen window. The front door bell rang again.

"Oh for God's sake" said Diana "this is preposterous, I'm going to phone the police."

The police however were uninterested, barely even sympathetic.

"Have they broken in or threatened or assaulted you?"

"No, not yet."

"Then the problem is just that they are in your garden, ringing on the bell, tapping on the window?"

"Exactly."

"I'm sorry but I'm not sure that justifies sending a car. You could get their names and apply for a court order."

"But it's harassment, isn't that an offence?"

"As I understand it Madam, it's only been going on for an hour or so. Sorry Madam but call us back if there is actually an assault or a definite threat of violence then we'd be happy to send an officer round."

Eventually Lucien managed to get through to Lily Harper-Smith and she too was unable to provide any solace.

"There's nothing that can be done to stop them I'm afraid. Obviously we'll need to look carefully at anything that's published in case it's defamatory. Perhaps you and I could agree a statement that could be released to them. I'll call you back later with a draft or perhaps we could meet in town tomorrow about it?" After which Lucien simply unplugged the phone.

There were no journalists or photographers outside when Diana ventured out the next morning to buy a newspaper. Normally she would not have bought "The Sun" but today the headline was inescapable *"Doc in the Dock, sex pest top doc charged."* Fortunately most other papers and all the broadsheets seemed to have relegated the story to a small paragraph or not bothered to cover it at all. Lucien doubted if they'd be as low key if he came to trial or a full GMC hearing.

"And what are you going to do to stop this nonsense going any further?" asked Diana sternly

"I'm not sure, I'll need to talk to Lily Harper-Smith, she's dealing with all that."

"You fancy her don't you, that's why you are letting her make the running so you'll have an excuse to see her."

Lucien was nonplussed; he'd hardly mentioned Lily and he never thought to wonder how he felt about her as a person. Perhaps female intuition had sensed something he himself had not spotted.

"Don't be daft – she's the MDU solicitor that's all."

"Well I think you should be doing something yourself. Find out if these two Libyan women really made complaints, try to find out from your friend in Tripoli whether he can provide any evidence that Gamal Ghanem was involved. Do something Lucien! God knows you are going to have plenty of spare time now – and don't think you can spend it all mooching around at home here. You need a timetable."

Once Diana put herself into organising mode there was little point in interrupting her – anyway she was a school teacher and timetabling was her forté.

"Thursday is your day at the college. I'm sure they won't stop you attending that, you're too hard working, too useful."

"But Thursday is your day off – it would be nice to be here together."

"In theory Lucien darling but maybe not in practice. I need some time to myself you know so you'll need some definite projects for other days. You could go fishing; you haven't done much of that recently. My cousin Rachel's husband has some rights on a river in Hampshire somewhere, I'm sure he wouldn't mind. I'll phone her."

Lucien was bemused by all this, not resentful. Like many senior men he was accustomed to competent women arranging his life for him, Pam his PA, his private secretary, his research secretary. He quite enjoyed it though it hadn't gone as far as with poor old Prof. Barcroft who'd found himself at the airport in Delhi and needed to phone his PA who had so efficiently organized his travel, to find out why he was there.

"Perhaps you should settle on some other regular days in the week, as well as Thursday, when you go off to do things. You've got your 'Freedom Pass' so the travel won't cost you anything."

This was a familiar script of Diana's; he was over sixty so he had a 'Freedom Pass' for free travel in London, she did not because she was still young, or at least younger than sixty, and as she was taking hormone replacement therapy and planned to continue indefinitely she would remain, she said, forever young. He had no problem with that. Diana need not have worried that perhaps Lucien might spend his 'gardening leave' gardening or just hanging around the house. Lucien was all too aware that in spite of years living in London his work, children and family had denied him a chance to enjoy it.

In the weeks that followed, now freed from the treadmill... having been pushed off the treadmill, he spent two or three days each week out of the house. Days passed wandering from museum to gallery to unvisited church. On Mondays he could be seen at the Wigmore Hall lunchtime concert. He travelled around mostly by bus whenever possible sitting at the front of the top deck as eager as any tourist and because he wanted to see London through naïve eyes he carried the Michelin Green Guide. Michelin properly followed never allowed important features to be overlooked. Lucien adored galleries and the paintings in them. Had someone offered him a curatorship or an obscure research role in a gallery for this period of his life he would have embraced it. His tastes were catholic and well informed though he had his preferences of course; the medieval and early renaissance paintings in The Sainsbury Wing of The National Gallery, the Impressionists in The Courtauld, primitive sculpture at The British Museum, Turkish pottery in The V&A, the Futurists at the new Estorick Gallery. In his wandering he even visited Tate Modern in its stark mausoleum on the South Bank trying again to like what he saw but abhorring the crude pretentiousness of most of it. What did it say on the wall? *"These artists sought to redefine art giving priority to concept, process and activity over the finished objects"*.

"Self-serving crap!" he muttered to himself so loudly that the German tourist next to him looked alarmed imaging that this required a response from him.

Lucien went into his club, The Athenaeum, for lunch on these perambulatory days always turning right into the members' bar as he came in so as to see who might join him at lunch. Often it was his friend Julian Scantlebury whose Pickwickian presence dominated the Bar; unmissable in his bow-tie, yellow checked jacket and red waistcoat. Julian would hail him as he came through the door.

"Hurrah, here's the handsome Lucien come to cheer my day with tales of gore. The usual dear boy?" and he would pat the stool next to him at the bar. He was so fat that he avoided the armchairs as they were difficult to get up from and far from the bar. Julian put his own extravert happiness down to the fact of being enormously wealthy, a bachelor, living in central London and enjoying food. He was a music critic for "The Times" and occasionally the restaurant critic though he preferred eating in restaurants he knew and who knew him. "There's no problem with the music" he said "they tell you in advance what's on the menu and if you know you're not going to like it you don't go. It's not like that in restaurants."

But for all the pleasures it was an odd life for Lucien and after a couple of weeks it began to pall. He resented the fact that he was not doing anything constructive, also the legal case wasn't going anywhere. Lily Harper-Smith had failed to get any response from the CPS, Lucien's attempts to contact Professor El Hammedi by phone had failed and there had been no response to his e-mail. The GMC wouldn't do anything until his pending court case was either concluded or abandoned. His enquiries had, however, involved two meetings with Lily, meetings which he embarked upon warily following Diana's presumption that he "fancied her". They met twice, once in her office in Lincoln's Inn and once, at her suggestion, for lunch nearby. Both meetings were strictly formal but as he sat looking across the table at her almost oval face, her high arched thinly drawn eyebrows, her slim neck and her pointed chin, brown hair pulled back into a tight chignon he realized that she was actually rather beautiful; part way between a Botticelli and a Modigliani. He focussed on the small cameo which secured her blouse at her throat but when he couldn't help noticing the hint of nipples beneath her blouse he felt a flush of confusion. She was perhaps thirty-five, about Lucy's age, and had Diana not raised the subject he would not have allowed himself even a whiff of 'fancying her'. Actually it wasn't a matter of not 'allowing' himself such thoughts, it was a reflex; as a gynaecologist he had seen and touched more half naked women that any Casanova could have boasted of but never had he harboured any sexual thoughts about them. Professionalism? Commitment to marriage? Both? Something else? Odd though – now he came to think about it. At lunch he watched as Lily daintily ate tiny scallops in *beurre blanc*.

"That was nice" she said smiling sweetly as if someone had just kissed her.

"No" thought Lucien wondering if in such company he could wipe up the sauce from his plate with the bread, French style. "No, I don't 'fancy' her" in the sense of wanting to slip his hand under the silk blouse. No he enjoyed her as he would a beautiful painting, simply admiring, nothing more. He explained this to Diana over dinner .

"How proper" she retorted "How sweet – I bet she fancies you though!"

The thought in all truth had not crossed Lucien's mind. Diana was in full flight now.

"Women like her relish the idea of an older, successful lover and you're handsome, still got most of your hair and you're in quite good nick for a man of your age. Pity about your chubby tummy though – you ought to take more exercise."

Lucien laughed it off but was slightly affronted. Although he made a point of regularly complementing Diana on her slim figure and her good looks, she rarely reciprocated. Perhaps he was indeed going to seed; if he was he hadn't noticed. He never weighed himself and mirrors were for practical tasks, combing hair, straightening the tie. He was familiar with the character in film and fiction who gazes into the shaving mirror, pulls down a lid to inspect the yellowing sclerae, plucks at the jowls and suddenly sees his true self reflected. The mirror as a short cut to self-knowledge. Certainly this didn't work for him. Lucien never considered his body, the visible parts anyway. He measured his blood pressure, occasionally ate a balanced diet, got his eyes tested but the fleshy bits and how he looked were not considered. If asked he'd have said that it was what he was that defined him not how he looked. Still Diana was probably right; he didn't take enough exercise, though he doubted if taking more would get rid of his chubby tummy, a feature of his age rather than his inertia. He toyed with the idea of reminding Diana what she too would spread a little in the same place if she stopped her HRT but decided against it.

She was right though he needed to take more exercise; brisk walking was claimed to suffice especially if the arms were swung vigorously as you walked. He resolved to walk more but without the Monty Python arm swinging.

Thursday 31st July. Tripoli, Libya

When Charlie O'Dwyer was admitted to Sandhurst Military Academy no-one was surprised; a recent graduate in Arabic from Oxford, a rowing 'blue' and a charming, articulate young man the Army was delighted to have him. At the AOSB, the Army Officer Selection Board, he scored the highest OIR, Officer Intelligence Rating, of his entry; in the tests of leadership, resourcefulness and physical prowess he excelled. When he was thrown out of Sandhurst just one year later he was not surprised and nor were the shrewder assessors who has predicted that his rebellious individualism was not compatible with a life of soldiering. For MI6, SIS, the Secret Intelligence Service, he was however exactly the sort of man they wanted; better by far than the cast-offs from the Foreign Office recruitment programmes and he was quickly and quietly assimilated. His Arabic made him an ideal posting for any of that swathe of difficult Arabic speaking countries that stretch from Morocco to Iraq. Charlie was in his element and found the training a lot more relaxed than the awful shouting and stamping at Sandhurst. Libya was his first overseas posting, ostensibly as commercial secretary. Once there his charm and easy gregariousness either helped him get at the information his masters were after or recruit locals who would find out what he wanted to know. His most valuable contact had been "inherited" from his predecessor – always a tricky change. The person, and it is a person not a 'joe' or 'an asset', is naturally wary of a new handler. Often if they cannot talk to the person they know they avoid contact and simply cut the link. For them it is, after all, often a matter of life or death or worse. It was a measure of Charlie O'Dwyer's charm that Professor Mohammed El-Hammedi stayed in contact. He was important not just as an articulate anglophile but also, best of all, a member of The People's Committee, a link that would give a clearer view of President Gaddafi's intentions than the flatulent, contrived meetings in his tent in the desert to which foreign dignitaries were invited so that they could be lectured. Not all the members of The People's Committee were quite so perceptive and helpful as Professor El-Hammedi. Gamal Ghanem for one, a self-serving thug, but as Minister for Trade a man much courted by the

British government. For Charlie O'Dwyer, as much conditioned by James Bond movies as by his SIS tutors, global politics was a matter of Goodies and Baddies, though he did admit having difficulty pigeon-holing the Jews and the Palestinians locked into their insoluble feud. It was easier in Libya. He knew that in spite of the British government's courtship Muammar Gaddafi was a Baddie. The Goodies were more difficult to spot but Charlie O'Dwyer's information confirmed that they were mostly to be found in the east of the country, in Benghazi and thereabouts and he, and his predecessor, had managed to persuade the powers in London to channel money and expertise to several of the groups especially the LIFG, the Libyan Islamic Fighting Group. OK they were fanatics, Islamists but they were intent on the overthrow of Gaddafi so well worth supporting. The lessons of Afghanistan about how that support might rebound had not yet been learned. Back in Tripoli he'd been glad to help Professor El-Hammedi's English friend, Lucien McCulloch, get out of the country though he'd been bemused by how difficult the man had found the stresses of uncertainty and risk. Charlie O'Dwyer relished such dangers and the deceptions; Lucien McCulloch clearly didn't. Once he'd heard he was safely back in London O'Dwyer had put him out of his mind until he received a memo from the ambassador's PA saying that Professor El-Hammedi hoped that Charlie would be at the reception at the ambassador's residence the next afternoon. Normally meetings with contacts are fraught with hazard for both parties and are kept to a minimum, but "The Prof" was in a different category. The ambassador made sure that as a senior member of the Libyan government he was invited to as many receptions and dinners as possible. Charlie as a member of the embassy staff could always arrange to be there though, in fact, he hated them; the ambassador busily pressing the flesh and his wife in her pearls and Laura Ashley frock smiling relentlessly at all-comers. To Charlie these occasions felt like never ending wedding receptions in the country houses of his Oxford friends – but with no alcohol. This time though he made sure he was paying attention, hovering within easy reach of "The Prof". He briefed Janet from the embassy to stay beside him so the contact looked natural.

"Hello Prof, this is Janet she works with me, she's OK to stay."

"Good afternoon Janet, how nice to meet you. If I may say so that's a very pretty dress." Dear Prof, so courteous, so old fashioned. "Now Charles there is more trouble from my colleague Gamal Ghanem. You'll remember helping my good friend Professor McCulloch. It seems now that Gamal Ghanem is persisting with this personal war against Professor McCulloch and has arranged for him to be arrested in London." Charles O'Dwyer looked sceptical.

"How can he arrange that?"

"I think he gets his friend Mr. Ashbury, your Minister of Trade, to arrange it. I don't know how. He seems to have a power over this Mr. Ashbury that I do not understand. Several of us in The People's Committee are concerned that though Gamal Ghanem is trying to set up important business deals particularly with oil companies, these are primarily for his own benefit rather than the Libyan people's and perhaps Mr. Ashbury is helping him. Also he is pushing the bid to release Al-Magrahi from prison in Scotland so as to keep Gaddafi on his side The rest of us know this will only annoy the Americans and make things worse for Libya" Charlie smiled and gestured to Janet.

"I'm just smiling at you for the watchers' benefit" he said to her and then to Prof Hammedi. "It's OK Prof I did hear what you said."

"Good – I was worried that you weren't taking me seriously" said Prof El-Hammedi speaking to Janet to maintain the charade.

"What are you telling me Prof?" asked O'Dwyer

"I'm telling you, you have a problem with your Minister of Trade, this Mr. Ashbury. I'm not quite sure what the problem is but Ghanem has control over him and it's not through friendship and I'm sure will not necessarily be in the interests of either of our countries." Charlie O'Dwyer looked bemused, "And presumably" El-Hammedi continued "Ashbury has people doing his dirty business for him in the UK, he couldn't personally arrange for my friend to be arrested surely? It's not Libya!"

"Ashbury certainly seems to have been an enthusiast for all things Libyan – we'd noticed that. Maybe we need to take a bit more interest in him. Thank you so much Prof. Perhaps we should go our separate ways now."

"It would be safer – goodbye Miss Janet it was nice to meet with you."

Charlie O'Dwyer took Janet's hand and walked her away. He was in no hurry to let her go – he had plans for the evening, but only after he'd talked to London on the secure link at the embassy.

Friday August 1st. London

Full of good intentions to become leaner and fitter Lucien decided that instead of going to the nearest station he would walk up to Denmark Hill Station and get the train from there. He calculated the walk would take him thirty minutes. Then he could get a train to Victoria and from there walk across Green Park to The Royal Academy in Picadilly, another half hour walk – spend an hour looking at the Hammershoi exhibition again, then walk to The Athenaeum for lunch, twenty minutes. All in all he could easily walk for a couple of hours in the day which was plenty. Lucien liked to have his day planned out in his head. He always set out with a clear idea of where he was going, by what route and how long it would take. He liked his life to have structure and predictability which was why the events of the previous few weeks had so unbalanced him. As he walked to the station he thought about the Hammershoi paintings, they'd disturbed him too but he didn't know why. On the surface they were just melancholic interior views, Danish, cold northern light washed across grey panelling, a woman in black sitting at a piano or standing by a table her face never seen. Perhaps he should just experience the paintings and not try to understand them. Perhaps he should approach Diana the same way. She'd seemed brisk and unsympathetic since his arrest. Perhaps that's how she expressed anxiety. Perhaps, heaven forbid, she didn't love him as much as he loved her. When she'd had problems it made him sad and even more attentive. To her his problems seemed an irritation. He should stop analyzing and just enjoy his walk, the fresh air, the flowers in the gardens he passed and the sun. At least he could feel it on his skin not like to two men who had been sitting on a motorcycle across the road when he left home. Black helmets, leathers, gloves, not an inch left with which to sense the elements or enjoy the sun.

By the time he reached Denmark Hill station, just across the road from King's College Hospital, he felt refreshed. As he stood waiting to cross the road someone shouted "Hey, doc!" he paused and turned and at that instant glimpsed two men on a motorcycle, the pillion passenger pointing a gun at him. A fraction of a second later as he threw himself to the ground he heard a rapid sequence of sharp bangs and the motorcycle accelerating away. In his head Robin's words from beyond the grave "when the shooting starts you get down and stay down". Lucien stayed down, then realizing he'd not been hit sat up. Around him people were shouting and a woman screaming. He could see two other people on the ground, the one nearest to him a black girl her hand clutching her neck, blood pouring from between her fingers and onto her shirt. Suddenly all his fears were over-ridden by his surgical reflexes. He glanced at the other person who was lying down, he was moving, breathing, eyes open, no signs of blood. The black girl seemed the more serious, blood was still pouring from her neck soaking into her clothes and splashing onto the road; she was now thrashing about, her breathing coming in harsh gasps. Lucien tried to examine her, tried to assess her wounds, stop the bleeding, move her onto her side, help her breathe, but cold despair gripped him. He had nothing with which to help, no endo-tracheal tube, no intravenous line, no surgical instruments, no-one else to help him. All he could do was try to press on the wound in her neck to stop the bleeding without obstructing her breathing. It was not like this in hospital and he could see King's College Hospital just 100m away. The girl was beginning to choke now, unable to speak, her eyes imploring him. He heard sirens coming closer. There was nothing he could do. He held her hand. Her eyes closed and her breathing whispered to a halt. The sirens stopped and he was pushed away by paramedics. Lucien sat in the road his head in his hands.

"You all right, sir?" it was a policeman, Lucien looked at himself; dirty, covered in blood, his jacket torn.

"I think so, thanks. Poor girl, that was meant for me and I ducked and then I couldn't do anything to help. I tried."

"Not your fault sir, let's just sit you in the ambulance and get them to take a proper look at you shall we?"

He was unscathed apart from a scrape on his knuckles but they wanted to take him to hospital.

"No, no it's not necessary, please could someone just find a taxi to take me home, it's not far," but they took him home in a police car. A pair of plain clothed detectives came to see him within an hour to take a statement but shook their heads when he tried to explain that he was the target, that the gunman had shouted "Hey doc" to attract his attention, that a Libyan called Gamal Ghanem wanted him dead, that the gunmen had been outside his house on the motorbike. They were having none of it. Could he be sure the men on the motorbike were the same as the ones shooting? No. Was he absolutely certain they shouted "Hey, doc". No. If the men outside his house were the gunmen why had they waited until he got to Denmark Hill to shoot? No, this was a typical south London drive-by shooting, probably black on black, the victim probably someone's girlfriend who'd cheated. The case would be passed to officers from Operation Trident, the specialist unit that deals with Afro-Caribbean gun crime. They might want to see him but probably not. With which they finished the cups of tea he'd made for them and left him sitting blood stained at the kitchen table which was where Diana found him when she returned for lunch at 12.30. Only three hours had elapsed since he'd left the house.

Diana was almost as skeptical as the police when Lucien claimed events as an attempt on his life.

"However, just in case Gamal Ghanem is arranging to get you killed you'd better be careful" she said pulling his blood stained shirt up over his head and dumping it in a sink full of cold water. "Perhaps you could take up Rachel's husband's offer of fishing. They've got a little cottage there too which you could use."

"Would you come too, that would be nice?"

"Lucien, you know I have to work, term ends this week but they don't let us off until the middle of next week. Also I don't fish."

Saturday 2nd August . Hampshire

The following day, Saturday, Lucien drove down to Hampshire trying not to let his concentration be blunted by recurring images of the day before. By late afternoon he found himself in a dark cottage near Fordingbridge fronting onto a small but picturesque tributary of the Hampshire Avon. Between the cottage and the river was just a field of rough grass some sheep and a donkey with white ringed mournful eyes who was inquisitive but not friendly. A field in the other side of the river sloped up to some woods, the tree tops occupied by a half dozen bickering rooks. There was no food in the cottage, the bed was unmade and felt damp but at least it wasn't raining. So he walked through the fields the mile to the nearest pub checking out the stream. There were a few rises here and there but it didn't look very promising. For the moment he was just missing London, Diana, his house and his daughter. Disconsolate, still shocked by the previous day's events. The pub was almost empty and the small cluster of locals joshing at the end of the bar obviously resented his presence in the corner with his pint of beer and an unappetizing pie with beans. The barman seemed to know nothing about the fishing.

The next day, Sunday, Lucien found his waders had a hole in them and his box of dry flies in disarray. All in all nothing gave him the confidence needed for a successful day's fishing but it was pleasant enough exploring the water, watching for trout in the dark eddies under the banks, floating his fly past the reed banks; the water was so clear that he could see every fish that ventured up towards the fly – and they could see him. But he landed two so it was grilled trout for dinner after which he felt more at ease. He phoned Diana but she wasn't in so he contented himself with a book and the sound of the rooks settling for the night into the darkening treetops.

The next morning, Monday, it was cloudy with a light drizzle; easily enough to dampen any enthusiasm for revisiting the same piece of river as the day before. What to do? Where to go? So easy in London, so difficult on a wet day in the country. He scanned the framed Ordnance Survey map on the wall. Salisbury was quite close; he'd not been there since childhood. Its cathedral was certainly worth a revisit. And then he remembered that Felicity, his girlfriend from University times, lived there or nearby and, barely legible in the little list of phone numbers that accompanied him from diary to diary, was her number. And yes the number was still hers, and yes she answered, and gosh what a long time since they'd spoken, and yes of course she'd love to meet him. So he drove to Salisbury.

They ate upstairs in one of those self-consciously 'olde' restaurants with low, dark beams, round oak tables and uncomfortable wheel-back chairs. The apple cheeked waitress wrote their order laboriously on a pad which she returned to the little pouch under her white lace pinny. She then came back to set on the table a pot containing cellophane tubes of ketchup, brown sauce and salad dressing; also two sets of cutlery wrapped in white paper napkins. She did not offer to get them a drink. Lucien was always bemused by how foreign these English county towns felt, how alien for a Londoner, more alien than Brussels or Rome or Copenhagen. The food was wholesome enough and he did eventually coax two glasses of wine from the waitress. Felicity and he talked about their time at Cambridge and managed to remember the names of friends and the places they'd been to together. She remembered them better than Lucien because for her Cambridge was an apogee, three years full of excitement, new discoveries, freedom and growing self-confidence; but after that there had been just anxiety and solitude. For Lucien it was a good time too but only a station en route to a fuller life, looking back from which the Cambridge years seemed as contrived as one of those Victorian bottle gardens, vivaria; luxuriant but as nothing without the glassy prison walls. Felicity's life was better than it had been when she'd last spoken to Lucien. Her mother was now in a nursing home and at last, at exactly the age of fifty, she had become married, to a widower who spend his weekdays in London; a kindly pipe and slippers man who gave up golf to spend the weekends with her.

"Would you come home with me for coffee Lucien? And then we have some unfinished business from Cambridge and I'd like to close that chapter on a happy note!"

She had come straight out with it looking him in the eye and giving him a big smile. He looked at her in amazement, reviewing her in a new light. Her hair was just as luxuriant, just as black though now perhaps with help, her breasts no less magnificent than they had been all those years ago, her smile as winning and as she talked she was tracing with her finger around the edge of his hand then she turned it over to stroke his palm but he could not help noticing how her rings were in a groove in the finger, her nails worn and the skin discoloured with the brown blotches of age.

"Well?"

"You're suggesting we go back to your place and make love to each other?"

"Yes, do what we never had the courage to do forty years ago – do it properly for once!"

"Oh Felicity, you flatter me but you know it's not on. Quite apart from the rights and wrongs it's just crazy. If it didn't work out you'd regret it, if we had a wildly enjoyable afternoon we might want to do it again and think of the trouble that could cause. Let's just have coffee, kiss each other goodbye and leave it at that shall we?" And that's what they did.

"How ironic Lucien" she said as they parted "All those times when I said no and now that I say yes, yes please, it's you who says no!"

As he drove back to the cottage he wondered why the hell he'd arranged to meet her again – what had he expected? Deep down in his subconscious fantasised that they would fall into bed together? Perhaps he wanted to test himself, test his relationship with Diana, see how close to the cliff's edge he could walk before fear stopped him. Anyway no harm had been done except perhaps to him. Closing the chapter with Felicity had made him sad, another mooring rope to the life he'd known had now been severed.

Later as the day waned he wondered disconsolately along the river with his rod, flicking the fly half-heartedly onto pools that had looked promising on his previous visit. He was in no mood to return to the empty cottage but it was almost dark. In the final pool under the stump of an old oak he could barely see his fly, a tiny silhouette drifting slowly across the reflection of the last silver streak of sky. Suddenly there was a swirl in the water, the fly disappeared and more through surprise than skill Lucien grasped the line firmly and flicked up the tip of the rod; the fish was hooked. It felt strong as Lucien reeled back the line little by little and within just a few minutes he had the fish on the bank, a brown trout, a pound and a half perhaps but old and battle scarred with ragged fins. The trout just lay on the grass without any more struggle, its eyes melancholic, its mouth turned down. "You poor old sod, you look even more depressed than me". Lucien rummaged in the bottom of his canvas fishing bag and brought out not the heavy 'priest' to dispatch the fish, but a pair of pliers with which he carefully crushed the barb of the hook and withdrew it, then slipped the fish back into the water where it lay for a moment before disappearing into the darkness. He plucked a handful of grass and wiped the fish's slime off his hand then rinsed it in the river and with it the last touch from Felicity. As he put the pliers back in the bag they chinked against his silver whisky flask, his father's. He took it out, '*To F McC from S McC 1945*" was engraved on one side of it in flowing italics. On the other "*L'Amour triomphe de Tout*'. He took a long swig and set off slowly back across the fields. The sky was full of stars, car headlights flickered between far off trees to the west and the lights of Fordingbridge tinted the sky to the east, but here engulfing Lucien was just a huge inky pool of darkness containing him and the distant light in the cottage window, utterly silent apart from the hooting of an owl.

Back in the cottage he phoned Diana.

"I'm coming back tomorrow. I'll be home by lunchtime."

"Oh dear, I thought you'd be away longer, I've got all sorts of things planned."

"I'm not staying here, I feel like a refugee; I need to get back and do something positive."

Wednesday 6th August. Tea with Pam

Diana was not at home when Lucien arrived back from Hampshire, just a note "Sorry not to be here, see you this evening D xx" so he made himself a cheese sandwich and sat down at his desk hoping to make his own stand against the problems that were besetting him. First he sent another e-mail to Professor El-Hammedi in Libya, more in hope than in expectation of a reply. Then he phoned Lily Harper-Smith but her secretary said she was "out at lunch and not expected back today." Next he phoned Pam his PA at the hospital.

"I'm so pleased to hear from you Prof – a lot has been happening; it's not a happy place here. I'm sorry about the reasons for your not being around but you're lucky to be out of it. Are you well?"

"I am, thank you." Lucien chose not to tell Pam about the attempt to kill him instead they talked for a while about what had happened in his department (he still thought of it as his), how the consultants had all been told that the number of posts was to be reduced and how they would need to re-apply for their own jobs. The nurses were spending their time doing 'dependency assessments' on each patient in an attempt to see how big a reduction could be made in the number of nurses and in beds. The secretaries had been told that most of them would go, to be replaced by digital dictation with the typing outsourced to India. A few would be kept for answering the phone. 'Customer Service Agents' they were to be called. Most people were looking for a job elsewhere. Lucien was appalled. He'd seen enough uninformed change during his 40 years in the NHS to know that most of the benefits expected by the new management would not occur; complaints and problems would soon rise and extra staff would be recruited, this would be followed by a return to the previous ways of doing things with none of the proclaimed financial saving achieved – just a trail of damage and disillusionment.

"Pam" he said "I need to take you out to lunch away from the chaos."

"How kind Prof, but I really shouldn't – not lunch, tea perhaps?"

"Tea then – tomorrow." Lucien had no idea where one took a lady for tea – or what was involved. "Tomorrow. I'll meet you by the ice cream van outside The Tate at 3.00pm."

"Are we going out for an ice cream?"

"No, no it's simply that I don't want to appear in the hospital and it's somewhere nearby that we both know."

He phoned Lucy.

"Lucy – help! Where would I take Pam my PA for tea?"

"I never done tea Dad but I believe clients of mine go to The Wolseley in Piccadilly, next to The Ritz. Don't go to The Ritz; it very vulgar and full of foreign tourists."

The Wolseley is simply a large, vaulted room entered directly from the south side of Piccadilly, the room shielded from the draughts by red velvet curtains just inside the door. As you slip through the curtains you enter a completely un-English scene; a high vaulted ceiling supported by black Doric pillars, the floor is patterned black and white marble, the tables black with white linen cloths. The huge chandeliers hanging from the ceiling are in black and the whole decor lightened by some patches of gilt on wall panels though with none of the glittering vulgarity of The Ritz next door. The waiters in black aprons seemed middle aged and attentive in a way that reminded Lucien of Vienna or Budapest. The tables were mostly full but he was pleased to notice a little staircase at the back leading to a narrow balcony from which the room and the red velvet entrance could be watched.

"A table on the balcony please." Since the shooting only five days ago Lucien had remained wary, anxious that another attempt might be launched at any time, catching him unawares in the street. Surely not here though. Lucien settled Pam into a chair and ordered tea. Tea to drink and "tea" to eat. He never normally ate at this time and the plate of finely cut little sandwiches, the slices of chocolate covered gateaux exuding cream reminded him of those childhood treats when his mother took him to Lyons Corner House and fed him cake to keep him quiet as she chattered to her friends. He took a slice of Battenberg cake and, just he had as a child, freed each pink and yellow square from the marzipan coating eating each separately.

Pam was, as ever, neither quiet nor demonstrative, not overdressed (dark blue pleated skirt, sensible light blue cardigan, single row of pearls) nor underdressed. Just the predictable, reliable Mrs. Pamela Jones that he'd known for twenty years. She'd chosen Earl Grey tea of course and was trying hard not to have more than one cake.

"How's Wilfred?" asked Lucien. He knew that Wilfred, Pam's husband, was about ten years older than her so perhaps seventy and he'd been in and out of the hospital with colon cancer during the previous year.

"He looks well, he eats what I put in front of him. He still goes to the pub on Friday evenings to be with his friends but how he feels I'm not sure. He doesn't talk about it. Men are useless when it comes to talking about their problems."

Lucien knew he was not included in this stricture as his relationship with Pam was absolutely neutral. They did not discuss each other's private lives and never had. She was fiercely loyal yet he wondered how she perceived the person for whom she worked and to whom she was so attached; perhaps her loyalty was to his position rather than to him as a person? The neutral relationship was automatic in the hospital but here tucked away in a dark corner of a restaurant she clearly felt less constrained.

"I'm sorry about you being suspended from the hospital, you must feel awful about it. Presumably you'll be back soon – as soon as it's all sorted out?"

"Of course I will, yes. Back to normal as soon as possible. But what about you, doesn't Wilfred need you? Have another pastry." He gestured to the tiered silver cake rack on which the downfall of their diets was so tantalizingly displayed. She took a small piece of shortbread.

"Probably he does but until he's obviously in the last part of his cancer I need to keep my own life going."

"Don't you want to do things together?" Lucien knew that Pam, with her unconstrained access to the hospital computer, must have seen the pathology reports and the scans showing that the cancer had already spread to Wilfred's liver.

"Not particularly. Over the years we've done all we've wanted to and could afford to do. All we want to do now is behave as if all is well. It's less stressful that way. Not be flustered."

"I've never seen you flustered, ever" said Lucien.

"Never in public – it wouldn't do would it." she replied sitting up straight in her chair.

Lucien looked at her thinking how lucky he was. He called the waiter over.

"A bottle of champagne please. The Pommery Brut. You're not in a hurry are you Pam?"

"In the circumstances of you having just ordered a bottle of champagne that would be impolite wouldn't it! Besides I need to go through this list of things that have come up whilst you have been away."

She put her spectacles on and produced two neatly folder pieces of paper from her handbag. One list, two copies, one for each of them. Typical.

"And there's this hand delivered letter which says 'confidential to be opened only by the addressee'. She handed it to him.

"Shall we look?" teased Lucien. He filled their glasses. The letter was from a senior civil servant at The Department of Health, someone Lucien knew well.

"We both know that some things are not for chatting about at the hospital don't we Pam?"

"Of course Prof."

"OK. This letter says that rumours of an unacceptable management style at RUH and deepening demoralisation of the staff have led The Secretary of State to be 'minded to commission an enquiry'. Before that they wish to talk to just a few people to confirm that what The Secretary of State has heard is accurate. It seems I'm one of those people."

"And who else?"

"It doesn't say."

Pam could barely contain her pleasure.

"Thank goodness someone is doing something. Is there anything I can do to help? I could make a summary of everyone's bad experiences and type it up for you. Also what Angela told me might be of interest."

"Angela?"

"You know, posh Angela, the NCT Breast Feeding Counsellor. She's married to a very rich city man. They were at a dinner somewhere and were sitting near Winston Arkwright our CEO who was puffing himself up about having been made CEO at The RUH and how it was probably partly due to having an MBA from The Harvard Business School. Angela's husband has exactly that, a Harvard MBA and reckoned from the conversation that Winston Arkwright was making it all up though he didn't say anything at the time and Winston Arkwright didn't know that Angela works at the hospital. She probably had her diamonds on."

"Lucien put down his champagne, very attentive – he'd heard rumours before but nothing definite."

"What's Angela's husband's name?"

"Robin, Robin Braithwaite."

"And how old is he?"

"Mid forties, about the same as Winston Arkwright."

"So he was probably right. Interesting."

They finished the champagne and Lucien helped Pam down the stairs. She refused a taxi.

"I live out in the suburbs at the end of the District line. I'll get the tube thanks." So he walked her to Green Park tube station and said goodbye, even now after twenty years no kiss on the cheek just a routine going home time parting. Their entirely satisfactory neutral relationship to be continued.

Friday 8th August. Department of Health, Whitehall, London

The next afternoon, safe in his study in Dulwich, Lucien did a quick internet search on Robin Braithwaite and confirmed that he did indeed have a Harvard MBA. Then he pulled up the CV of Winston Arkwright. He'd been sent this because he'd been on the shortlisting committee for a new CEO and sure enough there it was "MBA Harvard Business School 1994-95". He found the Harvard Business School website and negotiating his way past a large gallery of smiling and ethnically diverse graduates he checked the Alumni pages and with a frisson of embarrassment tried unsuccessfully to log in as Robin Braithwaite. No luck so far, no sign anywhere of an Arthur or a Winston Arkwright. So he tried a new tack and phoned the Boston number given on the website.

"Good morning. I'm trying to clarify some information on one of your graduates."

"Yes sir. Thank you, but I'm afraid data protection regulations do not allow us to give out information about our graduates."

"I just wanted to confirm which years one of your graduates attended."

"I'm sorry sir...." Lucien had hoped not to use his next ploy.

"That's most unfortunate. I'm calling on behalf of the UK Honours Committee – the body that advises Her Majesty to whom she should award knighthoods and other honours. There is a British citizen who has been proposed for an honour but before the nomination can be put before the committee we need to verify the accuracy of the nominee's curriculum vitae. I'm sure you can appreciate that we are most keen to avoid any embarrassment to Her Majesty by asking her to confer an honour on someone for whom it might not be appropriate. I know you will understand that this process requires both sensitivity and confidentiality."

"Yes sir, I can understand that but ....."

"Quite simply I'm just hoping that you just might confirm whether Arthur Winston Arkwright was awarded an MBA having been a student between 1994 and 1995."

Lucien had put on his most plummy voice for this hoping that the American lady on the other end of the phone would, like so many others, succumb to an English accent. She did, and confirmed that they had no record of a Mr. Arthur Winston Arkwright ever having been on the MBA course or indeed at The Harvard Business School.

"He might have been on one of our short leadership courses but there are many of those, some only a few days long and they're held all over the world including in England. We don't keep the name of those attendees on our data base. I'm so sorry sir."

Lucien wasn't surprised. He'd been suspicious of Arkwright's exceptional CV which didn't quite match the man, though they'd been told that the head-hunters had checked it. He was also not the only person annoyed by being told by Winston Arkwright that he'd been "at university in Oxford". Arkwright had not been so rash as to conceal on his CV that truth that the university in question was not Oxford University, the Oxford of 'Oxbridge', of embryo prime ministers, of Inspector Morse and the Sheldonian Theatre, it was instead the humbler Oxford Brookes University of which the Faculty of Business Studies is unromantically housed in an old teachers' training college miles outside Oxford. "No dreaming spires there" thought Lucien.

Just two days later having warily negotiated the train journey from Dulwich to Victoria and onto the District Line Lucien arrived at the quasi-gothic piece of brick built modernity in Whitehall that is the façade of The Department of Health, Richmond House. Actually he liked its brave quirkiness, not a virtue he identified with The Department of Health, an administrative monolith of truly Soviet proportions. Outside a security guard was remonstrating with a man sitting on the pavement holding a placard "You killed my wife! Take responsibility!" Inside he succumbed to the usual ritual of signing in, hanging a plastic "Visitor" badge around his neck and waiting to be collected. Within a few minutes a short, fat man rushed across the lobby hand out to greet him. He didn't look like an aspiring mandarin; red faced, balding and bursting out of a blue suit of which all three jacket buttons had ill-advisedly been done up.

"Lucien, how nice to see you again. Thanks for coming in. I've booked a room downstairs for us."

It was, as Lucien knew it would be, one of those over-bright, windowless, little rooms in the basement; a square table and eight chairs.

"Why on earth do we never just meet in your office and sit on comfortable chairs?" asked Lucien.

"Sorry. Meetings guidelines are specific and also we'll have to have a note taker with us."

"Sod that Humphrey, do you want to hear what I've got to say or not?"

"Of course I do."

"Then we'll go to the pub and your note taker can go and do something useful elsewhere."

"Okay. We'll walk along to The Clarence at the other end of Whitehall, The Red Lion is closer but always full of DoH people."

Lucien knew Humphrey Attwell from his time chairing the government inquiry into school age pregnancy and knew him well enough to know that he'd listen, be discrete and be unperturbed by Lucien's recent brush with the law and The General Medical Council. Once settled into a quiet corner of the pub with their pints of beer he showed Attwell Pam's list of "bullying events" gleaned from her friends. He then recounted details of the meetings he himself had had with the new CEO and with the CEO's 'top team'. None of it surprised Attwell.

"Don't think you and your people have been treated differently from everyone else Lucien – everyone we've talked to tells the same story."

Humphrey had already opened his second packet of crisps by tearing down the side of the packet to make it easier for his pudgy hand to get at them.

"You'll get coronary heart disease if you eat all those Humphrey" warned Lucien genially.

"I'll be okay. I don't smoke."

"I've thought about Arkwright since my last meeting with him and it's not just that he's a boor and a bully, it's the culture that's wrong. He's where he is because he fits into the new cultural fabric of the NHS so well."

"You don't think a BSD CEO is appropriate?"

"BSD, what's that?"

"City term – Big Swinging Dick – forceful, macho, ruthless."

"No, I don't think that's appropriate. We both know how this will turn out Humphrey. The Secretary of State will order an enquiry into the management culture at RUH, Arkwright and his team will be identified for what they are and The DoH will tut tut and say that there is no place for that sort of behaviour in today's NHS, no blame culture allowed, whistleblowers will be cherished and rewarded and so on. All that crap. Arkwright and his cronies will be eased out probably into some senior positions here in Whitehall and nothing will really change!"

Humphrey Attwell looked bemused.

"No point in you getting cross Lucien – it's the way things are."

"It's the way thing are that's wrong. The Department has always been hide-bound by its Command and Control obsession. Now there's also this belief that you can't trust professionals, you just have to set them targets and budgets and all will be well – it doesn't work Humphrey. Words like Care and Quality don't get used."

"Ah ha! Got you there Lucien! There's an Act just going through Parliament that will set up a "Care Quality Commission" to inspect hospitals to make sure they are providing good quality care. Got that Lucien? *Care* and *Quality*. But we both know that just bandying words about won't change anything. It's not easy. Poor care is not just the result of the way we run The NHS or the way the government runs the country it's other things too, things we can't change."

"Such as?"

"Nurses being better educated and not wanting to do the basic dirty jobs anymore, doctors bound by EU working hours and so constantly handing on problems rather than taking responsibility. A belief that the technology is more important than love and care."

"I never thought I'd hear you say love was important in The NHS Humphrey – you astound me."

"I'm a Christian Lucien, I believe in love." He laughed self-deprecatingly "but I think this department's love for Arthur Winston Arkwright is probably waning."

"Good. And if you are talking to your lawyers get them to check the qualifications cited in Arkwright's CV."

"We already have – but thanks."

When Lucien walked back past the entrance to Richmond House the man with the placard was still there, also a noisy group holding a banner "Save our Hospital". It didn't say which or why – perhaps they were appealing on behalf of everyone.

Over supper Diana was, as ever, the healer explaining that The NHS was not some unhelpable basket case but just another casualty of a government, like every government, incapable of letting go. Education is just the same she said, the habit of over regulation just as pervasive. Her primary school was saved by its small size, there was nowhere for managers to hide. They couldn't just demand this and that and then swan off into an office somewhere distant; they were all teachers with pupils of their own and they had to sit in the same common room as all the other teachers during break. No hiding place.

Diana made no secret of the fact that she found Lucien's passionate commitment to his job tiring, even irritating; responsible for sucking some of the life out of their marriage. Not that he'd have noticed. Diana, not normally one for discussing her feelings had unburdened herself to her mother about it on the phone just a few nights earlier.

"He hears me but I'm not sure that he listens to me. He spends all day talking to women about their problems so I suppose he has to believe that he understands us, can empathize with us but I don't know how much emotional involvement he commits to each encounter. It can't be much or he'd be even more knackered in the evening than he usually is. I'm always worried that perhaps I'm no more than just another woman, that I'm just another troublesome patient tacked onto the end of his clinic."

"I'm sure it's not like that Diana, Lucien loves you." Her mother was always emollient, always quick to assume that all was well and that relationships and events would comply with her romanticized home counties norms. She might have been more useful if her reading matter had ever extended beyond Barbara Cartland's books where "love" was always the panacea. Diana felt better talking to her but knew not to expect an insightful response.

Monday Aug 11th. Meeting with Charles O'Dwyer.

Nine AM, Lucien's mobile rang.

"Lucien McCulloch? Hi, it's Charles O'Dwyer. We met in Tripoli; I wondered if we might meet for a chat? Are you available?"

Lucien was free, indeed since his suspension from medical practice he was free most of the time, he'd be interested to meet Charles O'Dywer again.

"I'm in town for lunch at my club today, perhaps you'd join me."

"Sorry, no can do, how about a drink before lunch. The Old Star in Broadway opposite St. James' Park tube station. It's only a short walk from Victoria. Midday? I'll meet you downstairs in the Cellar Bar."

Lucien remembered the rush of presumptions, the staccato delivery from his only other contact with O'Dwyer.

"Fine, I'll be there – midday."

And convenient he thought, as it's an easy walk from the club. He didn't know that O'Dwyer knew that too, along with a good many other details of his life.

The Old Star is a nice enough place in a brown and cream old fashioned way. The Cellar Bar is somewhat claustrophobic but discrete, invisible from the road and has two staircases down to it, one at each end. When Lucien arrived Charles O'Dwyer was already there and half way through his first pint. He was wearing jeans and a black leather jacket. Lucky he didn't accept the invitation to lunch at The Athenaeum thought Lucien, they wouldn't have let him in.

"Nice to see you again, how are you? Sorry about all the stuff in the papers. Gamal al Ghanem again I presume. Like to talk to you about that, not here though, too many nosey coppers from The Yard come here to drink. Did you get your stuff back from Libya OK?"

"Yes thanks, luggage, passport, cards, even my old SIM card. They all came about two days after I got back – very efficient. I'm sorry that I haven't had a chance to thank you, I'd liked to have taken you to lunch."

"Sorry I'd have liked that too but not really appropriate. Finish your pint and we'll got for a walk."

They walked through to Birdcage Walk and into St. James' Park. Lunch time crowds of office workers were scattered across the lawns in little groups or singly. The girls' skirts hoisted up, their tops rolled down slightly in an attempt to capture some of the rare summer sunshine. Tourists milled about trying the photograph the flowers, the squirrels, the ducks or the views of Whitehall and Buckingham Palace beyond the lake.

"You're not the Commercial Secretary at the Embassy are you?" asked Lucien, not for the first time.

"Of course not" said O'Dwyer "as you'd probably guessed, I'm with what we teasingly like to call a non-attributable quasi-governmental information gathering team!"

"MI6, SIS you mean" said Lucien not sure which acronym to use. O'Dwyer grinned at him.

"The official part of my meeting with you is over, we have to log every contact we have with anyone outside the service – for those purposes our meeting today was simply to confirm that your possessions were returned intact from Libya. But now tell me about our old friend Gamal al Ghanem's attempts to discredit you, you must be pretty angry?"

"Of course, and particularly because the Foreign Office seems to be helping in the process which to my mind seems a bit out of order."

"May be, may be not, who's dealing with it there?"

"I'm not sure, it's all done through the GMC and The Medical Defence Union. The MDU's solicitor did mention a name once, Happyland, or something odd like that."

"Don't recognize the name – if we can though we'll see if there is anything we can do."

They walked on over the little bridge that spans the lake while Lucien updated O'Dwyer on what had happened including the shooting and explaining his reasons for not dismissing it as readily as the police had. O'Dwyer for once was serious and attentive. He acknowledged what Lucien had to say but was careful not to add any interpretation or offer to make enquiries. As they reached The Mall a Japanese tourist thrust a camera into O'Dwyer's hands and stood grinning next to his wife gesturing at Buckingham Palace in the distance. O'Dwyer took a picture of a couple in their orange linen hats and handed back the camera. The couple gave little formal bows "*Avigato, avigato.*"

"Glad I was never posted to Japan" said O'Dwyer "I couldn't learn to be so bloody polite and no way could I cope with the language. It was helpful to have a chat; I'm sure you'll be wanting your lunch. We're almost at The Athenaeum so I'll say goodbye."

At which he hailed a cab, gave Lucien his card and was off. Lucien did not know what to make of this quick-fire meeting, he looked at the card. On it was written "O'Dwyer" and a mobile number, nothing else. He sighed, climbed the steps to Waterloo Place and the relative tranquility of The Athenaeum.

O'Dwyer had taken the cab to the old Tate Gallery and then walked over Vauxhall Bridge to the big, bold, green SIS building on the South Bank. His desk on the 5th floor was part of an open plan office, no secrets here, except what was typed into the carefully shielded computer. He pulled up his log on the screen "Date: August 6th 12.00pm met Prof. L. McCulloch, confirmed safe return of property from Tripoli." As he logged off the door at the end of the office door opened and his boss beckoned to him.

"Charlie can I have a word with you please." John Fitzgerald, Head of Section, waved him to a chair in the silent, sound-proofed room. "Well, did you find out who in Whitehall is acting for Ghanem to smear McCulloch?"

"We might have guessed it, it's almost certainly that wanker Jerry Havilland, couldn't be anyone else. McCulloch remembered it as Happyland."

"So it's the eternally uninspiring Jerry. Which section have his FCO masters managed to find him a desk in?"

"South America. Presumably because he speaks neither Spanish nor Portuguese!"

"And he's purporting to be from the North African section. Naughty, naughty – do they know?"

"I doubt it but I'll check."

"And we know who Jolly Jerry Havilland was seconded to for the last three years don't we – the Department of Trade and Industry. And we know who he was the lapdog to there don't we Charles?"

"Yep, the minister himself Harry Ashbury. Admirer of the deranged old fart Gaddafi and friendly with his odious side-kick Gamal Ghanem their very own Minister for Trade."

"So we have a nice, neat set of connections. Gaddafi through Ghanem uses Ashbury to oil the wheels to get Al Megrahi sent home, Ghanem uses Ashbury to screw McCulloch with Havilland as the cutout. The McCulloch business must be trivial stuff to Ashbury compared to persuading Brown and Blair to snuggle up to Gaddafi and getting the Scots even to consider letting Al Megrahi go, particularly knowing how the Americans feel about it."

John Fitzgerald was quiet for a moment, elbows on the desk, fingertips together.

"Any ideas Charles? We can't let this thing go on and on, we can't let HMG back the wrong side in Libya. It never used to be like this. We were supporting opposition groups like the LIFG and now since the defence deal last year it's all changed and we're even complicit in helping the Gaddafi lot get their hands on the very people we used to support. I know it's a dirty business but Gaddafi will get the chop sooner or later and the UK mustn't be too close to him or we'll have no clout with whoever takes over. Ashbury seems to be the common denominator in this love fest with the Libyans, I'm not sure why. Your man Professor el Hammedi is probably right; there must be something in it for Ashbury. Obviously we need to have a sight of Jerry Havilland's bank accounts to see if he's being paid by the Libyans. Apart from that have you got any thoughts on how we might deal with all this? "

"Actually I do have an idea" said Charles "Obviously we can't be seen to have a hand in acting to undermine Ashbury or government policy even though we know it's foolish, also we can't investigate Ashbury directly; that would mean bringing in MI5 but the McCulloch business offers a chance. The British wouldn't like to see one of their own ministers encouraging foreigners to screw an innocent Brit, would they? Give me a few days and I'll see what options there are. One of the minister's close protection officers is an acquaintance of mine and I think I need to buy him a drink or two."

"Good, but don't put it in your log and I won't talk to anyone upstairs about it." Charlie O'Dwyer was looking pensive and made no move to leave.

"There's potentially another strand to all this and that's this shooting at Denmark Hill that McCulloch is sure was an attempt on his life. If he's right and Ghanem is behind that too then he might be using that cell he set up in London for the business of rubbing out Libyan dissidents. It was when he was in the Security Ministry, before he was Minister for Trade. Neither we nor MI5 ever really got to the bottom of that. I believe Five are fairly sure who they are but never had enough evidence to do anything about it." Charlie O'Dwyer was clearly keen to pursue that topic .

"Not now Charlie. Let's have a go at the Havilland/Ashbury matter first. If we restart the other business we'll have to involve Five and you know what a pain that will be. One thing at a time; so first of all you'd better talk to your friend."

But as soon as Charlie was out of the room and the door shut John Fitzgerald made some phone calls.

John Fox of the Special Branch was standing in a doorway near the pub when Charlie O'Dwyer got out of the taxi the next evening. He fell into step next to him, a tall, gaunt man in a black raincoat next to a fit young man in jeans and a leather jacket.

"Evening Charlie, nice of you to want to meet up again though I doubt if it's to chat about old times."

The pub was noisy and busy with people delaying their journeys home or just staying out of the rain. O'Dwyer found seats in the corner where they could sit with their backs to the wall and from where they could see the door. Just a habit and probably not needed tonight.

"And you'll be buying the drinks Charlie" said Fox "All of them, not just the first round. You're only here because you want something; you're a sneaky little bugger you know, like all your kind in that place," but it wasn't said with malice just the formalized animosity that divided SIS from Special Branch and MI5 "So what do you want? Is this going to be a two pint or three pint conversation?"

"That's up to you, I just wanted to talk to you about your current charge, the minister, Mr. Harry Ashbury."

"That's not in your patch Charlie, you know that."

"Yes I know that, we only deal with stuff outside the UK but it's his Libyan connections that interest us."

"OK, that's kosher."

"Bad choice of adjective, Johnny!"

"OK, not kosher but allowable. I've only been to Libya once with him though he's been more times than that as I'm sure you nosey bastards know. Actually, he's not at risk there. Their goons are unpleasant but quite professional as far as personal protection tactics go. The yacht trips were more fun for us."

"What yacht trips?"

"The ones on Igor Orloff's flash yacht. The one he takes all sorts of cabinet ministers , movers and shakers on. We liked those trips not because we went on the yacht you understand, we weren't allowed, the Russians have their own security, we'd just get the minister to the gangplank then wait in port until the yacht got back. Tough assignments you know, Nice, Cannes, Monte Carlo – really tough!"

"Who did he have with him on these trips?"

"No-one special, a PA usually but she was normally left ashore with us. It was only that twit Havilland, his aide, who was aboard with him."

"Any Libyans on the yacht?"

"Sometimes Gaddafi's son but usually the other one, nasty looking bugger, Gamal something."

"And in London?"

"Never any Libyans to my knowledge and we'd know as there's always one of us with him except in The House and on his evening jaunts."

"Evening jaunts?"

"Every couple of weeks." Johnny Fox sniggered to himself "Hanky panky nights I expect. He gets the driver to take him to Hampstead, then the driver and I and the car have to come back and then return to get him three hours later. We're not meant to let him out of our sight but he is always very adamant and rabbits on about his entitlement to privacy."

"Is he on his own on these trips?"

"No, usually has Jerry Havilland with him."

"So it's a mistress or a tart in Hampstead?"

"Dunno, might be two mistresses, two tarts, one for each," Johnny Fox guffawed at the thought, "or they could be gay, of course, Hampstead Heath's a happy hunting ground for that lot." He guffawed again "can't understand it myself – all wet and muddy."

"Do you drop him on the Heath?"

"No, always the same place, the petrol station half way up Haverstock Hill."

Charles O'Dwyer peered into his pint for a moment.

"Johnny you wouldn't let me know when the next jaunt is due would you?"

"Easy, this Thursday, the day after tomorrow. We normally drop them off by 21.30 at the garage. You're not planning anything naughty which I as a serving police officer would disapprove of are you?"

"Of course not Johnny! Another pint ? "

Fortunately, it wasn't raining on the Thursday when O'Dwyer parked his motorbike in the side street adjacent to the garage on Haverstock Hill. He hated surveillance jobs in the rain, it was so difficult to remain anonymous yet be watching when everyone else was heading for somewhere dry. Promptly at nine-thirty as O'Dwyer dawdled over buying a packet of crisps in the garage, the ministerial car paused at the kerb and disgorged the two men from the back before driving off. They were easy to tail, one short, fat man and one gangly, both intent on where they were going and having no idea that they were being followed, even though it was by someone on a motorbike. O'Dwyer had opted to bring his "wheels" in case the pair took off in another vehicle; a moped would have been more sensible but O'Dwyer couldn't bear the thought; he always felt more in command of any situation when on his MotoGuzzi though he knew full well that in this instance he was barely in control. It needs at least four people to tail someone effectively but that option was not open to him as John Fitzgerald would have had to put in a requisition and the twerps at MI5 would have had to do the job even if it had been allowed, which it would not have been.

Having spent an uncomfortable four hours on the streets of north London, following the two men, then watching a house, then tracking a van O'Dywer returned home reasonably confident that he knew what Harry Ashbury and Jerry Havilland's evening "jaunts" were about and as a consequence he knew what needed to be done next. The next morning he was closeted with John Fitzgerald in the soundproofed office well before nine o'clock. He recounted what he'd seen the night before and his deductions.

"I'm confident that I know how we ought to proceed. Do we have surveillance footage of the Igor Orlov yacht when it's been in port?"

"I'm pretty certain we would – if cabinet members are consorting with Orlov and accepting his hospitality we need to know who else is on board, so yes. We know Libyans were involved so we're entitled to ask for the tapes."

O'Dwyer explained that he wanted Fitzgerald's permission not only to review the tapes but also to share selected images with the French authorities. Fitzgerald agreed.

"Make sure they look like paparazzi shots – I don't want our Gallic friends aware of what we get up to in their jurisdiction, without having cleared it with them first."

"If we don't clear it with our own government then we can hardly be expected to clear it with the French can we!"

"Good point but remember the whole of this project is high risk as far as you and I are concerned. I dare not share it with Upstairs. After the Iraq dossier fiasco it's unclear where Upstairs' allegiance lies and what the hell they think we're here for!"

After reviewing the tapes it was clear to O'Dwyer that, as he had predicted, a trip to the French Mediterranean coast was needed, in particular Cannes. After hours of flicking through the surveillance tapes of Igor Orlov's yacht in the harbour by the casino at the west end of the Croisette he could see exactly what he wanted; details of the people boarding the yacht. He had printed off a couple of dozen A4 prints of some of those boarding and the vehicles that they arrived in. He'd even seen Johnny Fox just behind the shoulder of Harry Ashbury as he arrived on the dock but he hadn't printed that one out. There was one of Harry Ashbury and Jerry Havilland standing on the deck, champagne glasses in hand as the boat slipped its moorings prior to being out in the undeserved blue Mediterranean for two days. He printed three copies of that one.

On the following Sunday O'Dwyer flew into Marseilles airport and was met by a tall brunette in glasses wearing a smart two-piece navy blue suit. She kissed O'Dwyer on the lips and squeezed his hand.

"Welcome back Charlie, I've missed you."

"Hi, Clara; good to see you to but you do know that I'm here on business don't you?"

"You were last time! We'll see how it goes shall we?"

Clara Hurst had worked for the UK Border Agency since its creation in April 2008 and before that it's various predecessors. Her role was as liaison officer for the Marseilles' part of the global effort of the UK government to reduce illegal immigration. Marseilles has always been the place where the population of north Africa leaks into France, some legally, many illegally and Clara's enthusiasm, her colloquial French, quite apart from her charm and good looks allowed her access to every government agency in Marseilles and the surrounding ports, which included Cannes.

"Have you booked into a hotel Charlie?"

"No, I thought you might let me use your sofa" he said unconvincingly.

"You know bloody well I have a one bedroom studio and no sofa!"

"I'd forgotten."

"No you hadn't – you're an opportunistic little shit Charlie O'Dwyer you know that don't you?"

"Yep."

"So let's go and find a bar and you can show me these pictures you've brought."

By the time he'd left Marseilles, deservedly tired, two days later Clara had taken him into enough dowdy portside offices, regional HQ's of this and that and shown his pictures to enough uniformed hard-men and beetle-browed men in scruffy offices to be certain that he could persuade John Fitzgerald to let him take the next step. The cat-in-the-bag was now wriggling relentlessly and needed to be let out.

The next day, within a couple of hours of sharing his discoveries with John Fitzgerald, O'Dwyer met his contact from the Sunday Times and told him that as a by-product of another investigation, certain unsavoury habits of a cabinet minister had come to light. He added the briefest of outlines omitting to say how the information had been acquired.

"What I'm giving you is pure gold, but just you remember that this is a personal leak absolutely not authorised from above, even they don't know what I'm giving you, and I'm not giving you much. You'll need to do your own research on this one."

He gave him a date and time, the name of the garage on Haverstock Hill, an address in Chalk Farm and the name of a Camden Council care home. He also gave him a handful of photos including several of a minibus on a darkened quayside, French plates, and children getting out; in the background a floodlit and clearly named, sleek ocean-going yacht. There was a picture of the children being escorted up the gangplank. He also gave him the picture of Ashbury and Havilland drinking champagne on the same yacht with the same date mark in the corner.

"This will take a couple of weeks minimum" said his contact. "It's dangerous for us too, we'll need to ask around to see if there have been any hints of this before and if so whether they have been suppressed. There might even be a D notice on it, but if you're right about all this, it certainly is pure journalistic gold!"

Monday 18th August. London SW1.

What Charlie O'Dwyer did not know was that no sooner had he left
the room the week before after telling John Fitzgerald his Head of
Section about the attempt on Lucien McCulloch's life, than
Fitzgerald started phoning contacts and setting up a discreet meeting
with his opposite number at MI5 and a senior member of SO15 the
Metropolitan Police's Counter-Terrorism Unit. His contacts both told
him that from what he'd told them they needed to do some research
but a week later all three met at New Scotland Yard. The un-minuted
topic of the meeting was the simple question of whether the cell set
up in London many years before by Gaddafi's government to
arrange the "physical liquidation" of opponents to his regime was
still in business. All three men at the meeting were aware of the
balancing acts they had to perform to adhere to the policies of their
different organisations, acknowledge the current political stance in
relation to Libya and not forget the basic principle of keeping the
inhabitants of the UK safe.

"I'm concerned" said John Fitzgerald "that our information might
be correct and that the Libyan Minister of Trade, Gamal Ghanem
may be using his old contacts to arrange for a British citizen to be
killed here in London. We are in a difficult position because our
masters are currently intent on being friendly with Gaddafi and his
people. We all know what morally suspect actions that has already
led to. 'Six' was complicit in the rendition of Abdul Hakim Belhaj
and Sami Al Saddi and their families to Libya. The very people that
in the past we'd worked to protect we delivered up for torture and
imprisonment in the interests of good trade relations. I know all
three of us are very uncomfortable with that." The others nodded.
"Not much sign of Gordon's moral compass there then!" said the
MI5 man putting his briefcase onto the table and taking out some
papers. "I can tell you that we have a good idea of who the members
of this cell in London are, or were, but we don't currently have them
under surveillance – there is no need to as we are doing their dirty
work for them putting dissidents under control orders! But before

we go on John can we be confident that there really was an attempt on this chap McCulloch's life?"

"I've talked to the Trident team about it" interjected the crop-haired man from Scotland Yard. "They did the investigation after the shooting and say it had none of the hallmarks of a south London shooting. For a start they are not usually done from a motorcycle. The victim was a nurse, happily married, absolutely no criminal or gang connections and the gun was unusual. As best they can judge from CCTV pictures at Denmark Hill Station and from ballistics it was a 21mm Gyurza SR-1 pistol – Russian Special Forces weapon not seen in this country but we know that Libyan security forces had some. If the Libyans here are behind this shooting then we want them for murder. Simple as that. No politics and no turning a blind eye – straight forward police matter."

John Fitzgerald was relieved by this. It meant he was justified in pursuing this even if it upset the Libyans and HMG.

"I'm sure you'll appreciate that 'Five' is very busy" said the MI5 man primly adjusting his bowtie and taking off his spectacles to polish them whilst he thought, "but we might be able to assist here as we still have surveillance devices in the homes of two Libyans whom we suspect. Also a tracker in their vehicle. They are UK residents who got asylum here ten years ago on the grounds of being at risk from Gaddafi's security service if they went home. A bit rich really in the circumstances. They're 'sleepers' – just waiting."

"I know you're not watching them now but what did the previous surveillance show?" asked Fitzgerald leaning forwards hopefully. The MI5 man shook his head.

"Just the basics and that's several years out of date. Here's the details" and he handed them folders each containing a single sheet of A4 and two photos. No big 'Top Secret' stamp on them to attract attention. "They are hardly in the travelling international hit-man league. They're both in their 50s now, run a kebab shop at the wrong end of the Edgeware Road and live over the shop."

The three of them discussed their options. Raiding the Libyans' premises hoping to retrieve the weapon to match it to the murder carried not real prospect of getting a conviction without more to tie the Libyans to the attack, so they agreed that MI5 would simply recommence monitoring and would check that the vehicle tracker was working. SO15 would brief the team who would move in should the chance arise. And MI6 who, of course, have no role in operations within the UK? Charlie O'Dwyer could be kept on the case when he got back from France. They ought to tell McCulloch what was going on but he might take fright and go to ground somewhere. So without making a formal decision they decided not to rush to let him into what they suspected.

At his meeting with Charlie to discuss the visit to France Fitzgerald told him what had been talked about at the meeting and it was agreed that for now he would stay in London and be available. Fitzgerald had nominated him as the person MI5 or SO15 would liaise with if they needed to take action. Fitzgerald was well past the phase in his career that might involve running around waving a gun. He was simply pleased that all being well the McCulloch affair might lead to the resolution of two problems at once. Ashbury and the sleeper cell. Even if the government and the top floor at MI6 were taking the wrong approach to Libya there were still a few in the service who we willing to do the right thing.

Just two days later Fitzgerald got a call from MI5.

"You'll find this difficult to believe John but we've just monitored a phone call made to our Libyans here, *en clair*, uncoded, unscrambled made on a public telephone by Gamal Ghanem himself from an hotel in Malta. He'd have been reasonably certain that his own side weren't listening in but he clearly doesn't know that we are watching the guys here."

"What did the call say?"

"Mostly abuse actually, haranguing them for not killing McCulloch, telling them that if they didn't do as he said he'd get them sent back to Libya by the UK government and he'd deal with them when they got back to Tripoli."

"And their response?"

"Predictably they promised to finish the job and do it this week. They know his reputation."

"So can we not just arrest them?"

"No, we wouldn't want to have a case that was based on our intercepts as primary evidence in court, we try to avoid that." The MI5 looked pleased with this let out.

"So?"

"So we plan to wait."

"You can't do that. They'll probably kill McCulloch whilst you sit on your arse waiting for more acceptable evidence." What a tosser thought Fitzgerald, the mind-set of a civil servant and a low level one at that. "Look – if you don't agree to pick the Libyans up now and McCulloch or someone else gets killed I'll personally make sure that everyone knows who dragged their feet. OK?"

"Are you threatening me John?"

Fitzgerald made it absolutely clear that yes he was threatening him and shortly after it was agreed to get the SO15 unit to make the arrests as soon as possible. SO15 preferred an early morning raid but agreed with immediate effect to watch the Edgeware Road kebab shop in case the Libyans attempted something today. It was now 3.00pm. At 5.00pm Fitzgerald's phone went just as he was about to leave his office, it was the SO15 unit commander.

"The kebab shop's closed up. It looks as if they are not here and their van's gone."

"Where's the van – have you got the tracker information."

"No signal. It's either not working or they've found it or it's somewhere where we can't pick up a signal."

"Shit!" exclaimed Fitzgerald "They're probably going for McCulloch right now."

"Do you know where he is?"

"No – they probably don't either – we'll have to gamble that they're heading for his home."

"OK we'll go there as quickly as we can. We know the address. You phone him and warn him."

Fitzgerald had his jacket off now and was back in the office chair. He pulled up the McCulloch file on his computer "damn! no mobile number." He phoned Charlie O'Dwyer and told him to phone McCulloch at home, he knew him and was less likely to alarm him. Charlie called back two minutes later. "No-one there!"

"Where are you?"

"Downstairs; still in the building here."

"Is your bike here?"

"Yes."

"Draw a weapon and get down to Dulwich as quick as you can. You'll probably get there about the same time as SO15. I'll keep trying McCulloch's home phone."

Charlie knew that if he had to go through the paperwork needed to get the armourer to issue a weapon he'd be lucky to get to Dulwich is time for breakfast the next morning which he why illegally he kept a Browning pistol and why he'd stashed it in the pannier of his motorbike when Fitzgerald had warned him of the impending SO15 action.

As Charlie accelerated away from the MI6 HQ in Vauxhall, swooped around the Oval Cricket Ground weaving between the rush hour traffic, jumped the lights at the tube station and hit a roaring 70mph down the Camberwell New Road, he was exhilarated. This is what he'd hoped life in MI6 would be all about; action, excitement, chasing foreign villains with a gun in his belt. Fitzgerald phoned McCulloch's home number every five minutes, there was still no reply, anyway Charlie would be almost there by now. Charlie had been told the Libyans might be in a white Transit van, unmarked, one of a thousand others, but he did have the registration number – less reassuringly he also knew that they might not be in a van but on a motorbike. He throttled back and cruised slowly past the McCulloch house. No white van, no motorbike. Just a mother with a baby in a buggy, a girl on a bicycle and an old man with a stick slowly making his way down the road. No sign of SO15 but he could hear sirens in the distance. How would McCulloch come home? Walk from the station or perhaps from Denmark Hill. He wasn't in his car… there it was in the drive…a Jaguar XJS in British racing green. "Good choice" thought Charlie. He cruised slowly up to the station, along a few nearby streets and then back "Jesus what a panic!" he thought "He might be anywhere. On holiday, out shopping, on a bus, walking the dog." At which moment as the MotoGuzzi coasted into the McCulloch's road for the second time he saw a white Transit van parked immediately outside the house, then just 100 yards further on McCulloch himself on foot coming from the other end of the road. O'Dwyer flipped the bike onto its stand

and walked briskly towards the van his heart thumping, his hand on the grip of the Browning under his jacket. He dare not shout to McCulloch lest it warn anyone in the van. They must be in the rear part of the van as the side door onto the pavement was open. If they were in the driver and passenger seats they'd have seen McCulloch by now. O'Dwyer sprang forward onto the pavement by the open door of the van crouching down, the pistol in the two handed grip, just as he'd been taught. "Freeze – put your hands up!" he shouted and then repeated it in Arabic. The two men in white overalls inside the van looked astounded.

"You having a joke mate?" said the older one as he put his hands up. The other was stirring a tin of paint and took a little longer. At that moment McCulloch arrived, equally astounded.

"What on earth are you doing here Charles? Why are you pointing a gun at my painters?" At which instant Charlie O'Dwyer suddenly realised that in his haste and certainty he hadn't checked the van's number, nor until now seen the words 'Dulwich Decorators' stencilled on the van.

"Are you sure?" he said to McCulloch "Sure these are your painters?"

"Of course, had them for years."

Charlie O'Dwyer tucked the Browning back into the waist of his jeans.

"We think the Libyans have probably planned to have another pop at you today. Go inside quickly in case they turn up – you too," he said to the painters, "In case someone else with a gun thinks you're terrorists." He walked back and sat on his bike whilst he phoned the SO15 commander. "I'm at McCulloch's. He's here, he's OK. Where are you?"

"Just clearing up, we've got our two Libyans and the handgun. The van was in a lock-up – the tracker started working as soon as they set off. We picked them up in Clapham – easy job, not a shot fired. You can tell McCulloch to relax. I'm a bit tied up here I'll talk to you later."

"Make sure you question them about the motorbike will you," said Charlie, "I'd hate there to be another couple of blokes still out there."

Anyone else might have felt sheepish ringing the doorbell to be let in to explain but not Charlie O'Dwyer; sheepishness wasn't in his make-up. He explained what had happened, pleaded ignorance when McCulloch asked why he hadn't been warned earlier "though I'm obviously very grateful to you all" McCulloch added, embarrassed at criticising Charlie who appeared to have just risked his life on his behalf.

"You should be OK now unless Ghanem tries a different ploy. And that may depend on what the two Libyans have to say and whether Ghanem's name finds its way into the newspapers. I suspect HMG will be keen to make sure it doesn't." It didn't.

Thursday September 4th. London

All his adult life Lucien had spent the days working. He felt no resentment about that; he enjoyed it, it defined him. It was **not** working that he now found difficult. Suspended from clinical practice, excluded from the hospitals he worked in, little remained. Even the fact that he now felt safer walking the streets or travelling on the Tube or the train was not enough to restore him. Fortunately the Royal College had at the outset of his problems taken the view that the charges against him were unproved and therefore as his work for the College other than as an examiner did not involve contact with patients, it was perfectly proper for him to continue.

"It's an ill wind etc." the secretary of the College announced at a meeting of Council "the Department of Health's initiatives have heaped multiple new unfunded tasks on us all, so a Lucien McCulloch with time on his hands is manna from heaven."

At this the President had promptly created a new sub-committee with Lucien as Chairman. Now several weeks later Lucien had spent an uninspiring morning at the College trying to agree a plan of work for this new sub-committee and felt no need or obligation to drag the work through into the afternoon. Now that his would be assassins were locked up at Paddington Green Police Station "helping the Police with their enquiries" he felt free to wander about London again so he phoned Julian Scantlebury and suggested that they might meet for lunch at The Athenaeum.

Julian was prone to homilies, what he called "homilizing", particularly when he was gloomy – which usually related to yet another temporary relationship having shown itself to be just that, temporary, leaving no trace other than a mild sense of despair. Hence, the gloom. Today's homily over lunch was on the topic of ageing and in particular the irony, as he put it, that things get stiff that you don't want stiff and the converse.

"But you're a lucky bugger Lucien you're still young and you've a gorgeous wife – enjoy yourselves. One of the problems us "vagina decliners" have is that we have no children, no expectations of stable relationships, it's really very sad as we get old. Never mind, the sun is shining and neither of us has to go to work – and you at least have a proper home to go to." He looked out of the window at the lawns just beyond the dining room window as if willing some grandchildren to be playing there. "And Lucy will have children I'm sure."

After lunch Julian and Lucien went up the grand marble staircase that fills the centre of the Athenaeum and into the Drawing Room for coffee. The Drawing Room is a large, long sunlit room overlooking Waterloo Place, the coffee is, for a London club, drinkable and the armchairs scattered about the room unusually low so that there is no particular inclination to get up and leave. Julian and Lucien thus spent a pleasant hour chatting and reading the papers. In normal times Lucien would have been back at work by 2pm yet in these peculiar times one benefit of his tribulations was that he could sit here all afternoon if he wished. He'd told Diana that he'd be at the College all day but he'd decided not to go back there after his lunch with Julian so by half past three he was walking home from the station amidst the mums bringing their children back from school. This good natured hurly burly was much more appealing than the grim faced commuters rushing home at 7.00pm, so he meandered slowly down Village Road enjoying the feeling of freedom. A few hundred yards from home he noticed a man coming out of his driveway "another restaurant brochure to bin" he thought expecting the man to go into the house next door but he did not, instead he looked up and down the street, got into a parked car and drove off. Lucien shrugged and put it out of his mind.

Going into the house he heard the radio playing in the bedroom and the shower running. In the bedroom he noticed Diana's clothes strewn about the floor and the bed rumpled.

"Hi darling" he said around the bathroom door finding her toweling herself dry "the joys of coming home early! "

She looked nonplussed to see him so early

"Oh, hello, I've just been having a nap – I'll be down in a minute. Why didn't you phone?"

"Why would I, I'm not late, I've got my own key. It must be years since I was here at this time of day".

Lucien had no work to do, no briefcase had accompanied him to London. He had no phone calls to make. No worrying patients to check up on. No-one in labour. No-one recovering from an operation. It was, he decided, actually pleasant. He and Diana had time for a drink before supper, a chance to discuss what they'd read in the papers, watch some TV and then at ten o'clock they went up to bed.

In the bedroom Lucien picked up a dressing gown which had been thrown over the armchair in a corner of the room. Beneath it was a sleeveless yellow pullover, Pringle, cashmere with a pattern of large red diamonds on the front, a style he disliked. A man's pullover.

"Who the hell's is this?" Diana looked flustered,

"One of Robin's, I was wearing it."

Lucien looked at her and looked at the pullover:

"Diana, my darling, Robin God bless him would never, ever, have worn a diamond patterned yellow cashmere pullover!"

At that moment the image of the man he'd seen leaving the house earlier suddenly came back to him with the memory of the rumpled bed and Diana's scattered clothes.

"Do you want to explain?"

Diana sat up in bed, looked silently at Lucien for a while as if judging how best to say what she was going to say.

"Lucien I need to tell you something. Why don't you sit down."

Lucien sat down on the edge of the bed a sense of panic rising in him.

"I've been having an affair."

"An affair?"

"An affair."

"With another man?"

"Yes, or course with another man, the owner of the sweater."

Lucien felt his heart thumping, his brain not really comprehending.

"With whom? What? How? Why? How long has it being going on?"

"It's been going on for rather a long time."

"How long?"

"Five or six years" – Lucien was silent, pale. "I met him by chance in the Dulwich Gallery. There was an exhibition of Picasso etchings. I was on my own because you were away somewhere for a few days – I can't remember where or why – examining or doing something for the College, or at a conference – anyway we just said hello in the gallery and both went our separate tour round, it's quite small though as you know, so we both emerged at the same time and he asked if I'd like a cup of coffee. We sat in the café there for half an hour or so talking about this and that and the etchings, he said he was an amateur artist. In fact I was just enjoying having a conversation. Since the kids left home I used to get lonely when you were away. Anyway as it was late morning I said would he like to come home for some lunch. I made a straight forward salad lunch and we shared a bottle of wine, so I was a bit tipsy I suppose and I remember him telling me how good I looked – I suppose he meant for my age but I just took it as a compliment. He said how he liked my hair, what a strong profile I had and how he'd like to paint me."

What she didn't say when telling the story was how he'd looked into her eyes as he asked, then touched her cheek and when she showed some pleasure at that he stroked her breast, quite gently and said he'd love to make a painting of her naked. He was smiling at her and she relaxed. Emboldened by alcohol she said that if they were to go upstairs he could see her naked now. And they did and, of course, ended up in bed having sex not once but twice. And she didn't tell Lucien that far from being seduced she was an enthusiastic accomplice, that the time in bed had been exciting; vigorous and then cosy then vigorous again, and after it she felt not soiled or used but enervated, stimulated, satisfied and therefore it was hardly surprising that whenever a chance of a repeat came up in the following weeks, months and years she'd taken it. In addition to all that she did not tell Lucien that this seemingly chance meeting in the gallery was, in fact, with someone both she and he knew so this passionate denouement was in fact probably just a coalescence of previously undiscovered fantasies.

Lucien had been struggling to adjust himself to the simple fact of his wife's confession to adultery. She did not sound like the woman he knew.

"Didn't you feel guilty? I mean adultery is adultery!"

"Not at the time, to be honest I just felt elated."

She didn't tell him that she remembered standing naked in front of her dressing table mirror seeing herself glowing and the man crouched on the bed looking at her, admiring her, desiring her. Lucien felt himself part angry, part faint, part just distraught.

"But didn't you consider us, our marriage, the implications?"

"No, not really. I've always assumed that you've been having it off now and then when you were away at conferences so it was my turn."

"And what if I'd told you that's completely false and that since we married forty years ago you are the only person I've desired or made love to."

She smiled slightly and reached over and touched his arm.

"Then in fairness I have to say that I believe you, you're a good and honourable man, and I've probably just pretended to myself that you were unfaithful simply to justify what I really wanted to do."

"And are you going to tell me who this man is?"

"No."

"And are you going to stop seeing him?"

"No!"

"And us, what about us, our marriage, our life together?"

"I don't know; you'll have to decide if you want to divorce me."

Lucien held both her hands and looked at her trying to divulge from her expression what she really wanted, he couldn't, she seemed far away, out of touch. He felt ill, sick at heart, totally confused. He had no inkling, no suspicions, was unprepared. He had no script, he had absolutely no idea what to think or what to do. All he knew was at that moment a bond of trust had been broken – he had no way of knowing whether it could be repaired, and if so, how. Indeed at that moment he did not yet know whether even if he could repair it he wanted to. He got up and went downstairs and poured himself a large glass of whisky – no ice, no water. He sat down heavily, sweating, clutching the glass disconnectedly watching the traffic pass outside. He turned the TV on and watched it without seeing it. He felt numb. He did however manage to grope to one conclusion, tonight was not the time to sort this out. He was in no shape, tomorrow maybe.

When he went back upstairs an hour later Diana was asleep, her hair spread across the pillow. He kissed her cheek and went into the spare bedroom and got into bed, lay on his back and looked at the ceiling. He felt utterly devastated. This was the end it really was. Within a month he had lost his job, his professional standing, half his income, been arrested, denigrated in the newspapers, almost lost his life and now it seemed he'd lost his wife. After Robin had been killed he thought nothing worse could happen. At least then he had his profession, his work, his wife to sustain him. Now fuck all, absolutely fuck all. And for what? What had he done wrong? Nothing. The wheel for fortune was turning and crushing him slowly under its rim, completely unheeding. Eventually he fell into a troubled sleep dreaming of satyrs crouched over sleeping women.

Friday 5th September. To France

The next morning Lucien woke confused by being in the wrong bed. He reached across, no Diana, of course not. The events of the night before snapped back into his consciousness. He lay there picking up the unresolved agonies of what to do next. The house was silent, unhelpful. He got up, went downstairs to the kitchen, it was only eight o'clock but Diana had gone. There was a small note on the table "Gone to work – D x" She'd probably been keen to avoid further conversation.

Lucien sat at the kitchen table staring at the cereal packets and the marmalade jar, the plate laid ready for him. He was exhausted. "I have absolutely no idea what to do next" he said to himself. "I really don't know how to handle this. All my life I've responded to challenges promptly and rationally but this time I simply have no idea." The temptation was to have a stiff drink. He resisted it and made himself a cup of coffee. Talk to Lucy? No not fair on her. Wait for Diana to come home and talk to her again? No he couldn't bear to do that without any notion of how best to deal with the situation. "I can't believe I'm in a position where I need help". This realisation was almost as shocking to him as its cause. "I need to talk to someone" he thought. Who else but Julian.

"Hello Lucien how's things? You're phoning very early" said Julian from the other end of the phone.

"Things are not good Julian, can we meet. I need to talk to somebody."

"Christ! You sound dreadful what's going on. You were fine yesterday. No don't tell me let's meet now. Do you want me to come down to Dulwich or do you want to come here?"

"I'll come to you, thanks."

Less than an hour later he was at The Albany, that discrete group of 18th century apartments hidden away from the bustle and tawdriness of central London. A secret oasis just off Piccadilly for the well connected with long established claims. No nouveaux riches here; indeed The Albany remains one of the places where money cannot buy you entry. That Julian lived here was simply a reflection of his patrician background.

"Can I help you?" asked the uniformed porter at the door.

"Mr. Scantlebury is expecting me."

"If you'd just wait here for a moment please."

The porter retired to a cubby hole at the back of the lodge but could be seen through the glass phoning and nodding.

"Yes, that's fine – do you know the way?"

"I do – K2 – thank you."

What an extraordinary place this is thought Lucien as he walked through the neatly planted courtyard to K2 staircase just 100 yards from Piccadilly but the same as the courtyard of any Cambridge college, which was probably why Julian liked it.

Julian was waiting at the door of his first floor flat in a silk dressing gown, but his hair was perfectly combed, his round pink face looked as healthy and cheerful as ever.

"Sorry still to be in me pyjamas – long evening yesterday and then had to get my copy in." Julian's job as a music critic for The Times was hardly necessary in view of his large private income but he loved his music and it gave him something to do. "Brahm's violin sonatas at The Wigmore Hall" he said, "Lovely young soloist, beautiful bowing – the boy's Hungarian but not a touch of the gypsy in his performance – coffee?"

Lucien settled into an armchair by the unlit fire and admired, as always, the gilded glow of the priceless Claude Lorrain painting over the mantelpiece. A castle, a harbour, a misty sunrise, boats loading, people enjoying the early sun. It always reminded Lucien of Constable's comment that Claude paintings reflected "the calm sunshine of the heart".

Safely in Julian's flat, looking at the painting he felt calmer.

"Now then" said Julian returning with a cafetière of coffee, two delicate gold lipped porcelain cups and four Madeleines. "What's up?"

"Oh God – just one thing after another. I told you about the mad Libyan and the vindictive CEO before but now it's Diana. Last night she told me she'd been having an affair, boasted almost. Said it's been going on for years and she is not planning on stopping it. I never suspected, I just can't get my feeling about it in order, to be frank I have no idea what to do next."

"You poor sod, not like you to be so distraught, you're usually the model of statesmanlike calm."

"Thanks but not very calm today. What's made it worse was that I was completely unprepared. As we've got older I'd worked through the possibilities of losing her but only to some sort of illness, to cancer or Alzheimer's. I'd tried to imagine how it would be, I'd prepared myself like a boxer, working out, sparring until I knew I could repel a right hook to the head then suddenly there's this huge punch in my gut for which I haven't prepared and I'm down on the canvas. "

"Okay, have you asked yourself why Diana's having an affair?"

"No, to be honest I haven't, not in any detail except to blame myself. It's so out of character for her that it must in some way be my fault."

"Maybe – maybe not. Did you beat her?"

"Of course not."

"Did you ignore her?"

"No."

"Did you have affairs yourself?"

"No, never."

"Do you tell her you love her?"

"I keep telling her, I tell her she's beautiful, I cherish her, I share everything with her."

"Too compliant perhaps!"

"Oh, for God's sake!"

"So it could be the sex! How was that?"

"Good – well okay. I don't have much to compare it with. It's over forty years since I've sex with anyone else."

"Did you talk to each other?"

"Yes."

"About your relationship? About feelings? Knowing you I bet you didn't."

"No, I suppose we didn't. We got on so well I didn't seem necessary."

"So what are you going to do now, simper up to her, tell her you love her regardless of what she's done, beg her to give up this bloke whoever he is, and spend her waning years with you?"

"I don't know, something like that I suppose, negotiate a solution."

"Negotiate! Oh, for Christ's sake Lucien this is not another of your sodding board meetings. Where's the passion? The risk taking? Why don't you just leave her, she'll expect you to creep back, don't do it, just leave, go away. It doesn't have to be permanent but you certainly need to put some distance between you and her for a while."

"Go where?"

"It doesn't matter, anywhere, why not your place in France, you'll have plenty to do there and it'll stop you fretting. Also it will get you away from all the other crap they've been throwing at you."

"It would be difficult. What about all the things in my diary."

"Just cancel them, leave! Tell them to get stuffed, you're not indispensable, someone else can always be found. They'd have to do that if you died or were sick. Anyway you are suspended from everything so you can't have much in your diary."

"People will think I'm running away….which in a way I am."

"Look Lucien, just for once sod everyone else and what they think, just go. And you're not running away you're making a positive strategic move. Also don't tell Diana, just go!"

They drank their coffee in silence. The faint sound of a police car stuck in Piccadilly traffic was all that filtered through into the room.

"You're very good at counselling" said Lucien producing his first smile for 24-hours. "How come?"

"Ah well, we gays talk a lot to women you know, we enjoy each other's company, we share secrets and we share insights. When it comes to discussing this sort of business we talk tactics. And by the way, if you go away remember when you get there to keep Diana's goings on to yourself. It's tough being a cuckold, you're an outcast, it's really very primitive; you'll get no sympathy just derision, smirks, gestures. So if I were you I'd keep quiet about it. You're a pretty dignified guy usually so I reckon that the best stance to take is distain. By the way it is lucky I'm gay; do you know what Montaigne said? He said 'you can't tell a friend you've been cuckolded, not only may he laugh at you but he may also put it to personal use'!"

Lucien sat silently and reflected how good it was to have someone to advise him, he'd spent all his life advising others and now all of a sudden he felt the warmth of being able to let go and let someone else make the choices, push him towards an option that he wouldn't have taken if he'd been left just sitting in the kitchen in Dulwich, him and the whisky bottle. He'd have been drunk by the time Diana got home. No, he'd do as Julian said and be off, out from under.

"Julian you are a good friend indeed" he said carefully collecting up the cups. "I'll do as you suggest."

"And not blame me if it just makes things worse!" added Julian his chubby face bursting into another sunny smile. "Good luck."

So to France he would go. In the taxi on the way home Lucien decided he would go now, today, by the earliest ferry. The tunnel would have been quicker but he never used it. He felt trapped when in it; for the same reason he never took the Tube. Anyway he was in no hurry to arrive ; no-one was with him or waiting for him in St. Jean so he was happy to arrive late in the night, have a couple of big glasses of Armagnac and be tired enough to sleep well and forget. A plane would have been quicker but he couldn't stand Ryanair and anyway he always felt dislocated if he arrived too quickly at a destination; not really there, all a pretence, a movie. Only the train or the car gave him a real sense of leaving and arriving.

And so it was that having left Dulwich within half a hour of returning from The Albany, having left no note for Diana, he eased the Jaguar down the curling road cut through the chalk downs under Dover Castle and arrived at Dover Docks for a two o'clock ferry. The men in the French border control kiosk now transposed to Dover Docks were, as ever, lackadaisical knowing it really didn't matter; but he always felt anxious at any passport control, guilty, an escapee hoping not to be discovered. The difference today that he really was an escapee but felt elated not anxious. He was waved through. The docks were almost deserted, a thin line of cars creeping up the ramps onto the ferry, disconsolate little wisps of smoke from the funnel.

The Club Class lounge was empty apart from two elderly couples relishing the joy of quiet travel when school is back.

"Champagne, sir?"

"No thanks, just coffee and a sandwich."

Lucien sat looking out through the salt stained windows at the sea sliding by, the French coast slowly advancing. This was the first moment of proper reflection since his headlong bolt from this latest crisis. "What the hell am I doing?" he asked himself, thinking that perhaps in a moment of stress he'd allowed himself to be too easily swayed by Julian Scantlebury's solution. What was he expecting to achieve by bolting like this? How would Diana respond? Would this sudden absence jolt her into wanting him back or would she just use it as an opportunity to get her lover into bed – Lucien's bed! – as often as she wished. Simply leaving wasn't the solution to this new problem but he was now half way across the channel and some time alone in St. Jean might allow him to re-think his life. The last three months had derailed any prospect of a tidy completion of his professional life and any expectation of a contented retirement. Maybe all the recent jolts would force him to set a new and better course.

He spent the remainder of the journey laboriously sending texts: to Lucy "decided to take a break– will phone – Dad xxx". To his secretary: "Am in France. Best to assume I will be away for at least a month". To the RCOG "Regret unable to attend for next month, will phone to re-arrange committees etc". Then he turned his phone off.

The Jaguar had been directed to the very front of the car deck beside a row of trucks. At Calais as Lucien sat in his car waiting for the ramp to be lowered he watched the driver of the truck next to him, a short red-faced man with a bull neck and a florid moustache return to his truck: he climbed up and opened the door, reached inside and took out a pair of red velvet slippers which he exchanged for his shoes, then took off and carefully folded his black leather jacket and stowed it behind the seat. He saw Lucien watching him through the open car window and gave a little bow.

"To be comfortable in life you must be well prepared!" he said gravely and climbed up into the cab.

It was almost five o'clock French time before Lucien was out of the docks and onto the autoroute. By nine o'clock he had passed Paris and was on the A10 south towards Orleans, it was now dark and beginning to rain. The flip-flap of the windscreen wipers, the flashes of headlights in the smeared water on the glass, the streaked reflections from the tarmac were having a mesmeric effect. Suddenly the pain and stress of the previous 24-hours overwhelmed him and tears began to flow, his whole body ached, the thrumming of the tyres on the tarmac became louder. Suddenly immediately in front of him the lights of a big, red truck in the middle lane overtaking another but barely moving ahead. Norbert Dentressangle.

"Jesus Christ!" said Lucien out loud, foot hard down on the brake pedal "I've got to stop or I'll kill myself. Norbert bloody Dentressangle what a stupid name for a haulage company."

A few kilometres further on he was able to pull off into a rest area and find a quiet space to park. Within seconds of tipping back his seat he was asleep, his brain so numbed by stress and tiredness that even dreams were absent. Two hours later still aching and still confused he woke clear headed enough to continue the journey. The rain had stopped and he could see the stars bright above the pine forest beside the road. Lucien realized how rarely he'd driven down to St. Jean on his own in the last forty years; Diana would be with him to drive or sitting in the passenger seat occasionally resting her head on his shoulder or her hand companionably on his thigh. Tonight her absence was tangible. Waves of self-pity engulfed him and an overwhelming sense of loss; his lost son, his lost profession, the lost love of his wife. Driving on empty roads at night, his headlights picking out cottages or solitary trees, made for an unreal other world and not for considered reflection. Eventually at around three in the morning he arrived at the house in St. Jean. Before sleeping he sat for a while on the terrace in the cloying heat listening to the sound of frogs, watching silent lightning illuminating heaped up purple clouds on the horizon. A coming storm or one departing?

Saturday 6th September. St Jean.

Lucien woke with an ache in the pit of his stomach, hardly surprising as he had not eaten properly since his sandwich on the ferry and quite apart from that there were the effects of stress and his long drive. In the kitchen cupboards he found some biscuits, limp and uneatable, a half consumed pot of jam with a green, furry skin on the top, some coffee, sugar, an opened plastic bottle of long life milk and a couple of apples so dried up that they resembled large prunes. It was eleven o'clock, the Boulangerie should still have some bread and with any luck some of Mimi's croissants. Walking down the lane into the village he was, as ever, and in spite of all the misery that had engulfed him, overcome by the joy of this countryside; the cooing of doves, the sound of a distant tractor, the smell of grass from the verges and the sight of perfectly formed bunches of grapes hanging from the lowest stems of each manicured vine in the vineyards on each side. In the Boulangerie Lucien shook hands with old Madam Le Bon already at the counter, and after she had completed her long discourse on the state of the world with Mimi he, too, had the benefit of Mimi's radiant smile, a baguette and two croissants, also a pot of her home made Mirabelle jam. "Bon journée" it always sounded so much more heartfelt than the all American "Have a nice day"

Lucien was in no hurry to return to the empty house and its reminders. He knew that Jean-Luc at the café would give him a plate for his croissant as well as making him a *grande crème* coffee. He could see someone he knew already at his customary table outside the café; "TT" Terry Tufnall, the garage man. TT was in uniform, black sleeveless t-shirt, jeans, cigarette in mouth.

"Hello Luce, what you doing here all on your ownsome?"

TT with his carefully nurtured pecs, the tattoos on his bulging arms and the oil stains looked exactly as any garage man in South London might, but for the deep red sunburn, a pastis on the table in front of him and a copy of the Sud Ouest, the regional newspaper, open at the sports page.

"Just come for a break Terry"

"How long you here for?"

"You know I haven't decided that yet; a week, a month, don't know."

"That's not like you."

"I'm trying to develop the skill of relaxation!"

"Not like you either – you must come round to our place, Molly will feed you well – give us a bell, any day will do."

Lucien drank his coffee and ate his croissant in silence watching the slight wind ripple the leaves of the lime trees in the square. TT sipped his pastis, read his paper and then sat looking at Lucien whilst he lit another cigarette.

"Things aren't right for you are they Luce? Don't have to tell me but if there is anything I can do let me know."

As he left he squeezed Lucien's shoulder and walked over to his black 4x4 pick-up truck parked in the shade of the lime trees. "And you would too" thought Lucien. He mused that it was unlikely that TT would ever allow himself to get into Lucien's tangle of mishaps. If, however, the Libyans came looking for him TT with his rumoured SAS background might be just the man to get help from, the sort of robust knee in the balls and shoot to kill response that wasn't in Lucien's armamentarium.

Once TT had gone Lucien was alone amongst the chairs and tables outside; the square was empty apart from Jean Luc's dog lying under a tree scratching itself. Jean Luc came out and cleared away TT's pastis glass, flicked a finger at Lucien's empty cup.

"Another? "

"Merci, oui" said Lucien "Et un Armagnac, s'il vous plait"

TT had left his newspaper on the table. The usual stuff, a page of international news, some resentful reporting of government decisions in far off Paris; local stories, same mix as usual. Teenagers killed speeding, cattle thefts, promises of a good vintage, crimes of passion. A man had found his wife in bed with their neighbour and killed the man. Lucien did not think he'd have gone that far, probably just left the room. Civilized or meek? As he sat back in the chair, eyes closed, pondering this he felt a hand ruffle his hair, then a kiss on the cheek.

"Bonjour, Lucien cheri."

"Ah, bonjour Jeanette"

He stood up and kissed her on each cheek. He knew Jeanette well, petite, suntanned, with a sunburst of pale smile lines around the eyes. She was wearing a V-fronted T-shirt showing off her perfectly tanned cleavage. Her shorts were held up with a gold link belt, expensive sun glassed pushed up into her carefully tinted curly hair. Jeanette was the wife of Claude Jolliet a *negociant*, wine shipper, in Bergerac. He was her second husband to be precise the first having divorced her when he lost patience with her serial infidelities. Her age? Who knows, fifty, sixty may be a very well preserved seventy.

Lucien had never seen her quiet or reflective, she chatted, questioned, listened, smiled, talked, mentally always on the move. Diana called her the "little toucher" for her habit of always clutching someone or holding their hand when talking to them; which was what she did now as she sat down next to him.

"And why are you're looking so sad mon ami? No Diana? Suddenly here in St Jean unexpectedly? There is *un rupture* between you and Diana perhaps?"

Lucien knew that he had vowed not to tell anyone but he doubted if silence would suffice. In Dulwich yes, here in St. Jean, not a chance.

"You are a perceptive woman Jeanette."

"I am a woman. Why do you not come to lunch and we can talk about it. It's 12 o'clock now, I will expect you at one o'clock; now I must get bread from Mimi before she closes."

Jeanette and her husband lived in the grand 18th century "*maison du maitre*" next to the church, the gravelled path that ran straight to the front door was flanked on either side by neatly clipped yew trees; the facade of the house was five tall windows above and two on either side of the front door, perfect symmetry and order. At the back the kitchen led out through two pairs of long French windows onto a terrace surrounded by a low balustered wall sitting on which with a glass of wine in his hand Lucien could see south across the patchwork of vineyards towards the distant line of hills beyond which slid the River Garonne on its way to the ocean.

"Claude has a lunch meeting at the Maison des Vins in Bergerac so it is just you and me" said Jeanette innocently "but you need not worry he knows you are here, maybe he will join us for coffee. I don't have much food in the house but I have prepared a nice plate of *foie gras* with fig conserve, then a little salad and some Sarladaise potatoes. I hope that will suffice – and of course we have half a bottle of Claude's best Monbazillac to go with the *foie gras*.

She brought the two plates out to the table on the terrace and gave Lucien the bottle to open. She ran her hand through his hair and sat down opposite him.

"Now tell me about Diana; not the other things, Terry showed me the English newspapers so I'd heard all about the crazy allegations. I know they are not true, it will all go away, you see. No, tell me about Diana, that perhaps is the greater problem?"

She tucked into her *foie gras* with gusto, not looking at Lucien – he did not feel she was being inquisitive for its own sake, just concerned for him. Lucien and Claude, Diana and Jeanette, they had after all known each other for close on thirty years.

"Diana has a lover" he said at last,

"*Oui, naturellement*, she is an attractive woman."

"She has no plans to give him up."

"Ah, that is serious, when one's husband discovers one must always give up the man *toute de suite*."

"She asked me if I wanted a divorce."

"And you said?"

"I did not say anything, I was too shocked, we have not spoken since."

"Oh but that is so sad, so unhelpful. But mon ami, dear Lucien, what is to be done now? "

"I don't know, I really don't. I did not suspect that she was having an affair, indeed I thought we had a good marriage and it never crossed my mind that she would be unfaithful."

"But you do have a good marriage, and she has a lover, this is not so unusual, the two are not incompatible."

"Maybe not in France, but it's not how I expect a marriage to be" he replied a little stuffily.

"A little *affaire* need not harm your feelings for your wife you know; in marriage there is sex and love and friendship, nice to have all three. Love is crucial, friendship is good, sex is just *la garniture*, the garnish; perhaps you need to have a little affair yourself, then you would see what I mean."

"I don't agree, anyway one can't just go out and have an affair like hiring a car."

"Of course you can."

"Who with?" Lucien knew the answer before the question was out of his mouth.

"Well, me for example, you know I am very fond of you Lucien, I know you are married, I have no plans to upset that, if could be fun."

She touched his hand and laughed. She took out a cigarette lit it and leaned back in her chair mischievously enjoying Lucien's discomfort.

"So suppose you sleep with me" said Lucien …….

"So English? why the sleeping, there would be no time for that, why not just say have sex?"

"Whichever; and suppose it became a regular event – would you tell your husband?

"*Mais non*, of course not!"

"But once before you told me about these things in Paris, you told us about the swinger evenings, the after dinner entertainments."

"Ah, but that is Paris, it is just part of their showing off – here in the country we keep these things secret."

"If you can in a village!"

"One gets practiced at that. But you are right you'd probably hear gossip about it in the bar. The optimists, the no hopers, the chancers, but my lovers would not say anything."

"But if your husband found out?"

"He would pound the dung from you."

"He what ? Oh, you mean beat the crap out of me!"

"Same thing. That risk apart what do you think about the idea, shall we have an *affaire*, shall I be your *maitresse*? A man in your senior position really ought to have a mistress!" She stubbed out her cigarette "You think about it Lucien while I get some coffee."

He followed her into the kitchen.

"You are very sweet Jeanette, I don't need to think about it, so long as I am married to Diana, regardless of what she's done it would not be appropriate. It is not that I don't like you, an affair with you would be exciting, enjoyable but too much for my pathetic, old-fashioned principles."

Jeanette turned round from the stove reached up on tip-toe and kissed Lucien on the lips.

"Dear Lucien, I think that was the right answer. Your honour is intact. It is also the correct answer this afternoon because Claude has just come home to share coffee with us!"

As he walked back up the lane to his house Lucien thought about Jeanette's cheerfulness, her insouciance, how different from his own character. But honour? Jeanette had concluded seriously that his honour was intact. What an old fashioned way of looking at events. Honour, loyalty, love, commitment. He knew he'd have difficulty with accurate definition of these but for his own life he knew where the boundaries lay. Very different boundaries he thought wryly from those that Gamal Ghanem would draw. Honour to the Libyan probably involved killing Lucien! And if it had been the Libyan's wife who had been unfaithful rather than Lucien's, she would probably have been killed, possibly even with the acquiescence of the law.

And what would Diana's definition of honour be? Come to that what would be her definition of guilt. Lucien felt guilty about all his misfortunes. Intellectually he knew that he wasn't. He knew that his suspension from medical practice was all due to a scheming Libyan, but he still felt guilty that he was no longer looking after the patients he knew and who wanted him to care for them. A sense of guilt came too easily to him; perhaps that's why he felt so guilty in police stations and at frontiers. Too much guilt. He still felt guilt about Robin's death, as if somehow he'd been responsible for him joining the army. Too complicit perhaps. He even felt guilty about Diana's infidelity, God knows why though he accepted that marriage difficulties were rarely just the fault of one partner. He felt guilty about leaving London without explaining why to Diana or to Lucy or to anyone else, even himself! And what was he to do? Less guilt, more anger? Where would that get him? Try to patch it up with Diana? In his heart he knew that's what he wanted, to forgive her. Why? Because it would be honourable and would assuage his sense of guilt? Forgive her because he did not want to lose her? And why did he not want to lose her? Because he loved her or something altogether less romantic; horror at the thought of having to get out there and find a new partner! Trying to remember what to say, not knowing whether a woman just looks young because of the Botox, then all the anxieties about sex, when? how?

He'd enjoyed lunch with Jeanette, he'd been flattered and amused by her offer but now on his own in spite of the sunshine he was simply sad. He struggled to stop himself being drowned by sadness; the sadness of loss, the remembrance of the love he lavished on Diana and the pleasure that that love had given him. Or at least he thought it was love, it couldn't be anything else. The time shared, the laughter and the tears, also little things; breakfast brought to her in bed, fluffing up the foam on scented baths he'd drawn for her, her pleasure at gifts he'd brought. To be frank he'd even enjoyed the obeisance to her whims. Yet in her infidelity and it's secrecy it was as if she had set a naught each single gesture of love he'd ever made. And then there was the diary; he remembered how keen she was to know when he'd be home; they'd sit at breakfast comparing diaries, what was he doing - then "Oh you poor dear, a late committee meeting." Yet she was simply contriving the time she might spend with her lover; though presumably this depended on whether he too could find time to get away. Not so much a conjunction of bodies as of diaries!

Julian Scantlebury's male presumption was that Diana's infidelity was all just a search for better sex and if Lucien was honest with himself he realized that he'd never thought to analyze their sex life. "OK for her? OK for him?" He had to admit he didn't know. They both had orgasms at about the same time, fairly reliably. Were her orgasms good enough for her? He had no knowledge of that. All his professional life women had shared the failings and anxieties of their sex lives with him. He was after all a gynaecologist and fertility and infertility and the sex that they involved were his speciality. As he got older he'd been less willing to diagnose his patients' sexual problems and even less willing to offer definitive advice, but when he was younger he had no such compunction. He could describe a woman's anatomy to her, talk about the clitoris or the G-spot or vaginal orgasm. And if the patient preferred the exotic he could even talk about yoni massage or tantric sex, though he privately though the latter was the refuge of the timid or the ultra-cerebral. As for Diana, was the sex OK for her? He couldn't help coming back to the realization that he couldn't answer that. Women need to be practical and transparent or slightly mysterious and inaccessible. Diana definitely fell into the latter category. The whole issue was now going unhelpfully round in circles in his head. He thought about the other things, the things beyond orgasm that women writers talked about, "transcendence" he thought they called it. A sort of psychological calm, satisfaction; though Lucien reckoned that sufficiency of endorphins was probably all there was to it. Did Diana experience that "transcendence"? All he did know what that as soon as she'd had an orgasm she was away in her own world on her own side of the bed. Content rather than happy? Happy rather than exhilarated? How far along the continuum had he ever been able to take her and what happened with this lover that was so different? Or so much better that she wouldn't give him up. The mechanistic mind of Lucien wanted to think about it as simply that the mechanical parts of sex were, with this new guy, simply different or more drawn out or subtler. Oh, hell! He wasn't going to solve anything just sitting here thinking about it all and it was unlikely that she would tell him what the answer was. And anyway why all this focus on sex, what about all the other components of happiness the other ingredients in a happy marriage. If Diana could hear his thoughts now he knew she would be berating him for presuming that sex was the key. "Typical bloody man" she'd say. Anyway, maybe it was best not to start over-analysing. He seemed to remember that somebody, he had no idea who, had once said "over analysis equals paralysis". He went into the kitchen and picked out the best bottle of wine he could find, opened it, took it into the lounge, put Mahler's fifth symphony into the CD Player, turned up the volume and settled down to listen, drink and forget.

Sunday morning, 7th September. St Jean

Lucien woke late on Sunday morning and then only because of the insistent cooing of doves on the roof and the increasingly hoarse declamations of the cockerels beyond the oak copse. He felt calm, but lonely in the big iron bed with its thin summer duvet and Oxford sheets from The White Company. Diana's choices were everywhere. He wondered if Diana was waking up next to her lover, rolling over, stroking his prick to awaken him. With an effort he put the image out of his mind. This morning he would focus on the practical, the immediate and find solace in simple tasks in the garden starting with the laurel hedges on either side of the gateway. In the bathroom he was tempted not to shave, to declare his separation from the world of routine by letting the stubble grow, though he knew it would be grey and white and brown like a lost explorer's. The image of the awful, unshaved celebs in their black T-shirts, white trainers and two day growth of stubble persuaded him otherwise.

The trimming of the laurel hedge was almost finished when his neighbour Geraldine Makepiece came down the lane. She and her husband, Harold, lived in a converted barn on the other side of the hill behind the oak copse, they'd been there for ten years or more but contact with them was infrequent, the occasional shared bottle of wine on one or the other's terrace, pleasantries exchanged; the minimal currency of village life but no more than that. Indeed apart from a wave to Geraldine as she drove by up the lane there had been no contact for several months.

"Hello Lucien, nice morning. Is Diana not here?"

"No, she's in London."

"So is Harold, endlessly to-ing and fro-ing from here to London. I wish bloody RyanAir hadn't started the daily flight from Bergerac, it's become much too easy to flit." She was on foot, hesitating, loitering at his gate – he had no alternative.

"Can I make you a cup of coffee?"

"That would be nice." And she was through the gate in an instant as if that had been her intention all along.

145

Geraldine Makepiece was not someone who stood out in a crowd, nor would she wish to. Short, tidy, about sixty years old, her hair was neatly cropped grey, her clothes practical 'Country Casuals', quilted jackets, tweed skirts and flat heeled green suede shoes, but for all that she had a friendly manner, an engaging smile though spoke so quietly that Lucien had to incline his head to her to catch each word.

"With Diana not here you've joined the seperatees society, there seems to be quite a lot of us where one half prefers to be in France the other wants to be somewhere else. As I've got older I've got more attached to life here but Harold seems to be less and less so."

"What does he do?"

"Tries to pretend he's not sixty! We sold the business when he was fifty and he was happy out here at first painting, doing up the house and roaring around on his motorbike. Now he has all these daft plans; he's learning to play the guitar and to speak Spanish. That's why he keeps going back to London."

"Why don't you go too?"

"I prefer it here; anyway there are the cats and the chickens to care for. I'm content on my own tinkling on the piano and gardening. It's a peaceful life." She smoothed out her skirt with the palms of her hands keeping her knees close together. "I hope it doesn't seem forward but perhaps we might have dinner sometime, maybe in Bergerac, and perhaps ask Hans and Elsa to come along too?"

"What a good idea" said Lucien slightly surprised "I'm not sure how long I'll be here but perhaps next weekend?"

"You don't play bridge do you?"

"No, never."

"Pity, Harold used to be part of our bridge group in Bergerac but then stopped coming and some of the French ladies were quite miffed."

Hardly surprising thought Lucien, Harold Makepiece had affected the loveable, disorganized look for years; jeans, denim shirts, loafers, unkempt hair and a soulful look in his eyes like a homeless Labrador. It was hardly surprising that the French ladies would grieve his absence.

He was relieved when Geraldine left but he had no desire to wander about the kitchen cooking lunch for one in the empty house, it was too depressing; he would walk down to the bar and see what Jean Luc had as the *Plat du Jour*. It was bound to be more interesting than anything the he could cook for himself.

As he sat at his usual table outside relaxed by the sun and his glass of beer Thierry Desjoyaux joined him; normal village etiquette required that two people do not sit alone outside a café at separate tables. Thierry was a familiar figure in the village, tanned, in a sleeveless blue vest and jeans, floppy hair over his eyes, dark rings below them. Black, mocking eyebrows and two days of stubble all attesting to more time spent in the bedroom that the bathroom. Though usually found in the bar at the Café des Vignerons he occasionally roused himself to earn his beer money from odd jobs cutting grass, mixing cement, painting bedrooms and helping in the vineyards, as long as it was not too demanding. His main pursuit, however, was women, usually French and of any age up to fifty, indeed most agreed that he was God's gift to women. He was what the French called a *"chaud lapin"*, a hot rabbit. What Terry Tufnall called "a pussy hound". When he got the chance any female English tourist could be added to his conquests as they were easily bowled over by his fractured and heavily accented English. Never in history has there been an easier seduction than that achieved by a lithe, tanned, slightly sweaty, thirty-five year old Frenchman with a well-practiced set of chat-up lines. On hot summer evenings he would embellish his charms by strumming his guitar in a lazy kind of country-boy way outside the café "What beautiful fingers" one woman breathily observed clearly imaging uses beyond the guitar. This morning however he was in sombre mood.

"What's the problem Thierry?" asked Lucian.

Lucien knew Thierry well. Not just by reputation but because he was the occasional gardener at the Vieux Tour. After trimming trees or cutting grass he would sit on the terrace with Lucien and two cold beers. Diana usually left them alone to chat "Thierry's not my type". At the time it would never have occurred to Lucien to wonder exactly what that meant, he would have assumed it was just a turn of phrase meaning nothing.

"The problem Monsieur McCulloch is a woman."

"I didn't think you had problems with women, Thierry!"

"This is different; she wants me to marry her."

"Don't they all?"

"No, very rarely actually, most of the women like to have sex with me but realise I'm feckless, no good as a long term prospect – which is useful if a bit sad. This is different. Her husband found out and is divorcing her and has thrown her out of the house, the farm actually. So she wants to move in with me. Also her father has found out and is threatening to do bad things to me if I don't take on the responsibility for his daughter."

"Poor old Thierry – that's not how things are supposed to turn out in your world is it?"

"No it's not" and he lapsed into sullen silence, his fingers scrabbling ineffectively at the cellophane of a packet of cigarettes. "And my motorbike isn't working – may not be repairable."

He was dragging angrily at the cigarette now. It was difficult to tell which he considered the greater problem in his life, the sexual encounter turned sour or a motorbike that didn't work.

Lucien would not normally have probed any further but the Diana disclosure made him want to know more about how people like Thierry thought.

"Don't you feel guilty about this woman?"

"No, I didn't force her to have sex with me, *Le Bon Dieu* gave me a big dick and if women want to celebrate that okay."

This was said in all seriousness as he viciously stubbed out the cigarette – almost angry that God had bestowed this obligation on him. Lucien signalled to Jean Luc to refill the glasses.

"I hope you go to church to thank *Le Bon Dieu* for his gift!"

"I'm a good Catholic, I go to Mass, or at least part of it, I usually manage to get in and out in ten minutes, enough to get the bread and wine and do my duty."

"And confession?"

"Confess what? Anyway Pere Auguste wouldn't know anything about sex so it's no good confessing that sort of thing to him."

"Perhaps you could confess to screwing up other people's lives, husbands, partners, boyfriends." He realized immediately that he'd overstepped the mark. Thierry stared hard at him.

148

"Where's this anger coming from Monsieur McCulloch? Not my fault, your wife's off limits for me though I wouldn't mind ...... it's something else isn't it? That's great, be angry, it'll do you good but don't waste it on me." He got up. "Thanks for the beer" and shrugging his shoulders with truly Gallic contempt he was off though unable to make his usually noisy exit because there was no motorbike and angry exits on foot are difficult to pull off persuasively.

He's right thought Lucien. A lot more of anger is needed though to what purpose. He'd taught himself never to show anger, always to be in control but anger wasn't so easily assuaged. There were times when it remained invisible but smoldered away inside, hidden embers burning in a charred beam. No light, no smoke but just as destructive. He was on his own in a big, empty house in the country so where could he usefully direct any anger. Diana? No he couldn't face that. Her lover? He didn't know who he was. Gamal Ghanem? Too inaccessible. Fate? God? Even more inaccessible. Which just left Lucien James McCulloch. What was the phrase Lucy used? "Beating one's self up." No use doing that either.

Sunday morning September 7th. Libya

Far away to the south in another village in another country two other men were sitting outside a café on white plastic chairs, their sandaled feet scuffing the dirt as they sipped their chai in the inadequate patch of shade afforded by a torn umbrella. Nearby, against the whitewashed wall of the café an older man sat smoking silently, a white painted stick leaning against the wall within easy reach. His head was bowed. When he raised it towards the sun it was clear that he had no eyes. Also he had no left hand, just raggedly healed skin covering the wrist. One of the two young men was his son the other a cousin who had come from Benghazi in the east to this tawdry string of buildings that had sprung up along the highway into Tripoli, the café, a seemingly derelict but functional garage, a stall selling oranges and watermelons, a guest house of sorts and some shacks.

Half a dozen military trucks passed by at speed rising eddies of dust beside the road. Amidst the soldiers under the canvas awnings at the back of the trucks black Africans, mercenaries. The cousin from Benghazi spat onto the ground beside the table.

"The time will come Ahmed when all these oppressors will be gone and, God willing, Gaddafi with them. For now though we have one task which you've told our brothers in Benghazi you are willing to undertake. We will help you and soon our friends in Derna will provide the means – they will contact us here when they are ready."

"We shall succeed, Inshallah, God willing" said Ahmed more out of habit than conviction.

Ahmed's cousin went over to the old man, embraced him and kissed him on both cheeks.

"Your wait for revenge for what happened at Abu Salim will soon be over. In the name of the Prophet there will be revenge for all the tortured and the dead in that place. God is great."

In another world Ahmed would be at university or effortlessly moving up the hierarchy in a multinational company for he was handsome, tall, outgoing and intelligent. Here in the desert outside Tripoli denied an education or a supportive mentor, bereft of any important family connections the best he could achieve would be running this fly-blown café, serving tea or Pepsi Cola and making a pittance from doling out plates of rice and vegetables or mutton and couscous to hungry truck drivers. There was no money, no hope of a fine bride; perhaps no hope of any bride for his duty to his father would tie him to this life and this place. His mother had died just after giving birth to Ahmed, denied even the basic medical care which could have saved her. His father had a job in the kitchens in Abu Salim prison and it was he who had memorized the number of watches of the tortured and murdered that were brought to be cleaned before being sold. And his reward for letting slip this information was to have his eyes torn out and his hand and the wrist bearing his own watch hacked off. Why they let him live he had never discovered. Ahmed's clear purpose in life, next to his responsibility for caring for his father, was an act of revenge. It would be dangerous but he cherished the thought that afterwards he would return to his father and tell him the sweet story of retribution and of the satisfaction of honour served. All he needed was a vehicle, explosives and a way remotely to detonate them. His cousin had arranged for people in the East to provide the means so all he now needed to do was wait.

Sunday Afternoon 7th September. St Jean

Being on your own is bad it leaves too much time for thought and thought alone was not going to tell him what to do about Diana, their relationship or his own future. Just opening another bottle of wine and listening to Mahler was not the solution but perhaps all this churning of his memories was what he needed. Maybe Diana had got it right, perhaps any marriage however good it seems simply hasn't the kinetic energy in it to last as long as theirs had. Maybe they'd stayed in it out of laziness, subservience to a middle class myth? The fact that he was lonely on his own and wished Diana was there didn't necessarily mean she was the right partner for him. Maybe he didn't need a partner at all, maybe he could live without one. Diana or no Diana that was the only question he needed to answer right now. Could marriage to her still bring him happiness or joy – was joy still obtainable at his age? Life doled out the good and the bad pretty much at random and for most of his life he'd been lucky, the dice had come up with sixes more often than he'd had a right to expect and apart from Robin's death it was only now in his 60s that the laws of statistical probability had come back to taunt him at every throw of the dice. Laws he'd never understood. The statistician in his department seemed to have no problem. Throw the dice 60 times and you'll probably see a 6 ten times but the chance of throwing a six is the same every time the dice hits the table even if you have thrown it 50 times before and already had ten sixes, or twelve or even fifty. The next one may still be a six. Metaphysics not statistics. So here he was; his dice had come up with the wrong number, whichever one that is, multiple times in the last few months so could he expect the next event to be a good one? No it was just as likely to be another bad one and sometimes it only needed one bad throw to ruin your life. As he sat there with the sun on his face and the sound of bees in the flowers he remembered poor Felicity who brought sunshine into his years in Cambridge and who then picked the wrong man. Felicity, the bubbly one, the bright one, the scholarship girl. A sequence of sixes and then none from the age of 21 until she was 50, maybe not even then. Perhaps a run of bad luck can damage you irredeemably.

Monday 8th September. Sunday Papers

It was not until the Monday morning that Lucien saw the Sunday papers. It always took a day for the English newspapers to complete the tortuous journey from printing press to the *tabac* by the church at end of Place Gambetta in Bergerac. This was Lucien's third morning at St. Jean since leaving London and the memory of the events that made him leave England were softening a little. It still felt strange waking up in the big bed in the Vieux Tour without Diana beside him, odd to have breakfast on his own – it was such a big table. Now it felt strange to be sitting in the sun outside the café next to the *tabac* looking at The Sunday Times but not sharing out the sections between the two of them or discussing what they were reading. He didn't at first relate to the banner headline on the front page "Minister in Alleged Child Prostitution Scandal". It seemed that a cabinet minister had been filmed twice at a house in the Chalk Farm area of London to which at the same time children in their teens were taken by van, children seemingly of east European or north African origin some of whom it emerged were in the care of the local authority. When questioned the children said they were "at a party" and when shown photographs identified the minister as taking part in the "party". When challenged the local authority staff admitted that several of the children were in care having been "rescued" from traffickers and that two of the fourteen year old girls and one of the boys, aged only twelve, had previously been recorded as involved in prostitution. The article went on to publish a photo of the minister and his aide on the deck of a yacht in Cannes harbour and said children from a minibus had been recorded boarding the yacht and that local agencies in Marseilles had identified several of them as known child prostitutes. It was the next paragraph that made Lucien suddenly fully aware of what he was reading. *"Other guests on the yacht included Gamal Ghanem, the Libyan Minister of Trade with whom Mr. Ashbury in his role of UK Trade Minister was regularly in contact in relation to bilateral trade arrangements and the possibly repatriation of Abdel al Magrahi. The minister has denied any wrong-doing. He says he has no intention of resigning and is at present consulting his lawyers. A spokesperson for number 10*

Downing Street said that Mr. Ashbury retained the Prime Minister's full support." The reader was referred to the News Review section for a fuller report by the Insight Team and to editorial comment elsewhere in the newspaper. The inside article covered two pages and included maps of north London and the port of Cannes. There were pictures of the house in Chalk Farm and of the Russian Oligarch's yacht in Cannes harbour. Nowhere was it indicated where this investigation had begun and nowhere was Jerry Havilland mentioned apart from the caption to the picture of the champagne moment on the yacht's deck. The editorial referred very obliquely to the risk of blackmail inherent in the minister's peccadilloes but clearly with the paper's lawyers twitching anxiously in the background it skirted round the obvious implication that the minister's enthusiasm for Libyan causes might be to ensure a continuing supply of North African child prostitutes and to prevent his hobby of being exposed. The sub-plot of Gamal Ghanem's vendetta against Lucien orchestrated by the equally culpable Jerry Havilland didn't feature. After all who had ever heard of Jerry Havilland or, come to that, Lucien McCulloch?

As Lucien's car skirted the square in St. Jean on his way home, TT who was sitting at his usual table with a pastis held out his hand to stop him.

"Someone's been asking for you Luce and has gone up to your house; were you expecting them?"

"No, what sort of person?"

"Middle aged, Brit, hire-car. Want me to come with you?"

"No, as long as he doesn't look like a terrorist it'll be okay thanks!"

The gate to the house was open; a car on the gravel and a man in a linen suit was sitting on the terrace smoking.

"Hello who are you?"

"Harvey Brown, Daily Mail, sorry to have come right in unannounced – force of habit. Hoped we could have a chat."

"About?"

"I see you've got The Sunday Times with you, have you read the bit about Harry Ashbury the Minister of Trade?" Lucien nodded. Brown went on "great scoop for The Sunday Times, it's a story that's really got legs – Ashbury will eventually resign of course but yesterday our editor reckoned there's a lot more to it than what's in yesterday's Sunday Times. I noted that the Libyan Gamal Ghanem was named and I remember a story we were fed which involved you as well as him. Something about sterilising his wife without consent, we didn't publish it – does that fit with this story? Anyway I thought it worth the 7.00 am. red-eye to Bordeaux to catch you and see if we can squeeze some more out of the story."

"How did you know I was here?"

"Phoned your wife – she said I was to give you her love!"

"How do I know you are who you say you are?"

"You could phone 'The Mail' speak to the Editor's office." Lucien did that but having confirmed Harvey Brown's identity he still hesitated. Lucy Harper-Smith, The MDU solicitor, had confirmed several weeks ago that Gerry Havilland was the go between so there was a link. Havilland with or on behalf of Ashbury doing Gamal Ghanem's dirty work; but was it really worth letting it all out into the newspapers again? Lucien's continued sense of outrage reckoned that it was.

"Would you like some lunch whilst I tell you the story, you've had an early start?"

Over lunch Lucien recounted the whole story yet again now clarified and shortened by endless repetition in his head. He even recounted the Denmark Hill shooting. He did not explain why he was in France. Harvey Brown wrote salient points in his notebook but unknown to Lucien also recorded the whole conversation on a little digital recorder hidden in his jacket.

"Apart from being the conduit for the legal papers did this Mr. Havilland do anything else to help this vendetta along?"

Lucien had no knowledge of any but Harvey Brown had a list of possibilities. Had Havilland spread the stories about Lucien to the press and more interestingly had he influenced the CPS or the police to charge Lucien? After lunch while Lucien was making coffee Brown walked off to the edge of the terrace and made some phone calls then after coffee left so he could catch an early flight back to London.

"There might be something in The Mail tomorrow or on Wednesday. I don't know if it will help you but thanks for your information."

Tuesday 9th September. St Jean.

SEX SCANDAL MINISTER'S AIDE IMPLICATED IN PLOT TO JAIL TOP DOCTOR.

Following the revelation that Minister of Trade, Harry Ashbury, and his aide, Jeremy Havilland, have been implicated in a child prostitution scandal this paper can exclusively reveal that Jeremy Havilland has also been acting as an agent for the Libyan government Trade Minister Mr. Gamal Ghanem to pursue a personal vendetta in the UK against Professor Lucien McCulloch CBE internationally renowned expert on women's health. Mr. Havilland whose formal position is in the South America section of The FCO has been purporting to be working officially for the FCO when acting for Mr. Ghanem to persuade The General Medical Council, The Metropolitan Police and The CPS to harass Professor McCulloch. Full story page 6.

The fuller article disclosed what Lucien had not known – the direct approaches to The CPS had been made by Gerry Haviland and that it was he who, pretending to be from the North African desk at The FCO, had "validated" the affidavits from the two Libyan women who had claimed they were assaulted by Lucien. Also on the page in a separate fact box were biographical details about Lucien.

"Lucien McCulloch, sixty-two, married, son the most senior British officer killed in Iraq" all stuff from the internet *"lives in an £800,000 house in Dulwich,"* The Daily Mail never missed an opportunity at a house valuation, but then it concluded *"Professor McCulloch is estranged from his wife and is currently living in France"*. He was shaken by that, he had imagined that somehow the sudden upheaval in his married life could be kept not only in limbo, on hold awaiting his decision, but also secret. Diana had clearly been open with The Daily Mail man and now the word would be getting around his friends, colleagues, everyone would know that there was a problem. He was now just flotsam on the edge of the tide.

Lucien hadn't seen the European version of The Daily Mail until late on Tuesday morning when he went into Bergerac. Having read the revelations about Gerry Havilland he could see that the whole Gamal Ghanem nightmare might now come to an end, or at least The GMC and CPS processes might be stopped. He ruefully acknowledged that unless Gamal Ghanem had run out of vituperative energy he'd still have to be on the lookout for the next nasty idea on Ghanem's list. Perhaps another attempt to kill him?

What Lucien had not seen in the Daily Mail was a small paragraph noting that the Department Of Health had received and was considering the report it had commissioned on the management culture at their flagship institution The Royal United Hospital.

Sitting on his terrace having his little lunch of bread, cheese and paté feeling the sun on his back, sensing the ripening of the grapes he felt calm for the first time since he'd arrived in France five days ago. There was nothing he could do about The GMC or The Crown Prosecution Service or any of that but least he could try and resolve the problems with his marriage. However, for now he best thing to do would be to finish his lunch and then take a walk.

The road to the mill was not a through road, so prettily unkempt. None of the obsessional "fauchage" that leaves most French roadsides as featureless greensward. Nature was trying hard to reclaim this lane; questing strands of ivy and escaped vines reached onto the road and a mix of untutored trees intermingled above the green tunnel they'd made. At the end were the remnants of the mill, a complicated building in fine stone, overgrown but its little oak windows framed by freshly painted sky blue shutters. The river was still partitioned here and directed, silent and reflective in the pool above but fractured and noisy as it hurtled down the sluice past the rotted, unmoving wheel. Around the mill and on the island between the pools the owners had made a bracelet of little gardens, naturalistic and secret in places, formal and green in others. Beside the mill race a long lawn with fruit trees.

As Lucien approached he saw the owners Hans and Elsa Van Boeken standing side by side on the lawn. Hans had his left arm around Elsa's waist and was guiding her hand to a branch of a fig tree laden with purple fruit. Lucien had known for several years that Elsa had become blind though she was only in her early seventies, yet he was overcome by the sweetness of this vision of a man and a woman in the dappled sun beneath a fig tree. Elsa's hand moved out along the branch squeezing each fruit for ripeness before picking it and handing to Hans. Lucien felt he was intruding on a moment so personal it would be best to leave but Hans catching sight of him called out.

"Lucien my dear friend how nice to see you, come and sit with us."

Hans Van Boeken was a fine looking, tall, upright, white haired man. His face lightly lined and lightly tanned, his eyes as blue as his wife's almost as if they were twins. Her blonde hair cascaded wildly onto her Kaftan. The two of them looked as if they had just emerged from a video of a sixties rock festival which in a way they had.

"A glass of wine? Something to smoke?"

"Just the wine thank you." Lucien knew that amongst the garden herbs *cannabis sativa* had found a cherished place. Hans guided Elsa to a wicker armchair and went to fetch the wine.

"All on your own? No Diana? That's rare" said Elsa.

"I've just come for a few weeks quiet reflection on my own Elsa, I think I need to take a look at where my life is going."

He realised that this was perhaps too frank an explanation but to a blind woman whose perfect blue eyes looked towards him but not at him it seemed appropriate, safe.

"Have you never done that before?" she said smiling

"Since you mention it I realise that in fact I never have, life has just been a long unquestioning trudge into the future. I suppose that's one of the handicaps of being a doctor, it's difficult to justify not doing it and doing it fills your life from sixteen to sixty-five."

"But it has a purpose, every day has a purpose" said Hans returning with a bottle of wine and three glasses. "That is good, it absolves you from choices. For Elsa and for me it has been different; you know that from eighteen to twenty-eight we just dropped out, dropped out of making choices, dropped out of making effort. All we needed to know could be found in a Bob Dylan lyric."

"Didn't you enjoy yourselves?"

"We thought we did, but it was all very shallow – relationships were often meaningless, sex so freely available that it signified nothing. Most of the time we were stoned so we had a very hazy view of life! We thought that just being different from mainstream society was all we needed. But we loved it!"

"But it didn't lead anywhere" interjected Elsa.

"So we dropped back into society" said Hans "I became an investment banker and we got married to legitimize the two children who may or may not be mine but whom we love."

"Second choice for us" said Elsa "First to drop out, second drop back in again."

"Third drop out again in our fifties."

"So was that life change a considered choice?" asked Lucien.

"Yes and no, I'd made a lot of money, our children were grown up. The banking world I worked in was morally destitute so coming here to make beautiful gardens, restore an old mill and be happy amongst happy people seemed a good choice."

"And your choices?" asked Elsa reaching out hesitatingly to where she knew Lucien was sitting and touching his arm "What are they?"

"I really don't know. In medicine you storm along a single straight road then about now you find you've come to the end of that road and it just peters out, stops, leads nowhere in particular, an empty country with no definite horizon."

"Just peters out like our lane here" said Hans "But this lane leads to a beautiful watermill, flowers and the sound of water, a little paradise – what more can a man want except paradise?"

"But you've got Elsa."

"Any you have Diana."

"Maybe, maybe not that remains to be seen."

"Dear Lucien we can't help with that but if you can find a paradise as we have then you'll need to be sure you go in with the right person."

"Even Paradise is lonely if you're on your own" said Elsa "Now Lucien would you like some figs, I've spent all afternoon squeezing the little scrotums, it would be waste for them to go into a heap for the wasps. These purple figs are gorgeous stuffed with soft goat's cheese mixed with chopped mint."

Lucien laughed.

"What a developed taste - how we've all aged – I bet when you were hippies you were just squeezing and sucking them and quoting that awful DH Lawrence poem. I can't quite remember how it goes.

"The proper way to eat a fig in society
Is to split it in four holding it by the stump
Something, something, something
But the vulgar way is just to put your mouth to the crack and take
out the flesh in one bite
Then as I recall it becomes just an anthem to women's pudenda!"

Elsa screeched with delight,

"Yes we did, yes we did. We read it out loud as if it were a sacred text. Sacred I think because it was explicit. Sex is still sacred but much more private now. The hippies have gone."

When Lucien left Hans embraced him, almost too strongly.

"As we get older Lucien there's a lurking sense of despair; however we arrange our lives we cannot avoid that, don't waste too much time making your choices. We all assume we will live forever but we will not. Think of poor Anna in the Chateau all on her own now. It's three years since Hector keeled over with a stroke….. just standing looking at his vines with a glass of wine in his hand…… It could happen to any of us at our age."

Lucien walked along the river, pausing to watch a grey heron standing silently in the water at the edge of the *etang*. I may be slow to resolve this but I don't have his patience he thought and worked his way back through the vines up the hill to the house.

As soon as he got in he plugged in the phone and turned on his mobile. The first time he'd put himself back in contact since he'd crossed the channel. There were ten text messages. One from the College, one from his secretary, one spam and seven from Lucy all much the same "Daddy please, please phone me, I love you – Lucy xxx" There were no messages from Diana. Hell, he hadn't phoned

Lucy since he'd arrived and he'd remembered that in the text that he'd sent when he left she was the only person he'd said he would contact and he'd been so wrapped up in his own misfortunes that he hadn't. She answered her mobile on the first ring.

"Daddy!"

"Hi Lucy how are you?"

"I'm worried Daddy, why are you in France? You and Mum were meant to meet me for supper at the weekend. What's happened?"

"Did Mum not speak to you?"

"Yes, she just said you'd gone to France."

"Didn't she say why?"

"No. Tell me Daddy please, what's going on?"

Lucien wasn't prepared for this, explaining why at a time of family stress he'd simply done a bunk. Oh shit!

"Lucy darling, I thought Mum might have told you. She has been having an affair and has no plans to give the man up. It was all a surprise to me so I decided to come out here for a while to try to work out what to do. I'm so sorry."

There was silence, then he could hear Lucy sobbing on the other end of the line.

"Lucy?"

"Oh Daddy it's awful, how could this happen, you're such a strong couple, the two of you together are the fixed point in my life. When I was at my worst with the drugs and everything you and Mum and home were the lighthouse on firm land. I'd knew you'd be there, home was a safe place but now that's gone. Oh Daddy what are we to do? Who is this man? I'll go and kill him then you and Mummy can be together again."

The sobbing started again.

"I don't know who it is Lucy and I don't know what was so wrong between Mum and me that she felt she had to do this, I wish I did, it might help to put things right."

The sobbing had stopped.

"I'm going to hang up now Daddy, don't worry I'm not going to do anything stupid. I love you and I'll call you soon."

Lucien was about to phone Diana in Dulwich but still didn't know what he'd say so he just went and poured himself a whisky and took it onto the terrace with him. The sun was now low in the sky casting long shadows in the plantation of poplar trees on the other side of the valley. He adored with a pagan enthusiasm the poplar plantations that were found all around this part of France, usually a hundred of more trees planted with absolute geometrical precision, their trunks as tall and bare as telegraph poles, the grass between them chopped short, the grey-green foliage at the top all a-shimmer in the slightest breeze. Did he love them for some purely aesthetic reason he wondered or because they were so orderly. If he knew that, he concluded, it might tell him something useful about himself. Maybe he'd only be able to choose a future if he knew himself better, if he knew what he wanted from life.

Tuesday September 9th. Libya

Ahmed had been anxious as he waited for the vehicle, would it come, had he the courage to do what was planned. Had it all been a trap? But then a message that he should expect a delivery this day. The vehicle came in the evening and parked outside the café like any other, a battered Toyota truck. "VIP Ventilation Installation and Plumbing" said the writing on the doors in Arabic with an address in Sirte, Gaddafi's home town. In the back were lengths of pipe and coils of wire, air conditioning units and an old water container, a metal balloon a metre across, the sort you see on roof tops all over the Middle East. Ahmed's cousin gave him the keys, a forged requisition for a plumbing job at an address in Tripoli and lastly a small cardboard box labeled "Aircon Controls" in which was the type of remote control unit used for air conditioning units.

"This is the remote control for the explosives – don't touch it until you need it. It's been adapted to work at a range of up to 300 metres. To prime it turn it on with that little switch, to detonate rotate the temperature control around to 'max'. All you will need to do is park the vehicle outside the address on the requisition then taking the box with you walk away a couple of hundred metres and wait for the gates to open. Your target always travels by car and on Wednesdays always leaves promptly at 7.30. As soon the vehicle emerges from the gates operate the switch. I'll be waiting on the motorbike to bring you back here."

"Are you sure it will work?"

"The group who supplied it are confident."

"Who are they?"

"I don't know –in Benghazi my friends and I meet in secret to talk about how Gaddafi might one day be got rid of. Nothing ever comes of it of course, but someone in the group knows some people in Derna who are actually preparing themselves and who have received advice and equipment from outside the country."

"Who from?"

"I don't know; The British I suppose, maybe the Americans. Actually I don't care as long as the stuff gets to people who can use it against Gaddafi".

They sat for a while in the darkness outside the café, occasionally illuminated by the lights of passing cars. In the blackness beyond the shacks on the other side of the road the desert began but there was none of the sweetness of the desert air here, just the usual background smell of drains and diesel.

"So tomorrow morning then?"

"We must leave here at six-thirty to be there at seven-thirty."

Wednesday morning 10th September. St Jean

Although it was only six days since he had left London Lucien awoke without the shocks of memory that had dogged each previous morning. He had not woken in the night to spend a futile hour half-awake with the details and unstructured solutions whirling around in his head, he felt relaxed but animated. "If I was that way inclined" he thought " I would go for a run or a swim or do press ups". Instead he contented himself with a brisk walk down to the village savouring the air. Geraldine Makepiece was just coming out of the Boulangerie.

"Hullo, lovely day" said Lucien briskly, carefully avoiding the issue of dinner or bridge. Whilst he was paying for his baguette he felt someone squeeze his buttock; it was Jeanette – thank God it wasn't Geraldine.

"Bonjour cheri; still in St. Jean?" she said "wait whilst I buy my bread then we will have a chat." She led him over to a bench beside the church and patted the space next to her. "Now then Lucien, how are you ?"

"Well, thank you, calm and controlled and enjoying the tranquility of life here."

"But have you spoken to Diana?"

"No, I'm waiting for her to phone me." Jeanette took her hand off his knee and pushed her sunglasses up into her hair.

"*Mon Dieu* Lucien, this is not a child's game; you are behaving like a little boy who is sulking. You've decided to be the victim. This is not like you, normally you are so keen to sort things out, make sure everyone is pleased with you. That's a problem but this is a bigger one." Jeanette jumped up and stood in front of Lucien poking him in the chest with her baguette, "Be a man Lucien – do something!"

"But Jeanette I am just beginning to enjoy NOT doing anything, just letting time slip by."

"You are deluding yourself mon ami; enjoy this moment of calm but remember that sooner or later you must sort things out!"

"Yes I know that Jeanette. You are right". Jeanette had sat down again and replaced her hand on his knee.

"And what about the proposition I made on Saturday? I could teach you a thing or two, things that would make Diana want to keep you!" Lucien knew Jeanette well enough not to be embarrassed.

"Thank you Jeanette, I think there may be more to it than that. I will phone Diana. You're very sweet and if I become definitely unattached perhaps we can talk about it again."

"Too late Cheri, you only get one chance!" and with that she sashayed off, her baguette under her arm.

When he had returned home from his dressing down by Janette he had tried to phone Diana in Dulwich and was relieved to find no reply. He did not leave a message, instead he phoned his mother and arranged to visit her the next day. It was a long drive to Pau in the Pyrenees where she lived but it would take his mind off everything and anyway she was entitled to be told what was going on.

He'd ducked out of phoning Diana and she hadn't called him; just a childish game of chicken – who would blink first? He hadn't decided what to do next but at least she had the option of giving up this lover and opening a dialogue. He felt that the longer he waited the greater the likelihood of that happening. "So I'll have to sit it out on my own a bit longer" he said to himself "so I'd better learn how. I'll tidy up the house, pick up the towels, make the bed, tidy the clothes, sweep the terrace and learn to be a well organised bachelor again."

And it was when he was tidying the bedroom that he found the book under some others on Diana's side of the bed; a slim paperback book of a hundred and twenty or so pages, an English translation of a French author he'd never heard of, Frederic Beigbeder. The book's title "Love Lasts Three Years". It was not a book that he'd bought or seen before; there was a Waterstones' bookmark inside. Flicking the pages he noticed pencil marks in the margins and hoping for some clues to Diana's current state of mind he took it downstairs put his feet up and read it. It only took an hour. The book purported to be a novel but Lucien guessed it was autobiographical. The plot is simple: Author marries pretty, loveable girl. After two years his enthusiasm begins to fade so he begins an affair with someone else's wife, the core of which relationship seems to be lots of sex. His wife discovers, she divorces him in year three. The girl with whom he is having the affair at first refuses to leave her husband, then does, husband distraught. The two lovers are now living together. Fast forward; the end of the third year together approaches and will it all end in boredom and infidelity like the previous relationship? End of book. The book was irritating and typically French; self-indulgent, obsessed with sex, uncertain of the difference between love and lust, full of quasi-philosophical, quasi-insightful asides. One chapter was entitled "The Impossible Decrystallisation" which still sounded French even in translation. The marginalia, he assumed they were Diana's, had sampled accurately the shallowness of the philosophy.

"The fundamental rule when having an affair is never fall in love"
"Marriage the Institution-Which-Makes-Love-Tedious"
"Love is a glorious catastrophe"
"I don't believe empathy exists. I don't believe in anything. I don't even see the point of myself"
"Love lasts as long as it lasts"

And so on, a book waiting to be another black and white movie with subtitles. Yet another convoluted attempt to justify the habit of adultery. Lucien reached the end of the book and found, sandwiched between the last page and the back cover, a small folded piece of paper on which was written "*D. Infidelity is an existential obligation. H xx*" What crap! Lucien hurled the book across the room wanting to rid himself of this tainted talisman from what he assumed was Diana's lover "H". H who? He retrieved the piece of paper, folded it to the size of a postage stamp and put it in his wallet. Maybe he could identify the handwriting. He felt guilty pocketing something of Diana's, something that maybe she cherished. Guilty, even though by comparison it was a very trivial act of disloyalty.

Wednesday morning September 10th. Dulwich

Lucy let herself into her parent's house in Dulwich with a key she'd had for years. She hoped the code for the burglar alarm had not been changed. She keyed it in, her heart thumping whilst she waited for the beeping to stop. It stopped, the code hadn't changed. Now what to do? She'd come knowing that her mother would be out at work and her plan was to look for clues to the identity of her mother's lover. She'd asked Diana directly during an angry conversation that followed Lucien telling her what had sent him to France, but Diana had told her it was none of her business – which made her angrier. As far as Lucy was concerned anything that threatened her family was her business. So far however she had no idea of how to get the identity of the lover by other than loitering outside the house waiting for him to turn up. She wandered about the house, it was very tidy and she took care not to disrupt anything; perhaps there were hidden love letters, her mother would be sensible enough not to send or receive "love e-mails" if such a thing existed! If there was something to hide where would her mother hide it? In the bedroom. Where? In somewhere that was just hers. In the dressing table or among her clothes. Nothing hidden in the dressing table. No secret files in the wardrobe. But at the back of the underwear drawer was a large sponge bag, new, made of red and black striped fabric. In it some underwear of the sort Lucy would not have expected of her mother, crotchless panties and a tiny bra with peep holes for the nipples. Also a mobile phone, not Diana's usual one that she carried around with her. Lucy turned it on and flicked the screen to the call log. All the calls both in and out connected to just one number. With trepidation she moved to the file of saved texts, she felt this was really bad of her, perhaps they would be full of gushy love-struck stuff or explicit filth. Either way she didn't want to know, so she just looked at a few incoming texts in search of a name. Fortunately the first two she looked at were short, a date, a time, a place and signed 'H'. Enough. She wrote down the mobile phone number of 'H' . Also in the drawer she found another bag, a black velvet one closed with a drawstring. Inside a pair of handcuffs, some soft cord and a blindfold of the type airlines give their business class passengers "Oh

Mummy!" thought Lucy quite amused "What fun you've been having, and in your fifties too."

Lucy took the phone downstairs; she set it on the kitchen table, a small piece of high explosive. What to do with it. She took out her own mobile and phoned an friend.

Identifying the owner of a mobile phone number is, for most people, difficult and complicated but for Lucy, knowing the sort of person who could find out legally or illegally was one of the benefits accruing during her misspent past; there weren't many benefits but this was one and within 20 minutes she had the name and address she was looking for. Helpful Jim also offered to tell her where the owner's mobile phone was at that moment and if she wanted he would get the numbers of any other phones where the bill payer lived at the same address.

"You're a star Jim; tell me, would it be possible to arrange for all the calls sent from the mobile number I'm asking about to be automatically diverted to another number rather than the one dialled?"

She harboured a mischievous notion that it would be possible to arrange for all her mother's lover's calls to end up on his wife's phone rather than Diana's. Assuming he was married; she had for some reason presumed that he would be.

"Sorry Lucy no can do, but you can, of course, arrange for any of the texts and photos in the memory of the phone you have to be forwarded elsewhere; you can do that yourself."

"Thanks Jim, I think you may have told me what I need to do. Would you get me the mobile number for a woman, probably the wife, at the same address?"

As soon as she had that number she picked up Diana's phone and began, as she saw it, to set things right. Half an hour later she carefully replaced the phone in the bag and the bag in the drawer, made sure nothing was out of place, then she slipped out of the house.

Wednesday morning September 10th . Tripoli

Ahmed and his cousin arrived in the outskirts of Tripoli just after seven and made their way through the traffic to the smart residential area in the South West. The street they were looking for was narrow and one way with checkpoints at the ends each manned by two armed soldiers. Ahmed's cousin on his motorbike took the side turning just short of the first checkpoint. Ahmed eased the truck to a halt where red and white painted concrete blocks had been put down to narrow the road. The soldiers at the checkpoint took the papers Ahmed proffered, the fake requisition for some work at a building further down the road. The soldier nodded, walked slowly round the vehicle peering at the contents then beckoned him through. It was seven-twenty six a.m. The place where Ahmed had planned to park the vehicle was about 150 metres away but parked cars made it difficult to stop there. However one car pulled out from just the right place as he approached. It was in front of some gates and marked as a no parking area but no-one in Tripoli paid much attention to these except near military buildings. As he parked there the gates of the compound opened and a white Mercedes started to emerge. Ahmed's truck was blocking its exit. A bullheaded man got out of the passenger seat shouting and waving a handgun, Ahmed began to panic. Two hundred metres further down the street, just beyond the barrier at the far end, the car that had moved to make a space for Ahmed stopped at the kerb. The driver looked back and took something out of the glove compartment. There was a blinding flash of light and an explosion that was heard all over Tripoli. The truck, its contents and Ahmed disintegrated whilst a fireball engulfed surrounding buildings and cars including the white Mercedes and its occupants. There was total silence for a fraction of a second before a cacophony of car alarms, falling glass and screams took over. A huge gobbet of black smoke rose into the air. The soldiers ran towards the chaos; meanwhile the man in the car that had made way for Ahmed drove calmly off and a mile away stopped in a shopping centre car park to make a phone call before setting off on the long drive towards the east.

1200hrs Wednesday September 10th – News Flash. Reuters. Tripoli, Libya.

"At 7.35am this morning Tripoli was rocked by a huge explosion in a residential street in the South West of the City. The street is known to contain the homes of a number of senior government ministers and security is normally tight. It is believed that a car bomb was responsible. There is no indication at present of causualties and no-one as yet has claimed responsibility."

1800hrs Wednesday September 10th – News Flash. Reuters. Tripoli, Libya.

"It is now known that eight people were killed by the major explosion that occurred in a residential district of Tripoli earlier today. Although not confirmed it is rumored that one was Mr. Gamal Ghanem Minister of Trade and that others included his bodyguard, his driver, passers by and the suicide bomber himself. A call to Reuters has claimed to be from the "Martyrs of Abu Salem Brigade" a known Salafist group linked to Al Queda. The call also claimed that this was the first in a series of attacks that would lead to the destruction of the Gaddafi regime and establish an Islamic state based on the principles of Sharia law. Terrorist rebel attacks are rare in Libya and there have been no previous such bombings. There have been rumors of small uprisings in the Benghazi area but nothing before in Tripoli. Although Gamal Ghanem was known to be close to the British government, and one of the links through which bids to repatriate the Lockerbie bomber Abdel Basset Al Maghrahi from Scotland were made, it is not thought that his death will change the current pressure to send Maghrahi home nor upset negotiations on oil contracts with Libya. Gamal Ghanem was aged fifty-two. Neither his wife nor any of his three daughters was injured by the blast."

Wednesday evening September 10th. Chelsea

If you walk down the King's Road in London starting from Sloane Square with its plane trees and almost Parisian ambience, you'll be struck by how quietly opulent it is. None of the glitz of Bond Street or Knightsbridge. Indeed, none of the flamboyance and carefully paraded pop-culture that first made it famous in the early sixties. By the turn of the millennium all the remained of that was a gaggle of pink haired, pierced punks posing, for a fee, for tourists. Now well dressed people fill the pavements and cafes either shopping for something they like but don't really need or discussing it with a friend in a café. If you walk a few hundred metres from Sloane Square along the south side you'll pass Wellington Square which isn't a square but two rows of perfectly maintained Georgian houses admiring each other across a narrow strip of garden kept private by railings and locked gates. You wouldn't walk into Wellington Square because it doesn't lead anywhere and you might be inhibited by the unmistakable aroma of wealth and exclusiveness yet behind the glossily painted doors and the expensively swagged curtains there are the same joys and miseries, the same stresses and strains as in any other street... but it doesn't show. On this day in 2008 you might have seen a perfectly ordinary man in a suit carrying a brief case leave the stream of evening shoppers in the King's Road and walk along to one of the houses in the square reaching into his pocket for the key as he bounds up the four steps to the front door.

"Hello darling, I'm home" and he goes downstairs to the basement where the spotless, polished kitchen units reflect the expensively selected foliage in the courtyard garden through a sweep of sliding, glass doors. He's expecting to pour himself a drink, kiss his wife and ask what's for dinner – even though he's late, but his wife is standing arms akimbo silhouetted against the sunny garden.

"Sorry I'm late" he says.

"I'm surprised you came home at all! Wouldn't you prefer to be somewhere else – with your slut? Your whore!"

If you are short and broad and born of a Spanish mother and an Irish father you can do venom well. She had clearly allowed her anger to heat slowly and come to boiling point just as her husband came down the stairs into the kitchen.

"Teresa dearest, I really don't know what your mean."

"Of course you bloody well do and I know what's going on now too – I've had five messages forwarded to my phone today and two photographs. I don't know who from but the original messages are all from your phone to someone you call "D" and you tell her you love her, need her, want her all that sort of teenage crap, and there are dates and times when you expected to meet; then there's two photos, one of a woman, I suppose it's this D, with her nipples sticking out through holes in her bra and a finger and thumb, yours I suppose, squeezing one and then there's this picture of you, bollock naked, with a smug grin on your face holding your turgid dick and sticking your tongue out!"

"I, I,…." he stammered.

"Oh shut up, and they've all got different dates on them, the first you sent eighteen months ago and your nipple tweaking picture was tagged as taken just ten days ago – the day you were supposed to be away at a meeting." There was no stopping her now "How do I know all this? Because I had all fucking afternoon to look at them" at which she burst into tears and headed off upstairs; as she passed her husband she spat on the floor and then hit him in the face with the phone she was clutching.

"You're a deceitful, odious bastard!"

Ten minutes later he heard the front door slam as she left. He waited half an hour and then phoned 'D'. There was no reply and no messaging arrangements so he went to the pub, ate a plateful of pub food and drank a whole bottle of nasty Chilean wine. When he returned home his wife had not returned, nor had she returned by the time he left for work the next morning. Nevertheless by mid-morning she had returned to the house and was using her time to call in a locksmith and the collection service from The Red Cross charity shop. Then she took her husband's Audi and parked it on a double yellow line on Albert Bridge Road just south of the bridge before dropping the keys through the grill of a street drain. It would have been easier to move it into the King's Road but a few months earlier Westminster Council had stopping towing away such obstructions so she was relying on the less charitable Wandsworth Council to take the vehicle to their car pound in far off Mitcham. Her anger had not been entirely assuaged by what she'd done but she was pleased that she'd acted so decisively. And now it was time to join her friend Jo-Ann for lunch at Giorgio's Trattoria. Jo-Ann, in whose spare room Teresa had spent the night, was an American woman, thin as a beanpole, her age obscured by her husband's massive expenditure on cosmetic surgery for her. "If he doesn't like how I look he gets the look changed" she would tell her admiring friends. Today she was sitting in the window of the trattoria the sun shining through hair that was neither blonde nor pink but somewhere in-between and fluffed out into a halo as if by a charge of static electricity. The light twinkled in the diamond sides of her enormous spectacles, the lenses of palest blue. Jo-Ann's hobby was talking about divorce and marital breakdown. Her mental case book so full of other people's disasters that her skills of prediction were uncannily accurate and her advice usually sound.

"So Theresa, you gonna divorce him? Good choice honey! I've got a great lawyer who takes these guys to the cleaners for you. I'll give you his number."

"That's kind but I'm not totally sure about divorce yet, it's only yesterday that I discovered what he'd been up to."

"Plenty of time darling" retorted Jo-Ann " But your first response, your gut reflex was the right one, trust me, I know. Anyway it's not the first time he's strayed is it."

"No it isn't. Last time I let him persuade me that it wouldn't happen again. He's a smooth talker."

"And this time?"

"If I'm realistic I think I need to be done with him. It's my house, I've got my own business and I don't want us to stay together if I can't trust him. That's why I've changed the locks and given his clothes to the charity shop. I hated his taste in clothes anyway so I'm glad to be rid on them from the bedroom."

"Have you told him yet?"

"No, I thought you could help me compose a text to him"

"DON'T BOTHER TO RETURN. LOCKS ON MY HOUSE HAVE CHANGED. U CAN BUY YR CLOTHES BACK FROM THE RED X SHOP IN OLD CHURCH ST. PHONE WANDSWORTH TO FIND YR

CAR. MY LAWYER WILL CONTACT U. TERESA. PS. MAYBE
OWNER OF TITS WILL PUT YOU UP, I WON'T."

"Good gal" said Jo-Ann admiringly when Theresa had pressed the
button to send the text.

"Shall we have one of those huge chocolate nut sundaes to
celebrate. I think I can ignore my nutritionist's advice just this once
and by the way loved the thing with the car darling – inspired!"

"How about brandies with our coffees?"

As they were leaving the restaurant an hour later both rather
unsteady but particularly Jo-Ann on her bizarrely high heels, Jo-Ann
said

"Are you going to do anything about the trollop he's screwing?"

Teresa flashed her a huge smile.

"No need, the attentions of my soon to be ex-husband are all the
punishment she'll need and perhaps her husband, if she has one, will
give her the push and then my ex-husband will be all that she has!
That should be more than enough punishment."

The husband, the soon to be ex-husband, having received the text
from his wife had spent the afternoon frantically phoning Diana's
number and sending texts but her phone seemed to be switched off.
He tried phoning his wife but there was no answer. There was no
way he was going back to Wellington Square asking to be let in and
forgiven, he'd played that card before and it wouldn't work this time;
he knew his wife too well for that. Nothing for it then but to find a
hotel for now and phone Diana's number again in the morning or
maybe just turn up at her door. He'd go there on Friday when he
knew she'd be at home.

Thursday September 11th. A trip to Pau

Lucien was ten years old when his father died, one of the five hundred or so British soldiers to die during the long campaign against the communist insurgency in Malaya. His father at that time was a colonel in the Royal Army Medical Corps, the RAMC, and had been married to Lucien's mother, Sandrine, for eleven years. Sandrine Delmain was just eighteen when she first met Fergus McCulloch as the allied armies battled through Northern France in 1944. He was a young doctor in the RAMC and she a girl of student age but denied any higher education by the German occupation. She did, however, speak fair English and was the interpreter when this handsome young officer in uniform came to help with civilian casualties in Rouen where she lived. He was exhausted from dealing with the seemingly endless stream of casualties from the hard and bloody battles that had followed the Normandy landings. She was diminished by the rigors of the occupation and the unrelenting fear of discovery and reprisal she got from acting as a courier for the Résistance. One afternoon at the beginning of September she took him to visit Rouen cathedral, an enormous blackened monument to the sheer effrontery of medieval masons. Now its huge nave had been opened up to the sky by bombing, its stained glass shattered and the stone work pitted and cracked; the building no less impressive for that. At the west end of the nave some rows of chairs remained though covered in debris and dust. Fergus has swept the dust off two chairs and they had sat down together in silence, two young people older than their years. He took her hand and she rested her head on his shoulder. Whatever chemistry occurs at these moments was lasting and survived their parting after only a week as the Second World War moved steadily to its end. Early in 1945 Fergus McCulloch was able to make his way back to Rouen where he and Sandrine were married. Lucien was born almost exactly nine months later.

Fergus McCulloch died in Malaya in 1955, Sandrine McCulloch quickly remarried but that lasted barely a year, then married twice more. Her slimness, her elegance, her French accent and her instant warm attention to the life of the person she was communicating with ensured no shortage of suitors. The second and third marriages failed quite simply because she was still in love with the Fergus McCulloch that inhabited her memory. By the time she married her last husband at the age of fifty the images had faded a little and the new husband, her fourth, loved her enough to share the marriage with a young man in uniform whose sepia photograph in its regularly polished silver frame rested on his mantelpiece; but then aged only sixty-five he died and Sandrine unwilling to risk any more losses in her life retired to the city of Pau in that part of France that laps against the Pyrenees. She had no further children after Lucien but once he was qualified and safely married she had largely ignored him in the interests of trying to find a settled and happy place in the world for herself. She thought she had found that in Pau in a large penthouse apartment on the fifth floor of an apartment block on the Boulevard Des Pyrenees looking out to the mountains beyond, a long panorama of peaks capped by winter snow, sometimes washed pink by the setting sun, yet on many days absent behind a veil of mist making their re-emergence all the more magical.

Lucien had not seen his mother for almost a year – it was a long drive from St. Jean to Pau, which Diana disliked. Today though he relished the quietness of the Jaguar on the straight and empty roads through the pine forests of the Landes. Arriving just after midday in Pau he parked outside the train station which is in a valley below the Boulevard Des Pyrenees and took the ancient funicular with its narrow seats of varnished wooden slats up to the Boulevard, rising sedately through the tall palms of the Jardins Publics to arrive just a few yards from his mother's apartment block.

Sandrine McCulloch, the name to which she had reverted on her fourth husband's death, was still tall and beautiful at eighty-two. She had made no attempt to restore the colour of her hair, once a lustrous chestnut but now silver. The salon of the penthouse apartment was flooded with light through three tall windows; the Pics du Midi sharp against the horizon. Lucien noted, as on every visit, the framed pictures of his father on the piano and the glass case containing his cap badge and his medals. Of her other husbands no reminders except perhaps this apartment, brought with part of the fortune that came to her when her last husband died.

They ate lunch in the Brasserie L'Aragon nearby, escorted to Sandrine's usual table on the narrow terrace overlooking the Boulevard. This being France there was no problem about her little caramel coloured poodle Chou-Chou accompanying her to lunch. A water bowl for Chou-Chou was, as ever, already in place under the table.

"Lucien you sit there where you can catch the waiter's eye if you need to and I shall sit here where I always sit so that I can see who comes and goes along the Boulevard."

Sandrine clearly considered it inappropriate to discuss Lucien's problems whilst they ate, it might after all have spoilt her digestion, but there was no shortage of other things to discuss – the relationship of President Sarkozy with his new wife Carla Bruni being top of her list. It was only when coffee was on the table and Chou-Chou had been lovingly fed the bowl of scraps brought from the kitchen that Lucien's world was allowed to intrude.

"Now tell me about Lucy first, has she a man?"

"Not at present, as far as I know."

"A woman perhaps? I know she was uncertain of her affiliations when she was younger, has she decided yet?"

"I think she just wants love, preferably from a man but she has had some horrible, abusive ones in the past when she was on drugs – we hope she is out of that now. She says she would like a good man to settle down with."

"Dear Lucy, like all of us she would most prefer a tranquil life *a deux* ...which Diana is denying you?" Sandrine put Chou-Chou off her lap, sat up straight, folded her hands in front of her on the table. " Tell me please, what is going on?"

As they returned to the apartment Lucien recounted yet again what had happened. It was, of course, a simple story and completed just as they arrived at the door.

"My poor boy," Sandrine fetched a bowl of bonbons from a table and proffered them to Lucien as if he was still a child. "My poor boy – but what will you do? I do hope you can avoid divorce, it's a pitiless and hurtful process – I know, I've done it twice and both times I was the cause, yet still it hurt terribly – please don't do it. Have you not tried a rapprochement?"

"No mother, we haven't spoken yet."

"Well you should do so" she retorted sharply "And what about that other business with the Arab, have you sorted that out?"

Clearly Sandrine considered that the Diana business was now dealt with and that perhaps he could also settle the Gamal Ghanem saga with a phone call. There was a pause. Sandrine took Lucien's hand.

"Infidelity happens in marriages, it's either a symptom that something's seriously wrong or it can be discounted."

"How can I tell which?" asked Lucien

"Talk to her you silly boy – talk to her!"

Later as Lucien prepared to leave Sandrine put her arm around him and led him over to the photo of his father.

"Maybe I should not be telling you this but it is better that you know your real father rather than live with a heroic falsehood – your father was unfaithful to me, just as Diana has been unfaithful to you."

"And did you forgive him, you must have got together again?"

"We were never together again, I only discovered after he was dead and then most cruelly from the official report on the death. It all happened when he was in Malaya; the British were settling the population in villages as a way of controlling the influence of the communist terrorists. You father used to visit clinics in each village and in one village had a mistress – one day her husband discovered them together and killed them both, hacked them to death with a machete. I never had the chance to forgive him and that is a sadness I have carried with me forever."

"And I thought he was killed in action."

"In a way he was" said Sandrine wryly with a little smile. "Please try to forgive Diana; love and sex are like two children fighting for a mother's attention. Sex can be the louder and dominate today but it doesn't mean she has abandoned love." She hugged him very tightly "And now you must be off, it's a long drive back to Saint Jean."

As he left the apartment Chou-Chou the dog chased him into the hallway barking and had Sandrine not picked it up would have nipped his ankle. Typical, he thought, another male trying to get between him and his mother. Discovering the facts of his father's death had upset him. He would like to have talked more with his mother about the Diana problem, but she had ended their time together peremptorily, almost dismissed him but that was her style.

Through his father's death all those years ago Lucien had in a way also lost his mother for after it she was too intent on finding a new man to spare much time for her child. To Lucien the second husband Jack was simply evil and following a rash intrusion into the bedroom one afternoon Lucien avoided Jack. Lucien who was only eleven at the time had heard a banging noise upstairs and had peered through the bedroom door to be confronted by the sight of Jack and his mother naked, his mother standing pressed against the wardrobe, her lipstick smeared onto the mirror. Jack was forcing vigorous sex on her from behind, his buttocks and hairy back contorted by the effort. Seeing Lucien at the door, reflected in the mirror, he shouted "Get out of here you little bugger" while redoubling his efforts. Lucien fled from the house and from that day lost all sense of being part of a family; he arranged his life so as to have no contact with Jack who anyway was gone within a year or so. Although he now regretted it his relationship with his mother also became practical rather than loving. She was the person who took him to his boarding school and collected him at the end of team and in the holidays fed him, dressed him and tried to find someone for him to play with. There was little more to it than that. He'd once read that if a child loses a parent when very young they go through life thereafter always expecting another disaster, always presuming things will turn out for the worst. Re-running the film clips of memory about his childhood as he drove back to Saint Jean, he wondered, perhaps for the first time, whether his obsessive attachment to Diana and Lucy were not just his attempt to recreate family feelings lost by that confused eleven year old. Maybe his distress at Diana's infidelity was sharpened by the long shadow of those childhood memories. Of course they were! Did it help him decide how to approach her? No.

It was not until he was back in Saint Jean that he turned his phone on again. There was a voicemail from Lucy asking him to call her and a text from Lily Harper-Smith "*Important that you call me*". He called Lucy first, she sounded excited, she said there was a jewellery trade show she might go to in Paris on Monday; if she went would he be willing to go to Paris for a couple of days? She'd book a hotel for them for Sunday and Monday and would call him back with the details. Lucien could conceive of nothing he wanted more than to see Lucy and the arrangements partly banished the gloom that had beset him since leaving Pau. The call to Lily Harper-Smith would have to wait but the call to Diana should be made now before his resolve faded. He settled himself into a chair in the salon, poured a glass of wine and dialled the number. No reply. But he was prepared for that, indeed slightly relieved. The answering machine clicked in with his own voice; how strange, he thought, to have this spectral existence in the home that he'd felt he'd lost.

"Hi Diana, it's Lucien just phoning to make contact, see how you are, I'll call again tomorrow – I'm in St. Jean but I expect you've guessed that."

It was a hot and humid evening, the sort of evening overhung by purple clouds, a thunderstorm coming and the delicious anticipation of cooling rain. Lucien was by the open window trying to catch the first breath of the cool air and from the CD player the sounds of Gesualdo's Sabbato Sancto drifted out across the vines.

The phone rang.

"Hello Lucien, it's Diana."

"Hi, I'm glad you phoned, I wondered if you would."

"And I was waiting for you to phone me, I'm pleased you did. I'm sorry I was out."

"That's OK, would you like to talk about important things or shall we just make do with small talk this time."

"Small talk would be best. What's the music I can hear in the background?"

"It's the Gesualdo; Sabbato Sancto; it's a bit dour but there's a thunderstorm coming and it seemed appropriate."

"Gesualdo – wasn't he the Italian prince who caught his wife with a lover and killed them both?"

"That's the one."

Diana laughed, the familiar laugh that Lucien had so much missed.

"I hope you're not planning anything similar."

"It's on my list of options but I'd probably be satisfied by bringing the lover to a gory end. It seems a bit irrational also to kill the woman you love."

"And do you love me Lucien, do you still love me?"

"Of course I do but I'm having great difficulty understanding what's gone on – do you want to talk about it?"

"Not now, in a day or two maybe – anyway I can't hear you properly because of the music."

"I'll turn it down ….."

"No don't – we'll talk again in a few days; I'll call you. Lucy's fine by the way, in case you were worried. 'bye darling."

Friday September 12th. Dulwich

At eight thirty in the morning Lucy sent a text message to her mother's normal phone.
"SORRY MUM I FOUND YOUR OTHER PHONE. PLEASE DON'T BE ANGRY. CAN I COME AND SEE THIS AFTERNOON? LUCY XX".

There was no reply until midday when a text came back.
" COME ANYTIME TODAY. MUCH TO TALK ABOUT. NOT ANGRY NOW. MUM XXXX".

How useful texts can be to neutralize emotion.

"Why, why did you do it, why on earth did you start the affair with him?"
Lucy had arrived at Dulwich as soon as she could after getting her mother's text.
"Lots of reasons really. Loneliness, curiosity, desperation."
"Desperation?"
"I'm fifty-nine Lucy, I've been married to your father for almost forty years, I've been doggedly faithful, supportive, never complained about the medical lifestyle; but it's all about his life, our family, what we've done and what we need to do next; it's not about me. I realized that although I'd had lots of boyfriends before I met your father I'd not had one since; someone who'd make my heart flutter, make me sit on the edge of my chair waiting for his next move. In short I'd not been seduced and at fifty-nine there was not much likelihood of it happening in the future."
"But you're married Mum, you're not supposed to be up for seduction and anyway didn't Dad give you those feelings?"
"Well he did forty years ago but as the years go by it gets a bit formulaic. Each of you knows what the other is going to say or do."
"Even in bed? You don't mind me asking you do you Mum but I need to understand."
"Yes, even in bed. You both get to know what works, eventually slip into a pattern, if you've got a winning formula you stick to it." She smiled as much to herself as at Lucy.

"So did you just go out and look for someone who'd seduce you?"

"No of course not, but when someone came along who looked nice and said all the right things I was obviously ripe for it. Being a bit drunk probably contributed and once I'd done it once and found the pleasure outweighing the guilt, it was easy to keep doing it and to be honest Lucy the riskiness of it all, the secrecy, was part of the buzz. It was almost like being a child again wondering if Mum and Dad would find out if you'd been naughty and then when they didn't feeling so smug you'd push it a bit more the next time. The whole thing is something that's your own, your little secret and that's valuable."

"And the loneliness, you said you were lonely or was that just an excuse?"

"No I was lonely. Strangely I didn't feel lonely when you were off the rails, I had all that to occupy my mind even if it wasn't much fun." Lucy bit her lip and was about to say something but didn't. "Then Robin was killed and I had my grief and yours and your father's grief to deal with. Things haven't been right since that time; I've never got over the anger and loneliness. It is possible to be lonely you know even when you live with someone you love and who loves you."

"And did this affair, this little secret of yours, cure the loneliness?" Lucy stood up and walked away a little distance "Did it?"

Diana shook her head. "No, not really. It sounds a bit odd but loneliness, or some degree of loneliness is part of the human condition but it's taken all this business for me to discover that."

"But I don't feel lonely" retorted Lucy "or a least I don't so long as I know I've got you and Dad" she sat down next to her mother "that's why I did what I did – your phone, the texts, the photographs all that. I couldn't bear the thought of you and Dad separating and I knew you loved each other and that all this was just lunacy."

"Yes Lucy darling I know it's lunacy too, just temporary, I don't know why I didn't just say the affair was over when Dad found out. Too proud perhaps, too possessive of this thing, this exciting aberration I'd fashioned with another man, but it's all over now."

"Because his wife found out? Because I told her?"

Diana got up and was now wandering about the room, picking up the ornaments and books, looking at them and then putting them down again. She picked up the photo of Robin in dress uniform with medals and sword, gazed at it for a moment, brushed an imagined speck of dust off it with her sleeve and then gently replaced it.

"No not that directly, but it obviously caused a crisis which made me see things more clearly. Did you know his wife threw him out when she discovered and now she's going to divorce him?"

"I didn't know; should I be upset?"

"No you shouldn't. What happened next is that he came here this morning and told me he loved me, wanted to move in here with me and asked me to divorce your father. That really brought everything into focus."

"What did you say?" Lucy was aghast.

"Do you really want to know?" There was a wicked twinkle in Diana's eye as she guided Lucy back to the sofa to sit next to her "I told him he had a cheek even coming to the house without it being arranged in advance and there was absolutely no way he was moving in and not the remotest chance of me divorcing my husband. Then he started whining that his wife had kicked him out, changed the locks so he had nowhere to live. So I told him that wasn't a reason suddenly to come on all strong about love. The fact he was my lover didn't mean that I loved him."

This is not what Lucy had expected, she'd assumed that her mother had a really strong affection for the man – why else would she have refused to give him up when her father found out and why else would she have taken all the risks.

"I told him it was over, that it was time to leave. He said surely he meant something to me?"

"And you said?"

"I said he'd always been just peripheral to my real life and that being lovers didn't mean we were in love. It was just shorthand for having sex. Lover's a nicer word than adulterer or gigolo which is really all he was."

"Wow, that must have made him cross, being called a gigolo."

"It really did. He got very angry. He called me stupid, a stupid, stuck up cow, an arrogant bitch and said he hated me. So I said okay in that case you can just piss off. Which he did, so now I'm free!"

"You're free Mum, but what about Dad?"

"We spoke for a few moments on the phone last night, before all this happened. He said he still loves me. I realize that doesn't mean our lives can just go back to where we were as if nothing had happened. We'll have to be together somewhere to sort it out, it's not something we could do on the phone. Even if he doesn't want to leave me or divorce me then just staying together isn't enough. We'll need to lead a different sort of life. Or maybe, just maybe we should separate for a while, see how we get on on our own. I really don't know."

Diana by this time had become disconsolate, her ebullience at having disposed of her 'gigolo' now lost in the knowledge that that was the easier part. Restoring her relationship with Lucien, trying to redress the hurt, would need much more time, more effort and she still had to look at her own feelings to discover whether she really did love him, whether her desire to be together with him again was just an affection for the habits of marriage and its comforts. Was there still that fire burning somewhere that they could re-ignite? He must be having the same feelings.

Lucy had been in the kitchen making tea, the panacea. When she came back with the two mugs and four biscuits she said " I have a plan Mum. I know what needs to be done next."

"The plan ought to be only to eat one of those biscuits; you know we normally only have one each with tea or coffee. I might get fat then your father will never have me back!" she straightened her sweater and cupping her hands under her breasts hoisted them up a bit before smoothing her skirt.

It took very little time for Lucy to explain what she planned to do next and then she settled by the phone to arrange it.

"Lucy. There's a bottle of bubbly in the 'fridge, I'm going to open it and we are going to drink it. All of it! "

Friday September 12th. Libya

In the small town near Tripoli, in a small mosque with a low minaret covered in cracked stucco, the Imam was leading Friday prayers – the doors were open and just a short distance away sitting against the wall of an empty café the blind man was rocking backward and forwards, tears flowing from empty eye sockets. Crouched beside him clutching his remaining hand was Ahmed's cousin.

"We should go into the mosque, it is prayer time."

"I cannot, I will not, how can I speak of Allah as merciful when madmen who are obsessed with the words of his Prophet have murdered my son, my only son? Why did they do it?"

"It is said they wanted Ghanem's assassin to be seen as a suicide bomber to persuade Gaddafi that an army of suicide bombers was about to be unleashed on him. I swear to God that I didn't know that was their plan when they gave us the Toyota."

"Allah is cruel to take so much from me. My wife giving birth to my son, my eyes and my hand for exposing evil and now he has taken also my son. What am I to do?" He was hitting the ground with his stick.

"I shall care for you. I shall move here from Benghazi and take over from Ahmed. It is my fault that these evil men have done this to another Muslim, it is my fault and I shall come here to look after you so some small good may come from it. It will take a few days to arrange because I am due to be married but her parents would not let her come here to be the wife of a café worker in the west, so although we love one another we will part and I will be here for you."

"You are a good man and you will be rewarded in heaven. These madmen will not, they are simply obsessed with killing, they think it is for God but it is not, it is just to satisfy some lust in themselves. They are no better than Gamal Ghanem. We will go into the mosque now and I will pray to Allah today and every day in the future that they are not allowed into Paradise."

Saturday morning, 13th September. St Jean

Saturday morning in St. Jean, the sun shining, the grapes swelling, turning the sunshine into the sugary promise of a good vintage. Outside a pair of doves were searching for breakfast among the short grass and when Lucien opened the door flew up onto the roof with that creaky, rattling take off that he'd always found so odd in such elegant creatures. They sat on the roof, the one nuzzling the neck of the other.

Saturday morning in St. Jean and in just a week Lucien had already slipped into the comfortable torpor that summer here engendered. If he were in Dulwich he would be trying to organise the week's mail – none of it welcome and none of it personal; or he'd be waiting for Diana to get ready so that they could go so Sainsbury's for the weekly shop, or be driving up to the hospital to see his patients. Sometimes he spent longer looking for an empty parking space than he did at the bedside. But here on the terrace, just a warm, flaking croissant, a jar of Mirabelle jam and a full pot of coffee to negotiate. He didn't feel lonely now, just a lingering hint of sadness mollified by the prospect of meeting Lucy in Paris the next day. She'd phoned the previous evening to confirm that she was going to the jewellery trade show there on Monday. She'd booked the hotel for Sunday and if he got the early train they could have a late lunch together. She sounded mischievously happy.

Lucien realised he'd not done any laundry for a week – he'd been proud of his effective shopping, his cooking and he'd kept the kitchen clean with the washing up done after every meal, but he'd overlooked the laundry now loitering in the basket in the bedroom. He needed something clean to wear to supper at Geraldine Makepiece's this evening so it had to be done. It was as he was pushing it into the washing machine that the phone rang.

"Lucien? It's Lily."

"Lily?"

"Lily Harper-Smith."

"Sorry, I wasn't expecting you to call on a Saturday; don't you get the weekend off?"

"Yes, of course – but I have some good news for you. It's a while since we spoke and I wondered how you were."

"I'm fine thanks. It's nice to talk to you."

"Have you seen the papers?"

"Not since Tuesday. I read about Harry Ashbury and the civil service chap Havilland and the bit about me in The Mail."

"Yes, I saw The Mail too. I didn't know why you were in France until I read that." Lucien said nothing "The news that you may be pleased to hear is that Ashbury resigned from the cabinet yesterday and Mr. Havilland has been arrested and charged with misconduct in public office. So on the assumption that now the game's up Havilland will confirm that the allegations from Libya are a set up job, a conspiracy, I'll need to get in touch with the CPS and ask for discontinuance of the charges against you. I'll do that next week. They've said they can't do that yet but unofficially they say they probably will. Now that the man you blame for it all, Gamal Ghanem is dead the chances of this being pushed from the Libyan end must be remote."

"Ghanem dead! I didn't know. What happened?"

"I'm not certain, there wasn't much in the papers but I believe it was an assassination by a suicide bomber."

Lucien could hardly believe it, his nemesis, the man who wanted him dead – himself dead.

"How ironic, but he had a lot of enemies I believe."

A wave of relief spread over him. He sensed the release of tension he hadn't recognised. The wariness and anxiety that followed the attempt to kill him was already perceptibly slipping away.

"I'll be honest, I am extraordinarily relieved. I hope his wife and daughters weren't caught up in it. All that apart I suppose The GMC won't reverse my suspension until the CPS makes up its mind?"

"Correct and I'm sure you know how slowly these wheels turn. I expect it'll be a couple of months before you can return to work, but that can't be too bad if you're in France. Are you on your own?"

"Yes, for now, but I'm off to join my daughter in Paris tomorrow."

"That's nice. I love Paris, I don't get there often enough. No-one invites me!"

Lucien had a disconcerting feeling that if he'd suggested that she joined him there she would have said yes. He was right, Lily was at that moment sitting with the phone at the window of her flat in a tastefully converted Victorian warehouse overlooking the Thames, twisting a lock of her hair around her finger. She was toying with the image of herself on the arm of a distinguished older man, promenading the Avenue Foch in a slim pencil pleated skirt and a Dior hounds-tooth jacket. Later at an embassy reception in Rue Du Faubourg St.Honore in a floaty silk dress and Louboutin red shoes. Then even later on a satin bed in a suite at the Hotel Crillon.

"Perhaps when you're back in London we can meet to see if there's a way to speed it all up. I'm not sure about your position at The RUH though, I understand there is likely to be a bit of a shake up there when the DoH report on their management culture is completed. I'm not certain of course but I've heard rumours that it'll be very critical and the whole senior management team may be required to resign."

"What, fire them all? That sounds like a good idea!"

"Legally speaking that's difficult if the crime has just been bullying and general crassness, but maybe there's more to it."

"Firing that particular CEO would please me."

"Why?"

"It's a long story; part of a longer one. I'll tell you about it sometime."

Saturday evening 13th September. St Jean

Geraldine Makepiece's invitation to supper, "not dinner, supper, nothing posh" was for Saturday evening. It would be just four; Geraldine, Lucien, Terry and Molly Tufnall. Lucien arrived as bidden at seven.

"Terry has phoned to say he's delayed" announced Geraldine handing him a large glass of wine "do you mind being in the kitchen whilst I cook?"

Lucien would have preferred to go home until TT arrived but the option was clearly not on offer.

"When's Harold due back?" he said to get the conversation started.

"I don't know, though to be honest I think I don't care, but I am cross about not knowing. I'm presuming he's got a woman somewhere and that's why he's away so much."

"You don't care?" she was standing chopping vegetables with her back to him.

"He's unreliable, he's here less and less of the time and we seem to have little in common any more. It was bound to happen sooner or later" at which, hurling her knife down so that the vegetables scattered onto the floor she turned round to face Lucien "Of course I bloody care, he's had me for thirty years and hasn't even the courtesy to tell me if things are wrong."

"Perhaps he's embarrassed to tell you."

"What? You mean he'll tell me that he's lost interest because I'm older and fatter and greyer and don't fancy him the way I did twenty years ago?" She was crying now her mascara streaking her cheeks. She blew her nose on a piece of kitchen paper "Well he can bugger off, I'll be better off without him."

She gestured at Lucien with a half empty bottle before refilling her own glass.

"More?"

He held his glass out.

"Do you know who this other woman is?" he asked. She looked up – she was at least four inches shorter than him.

"No I don't, but I have suspicions." Lucien said nothing. "Where's Diana?" asked Geraldine her head on one side looking Lucien straight in the eye.

"She's got things to do in London."

"Might one of those things be my husband?" Lucien was wary but he already had Harold Makepiece on his list of suspects. Name began with H, pretensions of being an artist, house in London, known to Diana.

"I need to be honest with you Geraldine. Diana admitted last week to having a long standing affair. That's why I've come out here. It might be Harold but we can find out one way or the other right now."

He extracted from his wallet the piece of paper he'd found in Diana's book.

"Is that Harold's writing?" Geraldine wiped her eyes and put down her glass.

"No this isn't him – I'll get something he's written to show you. His writing is much more flowery than that" which it was, there was no similarity at all.

"And where was he on Thursday of last week?" asked Lucien

"Just for once he was actually here."

"Well that resolves it; Diana's lover was definitely in London on that day. Is that good news or bad?"

"Good I suppose, I've not real proof he has someone else it's just a guess; though maybe I'll divorce him anyway, he's a waste of space!"

Lucien didn't know whether to be relieved or not that Harold was off the list. He badly wanted to know who Diana's lover was and he knew he'd never come to grips with her infidelity until he had an identity for the man.

"Let me help you with these vegetables – they'll be okay if we wash them under the tap."

Standing next to Geraldine at the sink he put his arm round her and gave her a companionable squeeze.

"No-one teaches you how to deal with this stuff do they." Geraldine smiled wanly at him.

"No, so we'll just have to have another drink."

By the time Terry and Molly arrived half an hour later the bottle was empty and the next one open. Terry's arrival was announced by a scattering of gravel and a loud crunch as his big black pick-up truck demolished the terracotta planter by the front door.

"Sorry about that Geraldine darling" shouted Terry standing in the doorway resplendent in clean white t-shirt and red shorts with white socks and unsullied white trainers. Molly coming behind him made drinking signs to Geraldine and raised her eyes to heaven, a gesture make doubly impressive by her extravagant use of blue eye-shade.

"Very, very, very sorry we're late sweetie" said Terry embracing Geraldine clumsily and collapsing onto the sofa "We've been at a party. Watcha been up to while you waited?"

Geraldine smiled blearily at Terry and then at Molly and Lucien

"We were celebrating the fact that my current husband, Harold, is not currently having it off with Diana, who's currently Lucien's wife and currently having it off with someone else, currently."

"Ah, ha" said Terry pointing unsteadily at Lucien "I knew something was up you poor old sod, so if it's not horrible Harold that she's screwing who is it?"

Lucien didn't want to get drawn into this but was too drunk to avoid it.

"I don't know Terry, I don't know, though it can't be you as your name doesn't begin with H."

"Whazzat mean?"

"Lucien found a love note from someone who'd signed himself H" interjected Geraldine.

"Narrows it down to all the frogs called Hervé, Henri, and Hubert who want to shag her along with all the English fucking hooray Henrys, who want to, or are, or have. And what will do you when you catch Mr. or Messieur H eh Lucien? Can I have a drink Geraldine this sounds heavy."

"Terry you really shouldn't" said Molly, the only one of the four anywhere near sober.

"S-alright we can walk home. Go on Lucien" said Terry returning to the fray "Wotcha gonna do?"

"I don't' know Terry, it depends."

"Depends on what? This bloke H has been screwing your wife hasn't he?"

"Yes and no. If she was complicit that changes things."

"Complicit? What the fuck does that mean? Fact is mate she's your wife so you need to give him a going over and you're a surgeon so you could even cut his balls off; you could do it proper tidy too, small scar, no bleeding, know what I mean?" Terry guffawed and fell off the sofa.

"It would be very satisfying I agree" said Lucien who'd started to eat the food that Geraldine had now managed to put on the table "but the SAS approach to these things isn't really feasible."

"Course it is" retorted Terry who'd climbed onto his chair and was unsuccessfully trying to roll spaghetti around his fork "and by the way I wasn't in the SAS, just three years in REME, it's you bloody middle-class Brits who like to pretend I was, makes you feel better in some way. I don't know why, there're mostly fucking psychopaths, killers, worse that the bloody paras, but at least they do things instead of just talking. S-pose you and Diana'll be off for cosy chats with a relationship counsellor rather than you punching the bugger! And what you doing here on your own anyway? Did a bunk eh? Just fucking ran away instead of sorting it. Tosser!"

"Please don't Terry" said Molly smiling hopelessly at everyone else.

"Yeah, sorry, I'm drunk; sorry Lucien. Have another drink mate."

And by the end of the evening they were all the best of friends again. Sobering up slightly in the cold night air as he walked home Lucien wished his approach to life was a simple as Terry's seemed to be. In a way Terry was right, he had just run away from the problem hoping it would resolve itself without him having to act. Cowardice. Anyway there was nothing to do tonight and tomorrow he was going to Paris.

Sunday September 14th. Paris with Lucy

The journey from Bergerac to Paris by train takes between four and five hours. You can take a little TER cross country train to Libourne and then get the Paris train but there isn't an early one on Sundays so Lucien drove the Jaguar to Libourne and parked it in the station car park, then waited on the platform for the drama of the sleek eighteen carriage, half kilometre long TGV express sliding to a halt, the door of his carriage exactly beside the mark on the platform. From Libourne it's three hours to Gare Montparnasse in Paris; time for Lucien to reflect on what Terry Tufnall's drunken tirade had made clear to him. That he, Lucien James McCulloch, was in matters of personal relations, a coward. He preferred the status quo however unhappy, to forcing a resolution. Cowardice or laziness? Perhaps it was both, nevertheless one way or the other he must bring all this to a conclusion, but he'd talk to Lucy first. The last thing he would want to do was upset her.

Because it was Sunday morning the carriage was only half full; Lucien knew that the afternoon would be different as part-time country folk returned to the embrace of the city. On this train the seat opposite him was empty until the first stop at Angouleme where a woman approached down the aisle, ticket in hand, looking up at the seat numbers until she found hers – the seat opposite Lucien. She looked to be about eighty years ago and no more than 5 foot tall. Certainly not tall enough to get her bag up onto the rack, so Lucien did that for her and she sat down facing him across the small table with its pink plastic lamp.

"Thank you monsieur" and set her brown crocodile skin bag onto the table between them; as a barrier? Or a signal of expensive tastes? Lucien assumed from the perfectly coiffed hair, the silk scarf carefully tucked into a cashmere cardigan and her just perceptible air of distain that she was a Parisienne. He returned to his book "An Intimate History of Humanity" by Theodore Zeldin, a quirky, wise dance through human emotions. He'd started it some years earlier and not finished it but now returned hoping not for entertainment but advice, consolation, comfort, something like that. He'd found the chapter he'd half remembered, it was about escapism, the art of running away. An important topic as after all religion, art, humour, divorce, are just means of escape. Lucien remembered one intriguing little fact in that odd way one does with books and lectures. The fact was that a chemist called Henri Laborit had invented the tranquilliser Largactil and then retired on the profits to promote a philosophy of escape and non-aggression. The latter sounded less cowardly to Lucien than escape but Laborit was all about good French pragmatism, devoid of emotive moral tags like cowardice or heroism. Lucien read on. *"Avoid confrontation, says Laborit, because its only result is to establish an order of dominance, such as monkeys seek when they fight to decide who may mate with whom. Once you are caught in the competition for superiority, you lose your independence. The purpose of life – he speaks as a biologist – is to survive, which requires one to keep calm, to avoid stress.... Fighting and running away he concludes are alternative ways of countering stress; but fighting, if successful, becomes addictive and draws you into the stress of a competitive life; moreover there will be occasions when it is impossible to fight your competitors, so you will fight against yourself, and that will produce stress. It is better, he insists, to run away."* But as Lucien read further Zeldin reminded him that the problem with escape is knowing where to escape to. Then right at the end of the chapter just before the long and impressive list of references the concluding paragraph said *"to ask what the practical results of escape might be is to miss the point of escape, which includes escape from purpose. Those who want a purpose must look beyond escape."* How very French thought Lucien; teasingly obscure. He hadn't escaped to France to avoid a purpose but merely to avoid stress, though ironically the resolution of those stresses would leave him without a purpose. Put quite simply there was a question to be answered when the stresses were resolved:.... what was he to do with his life ? A question that was independent of whether Diana wanted them to stay together or not.

"Hmmm" he said out loud.

"Is monsieur bemused?" asked the little lady opposite him "I was when I read that book that you have in your hand, I remember it from the cover. In French the title was a little different. "Les Francaises et le'Histoire Intime de L'humanité" if I remember it right. The book, of course, isn't just about Les Francaises, they must have put that in to pander to our self-interest I suppose, or for our solipsism. The picture on the cover is interesting isn't it? Do you know the original, it's in the Louvre?"

"Yes I do, it's Gabrielle D'Estrées."

The little French lady leant forward in pleasure, moving her handbag to one side, her bony hands now together on the table in place of the bag, a gesture of acceptance, almost a handshake.

"That's very knowledgeable for an Englishman."

"Well it does say who she is on the book-jacket! But I do know about her, she was the mistress of Henri IV. She died from eclampsia giving birth to her fourth child. Which is unusual."

"Why so?"

"Eclampsia normally gets progressively better with each pregnancy."

"Ah, so you must an *accoucheur*, an obstetrician."

"I was one." He was annoyed that he'd slipped into the assumption that that was a past life, not a current or future one.

"My husband described himself as an *accoucheur;* he wasn't of course, his skill was *haute couture*. The babies were the dresses. We had our own couture house but it never thrived, he was too much the perfectionist, too traditional. We had to sell up and that's what killed him really. The new owners wanted simpler styles, things that could be easily mass produced and they wanted sales over the internet. They were interested in money not fashion or art. Dear Yves he would not, could not, change; it finished him. He was only sixty-five when we had to give up and so disillusioned that we left Paris to live in the countryside, but it wasn't a cure, he fretted, he was bored and he just died from it. He'd left Paris out of pique and wouldn't go back. Now I live in Paris again near the Luxembourg Gardens and I'm still welcome at the shows, no longer in the front row by the catwalk of course but still there, further back and they give me a cushion so that I can see! I live vicariously, but I'm content."

"I'm sorry about your husband, Madame" said Lucien. She lifted her hand momentarily as it to whisk away a fly or a memory "Can I get you a coffee or something from the bar?" he offered.

"Perhaps one of their little bottles of white wine, thank you."

When Lucien returned he asked her whether when her husband gave up the couture business he'd had a clear idea of what else he would do instead.

"No, he was so demoralised he didn't have the emotional energy to commit to anything else apart from a life in the country, keeping the house and garden in order, playing boule and meeting friends in the bar. He thought he'd escaped but of course he hadn't. If you escape you always take yourself with you and in this case he took the chagrin with him; took it to his grave."

"And you?"

"Oh I just cooked and dreamt of Paris"

"You never tried to persuade him to go back?"

"No, of course not. He was my husband. But I'm happy now, getting older is a skill that can be learned."

When they arrived in Paris Lucien helped her into a taxi and carried her bag up the stairs to her apartment so he was later than he'd expected arriving at the hotel.

Lucien called Lucy on her mobile. She was already in the hotel, a hotel in the Rue Des Ecoles on the left bank just south of the Boulevard St Germain but away from the tourist hot-spots; central, adjacent to the Sorbonne and a short walk from what Lucy knew was one of Lucien's favourite museums the Musée Cluny, the museum of mediaeval art.

"I'm so sorry I'm late Lucy. You'll be wanting your lunch."

"It's OK Dad, just check in, I'll meet you in the lobby in ten minutes. I'm so glad you're here I can't wait, I've got a lot to tell you."

Lucy came out of the lift, ran across to embrace her father. She didn't stop smiling.

"I really have important things to tell you Dad."

Lucy was always happy in Paris. She'd dropped out here after refusing to go to university and had relished her time, happy to be with university students, talk philosophy and politics with them, sleep with them, drink with them, but never to join what she considered the uncool part, lectures, exams, the hard grind of a university course. She admitted that was through a mixture of fear and laziness but reckoned that her life in Paris had taught her four fifths of what university students learned and possibly a lot more.

"Shall we talk over lunch Dad, we're both hungry? It's a lovely day so we could walk down to the river; it's only 5 minutes and I know a little Brasserie with a view of Nôtre Dame and a good menu."

They walked down to the Seine and stood leaning on the stone parapet looking across at the long side view of Nôtre Dame, almost the best view but not the one on the postcards. Beside them a stall selling old books and prints was doing no business at all, the stall holder quite contentedly sitting on a stool with a cigarette in his mouth reading. To their right on the little bridge, that leads into the gardens on Ile de la Cité, the Pont de l'Archevêché, a couple were embracing vigorously. They then began to attach something to the steel mesh under the handrail at the edge of the bridge.

"What are they doing?" asked Lucien pointing them out to Lucy.

"Oh, just fixing a padlock to the bridge. It's a fashion. It happens mostly on the footbridge over the river up by the Musée d'Orsay but they've started doing it here too. If you're in love you're supposed to fix a padlock on the bridge and throw the keys into the river to ensure your love will last forever. When I was here boys sometimes asked me to do that with them. They thought that if we did then it was OK to sleep together. But I always said I wanted to keep one of the keys!"

A big *bateau mouche* swept past on the river below them crammed with tourists trying to take the best photo of Nôtre Dame.

"Let's go and sit down and you can tell me the news – I know you're bursting to."

Lucien guided her to a quiet table by the window just inside the restaurant that Lucy had already chosen. When they'd ordered their food and the wine was open on the table Lucy began, hesitatingly at first as if it was the first run through of a play and she was not sure of the script.

"I spent the afternoon with Mum on Friday. I went there to apologise for something I'd done" and she recounted the whole sequence starting with finding the phone, though she didn't mention the handcuffs. She explained about forwarding the texts, but she didn't mention the photos. Then she told Lucien what had happened on Friday morning and how her mother had thrown the man out and ended the affair. Lucien sat reflecting on this for a moment as the waiter slid their salads onto the table.

"She didn't need a second phone, I would never have spied on her by checking her phone." There was a pause "So who was it – who's the man?"

Lucy looked embarrassed.

"Dr. Lightwood, Henry Lightwood, your colleague at the hospital."

Lucien did not respond at first. He took a piece of bread from the basket and began to tearing it into ever smaller pieces.

"Yes of course, the bastard, I should have known!"

"Why?"

"Oh just the odd snide comment he'd made over the years, and there was the party a couple of years ago where I saw your mother kiss him. It was at the hospital; one of those team building jollies they have for senior staff and their partners. I was already there and your mother was coming from home to join me. It was in the winter and she was in the lobby outside the room, taking her coat off. I could see her outlined in the doorway – then Henry Lightwood came into sight and kissed her, that's all, then she joined the party. I put it out of my mind but I shouldn't have. I guess I just wanted to repress what I'd seen. It wasn't a normal social kiss, a kiss on the cheek. It was a kiss on the lips and she put her hand on the back of his head momentarily her fingers in his hair to stop him breaking away. It can only have lasted a few seconds. I can still see that image, those silhouettes in the doorway. I don't know why I didn't do anything then."

"It's all over now. Mum says he got very cross when she said he was just her gigolo."

"I bet he did; he's always struggled to inflate his importance. He'd like to have been thought of as the great lover not just as an unpaid gigolo. I presume he was unpaid?!" At which they both laughed, relieving the tension a little. "I'm glad it wasn't a love affair that would have been harder to deal with, though in a way it would have been easier to forgive. Love is always a forgivable failing.... even perhaps if it had meant the end of our marriage. As it is ....."

He fell silent, pushing the food about on his plate. He took a swig of wine, then got up. "I'm just going outside for a moment Lucy – I'll be back soon, I just need some fresh air."

Lucy watched him cross the road and pace up and down on the opposite pavement overlooking the river, the view of him sometimes clear, sometimes hidden by passing buses and cars. She couldn't make out whether there were tears on his cheeks. She could see him clutching his hands together on top of his head as if trying to squeeze out an important thought. Another *bateau mouche* was passing out of sight below the parapet, the loud, over-zealous commentary echoing off the walls. It drove Lucien back to the table.

"I mustn't start apportioning blame, It would be easy to lay the blame on Henry Lightwood or even your mother but that won't help at all. She and I will just need to take this as a signal that we must decide whether to stay together or not. And it's not just about the marriage, it's about what we do with our lives from now on. We can fix our marriage if she wants to. It won't be the same as it was of course but we've shared too much to let all that go and we're probably too old to give up what we have and start again. Maybe we need together to start a new life. It'll be difficult to go back to the hospital if Henry Lightwood is still in post and I don't really think I want to anyway. On the other hand I'm not so naïve as to think we can just disappear to St. Jean and live a life of rustic simplicity. Hans and Elsa seem to have managed that but I'm not confident that your mother and I could unless we take back the vineyard and learn how to make wine. Anyway we'd miss being close to you."

"Perhaps I'd come and join you" said Lucy. Lucien laughed.

"We'd love that Lucy but it rather diminishes your chance of finding the man of your dreams – unless it was Thierry Desjoyaux!"

"I quite fancy him actually – but you're right he's certainly not a long term prospect."

"I need to talk to your mother." Lucien was serious again and now Lucy played her trump card.

"Then you'll need to be at Gare Du Nord tomorrow at midday to meet her off the Eurostar from London!"

Monday morning Sept. 15th. Paris with Diana

Lucien had always loathed the breakfasts in tourist hotels. The attempt to ensure no nationality feels ignored and all are free to graze on indeterminate cereals, dry ham, white cheese, unripe fruit and a selection of pastries garnished from tiny jam jars and washed down with insipidly dilute orange juice. So Lucien and Lucy took themselves off to a bar nearby sensibly sited next door to a boulangerie so that its patrons could enjoy fragrantly fresh croissants with their big cups of hot milky coffee. Lucy had to go to her jewellery trade exhibition and then, so that she could be back ready to open the shop in South Molton Street next morning, had booked herself onto an afternoon train to London.

"Anyway" she said "you and Mum won't want me around so I'm going to try to be adult about all this and just say I hope you can sort it out and be together again." She kissed Lucien on the forehead and was gone before he could reply. She didn't look back – Lucien had already sensed how anxious she was feeling; it made him sad – it all seemed so unnecessary. He ordered another cup of coffee and whilst the patron frothed the milk at the expresso machine went to look at a framed sepia photo on the wall. A man with big ears, a walrus moustache and short pointed beard frowned at him out of the frame "Pierre Jules Renard 1864-1910. Author". Ah Yes! The author of the quote after which the Bar "Le Sablier," The Hourglass, was named. And in flowing italic script on a wooden plaque next to the photo there was the quote *"L'amour tue l'intelligence. Le cerveau fait sablier avec le coeur. L'un ne se remplit que pour vider l'autre."* Below it in English the somewhat inaccurate translation " *Love is like an hourglass, with the heart filling up as the brain empties"*. Lucien took his coffee back to the table reflecting that he'd like both his head and his heart to be working effectively when he met Diana. Before that he had time for a quiet walk around the Musée Cluny to settle his nerves contemplating the mysteries of the Lady with the Unicorn.

In the Gare du Nord Lucien stood at the end of the platform straining to catch a first glimpse of her just as he had on that cold

January day at Waterloo station over forty years earlier. A stream of people trailing suitcases passed him, little electric service trucks dodged amongst them going the other way. No Diana; but then there she was, catching sight of Lucien she waved and he went down the platform to meet her.

"Hi!" He reached out to take her suitcase "Welcome to Paris" he kissed her cheek and turned to walk along the platform beside her "Good journey?"

"Yes thanks, are you well?"

"Yes thanks." The tick-tock of meaningless pleasantries.

They went out of the side door of the station and stood behind the barrier at the taxi queue.

"It'll take at least ten minutes to get to the front" said Lucien "would you rather take the Metro?"

"Let's just stay in the queue, the Metro will be awfully hot."

Five minutes went by nothing being said, Lucien pushing Diana's suitcase forward with his foot as the queue gradually shortened.

"Have you talked to Lucy?" said Diana eventually.

"Yes."

"So you know everything?"

"I know who is he is and I know what Lucy's done about it and I know, or I think I know, what your response to all that was."

Standing beside him but not looking at him, Diana took Lucien's hand. They reached the head of the queue and squeezed into the back seat of the taxi, Lucien with his arm around Diana. She leaned across and kissed his cheek. The taxi set off like a startled cat; the driver looked North African, impatient .

"Is honeymoon?" smirked the driver into his rear view mirror as he simultaneously waved his fist at a pedestrian and jumped a red light.

" Peut'être…. maybe" said Diana clutching Lucien's arm.

"Is nice- but you guys pretty old!" said the driver accelerating down the bus lane, his moustache twitching.

"Never too old" replied Diana looking directly at Lucien for the first time. "Never too old. "

Lucien, leaned across and kissed her.

Monday afternoon, September 15th. Paris

"Now what?" said Diana.

They were lying side by side on the bed, the room bright with the afternoon sun – there had been no time or inclination to close the curtains when they came straight up to the room from the taxi, threw off their clothes and by the simple business of sex reclaimed each other. They were lying side by side and if this had been a movie they would have been smoking and a sheet would have been drawn up improbably high to cover her breasts. It was real, it wasn't a movie. They were lying there naked, Lucien's finger idly drawing circles around her nipples.

"Now what ?" she repeated.

"Now perhaps we can start again" said Lucien, "Maybe we can tell each other what was wrong and maybe we can make those things right. But then maybe we don't need to discuss it at all, stay away from the forensics and just get on with our lives?"

"As if nothing had happened ?"

"I suppose so, yes."

"But something did happen. You probably just think it was all about sex but it wasn't- well it was slightly- but mostly it was about our marriage and what it was doing to us. In the last few days since dumping 'the gigolo' and talking to Lucy I've thought it all through many, many times. I'm clear now that it's actually about our marriage. We've always dealt with the world as a couple rather than as individuals. Maybe that's how marriage is supposed to be, but to be honest darling it's become a bit claustrophobic. I'm worried that there's an individual in me that hasn't developed fully and never would if we go on living together as we have for the last 40 years. It's not your fault but you only conceive of me as one person in one role- as Mrs. McCulloch. I need to be more than that."

Lucien was sitting up now looking down on Diana stretched out along the bed. The joy of the presumed rapprochement had evaporated as quickly as it had arrived.

"Are you telling me that you don't want us to go on living together?"

"Yes I suppose I am. I don't see how I can become a fully grown person so long as I'm always having to think about how you might react, or how it would sit with the day to day realities of our living together."

Lucien was confused. He'd always thought marriage, including their marriage, made a couple into something more than they would have been on their own. He'd thought that marriage made the sum of the 1+1 to be more than 2, but here she was telling him that in fact 1+1 added up to less than 2.

"Are you telling me you want us to get divorced?"

"No, absolutely not, I love you, I always have. No, I just need my freedom."

"Then what the hell are you doing here in bed with me in Paris in the middle of the afternoon behaving as if all the problems had been cancelled out?"

"I wanted to be here to explain, to try to get you to understand."

"I understand well enough Diana, it's all the familiar stuff from Women's magazines about the importance of 'finding yourself' – so much more important than making a happy marriage, a marriage that works, though to get that compromises are always needed. And I suppose this new 'freedom' of yours will allow you to take on a new lover if you come across someone else you fancy after a glass or two of wine?"

"That's unfair Lucien"

"Well does it or doesn't it?"

Diana had started to dress, her back to Lucien.

"Unfair. But yes I suppose it does."

"Knowing that would mean divorce?"

"I hope it wouldn't."

"I'm telling you it would."

"Even if the affair meant nothing?"

"If it meant nothing then you shouldn't do it!" With that they lapsed into silence, Lucien standing at the window his brain a whirlpool of incomprehension and anxiety. "Shall we go for a walk then find a good restaurant and talk about something else- happy times we've had?"

Diana came over and put her hands on his shoulders.

"I do love you you know."

206

"Odd way of showing it" said Lucien lifting her hands off him one by one. "Let's go for that walk."

They walked slowly along the banks of the Seine looking down on the Quais where lovers embrace and promises are made. They walked along holding hands. Out of habit? Maybe hoping that some different message would pass to each other through their palms, something to do with the love they both professed but somehow couldn't clarify. On the deck of a houseboat, a converted barge moored at the bank, a couple were sitting at a little table a bottle of wine between them their ankles twisted together companionably under the table. On the hatches tubs of geraniums. Leaning against the rail a couple of bicycles. A little dog raced along the side of the barge as Diana and Lucien passed; it had to stop when it reached the bow but carried on barking.

"I just want to know specifically what it is that you really want. If you'd just tell me what that is for God's sake then I could help you find it."

Diana leaned, straight armed, on the parapet looking across the river at the Louvre.

"But I don't know what it is! I don't bloody know what it is, I just know that I need some space to find out, room to see if I can breathe more easily, time to discover who I really am."

"Oh Christ, more crap out of a woman's magazine !"

"Don't diminish me Lucien, perhaps that's the trouble, maybe that confirms that I ought simply to make my own decisions now, never discuss them with you first. I expect you think this whole thing is just selfishness on my part ?"

"To be frank, Yes, it does look like that."

They walked on further not speaking, no longer holding hands; impervious to the rest of the world circling around them.

"You know what the problem is Lucien. You don't really love Me. You fix on an image of me as the woman you want me to be, the perfect woman and wife, an object. Something that I'm not. Maybe the problem is that I'm the only woman you've really had a proper relationship with. Certainly from what you've said your relationship with your mother wasn't very loving. Maybe it's not just me that needs some space; maybe you do too. Perhaps by leaving I'm doing you a favour!" Diana nodded to herself, looking down and nodding again as if simultaneously she'd just had a great truth and a great solution revealed to her.

They had reached the Musée D'Orsay. The swirl of evening commuter traffic fought for space with the tourist buses trying to load the hordes of teenagers corralled together for their pre-booked, unasked for culture. The other tourists pushed out at closing time were being harrassed like herds of wildebeest by the touts, the postcard sellers, the musicians and jugglers and the men with dustbins of iced water filled with tins of soft drink.

They turned away from the river and the hubbub into quieter side streets towards the Boulevard St Germain. They settled into a quiet corner of a bar in the Rue du Bac.

"I'd find this easier to cope with if I knew what I'd done wrong" said Lucien staring disconsolately into his beer.

"You haven't done anything wrong darling, that's half my problem, if you had it would be easier."

"I give up; so is it to be a...what do they call it....a 'trial separation'?"

"I suppose so."

"So tomorrow I'll go back to St Jean and you will go to London and then we'll just see how it goes?"

" I suppose so. Will you keep in touch?"

"To remind myself of the stupidity and futility of all this? To get an update on your new lovers? We'll just leave that open shall we?" For the first time he was now on the verge of anger but he knew that would, as ever, resolve nothing. "For now let's just go and find a restaurant and get pissed before I get too maudlin."

Two hours and two bottles of wine later they staggered back to their hotel arm in arm and fell back into the unmade bed where they had started the afternoon. Even drunk Lucien knew it was best to stay on his side of the bed and so they passed the night as awkward and uncertain as they were on that New Year's night, 40 years earlier.

Tuesday September 16th. Back to St. Jean

Lucien didn't wait to have breakfast with Diana the next morning, nor wait to go with her to the Gare du Nord for her train back to London. It didn't seem appropriate. Maybe he was just escaping again but he knew her mind was made up so whilst she was still half awake in bed he'd packed, kissed her, paid the hotel bill and left to get the early train from the Gare Montparnasse heading back to Libourne and thus St Jean.

The Gare Montparnasse is a building of brutalist, unfinished concrete of quite astonishing ugliness. A bomb shelter for trains built, it would seem, by a fascist dictator short of money.

Inside no Diana for company at breakfast, just a stale roll, some oversweet jam and a cup of lukewarm coffee served by a surly man at the station café… an apology for breakfast now in front of him on a sticky table at the side of the concourse. 8.00am. At the further end of the concourse jostling rivers of workers from commuter trains flowing down the steps and out of the concourse towards the Metro or the sun. There was half an hour to wait until his TGV left and even it, resting at the platform nearest to the café was drab, its blue and silver livery peeling and discoloured, its snout smeared with dirt.

He presumed that outside the station people were enjoying the Paris summer, greeting each other with kisses, smoking, reading the newspaper in the sunshine. Here inside this grey concrete ant heap nothing seemed happy. A pair of shaven headed young soldiers in lopsided berets slowly patrolled the concourse their assault rifles at the ready. Perhaps they were there to arrest anyone showing any hint of *joie de vivre*. Last year when he come to this station he'd arrived outside just after a man had killed himself by jumping from the top of the 60 storey skyscraper that dominates the bleak station plaza. Lucien had walked past the shape under a blanket that didn't quite cover the crushed cranium or conceal the splodges of blood and brain on the pavement. Some gendarmes in their big boots and black battledress were standing about not looking. Parisians rushed by, not looking, not even wishing to think what personal anguish had led to that leap. None of their business. Today Lucien was likewise ignored in his rubbish strewn corner of the station waiting to be allowed to board the train, a one legged pigeon pecking at the crumbs of his breakfast.

Slowly, slowly the train wriggled out from under the concrete. The buildings alongside are covered in graffiti that is almost uniformly incomprehensible. Arabic, Cyrillic, cryptic logos and just the occasional legible scrawl: "FUCK US". Was that "Fuck U.S." or was it "Fuck Us"? did it make any difference? Either way it was the sort of quasi philosophical item which could consume half an evening's conversation at a Parisian dinner party. Lucien was glad to be escaping back to the country. His part of the carriage was deserted apart from a young man communing with his laptop, the screen reflected in the lenses of his steel framed spectacles. He had not even looked up when Lucien sat down opposite him. The train sped up until the houses beside the track became a blur and then blasting out of a tunnel raced along beside the Autoroute outpacing the cars with increasing ease as it reached full speed. To Lucien it felt as if this race into the sunny countryside would get faster and faster until they reached escape velocity and transferred into some different universe. He wished they could. The man opposite him continued his arcane interactions in cyberspace occasionally pausing to tap messages into his phone. In the carriage it was silent apart from the metallic rush of the train. Lucien tried to organise his thoughts about what had happened in Paris and set into context everything that had happened before. He had been unthinkingly desperate to repair the relationship with Diana but that, he now acknowledged to himself, was just a reflex, heedless loyalty not to her but to marriage, the family, the home, the whole cosy edifice. Maybe that loyalty was not deserved. Thinking back on the previous 24 hours he realized that not once had Diana asked him how he was feeling, how he'd cope with separation. Not the way she was normally? Perhaps her normally outgoing nature had run its course, run out of steam. Her habit of thinking about others, asking about their relatives and their feelings and their plans and the daily grind of being nice to the children she taught, asking what they'd done or thought or made or read had eventually reached its limit. Maybe years of supporting Lucien had contributed. "Donor Fatigue" the charities called it when people stopped giving. Maybe Diana had Donor Fatigue and needed a period of selfishness.

On the other hand maybe this new Diana was the real Diana declaring herself, slipping out from under a pall of middle class politeness and carefulness that had been suffocating her. But, but, he told himself he hadn't the whole story. Probably never would now. He had not told Diana or Lucy about the slip of paper he'd found in Diana's book. *"infidelity is an existential obligation"*. What he'd also kept to himself was the knowledge that the handwriting was not only not Harold Makepiece's but it was also not Henry Lightwood's. Lightwood was in the habit of scrawling handwritten addenda onto letters he'd signed, or of writing marginalia in letters he'd received then returning them to the sender. He knew Lightwood's writing very well and the writing on the slip of paper still in Lucien's wallet was not Henry Lightwood's. He took it out and looked at it again to check. No, Not Henry Lightwood's, someone else's.

The more he sat and ruminated the less Diana remained unsullied in his memory. He realized that overall she was somewhat self-regarding; she liked to dress well probably for herself rather than to improve the view for others. In sex she enjoyed what was done to her, occasionally with her but it probably never occurred to her to do anything more for a man other than what was needed to ignite his lust. Did Diana love Lucien? He believed she did, yes, in a way, as a comfortable companion. Did she in any way have the same sort of feelings for him as he had for her? His obsession with her happiness? Probably not he concluded and indeed perhaps his obsession was his problem. His pleasure in the trappings and rewards of his obsession were just as self-centered as her self-obsession – simply different. An odd trick of the mind delivered up a long forgotten phrase from Keats: "Selfishness, Love's cousin". Well even if this separation they'd agreed upon was to be temporary he'd need to avoid spending time looking backwards or wondering how to arrange a reconciliation. He needed his own dose of self-interest, the option to look about and see where that led him. He'd agreed with Diana that she'd remain in the Dulwich house and when the time came to return from St. Jean, and he had no idea at this moment when that would be, he'd find himself a flat somewhere in London. What a grim prospect he thought; a flat reeking of temporariness and solitude.

"Angouleme, Angouleme, Deux minutes d'arret" announced the tannoy. The man opposite him shut the lid of his computer, slid it into a dedicated compartment of his special computer nerd's backpack and without a glance at Lucien left. "Perhaps", thought Lucien, "I really am invisible!"

It was after midday when he arrived back in St Jean having retrieved the Jaguar from the station car park in Libourne. He toyed with the idea of stopping at a restaurant along the way for lunch but decided that all he really wanted was to be back in the warm embrace of St Jean comforted by its familiarity and a cold beer at the Café des Vignerons.

Lucien waited until 7 o'clock that evening to phone Lucy, it would have been unfair to phone her at work and if the call was about to upset her it was better that she was back in her flat. In fact she wasn't upset at all.

"I guessed that's what might happen" she said "Mum wasn't going to give up her habits that easily." and then they began to talk practicalities as if this happened all the time. Lucien sitting in the kitchen in St. Jean shook his head; he'd been expecting a fraught and tearful recitation of all the reasons why he and Diana should not part but instead Lucy was just asking him when he would be back in London.

"You'll need to sort out some clothes and papers I expect and maybe lock away personal things in Dulwich. Then maybe we could look around to see the sort of area where you'd like a flat. It would be nice if it were near me so I could cook for you now and then, stop you from starving. Actually if you're coming over for a few days why don't you stay in my flat with me. You probably won't want to be in Dulwich and my sofa turns into a bed. Mum's going away to a conference in Nottingham in a couple of weeks' time you could come then. It's a weekend do so I'd be around and I could help you sort out whatever you want in Dulwich."

Lucy, it seemed, now needed to go and wash her hair so having confirmed the dates for Lucien's visit to London, October 3rd to 5th the conversation was over. Lucy certainly had her mother's genius for fixing on practical issues in the face of emotional chaos.

Wednesday September 17th, St. Jean. Jeanette's invitation

Back in the Vieux Tour, Lucien was intent on arranging for his life to be as normal as possible. He got up at 8 am. Shaved, showered, walked down to the Boulangerie for his fresh croissant and baguette, ate the same breakfast as on other days, did the washing up and made the bed but trying to clear his head of the events and conversations of the previous few days was turning out to be impossible. He was harassed by the unedited recording replaying in his head. He tried to extricate himself from the endless loop by looking for some positive side to what had happened. An excess of Fidelity he concluded, not for the first time, had been his problem. Fidelity to his marriage, to Diana; mindless fidelity, fidelity as a failing not a virtue. An image of Greyfriars Bobby came into his head. Greyfriars Bobby, the scraggy terrier who had sat by the grave of his dead master day in day out for years and been rewarded by the little bronze statue on a column that Lucien noticed every time he passed it in the taxi taking him from Waverley Station to the College of Surgeons in Edinburgh. He doubted if his own faithfulness would be rewarded. Perhaps it was the cause of the trouble, cloying, claustrophobic good behaviour; a futile habit best abandoned. "Move on Lucien, move on" he said to himself ,at which point almost on cue there was a knock at the door, Jeanette. Jeanette with her sunglasses in her hair, a crisp white shirt, a denim skirt and a basket over her arm.

"Bonjour Cheri. I saw the car was back but guessed you'd still be on your own so I brought you some healthy vegetables from my *potager*; courgettes, tomatoes, some little peppers and half a dozen peaches from that tree you so admire on the garden wall. Also I have come to see how you got on in Paris? May I come in?"

"Of course...coffee?"

As he made the coffee with Jeanette next to him in the kitchen he explained what had happened...there seemed to be no point in concealing it but he was glad to be busying himself with practical things so Jeanette could not read in his face the shame and embarrassment of his loss.

"Poor Diana….poor Lucien…and poor Lucy too. Diana must have been suffering to make this choice."

"Suffering! It didn't show" retorted Lucien defensively.

"Maybe you just didn't see it and now 'poufff', too late, she's gone".

"It's only a trial separation, It's not permanent"

"But dear Lucien it will only be of value to you and to Diana if you behave as if it is to be permanent... et alors therefore you must find a new woman. Can I smoke since Diana's not here"

"I don't want a new woman" said Lucien.

"Probably not right now Cheri but a sign that you've moved on will be that in due course you will have decided you do need one. What else will you do? Become a miserable bachelor living alone in a basement flat somewhere. Or living in your Club. Isn't that what you Englishmen do…stay in one of those femme-free zones. Forgive me for lecturing you Lucien but it's time to get real. Explore the world, come out from that domestic prison you and Diana locked yourselves into. Be brave…'life shrinks or expands in proportion to one's courage' not a quote you'll know. Anais Nin, *proto-feministe*. Get a new woman Lucien."

Lucien looked at her anxiously for a moment then just as he was about to speak Jeanette held up a finger. They were sitting at the kitchen table, on opposite sides.

"And before you even think it Lucien, that new woman is not me. When I suggested we had an *affaire* circumstances were different. I was just offering a diversion. A diversion? Is that the right word? *Un divertissement*, an entertainment; I was not offering to be a replacement for Diana. You need to get away from the easy options and the familiar Lucian. Explore."

"You're right Jeanette, you're usually right. No mooching about reflecting on what's past. Maybe Diana wasn't suffering as you said but maybe just bored. Maybe our marriage was, too tidy, safe, predictable, dull….. like Switzerland."

Jeanette reached across and stroked his hand.

"We shall all encourage you, so you must come to supper, meet some new people, pretend you are a bachelor again. But now I must leave though I shall wash up the coffee cups first; you see I have already acknowledged your new status- If Diana had been here of course I would not do the washing up."

"I'll walk you home."

"How sweet, how English – a Frenchman would not do that unless he was expecting to come upstairs when we got there!"

As they came into the lane outside the Vieux Tour Lucien was surprised to see, just ahead of them, Geraldine Makepiece and yes Harold Makepiece; his arm draped around her shoulder and her hand in the back pocket of his jeans, they were laughing. Lucien raised his eyebrows at Jeanette, lifting his head quizzically.

"Oui, he's back. I don't know for how long but they seem happy for now."

After Lucien had walked with Jeanette to her door, kissed her on each cheek and promised to be there for supper on Friday evening he returned to the square where the Makepieces were sitting outside the Café des Vignerons with a full bottle of wine open on the table in front of them.

"Come and join us" shouted Harold waving his glass. Geraldine Makepiece proffered an embarrassed little smile and an almost imperceptible shrug.

"Good to see you Harold, I thought you were in London…or Spain was it?"

"Both but I've come back now. Suddenly realized the pointlessness of all that running around. Reckoned it was just menopausal madness so I'm back " and he put his feet up on a chair.

"And he's given up the guitar thank God" Geraldine added. Lucien wondered whether in fact the rumoured Senorita in Spain had given him the push and he'd simply come back to home base for a while.

"Where is the lovely Diana?"

"London." Which seemed sufficient for Harold, more interested in himself perhaps or maybe Geraldine had already briefed him.

Lucien was just leaving the house when the phone rang. He was about to ignore it but didn't; it might be Lucy.

"Hullo Lucien, Lily here again. How are you?" All suddenly very informal mused Lucien though there was a frisson of pleasure at hearing her voice .

"I'm well thank you Lily, and how are you?"

"Oh you know… usual thing, working too hard, need a break. Look there are some papers I need to show you and a new statement to sign for the GMC. Can we meet?"

"Well as you know I'm still in France… can't you e-mail them to me or post them?"

"Yes of course I could, absolutely but I thought we might rather meet."

"Meet where?"

"I wondered about Paris?"

"Paris… I suppose that's feasible… when?" He was flushed now with a tingle of apprehension.

"It's awfully soon but how about Friday week? I can get a train about lunchtime and be there by 5pm. Assuming you'd say yes I've provisionally booked at the Hotel Marianne in Montmartre, I'm told it's very nice and it's on expenses …though you may have pay for your own dinner." She laughed.

"It's a nice idea, I'm flattered. There's nothing much to do here so I'd love to see you in Paris… Friday week, Hotel Marianne, Montmartre late afternoon."

"Rather a special place I'm told, not easy to find by the way, it's off an alleyway at the top of a hill. Apparently you go in through the garden gate. Must go… client's just arrived. See you in Paris!"

Lucien imagined her uncrossing her elegant long legs, sweeping her hair behind her ears, replacing her spectacles and going to the door, all smiles to greet the client. Probably another doctor in trouble. Though without, he hoped, the bonus of a date with his glamorous solicitor. Did she really mean it? She sounded so coquettish, slightly drunk perhaps. A date! God, when had he last been on a date? Decades ago! And how would he cope with Paris just two weeks after the debacle with Diana there. Well it would be a test of whether he was able to get on with his own life, but he was glad the focus was to be Montmartre, nowhere near the hotel he'd stayed in with Diana. He planned not to tell Lucy, she would be horrified to think of him spending the weekend with someone other than her mother. Lucien was desperately anxious that exploring his own independence should not leave Lucy feeling abandoned. Indeed Lucien, excited by the notion of a secret assignation had decided he would tell no-one, he would simply absent himself from St Jean for a few days.

Friday 19th September. St Jean. Supper chez Jeanette

It was a formal dinner party, very formal for St Jean. Jeanette was in the kitchen and there was a maid to open the door and take the guests through to be greeted by Claude with a tall glass of good champagne. Of the eight guests Lucien knew only one, Anna, widow of Hector Ponsonby the barrister who'd died of a stroke 18 months earlier. Claude introduced her formally as the Chatelaine, the mistress of the Chateau Montbelle though she had none of the pretentiousness about this that other expats might easily have taken on had they been in that position. Lucien knew her only slightly for she and her husband were rarely seen in the village, certainly never to be found drinking outside the Café des Vignerons. Lucien and Diana had been to summer parties at the Chateau and to celebrations to mark the end of the *Vendange*, the grape harvest, but not much else though Lucien had met Anna's son George several times when he'd come to the Vieux Tour during a romance with Lucy five summers earlier, or was it ten? He really couldn't remember. George had been keen but Lucy, as was her wont, had found someone else after a few months and moved on. Now however here he was commanded by a little cream coloured card in a silver holder to sit next to Anna.

As he unfurled his napkin Lucien noted the veritable armoury of cutlery and the four crystal wine glasses glinting at each place. It was going to be a long night! Clearly this was not to be "just supper" as Jeanette had offered when she invited him. Lucien was relieved that he'd at least put on a new blue linen shirt, ironed his chinos and polished his shoes. He'd also put on the Cartier gold watch that a grateful sheikh had given him when he'd delivered one of the wives of a healthy son. Lucien resented the messages that such baubles were intended to send but had made an exception tonight…because he was on his own? Anna was talking to a dumpy woman seated opposite her, the wife of some notable in Bergerac Lucien presumed but it gave him a chance to study Anna. A strong almost aquiline nose, dark, glossy but disordered long hair held back by a green velvet Alice Band. A wide mouth with full lips and a surprisingly dark complexion for an Englishwoman. That together with her very brown eyes flecked with gold made him wonder; a Mediterranean mother perhaps? Her hand was resting on the table next to Lucien… a large emerald ring with a wedding ring and on the little finger an antique signet ring bearing a coat of arms …unusual for a woman. She certainly didn't look like a murderess. Gossip in the village was that Hector had not died of a stroke but been bludgeoned to death by his wife. Why else would the gendarmes have spent so long at the chateau? She didn't look like a murderess, but then Lucien admitted to himself that in a line up he would not been able to distinguish a murderess from a nun or a nurse.

The meal lived up to Jeanette's reputation as a cook. Her homemade *Foie Gras* served with thin slices of warm brioche was followed by a small orange salad decorated with nasturtium flowers, then dainty little fillets of sole in sorrel sauce with a salmon mousseline.

"Has she added chopped pistachios to the mousseline?" Lucien asked Anna as a means of extricating himself from the deputy mayor of Bergerac who wanted to talk about his wife's gynecological experiences.

"Yes, I think so. Inspired!" Anna retorted savouring a little more of the mousseline first. "What a treat, I love these formal dinners at Jeanette and Claude's, there's always a surprise like this and then, predictably, duck for the meat course though prepared differently each time. There's ten of us here tonight so it'll be a challenge."

"*Et Voila, le Magret de Canard*" announced Jeanette "tonight baked in an egg and salt crust so that each of you shall have your meat at the point of perfection" which it was, accompanied simply by cubes of potato and of apple sautéed in goose fat.

"I'm so jealous" said Anna "Jeanette has managed to get all this meat to the table at perfect temperature and pinkness. I love it pink, 'pink as a tart's bottom' Hector used to say. I'm not sure where he got that phrase, perhaps he had a penchant for spanking that I'm not aware of! And how flattering, Claude is serving us wine from the Chateau to go with the duck." Lucien noted how quickly she changed tack when Hector's name came into the conversation.

The cheese came round.

Lucien had a problem with cheese! He knew with absolute scientific confidence that it was bad for him. Too much fat, too many calories, too much salt. Even by opting for Brebis or Roquefort to get the low fat benefits of sheep cheese or starting with just a thin slice off the side of a sour-salty-sweet pyramid of Pouligny goats' cheese all was then lost in the face of a hard, crusty Salers or an oozing Brie. Without fail he ate too much of the stuff. Tonight was no exception.

"How's George?" he ventured, trying to take his mind off the cheese board.

"He's OK. Lives in Islington and runs a sort of antique business looking out for antiques that the Russians and the Gulf Arabs might like to spend a fortune on."

"Is he married?"

"No, he has the occasional steady girlfriend but nothing permanent. To be honest he never really got over Lucy."

"Oh dear, she'd be upset to hear that, she was fond of George but was a bit flighty in those days, never stuck with anyone or anything, she's different now."

"My friends" said Claude, perhaps we should go out into the garden whilst the table is cleared and we can return for coffee and a *digestif* in a while."

"I suppose this is the point where the ladies used to leave the gentlemen" said Anna putting her arm formally into Lucien's as they went out. "Now the gentlemen have to come out here for a fag- not enough time for a cigar!"

"Odd isn't it" said Lucien" This used to be the main tobacco growing area in France, the countryside is still dotted with lovely drying sheds and Bergerac was the commercial capital for it all, now these grandees aren't even allowed to smoke indoors."

"Hector used to, he was a cigar man. It was part of his persona along with the red braces and the stripy double breasted suits. It's one of the things I miss now he's gone, the reassuring whiff of an expensive cigar confirming that he was somewhere about the house. I've kept a box of them so I can have a sniff if I'm feeling sad."

"Does that help?"

She smiled at Lucien and clutched his arm a little tighter.

"Not really, it can't bring him back."

"You must miss him?"

"Of course, he was a large, loud, happy man; he filled a big space...impossible not to miss him." She paused,"Isn't this a gorgeous evening, a bit hot perhaps, we could do with some rain to cool things down. Not too much though; it's not going to be a good year for the grapes and too much rain will make it worse." Lucien wanted to talk more about Hector but she'd clearly chosen to change the subject.

"The *Vendange* seemed to be the main topic of conversation at dinner, how it will be very late this year, low yield, poor quality and so on."

"It's just a form of group therapy...they like to feel they'll all be equally badly affected."

"And how about your vines? I hear you're carrying on solo."

"Yes I am but Hector never really took much responsibility for them, he was too busy making his fortune at the bar. To be honest it's not too big a burden. I've always made the business and marketing decisions but I have Victor and Franck to do the hard work and make the decisions about the vines. Victor is the *Chef de culture*, the vineyard manager, and Franck the *Maitre des chais,* the cellar master. Or is it the other way round I'm never sure, they both do everything. When to pick is a sort of group decision, everyone talking on the phone and chasing the analysis results from the lab in Bergerac."

"From the oenologue, the high priest?"

"Yes, the oenologue. Nice sounding title, crucial skill."

"I really ought to know more about it after all these years. I'd wondered about taking back our vines and trying my hand at making wine." He gave Anna a look that confirmed that this was a question not a decision.

"What does your wife think?"

"Ah well, that's why I'm toying with the idea... we've just separated so I'm looking for a new life."

"I'm sorry. Do you want to talk about it?"

"No, not really, not now ...it's all a bit raw at the moment...another day perhaps. Thanks though."

"I'm sorry Lucien. Making wine is difficult you know, start-up costs are high, it takes a long time to learn and if you haven't the nose or the acumen you can fail spectacularly. How many hectares do you have?"

"Ten."

"Not enough really. Why don't you come over sometime and you can look at how we do it at the chateau and talk to Victor and Franck. In fact I'll ask them to come over to you first and look at your *Chais* to see if they can be resuscitated for winemaking."

The remains of the evening offered no respite from wine talk and sure enough as the effects of the champagne and the wine and the Armagnac took hold the usual topics came round again; how the winemakers of Australia and South America are flooding the market with uninteresting predictable wines, getting the price down by soulless industrial scale production and by using screw tops or plastic corks. How shocking that even some French growers were resorting to such travesties, even selling their wine in plastic bags in boxes. Not producers in Burgundy or the Loire or The Rhone or Bordeaux of course but co-operatives in the Languedoc for example. Lucien had heard all this before, it was just as current in the Café des Vignerons as it was in this politer gathering. It saddened Lucien and Anna said it depressed her too, the facts as well as the chat. The endless talk of terroir and tradition from people with big histories and small vineyards.

Monday 22nd September. St. Jean. Wine

Victor and Franck arrived promptly at eight-thirty in the morning in Victor's thirty-year old caramel coloured Citroen van. Victor at barely five foot three inches was happy in this tiny vehicle that he'd had all his working life – he was sixty-three – conceived as France was liberated at the end of World War II, hence his name Victor. Franck, twenty years his junior and six inches taller, unwound himself stiffly from the van, the two men could not have been more different or more archetypical. Victor, skin like chestnut wood and hands as wrinkled as vine trunks, had spent a lifetime among the vines, indeed if his father was to believed he was conceived among the vines. His knowledge of grapes and vines, soil and weather and how to craft the best wine had all been accrued at first hand. Franck by contrast was one of the new young wine technocrats, a graduate of wine college, apprenticed at one of the finest Bordeaux chateaux; he'd even been to California to see what they did differently, maybe even better. Nothing, he concluded. Now here he was in his leather jacket and jeans, unreadable behind his wrap-around sunglasses and yet a harmonious relationship with Victor had developed. Victor didn't seem perturbed by being drafted to talk to Lucien, interested in fact, but Lucien sensed some hostility in Franck. Put out by being drafted to look at someone's old *chai*? Or put out by something else?

Lucien took them to the big building at the back of the house; the family had always called it the barn but, in fact, in past times it had been the *chai*, the winery. The children had played in there hiding behind wine vats and the old machinery. Now it was just a garage and a place to keep the lawn mower. Swallows nested under its eaves, lizards scuttled across the walls and bats hung from the highest of the oak rafters like a row of black socks on a washing line. Sunlight sparkled through the tiny chinks between the roof tiles. Victor was delighted with it.

"*Charmant… historique.*"

The centre of the barn was dominated by a giant basket press two metres across made of vertical oak slats bolted to iron hoops. Grapes would have been pressed here, the top was gradually wound down, wine oozing out between the slats and away into a gully below. At one end of the barn were half a dozen oak barrels, each big enough for a man but the hoops rusty and the staves dry and split. In the far corner several concrete vats their lids attached to chains on pulleys. Some rusty machinery. On hooks lengths of yellow hose. No wine though, no smell of wine, no bottles waiting to be filled, just dirt and cobwebs and some abandoned children's toys.

Franck looked about scornfully,

"I'm afraid monsieur that if you wish to make wine in here all this would have to go. You'd need new stainless steel vats, refrigeration, pumps, a modern tank press and a de-stemmer as a minimum. Also, re-make the floor, these terracotta tiles are very old and very decorative but could not be cleaned enough."

Outside they walked between the rows of wines each with ripened bunches of black grapes hanging from beneath, just above the ground.

"Mostly Merlot but your neighbour keeps them well" said Franck "but not enough and if you're to make some red wine you will need another variety as well, Cabernet Franc perhaps but you'd need to re-plant for that. Come and see us tomorrow we'll show you what we do at the chateau."

Lucien was unsurprised by their conclusion; as he pushed the creaking doors shut and secured them with the long oak crossbar seating it firmly in its rusted iron brackets he acknowledged that he liked it just as it was, lurking in shadows of the past.

The next day he walked to the chateau and round to the side. The wine making part of the chateau had always been so integral to the life of the chateau that a whole wing stretching back a hundred metres from the facade had been built simply for the work of wine. The ground floor was clean and sparse; bare stone, a beamed roof, doors large enough to let carts or, nowadays, tractor trailers through carrying grapes. Four large stainless steel tanks glistening with purpose, fronted with dials lined one side. Fixed pipes coursed along the walls, other machines whose function he couldn't deduce sat squatly amongst pumps and pipes and at the far end rows of new barrels in amber coloured oak. Franck was checking the new barrels,

Victor was hosing down the floor, he stopped to offer his forearm for Lucien to shake.

"I'm cleaning up before the *Vendange*, there won't be any time for this sort of work once the picking starts."

Franck looked more at ease today, safe on his own territory. By the time he'd finished explaining what was what Lucien's brain was numb. Franck told him what each machine was, why the grape juice first went there and how it was when it came out here. Also the importance of controlling the temperature there and how to let the grape skins impart tannins and colour and character to the red wine in that container there but for just the right length of time before the wine was pumped over into that container there and into those barrels down there and how they knew how much sulphite to use and the difference between *vin de goutte* and *vin de presse*. At last at the far end of the enormous space Franck led him down a flight of stone steps turning on the lights as he descended.

"And all these" he said indicating a regiment of barrels stretching away into the gloom "are ready for bottling. We should have done it already but it can wait until after the *Vendange* – here you will need to taste some." He took a pair of tulip glasses off a shelf and handed them to Lucien. "Hold these" and he opened an unlabelled bottle from a row on the shelf. "That's the 2005. It's a bit young but it's going to a good vintage."

Lucien sampled the wine being careful to inhale its aroma and let it roll along his tongue.

"It's good as far as my uneducated palate can tell."

Victor had joined them.

"Madame will be pleased. She's outside waiting to see Monsieur McCulloch."

"I'll catch you up" said Franck disappearing towards the far end of the cellar. As they reached the top of the stone steps up into the winery Victor tugged at Lucien's sleeve, checked that Franck couldn't hear and with a toothy grin asked

"Monsieur McCulloch are you going to marry Madame?"

"I hardly know her" retorted Lucien startled by this unexpected question. Victor shrugged,

"You could do worse Monsieur and you're the sort of person she needs. Better then her just relying on ...... locals for ...... you know."

If he was truthful to himself Lucien would have to admit that now he'd crept out from under his blanket of self-pity he was indeed half looking for a new partner but he had no intention of sharing that with Victor .... Or Anna. Looking for a new partner! The concept intrigued him. One of the deals you make with fate when you marry should be that you don't spend time thinking that there must be many other people out there, maybe someone you know or the person you've just passed in the street who would make a better wife or husband than you've got ....even when you are happy with the one you have.

Anna was outside where the little roads from the vineyard converged at the winery doors, blindingly bright, the sun reflecting off the limestone gravel and the stone walls. She looked ravishing, a white bandana, big sunglasses, a denim shirt and jodhpurs. Straining at their leashes two big hounds, grey and white with black marKing's, floppy ears and big doleful eyes. Straining not to attack or escape but to be friendly. They licked Lucien's proffered hand.

"This is Marguerite and this is Marcel" said Anna ruffling their ears. "They're supposed to be for the hunt but they are useless at it so they're just house dogs. Very English. French hounds here are kept in kennels outside. These two are softies and they sleep in the kitchen or at the bottom of my bed". She put her arm in Lucien's "Let's get out of the sun. Thank you Victor." Victor gave a little bow and went back into the dark cavern of the winery.

"How did you get on?" she asked.

"My place certainly isn't equipped – which I knew. The winery here is most impressive and you're lucky to have Victor and Franck."

"Ah, yes I am. Dear Victor isn't he sweet. And Franck so handsome and a good manager too. I'd ask you in for coffee but I need to be somewhere else. How about lunch in Bergerac next week at The Vigne D'Or after the market? Midday?"

And that was it, dismissed. As Lucien walked away down the drive towards the tall pillars of the entrance gate he noticed Franck waiting at the wheel of his car by the side of the chateaux. Waiting for Madame?

Friday Sept. 27th - Sunday 28th. Paris with Lily

When Lucien had climbed the long cobbled steps towards the top of Montmartre, found the bell push beside the small brass plaque with the name Hotel Marianne almost polished away he was let through the door in a high wall into a large garden of cedars, gravelled walks and fountains; completely unexpected here amongst the tight and winding streets of Montmartre. At the end of the garden, approached up a flight of steps, a graceful 19th century mansion that was now the hotel.

"Professor McCulloch, welcome sir, we are expecting you. Just sign here please. Now here is you key card, you are in room 103 on the first floor. Madame has not yet arrived. Raoul will carry your bag."

"Thank you I can manage, it's very light." He never let porters carry his bag, he travelled with so little that it seemed pointless or perhaps his Scots genes just resented the tip. The staircase wound around a huge chandelier, the steps were broad and shallow, fresh flowers in alcoves between mirrors. The softly carpeted first floor corridor was wide with windows on one side. Room 103 was larger than he'd expected but then he didn't usually stay in hotels as smart as this. Two long windows opened onto a balcony overlooking the garden and through the trees a vista of Paris to the Eiffel tower and beyond. Piano music was playing softly in the background, almost inaudible. Chopin? Lucien dumped his bag on the bed, took off his jacket, explored the room, poured himself a beer from the minibar and settled himself into an armchair by the window with his newspaper "Le Figaro", his mobile on the arm of the chair waiting for Lily to phone and say she'd arrived. There was no call but half an hour later he heard a click as the door opened behind him, it was Lily. He got up and kissed her on the cheek.

"Hi Lucien, isn't this a super room?"

"It is, I hope yours is as nice."

"This is mine…ours I suppose. Did you think we'd be in separate rooms?" she giggled, "Oh, how sweet Lucien, the perfect gentleman. Would you rather have a room to yourself, I'm sure it can be arranged." The answer of course was no but Lucien had only fantasized about this… he was taken aback.

"No, no of course not, wonderful, but not what I'd expected." There was a knock on the door, Raoul with Lily's suitcase. It seemed inordinately large for a weekend trip and Lucien was left standing by the door as she started to unpack hanging half a dozen dresses in the wardrobe.

"And now if you don't mind I'm going to have a bath" she announced "it was very hot on the train."

Lucien tried to concentrate on his newspaper as the bath was run, he could hear Lily getting into the bath, there was a pause and he could hear her humming to herself.

"Come and talk to me Lucien and bring the bottle of champagne that they said is awaiting us in the fridge." The bathroom was entirely fitted in white marble, the bath surrounded by a marble shelf on which were rows of candles in tinted glass containers, also a large bowl of rose petals. "This is what you get when you book the 'romantic weekend' package. Sprinkle some rose petals Lucien. No actually don't be so silly, why don't you just open the champagne!" Lucien poured two glasses and handed Lily one trying to ignore her body barely concealed by the little puffs of foam on the bathwater, a body as sleek and mysterious as a mermaid's. Lily seemed completely unselfconscious about her nakedness, indifferent to the presence of a fully clothed man sitting on the edge of the bath.

"You must think I'm an absolute hussy persuading you to come to Paris and presuming we would share a room. I bet that's what you're thinking."

"No I'm just thinking what a pleasure it is to be sitting on the edge of a beautiful woman's bath drinking champagne."

"And?"

"But a woman about the same age as my daughter, which seems a bit improper."

"Oh come on Lucien, you're not exactly consorting with a juvenile. I'm 36, also I'm not in a relationship. Neither of us is cheating on anyone."

"OK, OK, but what are we expecting from this weekend Lily?"

"I know what I'm expecting. To see some parts of Paris I haven't seen before, eat some gorgeous food, drink some good wine, enjoy your company and maybe have some nice sex." She paused "Is it that that's troubling you?"

"Not troubled, just confused."

"Look Lucien, we could have sex for lots of reasons. It could be because we thought we were in love, which we are not, or because we wanted to be in love, which we are not planning or we could do it simply because we might enjoy it. You might do it to punish your wife I suppose. For my part it's just a potentially nice part of an enjoyable weekend, no more no less. Is that problematic?"

"No, of course not." Why would it be, but it all seemed strange to Lucien. For a start he irrationally felt he was cheating on Diana and then there was this new Lily that he barely knew. Like most professionals he and presumably she, kept a rigid boundary between themselves and their clients, patients; offering nothing more than the most superficial chat about families or what they'd done on holiday. Nothing about what they believed in or wanted or what their dreams were. Apart from a couple of relaxed lunches he had been until now just a client. But this was a different Lily getting dressed not in a black skirt and white blouse demurely fastened at the throat but now in a short skirt and a red blouse, her cleavage barely concealed by a silk scarf; lips and nails no longer a discreet pale pink but a shade of red confident but not garish. Her hair normally in a tight chignon was now just a pony tail held with a red ribbon.

"This is the informal me rather than the solicitor me" said Lily.

"Which one is the real you?"

"Both!"

"I got on OK with the solicitor you so let's see how it goes with the other you shall we. I think we should go out whilst it's still sunny. It's a glorious, warm evening, we could walk along to Sacre Coeur then look for somewhere to have dinner."

As they came up the cascade of steps that leads to Sacre Coeur the low evening sun was reflecting off the white stone of the basilica so brightly that it looked new, as if the building had suddenly descended onto the hilltop fully formed. To Lucien's jaded palate Montmartre and Sacre Coeur were a series of tiring steps to be negotiated and tourists to be dodged but Lily's enthusiasm was infectious. Even the people on the terraces outside passing themselves off as silent statues of the famous and familiar enthused

230

her though she must have seen the like before in Trafalgar Square or along the embankment in London.

"How do they keep so still?" she asked, "and in those awkward poses? You must be very uncomfortable posing like that all day?" she said as she put a Euro in the hat beside a diminutive Charlie Chaplin who simply smiled and shrugged and twirled his cane. It was after 6 o'clock and as they went into the darkening interior of the basilica Lily put her scarf over her head and tied it under her chin; inside she genuflected and crossed herself at the entrance to the nave. Lucien was about to speak but she put her finger to her lips and they sat quietly as the sounds of the Latin mass drifted through the smoke of incense towards the cupola.

"Are you Roman Catholic ? I didn't know" said Lucien as they came out.

"Why would you; I'm just your solicitor, there's a lot you don't know about me. But I was a convent girl and old habits persist; irrationally sometimes."

Emerging from Sacre Coeur Lily took Lucien's arm as they walked along to the Place du Tertre once the haunt of bohemian, drunk, whoring, but now globally famous artists whereas today every available space under the trees is filled with pastiche paintings mimicking these famous names; competent, not original but what the tourists want. The square was as usual busy. As they wandered past the paintings Lucien was grateful that Lily showed no inclination to buy anything though she was intrigued by the artists at the south end of the square making portraits of whichever passer-by could be persuaded to sit.

"Please, pretty lady I will make your portrait" urged one eager young man with luxuriant curly hair emerging from beneath a beret . " Come, see what I can do" he said stretching out his hand to her. She looked at his pictures displayed on the ground.

"But these all look like Modiglianis !"

"Yes" he laughed "but it is quicker and easier to do in that style- it is why I am cheap- only 40 euros. Also mademoiselle you are as beautiful as any Modigliani that exists…it would be a privilege for me." at which there was a pause in the patter as he smiled up at Lily from his little stool and began to arrange a new sheet of card on his easel. "Or I could paint you as a Picasso….or Van Gogh or Matisse?... or Cubist?"

"How about Pointillist ?" asked Lucien mischievously.

"Mais non monsieur it would take too long and I think you and mademoiselle may have other plans for the evening!" Lily had been tidying her hair and was already posing herself in the sitter's chair .

"OK" said Lucien, "how long will it take?"

"Half an hour."

"You could go and have a beer" ventured Lily proffering her cheek for a kiss.

When Lucien returned the painting was finished, a classic Modigliani: oval face, arched eyebrows all simply and explicitly defined; but it looked unequivocally like Lily.

"I hope that Monsieur is pleased and also that he enjoyed his beer. Mademoiselle and I have had a good conversation" and he kissed her hand helping her up from the chair. Lucien felt a stab of jealousy, quite unexpected. In fact quite alarming.

Lucien wanted to eat at "Au Virage Lepic" in Rue Lepic to avoid the tourist food and high prices of the Place du Tertre but Lily preferred to stay and share the buzz of the place, watch the people inspecting paintings, see if anyone bought one. So they stayed.

Dinner was to Lucien's surprise very good and they lingered over it for almost two hours after which for the first time he felt that he knew Lily. He'd heard about her life as a solicitor working with the GMC, about her flat where she lived happily on her own overlooking the Thames at Tower Bridge. He learned about her childhood in Brighton; the only child of an alcoholic antique dealer and an actress. About how hard they'd fought to persuade her to go to university.

"I just wanted to hang out with boys, play music and sit on the beach, maybe train to be a dancer but I'm glad they prevailed."

"But why the Law?"

"Because you're not selling anything. Well you are if you are a barrister but not as a solicitor. One's just explaining the law or the truth to people even if they don't want to hear it. Both of my parents were out to sell something."

"But your mother was an actress."

"Selling her performance, telling an untruth about herself to sell the character she portrayed."

Lucien had begun the day very apprehensive about where this unlikely weekend might lead but now right on cue as they left the restaurant an accordionist began to play in a pool of light under the trees. Lucien realized without even a hint of guilt that he had not thought about Diana, or London or St Jean all evening; he put an unselfconscious arm around Lily's waist as they walked slowly back towards the hotel.

"Thank you Lily" said Lucien when they were back in their room and had retrieved the remaining half bottle of champagne, "I enjoyed this evening, I'm glad you had the painting done."

"Wasn't he sweet. He's called Jean Francois. He said he'd like to do a full length picture of me. He's an art student. He could do it tomorrow. He even put his phone number on the back of the painting." Lucien felt a jolt of jealousy again.

"That would be a Modigliani style nude I suppose."

"Yes, I suppose so." She sounded completely matter of fact about it.

"A pretty transparent chat up line" and all hideously familiar. Diana's recounting of her first meeting with Henry Lightwood flashed back. With an effort he repressed the memory.

"Yes, very transparent!"

"Would you like to pose for him Lily ?"

"Don't be silly, I'm here with you. Besides he's young and dangerous."

"And I'm not?"

"Not young Lucien but definitely dangerous!"

The next morning they were sitting contentedly having breakfast at a little table in the garden, a pair of cheeky sparrows pecking up the crumbs from the gravel underfoot.

"Yesterday evening...why did you say I was dangerous?" asked Lucien. Lily looked him in the eye almost quizzically, as if he ought to know the answer.

"Because I suspected a deep well of unexpressed passion in you"

"Oh goodness! That sounds a bit dramatic." Lucien was embarrassed.

"And last night we drew from that well you may recall, so I know it's there, Oh yes I certainly do!" She popped a piece of flaky croissant into her mouth spilling more crumbs for the sparrows.

"Perhaps it's just something to do with being in Paris."

"No, I think it's been there for a while." She signalled to the waiter to ask for more coffee "and an apple...*un pomme s'il vous plait*". Which was brought on a gold rimmed plate with a pearl handled knife. She held the apple up on her fingertips.

"Would you like a piece?"

"No thanks, we might get expelled from the Garden of Eden. Anyway it's 10 o'clock and the sun's shining. Shall we go and do the tourist thing" suggested Lucien to outflank any further delving into his persona. He just wanted to enjoy an uncomplicated weekend.

They criss-crossed Paris on foot and on the Metro. First the Picasso Museum, then lunch overlooking the sloping piazza by the Pompidou Centre. Then the long haul out to see the Monets at the Marmottan Museum. They walked from the Eiffel Tower over the river and up the grand sweep of the Trocadero, along the Avenue Kleber, climbed the 284 steps to the top of the Arc de Triomphe then wandered down the Champs Elysée. At last exhausted they arrived back in Montmartre, found somewhere to eat and went to bed early.

Pulling back the curtains on Sunday morning revealed a grey sky and drizzling rain so they ordered breakfast from room service and stayed in bed. Lily insisted that they had breakfast IN BED, not sitting at the little table with its low chairs. In bed, squatting on the bed as if for a picnic, Lily in a T Shirt and Lucien in his boxer shorts, the tray in front of them, coffee in a silver jug, porcelain cups, confitures in cut glass jars with spoons, freshly squeezed orange juice in tall glasses topped up from a half bottle of champagne. And for Lucien, joy of joys, perfect Eggs Benedict.

As they were eating Lucien asked something that he knew he should have asked long before.

"Lily. Seriousquestion. You are a solicitor, I am your client. What would your professional regulator, standard setter whoever that is, have to say about our spending a weekend together? It's OK is it?"

"Yes it's absolutely fine. The SRA, that's the Solicitors Regulatory Authority, the SRA Code of Practice doesn't say anything specific about sexual relationships with clients, it just says simply that I must at all times act in the client's best interest and provide the client with the highest possible standard of service. You are my client of course Professor and I hope you'd agree that our relationship this weekend has been in your best interest and that I've provided a high standard of service!"

"You have, would you like a formal letter of appreciation?"

"Not at the moment. However we need to remember that ostensibly this weekend is about business... The GMC, the MDU and the CPS. All the hassles at the hospital are depressing for you but there are no legal issues that the MDU needs to address unless the CEO, this Winston Arkwright is rash enough to slander or libel you." She got off the bed and brought back a folder of documents from the wardrobe. She sat cross legged, spectacles on the end of her nose and spread the documents out on the satin counterpane.

"Now then Professor, This is the most recent communication from the CPS, it's from Mr Fletcher-Pratt the man who was in court when you appeared on July 21st. He'd asked for a 4 week adjournment which was up on August 18th but he failed to have his case together by then. No reason for that other than incompetence. So instead of throwing the case out the magistrate allowed a further 4 week adjournment which brings us to September 15th. I discovered that at that point they had still not interviewed the Foreign Office man Gerry Havilland about the veracity of the paperwork from Libya even though the CPS had already charged him with Misconduct in Public Office. What's called "The Full Code Test" must confirm that evidence is credible and is reliable and I've pointed out to the CPS that the evidence from Libya processed through Gerry Havilland will almost certainly prove neither credible nor reliable. Nor is there much prospect of getting the alleged complainants to court so last week I formally requested Discontinuance under section 23, Prosecution of Offences Act 1985. The CPS have unofficially confirmed that the notice of Discontinuance will be issued this week. The GMC will then need to agree to abandon any actions they have underway and formally lift your suspension, then the London Clinic for Women and Children and the RUH will also need formally to lift any restrictions on your practice. However much your *bête noire* Mr. Arkwright may not want to reinstate you he has no choice. I

235

reckon that the whole process might be concluded by the end of October at the earliest so you have at least another month of idleness to enjoy. Also when all this is over you will need to decide whether you want to sue anyone for defamation or make an official complaint about the CPS' indolence or just go quietly back to work and pretend none of this happened. Is that all clear and are there any questions you wish to ask me Professor McCulloch?"

"No thank you Miss Harper Smith but if would you pass me the honey I think we might find something interesting to do with it!"

Lily reached over and smacked Lucien on the head with a plastic folder.

"You're not taking this seriously. All the work that I've put in to get you back to work and yet the impression I'm getting is that you don't want to go back to work at all. You're hopeless. I might as well give up now!"

"Actually you're almost right. I don't want to go back to living the way I was and that's partly your fault Lily."

"Well don't think you're going to be living with me ! This is a one off weekend which ends tomorrow when we go back to our separate lives".

It was still raining so they lay in bed and watched right through the film "Charade". Carey Grant and Audrey Hepburn. They didn't choose it, it was simply there on the TV, though Lucien given a choice might have picked it for Lily was as close to a modernized Audrey Hepburn as he could imagine. As the credits rolled she turned onto her side facing him.

"On balance Lucien I think you are more handsome than Carey Grant . Don't let it go to your head though! Come on, it's stopped raining and I want you to take me somewhere nice for lunch."

Saturday September 27th. Dulwich. Cricket

Diana's Saturday afternoon had been spent debating with herself whether her new freedom was really worth having. She'd started the afternoon in the pavilion by the Dulwich School cricket ground making cucumber and Marmite sandwiches and counting out cupcakes from a box someone had brought in. Why? Because this was the afternoon of the end of season cricket match between two teams of local teachers and her new friend Colin was playing. In truth, not actually a new friend; he taught at the same school as Diana and she'd been on flirty terms with him for several years; now she planned to discover how much intent there was behind the flirting though from Diana's point of view it would be on a strictly on a sale or return basis. That was an advantage of her new status. Commitment was optional.

Sitting on the plank steps of the pavilion she was able to admire Colin from a distance as he snickered a ball into the outfield disturbing a pair of pigeons. Cricket whites do flatter a man but particularly suited his leanness, his tallness and his mop of sandy hair. She wondered if his similarly of build to Lucien contributed to his attraction. Seeing Diana in her shorts sitting on the steps may momentarily have distracted Colin from the next ball which smacked into his wicket taking one stump clean out of the ground. Raising a hand in acquiesce he loped back to the pavilion pulling off his gloves, flopped down next to Diana on the steps and put his arm round her waist very publically if claiming a prize.

"Just another five overs to go. I expect you'll want to stay for a few beers with the boys afterwards. Shall I take you out to dinner tonight? The Café Rouge in the village?"

Diana was prepared to put up with this as she was fond of Colin but ruefully reminded herself that it was not the bright lights and adventure that she'd hoped would mark her new stage in life. Warm beer and then the Café Rouge? Definitely not, but she had plans for later and then there was all of Sunday together. She'd actually imagined evenings of cocktails, Michelin starred dinners and dancing; perhaps she might move on to that next time. Beer and the Café Rouge, oh dear! It turned out to be even worse and when they got back to the house instead of sweeping her off her feet and into the bedroom Colin turned on the TV and offered to make her tea. Colin the lonely, divorced teacher was looking for comfort and companionship not passion though over the next days Diana discovered that to her surprise she didn't mind that. Colin's passions were cricket, jazz (he played the saxophone) and mathematics. In practical matters he was useless, dependent. The sort of man who could neither boil an egg nor change an electric plug and who has to have woman with him when he buys a shirt. For her part Diana found that making the choices, setting the pace was pleasing, satisfying. It hadn't been like that with Lucien, he made the decisions and without any resentment she'd followed along. It was how it had always been. For now she enjoyed being in charge even if she had to tolerate the cricket, the saxophone, the cryptic crossword and the sudoku. Not that sudoku, fiendish version, took him long, damn him!

The sex was pedestrian but at least it was different.

Colin would do for now.

Back at school next week the liaison with Colin had, of course, been noted and broadcast with enthusiasm. Diana was supervising mid-morning break with Caroline who taught Year 3 and shared the daily chore of, in theory, ensuring that the little darlings played nicely together and came in promptly when the bell rang. These days though this Victorian echo had long faded and now they were more likely to be making sure children didn't stab each other or accept drugs through gaps in the railings.

"What are you up to with Colin?" Caroline came straight out with it whilst simultaneously separating two little girls who were fighting. "Has you husband left you?"

"No, the other way round I've left him, well separated actually."

"Why? He's lovely – he's good looking, successful, rich. If you don't want him I'll have him!"

"He might like that… you're twenty years younger than me and prettier! Maybe he'd like to have a thing going with a younger woman to test his virility!"

"Wouldn't it upset you?"

"Yes, of course it would, but maybe that would be good for me. At the moment I'm selfishly just assuming he's sitting on his own in France pining for us to get together again ….." she broke off… "Mary-Jane stop that immediately!" and she rushed across the playground to prevent a girl from pulling the shorts off a little curly-haired boy who was being sat on by two other girls. Then the bell went and Caroline was left to draw her own conclusions about Diana's behaviour.

Sunday September 28th. London. Royal United Hospital

It seemed very strange to be sitting alone in her empty office at 9 o'clock on a wet Sunday morning, no secretary in the outer office, a phone ringing unanswered down the corridor. As chairman of the Royal United Hospital Trust Margaret Ashbury, Dame Margaret Ashbury, would not normally come anywhere near the hospital on a Sunday or, come to that, on a Monday, Wednesday or on a Friday. As part time Chair two days usually sufficed together with the awful formal evening events. She was much too busy with her other responsibilities to spend time in a hospital. Not for nothing had the press labelled her "The Quango Queen". Chairperson of half a dozen worthy bodies and member of a few others, though nowadays she was really only prepared to be the Chairman, Chair, Chairwoman, Chairperson, whatever. The specific title didn't matter. She just liked to be in charge and always had. In fairness the detractors, and there were many, would usually admit that as a chairman she was masterful... always on top of the agenda, charming or rough by turns to have the business go the way she wished. She was a valuable commodity. Tall and grey haired, a thin, slightly hooked nose and eyes half closed by hooded upper lids, like Margaret Thatcher, "The eyes of Caligula," she was striking without being beautiful or even handsome but had a presence and she invariably found her way to centre stage. Nowadays she achieved this on her own merits but 30 years earlier it had been by the simple expedient of marrying a rising star of the Labour Party, Harry Ashbury, a champagne socialist whose relentless pursuit of position and friends of influence Margaret echoed to perfection. Who could forget those summer parties in the garden of their house on the edge of Hampstead Heath, the Bollinger flowing, cigar tips glowing in the dark beneath the trees as deals were struck and sometimes with a little help from the hostess, trysts arranged. Loyal to the party and the wife of an influential MP she was soon swept into those posts where her absence of academic qualifications or business experience was of no importance. What was of importance was not what she was but whom she'd become. Success bred success; success that knew no limits once she had been made a Dame, though no one was sure on what basis it was awarded. In recent years, eagerly sought for her title and connections, she had taken only those posts that paid very well for very little work. Her career model was Pamela Harriman, daughter in law of Winston Churchill and eventually US ambassador to France, admired for the sheer bravado with which she used her social skills, her charm and her willingness to be seduced to service her ambition. Margaret Ashbury acknowledged that she was not remotely in Harriman's league, she'd never really been able to use sex to get her way. It was not that men of power and influence did not try to get her into bed it was just that she wasn't willing to be bedded. It was nothing to do with moral scruples simply a basic distaste for the practicalities of sex...which extended even to her husband. How Pamela Harriman would have laughed; famous for her "extensive knowledge of the bedroom ceilings of the rich and famous". All Margaret Ashbury wanted was a divorce and a change of name. As her husband was now awaiting trial on charges of procuring underage girls for sex he'd become a liability and with him out of the cabinet, out of parliament and potentially in prison her chances of getting the peerage she so craved would be slim. "But" she thought getting up to check her hair in the mirror "I've still got my own friends in government so I may yet get there though I'll have to play the problem that's brought me here today very warily. I must be considered to have dealt firmly with the matter whilst not being seen anywhere near it. No photographs, no interviews, no press statements."

Hearing the ping of the lift arriving on the floor she went to unlock the outer door of the Executive Offices.

"Good morning Winston. Thank you for coming in on a Sunday."

Winston Arkwright was deliberately as informally dressed as he could contrive. A polo shirt, shorts and boat shoes with no socks.

"Morning Margaret... I'm assuming you wanted me here to decide how we're to handle this report from the Department of Health. They couriered a copy to me yesterday and of course I've read it through in detail, all of it not just the Executive Summary!"

Winston Arkwright was still standing and Margaret Ashbury sitting behind her desk. Normally they'd have sat in the two soft chairs by the window and she'd have asked him whether he would like coffee but there was no coffee on offer today. Winston noted the new frosty format and pulled up a chair to one side of the desk; not so close as to be familiar nor so distant as to seem subservient. "two can play at this game" he thought.

"And how do you think the hospital should respond to this?" she said pointing at the shiny, bound report resting at the centre of her desk.

"Oh I think we should welcome it don't you?" said Arkwright "but we don't need to do much except say our management style needs some fine tuning; say we will learn from the message in the report. It's all just political, they have to be seen to be listening to the whingers but what they actually want is for me to get on and deliver some headline goodies for them."

"Then I think, Winston, you have misread the document or misinterpreted its conclusions. I will read you some quotes" she picked up the report from the edge of which protruded half a dozen red markers.

"Staff gave multiple examples of the suppression of inconvenient information and the persistence of an inappropriate and aggressive management style."

"There has been widespread adoption of a blame culture."

"Middle management staff have begun emulating the aggressive management style displayed at the top of the organisation."

"A radical shift is required from a top down management style to a more collegiate form of working."

"The whole report is shot through with comments like this. In summary they are saying that the whole management culture here, starting at the top of the Executive, is wrong and must be changed. Their solution, which is not actually in the report, but which has been conveyed to me by the Minister is that you will need to resign from your post as CEO."

"But that's ridiculous!"

"No, it's what the Minister wants and it's what is going to happen."

"But I'm just being used as a scapegoat. The Department has put the pressure on Hospitals so much that they need people with my skills to deliver what they want, that's why they appointed me for Christ's sake. Now you say they want my resignation."

"Yes."

"And if I refuse?"

"Then I'm afraid Winston certain irregularities in the CV you submitted at the time of your appointment will, shall we say, come to light and the Board would then need to terminate your employment here with immediate effect and additionally, as you probably know, you could potentially face a criminal charge of 'obtaining pecuniary advantage by deception'."

Arkwright sprang to his feet, his face red, his fists clenched.

"The bastards!"

"They don't see it that way. The Department's report will be issued to the media today and embargoed until midnight. I want you to sign this letter of resignation now." She extracted a single sheet of paper from beneath the report and placed it in front of Arkwright. "Tomorrow will be the last day of your employment here so I would like you to brief the Executive Team at your morning meeting tomorrow and then be out of the building by midday. I hope that is clear."

"And who is supposed to replace me?"

"The Medical Director, Dr. Lightwood, will act as CEO until such time as a replacement is appointed."

"This is preposterous!"

"No Winston, it's the way it is."

Arkwright sat down sweating profusely, there was a long pause. Margaret Ashbury waited, her bony hands clasped patiently in front of her. Winston Arkwright looked out of the window, scrawled his signature gracelessly on the bottom of the letter, then stood up.

"Well, to hell with the lot of you then! And I'll be expecting a decent payoff."

"You'll need to discuss that with the HR director in the morning but in view of the likely response of the Press to all this you'll need to be satisfied with what's defined in your contract, no more. If we were to fire you you'd get nothing."

Arkwright knew the meeting was over, it was clear from her demeanour, so without a further word he walked out. Margaret Ashbury stood at the window and a few minutes later watched as he climbed into the yellow sports car he'd parked in the "Ambulances Only" bay by the main entrance to the hospital. She returned to her desk and phoned the Minister at home.

"Done" she said "just don't mention me in any press releases…as we agreed."

The next morning as Winston Arkwright entered the Committee Room at 8.30 for the weekly meeting of the Executive Team there was silence around the table. In front of every member of the team a copy of the Department of Health report and stapled to the front of each a brief note from the chairman of the Trust Board noting that 'To help the hospital revise its culture in the light of the report Winston Arkwright had generously proffered his resignation as CEO, which had been accepted with immediate effect.'

In fact Winston had earlier only skim read the report so he flicked through it again whilst the rest of the team read theirs.

"Winston, you don't have to go you know. It's all of us that's at fault" said The Director of Nursing plaintively, breaking the silence.

"I think it would be better for the Trust if I did" said Winston spreading his hands in a humble gesture of benefaction. "Besides, you will have seen my resignation in the papers this morning and heard the News. They wanted me on the 'Today' programme this morning but I thought it more important to be here with you, my friends and colleagues."

What he didn't admit was that the last thing he wanted on this day was a grilling from Jon Humphries that would certainly be aggressive and unsympathetic. He knew the format and admired the technique, but No, not today, or any day come to that.

"You will need to talk to the Press at some time though Winston". Samantha was standing at the door "they'll all be here soon with their microphones, their cameras, their vans with satellite dishes and their preconceptions! I've corralled the first few in my office. Security are keeping the rest out of the building. Come when you've finished here." He followed her into the corridor, grasped her arm.

"Samantha, what about us?"

"Us? I'm the Director of Public Relations, you are the ex-CEO. I'm staying."

"But when I left the last job you came with me."

"Winston. Your successor there was a woman! Anyway I'm in London now. I'm in a top job in a top place and looking forward to giving your successor Dr. Lightwood all the advantages of my considerable experience! Come and talk to the press when you're ready." At which she walked off down the corridor as firmly as any model on a catwalk, each high heeled shoe placed exactly in front of the other, her hips swivelling. Arkwright slunk back into the Meeting Room. He was in no mood even to look at the Agenda. Henry Lightwood had already, in the few moments that Winston had been absent, arranged himself pertly in the CEOs chair.

"Well it's over to you then Henry." And he left, went down an echoing back staircase to the car park in the basement, got into his BMW and drove out throwing his copy of the Report out of the window as he did so.

245

Monday September 29th, Paris

Lucien woke from a deep sleep with Lily whispering in his ear.

"Wake up Lucien, I've got something to show you that will give you enormous pleasure." He opened his eyes.

"Lily, there's nothing new to show me, every part of you gives me enormous pleasure!"

"No silly, look at this, on my laptop"

Lucien struggled fully awake, Lily had clearly been awake for some time and was sitting up in bed, her laptop open in front of her; open at the BBC news website.

'*Breaking News. NHS Flagship Hospital Chief Executive resigns in wake of critical Government report".*

There wasn't much more than the headline nevertheless the RUH and Winston Arkwright were clearly identified so there was no doubt.

"Lily that is fantastic. I cannot think of a better end to a wonderful weekend. My faith is restored."

"But does this mean that in spite of what you said yesterday you might want to go back to work at the hospital?"

" I honestly don't know but I do know that this weekend with you has shown me that if you start looking at life from a different vantage point you wonder why the hell you've led life the way you have."

"That's good. I wouldn't want you to think you'd just been here to keep me company. This morning however I'm going shopping on my own and then I'm off back to London. And you?"

Lucien had not expected quite such an abrupt end to the weekend. He'd expected to take her to the Gare du Nord for a traditional lovers' parting at the gate.

"Back to St Jean I suppose. When will I see you next?"

"When, as your solicitor I need to sort anything out with you to do with the CPS or the GMC. This was not the start of something Lucien. You know that. It was fun and now we both go back to our normal lives."

Later as he walked away back down the hill towards the Metro station, Montparnasse and St Jean he wondered if the last few days had actually happened, if the Hotel Marianne really existed. He wondered whether if he were to retrace his steps he would find no door in a garden wall, no garden. All perhaps just the fantasy of a confused 62 year old separated from his wife. What did he take away? Just the small bag he'd come with, the pyjamas he'd not worn, the phone he'd not turned on, the book he'd not opened but crucially also the realization that his life could indeed be lived differently and that were unused parts of his persona that were asking to be explored.

He walked down to the Metro station on Rue des Abbesses. He loved the Paris Metro infuriating as it might be with its steps and ugly angled corridors and its hot, crowded trains with over eager flip-up seats. But he loved the double tracks, the closeness to the surface, the air, the smells of streets and the glimpses of sunshine. He liked the way in some stations you could stand at the platform edge, peer into the tunnel and see the people standing on the platform of the next station. He liked the hiss of the trains that run on rubber tyres and the acerbic claxon warning of closing doors. It was all so specifically Paris Metro, there was nothing else like it. Today though all this was buoyed by the warm feelings left by his weekend and the surprising pleasures of his new freedom. Lucien was standing by the door of the train when a girl perhaps thirty-four weeks pregnant got on, glossy hair and a happy face; a blue striped, figure hugging T-shirt dress accentuating every joyous curve, the baby bulge, the breasts, the extra fullness of her hips. He realized that he was looking at her not as an obstetrician might but as a normal person would, sharing her pleasure. The obstetrician and the gynaecologist were not with him in Paris this weekend and it had not occurred to him to ask Lily whether she planned to have children, if so when and was she aware of the problems of delay? None of this had entered his head. Also he realized the topic of contraception had not been mentioned, he'd assumed she was on the pill. A dark thought sprang into his mind. Perhaps Lily did, indeed, want a child and had marked out Lucien as the father – the gene donor. It happened; he'd had patients who'd done it. What if Lily had simply arranged this weekend for that purpose. "Don't be silly Lucien." He could hear her voice laughing off an anxious enquiry. "Don't be silly Lucien, forget it" Anyway time to get off, here we are at

'Montparnasse Bienvenue'. 'Montparnasse Welcome' a stupid name for a Metro station, ill-named too as there is half kilometre walk from the Metro to the train station.

Monday Sept. 29th. London. Charlie's enquiries

The SO15 commander had called a meeting at short notice to update them on the progress of the Denmark Hill murder enquiry. John Fitzgerald sent Charlie O'Dwyer in his place to which the man from MI5 responded sniffily as if sending someone of lower rank in SIS was intended as a personal insult. Charlie barely noticed, the man was an ineffectual, chinless tosser anyway so Charlie didn't mind what he thought; in fact he enjoyed the man's irritation.

"These Libyans that we have had in custody for two weeks – it looks as if we are going to have to release them." Announced the SO15 Commander.

"You what?" expostulated Charlie

"We are going to have to release them. Firstly, ballistics cannot match the weapon we recovered from the toolbox in their van to the bullets recovered at the scene. Secondly, there are none of their prints or DNA on the weapon. We could charge one or both of them with possession of an unlicenced firearm but if they get a half decent brief it would be difficult to make it stick. There is nothing else we can hold them on. Simply receiving a call from this man Ghanem in Libya might allow us to hold them under anti-terrorist legislation but since Five have said we can't use their intercepts as evidence.

"Tell me, did anyone find the motorcycle?" asked Charlie O'Dwyer.

"No, and unfortunately, there is no registration number visible in any of the CCTV views."

"Which means the killers, their motorcycle and the weapon are still out there somewhere. But there must be a link with the Libyans you've got in custody because they received the call from Ghanem. Didn't they cough up anything when they were interrogated? You've had them for two weeks."

"Nothing, but I guess they were more frightened of this man Ghanem than of us even though he's now dead. We did tell them that he'd been assassinated and that it was now okay to talk to us but that didn't persuade them."

The man from MI5 had been sitting superciliously quiet during this exchange.

"The answer, before you ask whether we have records of any contacts of the two you arrested is that no, we don't."

"Then are you going to start looking?"

The MI5 man looked witheringly at O'Dwyer.

"Clearly you have no idea how complex such an enquiry would be. It's out of the question. If we thought they might be Al-Qaeda sympathisers or home grown Islamists out to kill just anyone then that might alter things, but they are not. Maybe you could make some enquires in Libya when you go back; I understand you are a junior member of staff at the Embassy there."

Charlie ignored him. The meeting limped on for another twenty minutes but by the time it was finished it was obvious to Charlie that the police had no leads and MI5 had no inclination to help. He'd have to make some enquires himself though he only had one more week before he was due to return to Tripoli. At least John Fitzgerald would be sympathetic if only because there was the prospect of getting one up on MI5.

"Charlie for God's sake be careful" said John Fitzgerald the next morning "So far no-one has worked out where the story about Ashbury and Haviland's peccadilloes came from but we need to keep below the radar for a bit."

To Charlie 'keeping below the radar' meant not telling anyone what he was up to and not logging it on his computer. So that afternoon he took an undocumented trip up the Edgeware Road on his motorbike. North of the flyover where the M40 traffic as last reaches the end of the Marylebone Road the character of Edgeware Road changes, heading progressively down market and becoming an uninspiring confection of small, scruffy shops along a road perpetually choked by slow moving traffic, the bus lane obstructed by delivery vans. A Halal butcher, a KFC, Ali's Travel, the Walwajid supermarket ('we sell hot nuts'), car parts, electrical shops with the signs in Arabic, currency exchanges and this is all to feed the poor end of the Arab market, Iran, Iraq, North Africa. The kebab shop was closed up, no note in the door to explain why. The windows of the two floors above were obscured by dirty net curtains and the door beside the shop had a cobweb across the corner and no marks in the dust around the keyhole or on the handle. If the killers came from here – and Charlie had no proof that they did apart from the one phone call from Ghanem – they'd gone. Time to do his own detective work. He crossed the road and went into the Ali-Baba shisha lounge; apart from the man behind the bar it was deserted. Dark, heavy velvet curtains cut out most of the light; the rest was absorbed by the stained red flock wallpaper. Most of the illumination came from lights above the glass shelves of the bar and from lighted alcoves in each of which were displayed brass and coloured glass, silk tassled hookahs, shisha pipes.

"Can I help you Sir?" the barman was North African, curly black hair, black eyebrows and a dazzling set of smiling white teeth.

"A tea please."

"English tea?"

"No, mint tea please, *Chai bil n'ana*" he used the proper Arabic not dialect.

"You speak Arabic?"

"Not much but I like to wander up and down the Edgeware Road occasionally to remind me how it sounds, how the food tastes. By the way what's happened to the kebab shop across the road?"

"Rashid's. I don't know, it hasn't been open for a couple of weeks."

"Are the boys still around?" Charlie knew this was a gamble based on a hunch.

"The boys? Oh, you mean Mohammed and Hisham; no they disappeared too. They used to come in here on Saturday nights when we had the belly dancer but they haven't been here for a month or so. Maybe it's because the place is almost dead now, people have stopped coming since the law about smoking in public places came in and they told us our customers can only smoke the shisha outside and who'd want to do that on the pavement of the Edgeware Road with the buses going by?" He'd been making the tea and now poured it expertly into the little glass raising the kettle as he did, his aim perfect. "Would you like a pastry to go with that?"

"Great, have you any Balghas?"

"Baboushes" said the barman using the French "Sure help yourself" putting the plate on the bar.

Charlie helped himself to two of the little slipper shaped pastries.

"I'm sorry Mohammed and Hisham aren't around I used to enjoy talking to them about motorbikes." Another gamble.

"Yeah, it was Hisham's actually but they shared it. I think he got a new one recently. Just before I last saw them actually."

The barman seemed happy to chat but there wasn't any more information to be had so after a second cup of mint tea Charlie left. Mohammed and Hisham, that was a start. Charlie weaved his way through the traffic to Marble Arch then broke the speed limit down Park Lane out of sheer joie de vivre. Back in the office at MI6 he turned on his computer and began to search. Electoral Roll? No-one recorded as resident at the kebab shop's address. No point looking in the census, anyway the last one was in 2001 too long ago. What next? Brain wave! He phoned Westminster Council Environmental Health purporting to be from the Home Office.

"We believe that some workers at a kebab shop in your borough may not have the right to work in the UK."

"Well that would apply to almost everyone in the restaurant business here! Anyway it's none of our business we just inspect."

"Exactly. I believe complaints have been made about the particular kebab shop we are interested in and you will therefore have inspected it. You keep these records presumably and you will have recorded the names of the staff in the food outlet."

And within minutes he had the names and dates of birth. Mohammed Al Mahdi aged twenty and Hisham Homeri aged twenty-two, same address as the kebab shop. He was on a roll. Now he phoned the real Home Office. No need for pretence this time it was his regular contact in the Border Agency that he was speaking to, 'Audrey the Arab' as she was known. An English mother, an Egyptian father, a childhood in the politest parts of Alexandria and an adult life spent entirely working for the UK government outfoxing people who didn't realise she could speak their language with absolute and colloquial fluency. Charlie could visualise her dyed black hair and her black rimmed, purple tinted specs hunched over the computer terminal, phone in hand.

"Hello Charlie darling, what can we do for you today?"

O'Dwyer gave her all the details he had. Ten minutes later she called him back.

"They're both Libyan, both entered the UK on the same day four years ago on one year student visas for the Charrington School of English in Oxford Street and surprise, surprise forgot to go home.

252

No contact details or addresses in the UK. There doesn't seem to have been any attempt to determine if they were a terrorist risk so they were ignored – low down on our list of 100,000 or so visa over-stayers. I'm sorry I can't help any more. There's not much on file but I'll get out the original paperwork and see if I can add some background."

As efficient as ever she was on the phone again half an hour later.

"I've got out all the original paperwork on these two lads you are interested in. The only thing that might interest you is that the older one, Hisham, has a father you probably know. Zahir al-Ghanem, Head of Security for Ghaddafi's household and brother of that chap who was assassinated recently Gamal Ghanem."

Charlie phoned The Charrington School of English and was not surprised to find the elusive Mohammed and Hisham had failed to show up for their course and no, that had not been reported to the Home Office. No address on file. Probably nothing on file thought Charlie except the receipt of the fee and the issuing of a letter to get the visas. All bloody corrupt the lot of them. One last grain of an idea. The motorbike. Charlie had noted a motorbike dealer a couple of doors down the Edgeware Road from kebab shop. Back on his motorbike, back up Park Lane too fast, he parked the bike around the corner and went into the shop 'John the Bike' and flashed a warrant card purporting to show him as a Metropolitan Police Officer. The owner of the shop had a big scar on his face, a shaven head and a tattooed line around his neck marked 'cut here'. He seemed unsurprised by a visit from the police. It was certainly not his first.

"I understand that a Mr. Hisham Homeri part-exchanged a bike here probably on or just after August 1st. We are interested in the details of the bike and any subsequent motorbike that he purchased from you."

"What? You think it's a stolen bike? I hope not I've still got it here."

"Good. Then I need to see the details in your records please and don't touch or sell the bike that you part exchanged until my forensic colleagues have visited to inspect it."

And within five minutes Charlie was outside with descriptions of the previous motorbike and the new motorbike and their registration numbers but he still had no phone number and no address for Hisham

Homeri or Mohammed Al Mahdi other than the empty kebab shop.
Enough for today.

At 08.30 the next morning sealed in John Fitzgerald's office
Charlie O'Dwyer proudly explained what he'd discovered.

"They ought to put me in charge of Five, all that info in just a few
hours and they hadn't a clue."

John Fitzgerald was unimpressed.

"Before you get too smug Charlie just remember that you've not
got anything that'll help find them; no address, no phone number, no
computer details just the number of the motorbike which may not be
much use as often it doesn't show on the cameras."

"OK, OK, but we do know who they are and where the previous
bike is."

"Well that's a start I agree. I'll call SO15 with that when we've
finished. Now that Ghanem is dead I presume they'll not still be
after your man McCullock though you'd better update him."

Charlie looked pensive.

"He's probably not at risk but one of the motorcycle men is the
nephew of Ghanem and completing Ghanem's orders may be a
matter of honour for him. You know what these guys are like when
family honour is at stake."

Back at his desk Charlie called the McCulloch home in Dulwich,
Diana McCulloch answered.

"Oh, hello. My husband has told me all about you" and then
without explaining why, she recounted that Lucien was in France
"for a while" but she expected him back for a couple of days soon.

"I'll need to talk to him before then – perhaps you'd get him to
call me."

"By the way I don't know whether it's important but a couple of
nice young men came to the door looking for him this morning."

"What sort of young men?" asked Charlie.

"North Africans of some sort I'd guess. Said they had a present
for him from a friend in Tripoli and wanted to deliver it personally."

"And did you tell them when he'd be back?"

"Oh yes, next weekend. I'll be away at a conference myself but
he'll probably be home for some of the time to look at his mail and
sort some things out."

Wednesday October 1st, Bergerac. Lunch with Anna.

The town was busy and the restaurants full by just after midday as the long French lunch break swung into its daily routine. Lucien was glad to avoid the tourist restaurants in the Place Pelissiere, a pretty enough square sloping down from Saint Jacques church. Instead he headed through a back alley to the Vigne D'Or restaurant hidden in one of the secret courtyards that open off the medieval streets of the old Quartier where Anna was waiting. She appeared to have the ear of Jacques the restaurateur for the best table suddenly became available and Lucien noted that Jacques' kiss was a little more considered and prolonged then required by simple politeness.

"I prefer this table by the window away from the door. Jacques always keeps it until twelve fifteen. If I don't appear he lets someone else have it; it's a nice arrangement which saves me booking."

Lucien noticed that the table was set for two and wondered who normally joined her for lunch. Without seemingly having been ordered two champagne cocktails appeared on the table and small plate of *amuse bouche* canapés.

"Didn't you do any shopping in the market" asked Anna.

"I've left it in the car down by the river."

"Good, you can give me a lift home after lunch."

"Didn't you drive?"

"No I don't drive. Franck brought me in; he's very good at looking after all my needs" she said without obvious irony or *double-entendre*.

"So what do a beautiful chatelaine and a currently unattached, unemployed gynaecologist talk about when they meet for lunch?" asked Lucien. This was a bit cheeky, a bit glib but he felt animated and somehow licensed after his weekend in Paris, so why not.

"I thought we were going to talk about your aspirations as a wine maker, but maybe we should find out about each other first. You start."

"You look very Mediterranean, are your parents both English?"

"My mother was Italian; she's dead now and yours?"

"My mother is French. Still alive, lives in Pau. Did you have job before you married Hector?"

"I worked in the Courtauld Gallery in London as an arts administrator. It's near Lincoln's Inn, that's how I met Hector, in a pub on The Strand. Have you done every done anything except be a doctor?"

"Not yet."

And so it went on Q and A, to and fro like a long rally in tennis. Factual not personal until Anna suddenly asked

"How do you view yourself?"

"What do you mean?"

"Just what I said. When you look at yourself, you the person from the outside, what do you see or maybe more importantly what sort of person would you rather see. Hero, actor, intellectual, lover?"

Lucien thought for a moment or two, tapping his knife on the table like a metronome.

"Well I'm a loyal husband when I'm allowed to be. I'm a hard working doctor, someone who cares about people and wants to help them."

"You mean worthy but dull!"

"I suppose so."

"Enough to get you into the Kingdom of Heaven but maybe not much fun. So Lucien…. now that the husband and the doctor roles are denied you perhaps you feel a bit washed up, washed up on the shores of a desert island having to decide what to do to keep yourself alive?"

She was taunting him just a little, a half smile and wrinkled eyes as she twirled the wine in her glass. Apart from leading the life he'd always led Lucien had no particular plan, certainly no overwhelming ambition – he wished he had. So instead they talked about food, how best to cook a duck breast, why the French do not eat chutney, had he tried Madame Hulot's cherries in Armagnac and then they talked about the chateau and the long and expensive struggle to bring it back to its past glory. Perhaps if Hector's clients had seen the restored panelling in the library, the re-carved stone doorways, the waxed chestnut floorboards, the perfectly clipped box bushes or the lemon trees in their Jardinières they would not have resented so much his enormous fees.

"Enough of all that we need to talk about your plans to make wine."

"Ideally what I'd like to do is make either a really good red or a fantastically good sweet white."

"A sweet white, a *vin liquoreux*? Lucien, that means you are very rich with money to burn or very ignorant."

"But our village is half way between Monbazillac and Saussignac and they both make world class sweet white! Why couldn't we do that in St. Jean?"

Anna looked pained, like a school mistress taxed by an enthusiastic but not very bright pupil. She walked over to the side of the restaurant and came back with a wine list. The restaurant's list was long and sheathed in a russet leather folder embellished with a gold tassel.

"Here are the Monbazillac wines – look at the prices. Less than 30 euros a bottle and that's restaurant prices, If the producteur gets even half that he's lucky. It's cheaper than a good St. Emilion red or a very good Bergerac red. The difference is that the time and effort required to make the *vin liquoreux* is maybe three or four times that for a normal wine and the yields per hectare are much lower. It's not a way to make a wine that only a few people want to drink. It's almost impossible to make it pay."

"I thought you just waited for the grapes to get mildew on them before picking; what's it called? 'noble rot'?"

"Botrytis. It makes the grapes shrink and increases the sugar content and imparts a particularly unique taste to the wine. It happens at the end of the season and it doesn't affect all the grapes in a bunch so you have to pick them individually and at different times. You have to know which ones to pick which is a difficult skill to acquire. Also if it's too dry there's no botrysation, if it's too wet it dilutes the sugar and the grapes just rot. What you need is that magical early autumn weather of cool, foggy mornings and warm, sunny afternoons. Those days when everything seems gold in the evening light; the wine too is golden. It's a labour of love and it needs a lot of experience – which you don't have and neither do I actually. Also, by the way, you need Semillon, Muscadelle and Sauvignon grapes none of which you grow! Have I said enough?"

"You're not very encouraging."

"There is nothing more dangerous than romantic over-expectation, you know that don't you?"

"It's just romantic optimism in my case, but I'm getting your message that on balance the chance of my being able to make wine from my few hectares seems slim."

There was silence for a moment. The desserts were brought.

"If wine isn't one's métier there is not much else around here to do" said Lucien with a shrug "so perhaps I'll just retire, live the quiet live and grow vegetables."

"On your own? I doubt it." And they lapsed into silence again both of them living on their own so both reviewing the possibilities.

"Shame about the *vin liquoreux*; it seemed a good idea. I'm sure if one is to make a new life one must have a passion and a specific, new, hard to achieve objective. In my case though probably not *vin liquoreux.*"

"No, you'll need a different object for your passions, a woman perhaps."

She raised her eyebrows and almost imperceptibly pursed her lips into a half kiss which Lucien affected not to have noticed. Her eyes were crinkled into a smile so he was unsure what to take from her comment. She was still toying with him.

"Would you like a *digestif* with you coffee?" he asked.

Anna was not so easily distracted.

"Are you coping on your own? Is someone cooking for you?"

"Thanks for your concern. Actually I'm not a bad cook and I enjoy it though to be honest there's not a lot of pleasure in cooking for one and more often than not I end up at the Café eating whatever Jean Luc has concocted."

"Why don't you ask me to lunch then!"

"I'm off to London on Friday for a few days but I'll be back on Sunday. How about Monday?"

"I'll be there, I'll bring a Tarte Citron from the patisserie."

Saturday October 4th. Lucien in London

Lucien wasn't entirely sure that he wanted to go to the house in Dulwich. He knew there were things to be sorted out there….that was all he would do. More importantly he'd been able to see Lucy. She'd met him at the airport with a tear, a trembling lip and a long hug but once they were in her little Fiat buzzing down the M11 bound for her flat in Highgate, she was bright and chatty and Diana was barely mentioned. It was all about the present and the future. "How was St. Jean? Was it sunny there? When are you going back to work? Shall we go flat hunting this weekend?"

Lucien didn't consider it a father's role to be other than upbeat and positive with his daughter so none of his uncertainties about his future were allowed to surface. Lucy had offered to go to Dulwich with him but he wanted to be alone for the visit, unclear how he'd respond to being back in an environment he'd blanked from his mind for over a month; blanked so successfully that it might not have existed. There was also the brief phone call from Charles O'Dwyer, now back in Libya, updating him and warning him to be wary this weekend if he went home. "Call the police immediately if you see anything suspicious."

Lucien stopped under a tree on the opposite side of the road about two hundred yards from the house. Everything seemed quiet. It was odd to be so hesitant about approaching a place he'd lived in for the last twenty-five years but there it was, not beckoning him just there. Neutral. A double fronted, two-storey Edwardian house, a low brick wall, a privet hedge and a Japanese maple tree in the middle of the small front lawn. He looked up and down the street. A couple of vans and a few cars were parked but no motorcycles, no pedestrians either. He walked briskly to the house and let himself in. A man in a blue van parked further along the road got out and stood beside the van his phone in his hand.

The burglar alarm was not on and the mortise lock had not been used. That was odd. From the hallway Lucien could hear that the television was on in the lounge. Football and very loud. He pushed open the door quietly, a tall man with sandy hair wearing a polo shirt and slacks was lounging on the sofa, a can of beer in his hand, his feet on the coffee table, he didn't look dangerous.

"Who the hell are you?" asked Lucien. The man looked appropriately surprised and alarmed.

"Err, umm hello I'm Colin Brown, are you Mr. McCulloch?"

"I am and please take your feet off the coffee table, it's an heirloom and it's fragile."

"Err, sorry okay."

"And what are you doing here?"

"Err; I'm a friend of Diana."

"Does she know you're here?"

"Not really... she's away this weekend.... I'm err, err, house-sitting."

Lucien felt anger rising, an unaccustomed emotion for him. Not angry with his man in particular, he seemed innocuous; just angry that this should be happening in his house without him knowing. The feet on the coffee table, Lucien's table, implying that Lucien was no longer the master.

"Well the house sit is over" said Lucien turning off the TV. "Would you leave please, this is my house not yours."

"But Diana....."

"My house! Leave now please."

And Colin left meekly, his unfinished beer in his hand. Lucien kicked the front door shut. The anger turned quickly to distress "It's my house, our house, our house" he said out loud. The pictures we bought together, the fabrics we chose, the wallpaper we decided on after weeks of sorting through sample books hand in hand like newlyweds. Our bloody house. The grandfather clock tick-tocked gently in the hallway one beat per second, sixty a minute softening his heart rate. He'd brought that clock for Diana on the day they moved into this house. The house was as he'd left it when he walked out just a month ago. It seemed unreal, as if he could just stay here and the month would be expunged. Diana would come home from her conference tomorrow, greet him with a kiss, they'd have supper, watch some TV, go to bed and then on Monday he'd go to work.... same as usual. He shook his head to clear the image. He was here to sort out his mail, collect a few things and go. Get real Lucien.

There was no mail for him in the hall just a buff envelope for Diana marked 'Confidential. Only to be opened by the addressee'. On the back King's College Hospital was identified as the sender. Lucien didn't open it but put it on the kitchen table propped up on the biscuit tin. Lucien had a study at the back of the house converted from an old utility room but it had a window and a door onto the garden and it was his space; it had his books on the shelves, his certificates on the wall, it was his own space and no-one had moved anything. Entering the room was a simple pleasure; the pleasure of being back in his own territory in what Americans would call his 'den'. He sat at his desk, drew his fingertips across the familiar grain of the leather desk top. In the garden the annuals in the border had 'gone over'; work was needed. He looked around the room calmly and happily. The books, the familiar box files, the picture of Lucy and Robin arm in arm as teenagers, in a gap on the shelf nested the photo montage Diana had made and framed of Lucien receiving his CBE from the Queen, Lucien at The United Nations with Kofi Annan, a wedding photo and pictures of family on the steps of the Le Vieux Tour on the day they moved in. How far away St. Jean seemed. Amongst the mail was a large envelope unmistakably addressed in Pam his secretary's hand presumably containing his mail from the hospital. He felt a surge of curiosity and wondered what was in there; he gathered up the envelope and the few letters that were not junk mail put them in an old briefcase along with his laptop. He'd been intending also to collect some clothes but couldn't face going upstairs to the bedroom. The bed perhaps unmade, soiled. Another man's clothes on the chair, another man's book on the bedside table. He left the house. He'd been there a mere thirty minutes. His departure was noted by the man in the blue van.

Sunday October 5th. Dulwich

Sunday afternoon. Lucien was on his way to the airport for the plane to Bergerac. In Dulwich Colin, undaunted, was back at the McCulloch home letting himself in with the shiny, newly cut key Diana had given him; the sort of love token Colin cherished. Diana had seemed rather cool this week so Colin was doubly determined to play the part of the useful man friend. He didn't want Diana to abandon him as easily as had his wife. He wanted, as he put it, "to make a go of it" with Diana, not understanding that for Diana the option of temporariness was the appeal. Subliminally aware of his shortcomings in the kitchen he'd spent a careful hour in Waitrose collecting all the components of what he imagined would be a grand welcome home dinner for Diana when she returned tired from her conference. A bottle of Prosecco, a pack of smoked salmon, a sliced brown loaf (he knew you had to cut the crust off, butter the slices and then cut them into triangles to eat with the smoked salmon), a box of organic vegetarian lasagne that could be re-heated in the microwave and to go with it a pre-dressed salad in a discus of clear plastic. Then some trifle in a plastic pot like a goldfish bowl. He'd been careful to keep it upright on the car seat so the pattern of cream piped onto the top was not spoiled. Then (and he was particularly pleased with this) the cheeses: plastic wrapped squares of Leicester, Cheddar and Stilton snug in a little basket with some crackers, the whole engulfed in a sachet of cellophane with a pink bow at the top. And to finish he'd make coffee from the expensive, fair-trade, Ecuadorian freeze-dried coffee he'd bought. He'd noted brandy in the cupboard in the lounge. Perfect. All in all a dinner to amaze and enchant her or so he hoped. Having carefully installed his ingredients in the fridge he went back to the lounge opened the Sunday Telegraph and put his feet up on the coffee table. He was damned if the unwelcome and angry appearance of her ex-husband was going to frighten him away. Diana didn't know he'd be here but she'd given him a key, what clearer evidence of a right to be there could one ask for?

Outside it was quiet, unusually quiet, for a Sunday. A man was cleaning a blue van parked in the driveway opposite and further down the street some contract gardeners were cutting the hedge and hoeing the flowerbeds. Colin's hearing was slightly less than perfect – actually the effect of age but he attributed it to the more glamorous dangers of playing in a jazz band – so he didn't hear a motorcycle stop at the gate or hear the pillion passenger still with his helmet on come to the front door unbuttoning his leather jacket. The man cleaning the van on the other side of the road did, he banged the side of the van and spoke urgently into a microphone attached to his collar. Colin heard the doorbell, looked at his watch and assuming Diana has returned early went to the front door and flung it open. The huge smile of his face disappearing instantly as he was confronted by a man in a black helmet and a leather jacket pointing a gun at his face.

"Mr. McCulloch?"

"No, no I'm just a friend, a friend of the family."

"You look like Mr. McCulloch…" The man twisted around as he heard the motorcycle engine gunning and within that single turning motion encompassed the sight of half a dozen men in baseball caps approaching at the run, weapons in their hands, two others rising from behind a car, carbines with telescopic sights trained on his head. The sound of the motorcycle was loud but still audible as was the amplified "Armed Police, stand still, drop your weapon!" then a crash as the motorcycle hit the van that was reversing out of the driveway two doors away to block the road. Distracted he turned toward the sound but within a fraction of a second, realizing the danger of movement, let go of his gun and dropped to the ground. Too late. One of the standing men fired three shots in quick succession but the target had gone, instead there was Colin reflexly slamming the door. Three bullets passed where the motorcyclist's chest should have been and smacked into the door splintering the wood, one ricocheted into Colin's shoulder. Colin dropped to the ground with a shriek just as the police reached the door handguns pointing at the now prone motorcyclist.

"Why the fuck did you open the door your stupid bugger?" shouted the man with the carbine, later during the enquiry to be identified as Officer 16, only two weeks into his posting with SO15.

"Help me" said Colin wiping blood from his face which had been cut by splinters of wood from the door.

"And who are you?" asked another officer. A man with a video camera crouched down behind him for a better view.

"I'm a friend of Mrs. McCulloch."

"Does she know you're here?"

"No."

"Your own bloody fault then, the house is meant to be empty. Just sit there quietly an ambulance will be here shortly."

The video cameraman had shifted to the motorcyclist lying prone on the front path his arms now handcuffed behind him. He videoed the man, then the gun lying in the grass, then the policeman taking off the man's helmet and squatting down beside him.

"Is your name Hisham Homeri?" The man nodded.

"Do you speak English?" The man nodded again. "Then you will understand when I tell you that you're under arrest. You do not need to say anything but anything you do say will be taken down and may be used in evidence. Do you understand?" The man nodded again.

"Is my friend okay?"

"He'll live; he was trying to leave without you - not much honour there eh?"

The street was now a melee of vehicles. An ambulance, three police cars, marked and unmarked police vans and amongst them uniformed police on foot reassuring neighbours and the curious, chivvying them back into their houses or behind the blue and white plastic tapes that were being stretched from tree to tree around the front of the house. A black Range Rover with a removable blue light on its roof coasted to a halt and the SO15 commander in sports jacket and cavalry twill trousers, summoned from his Sunday golf, got out. The Video cameraman did not record him being briefed. He beckoned over Officer 16, the marksman, who'd narrowly missed killing the hapless Colin.

"Didn't they tell you that when covering a suspect you make sure there is no-one standing behind him?"

"Yes sir, I'm sorry sir I let the team down."

The commander put his hand on the man's shoulder

"I doubt if you'll do it again. It's your first operation and I know the stress of these encounters. The do-gooders at the Police Complaints Authority might like to have a go at you so when you've drafted your statement and before anyone else sees it, send it to me so that I can check that the right words are being used okay? Also you'd better take a couple of days leave."

"Yes sir, thank you sir."

"You and the team have done well. You've apprehended a probable murderer and prevented someone being killed. Live and learn. Live and learn."

Then he walked back to the Range Rover, took the blue beacon off the roof and drove away. End of operation.

When Diana arrived home three hours later everything had returned almost to normal. Access to her house was closed off with blue and white plastic tape; a bored WPC beat officer was standing guard at the gate, her colleague sitting in their car eating a sandwich. Diana saw all this as she came down the road. She knew something had happened at her house and broke into a run, her wheeled suitcase bumping erratically over the paving slabs.

"Sorry Madam but you can't come in here it's a crime scene."

"But this is my house, I'm Diana McCulloch. What's happened?!"

"If you're Mrs. McCulloch you'll have to show me some ID please."

"What's happened ?" Diana repeated.

"We've had a shooting here this afternoon."

"Oh God! My husband is his okay? Where is he?"

"He's not badly injured he's in King's A&E Observation Ward, that's all I'm able to say at the moment."

They let Diana leave her case at the house and the other PC having finished his sandwich drove her to King's College Hospital where after twenty minutes confusion looking anxiously for a Lucien McCulloch the staff eventually realized it was Colin Brown she was looking for, a bewildered Colin too sorry for himself to be able to play the hero.

"Our supper's in the fridge" was the best he could manage as they stood outside the hospital and he hailed a taxi with the arm that wasn't in a sling. He'd not been badly injured and Diana's sympathy was limited, so later that evening after eating as much as she could stomach of Colin's specially contrived dinner she put him in her car and drove him to his flat before returning home on her own to inspect the door from which two bullets had been prised by the forensic team and to grieve over the grandfather clock in the hallway the glass of whose face had been broken by the bullet that had just passed through the muscle of the arm just below Colin's shoulder. She was more concerned for the clock than for Colin.

Monday October 6th. Lucien phones Diana

"Have you seen the papers today?" Lucien was half way through lunch with Anna at Le Vieux Tour when the phone had rung. It was someone called Fitzgerald who said he was a colleague of Charles O'Dwyer. " I thought that you'd like to know that he police appear to have caught your would be assassin outside your house in Dulwich yesterday afternoon though unfortunately in the fracas someone was shot, not your assassin."

"Good God, Who?"

"Not your wife - a man - I don't have any details I'm afraid but it'll be on the Internet, in the papers and on the radio. Do you not have these?"

"No – it may seem strange but no I don't."

"We'll go over to the Chateau with your laptop; we've got wi-fi there" offered Anna and half an hour later he knew as much as anyone else about the events in Dulwich the previous afternoon.

"Who's this Colin Brown?" asked Anna.

"He claimed to be just Diana's friend but I guess he must be her current lover."

"She'll be upset then. Shouldn't you phone her ?"

Phoning one's estranged wife to console her because her lover has been shot didn't seem to be a priority but phoning her because she might be distressed? That was different.

She answered on the first ring. He asked how she was.

"I'm fine. The carpenter is here fixing the front door and the police have gone."

"And your friend?"

"He's OK. It was his own fault. I'm more sorry for the policeman who shot him."

"Anything you want me to do?"

"No, nothing thanks. Look I'm just going out perhaps we can talk another time" and she hung up leaving Lucien to wonder why he'd phoned. Unbidden all the hurt and dismay of his separation came flooding back; everything that he thought he'd risen above. He sat silently for a moment the phone still in his hand. Anna put her hand on his shoulder.

"Come on Lucien, we'll get the dogs and go for a walk."
"There's something she's not telling me."
"She's an adult Lucien. She'll tell you if she wants to."

Friday October 10th. King's College Hospital, London

Wednesday had not been a good day for Diana. She felt embarrassed that in her early enthusiasm for Colin she'd given him a key to the house. The consequences of him spending the weekend there uninvited were mostly his fault and she was sorry about his injuries, though only sorry in a neighbourly sort of way, not sorry enough to distract her from telling him that their affair was now over and that she'd like her key back please. If she'd believed that her new freedom would make moving on any easier she was mistaken; Colin was in his own words "gutted" and weepy too.

"What have I done wrong to deserve this" he begged" last week you were all over me like a rash and now you want your key back. It's not fair, you're a … a…" He couldn't find the right words… "you're a loose woman, just a trollop; you're not safe to have around and I'm going to make sure everyone at school knows that". He huffed and he puffed but it only made Diana more certain that divesting herself of Colin was the right move. She'd need to be more selective next time.

And then there was the letter from King's College Hospital, the one Lucien had left unopened on the kitchen table. She'd been for a routine screening mammogram in the previous week, they'd always been OK in the past so she assumed this one would be too but the letter told her that more tests were required and she should attend the Breast Clinic at King's on Friday. She knew that if Lucien had been at home he'd have explained it all, hugged her, and reassured her but now she had no one to do that. Perhaps she could phone Lucy. No she wouldn't do that, she was an independent educated woman, she could manage this perfectly well on her own. She did however open a bottle of wine to have with her supper even though normally she was careful never to drink alone.

Now it was Friday morning and she was on her own at King's waiting to be seen in the clinic. The eight rows of eight blue plastic chairs that filled the centre of the room were full; the late arrivers queuing to register with the single clerk at the desk would have to stand. Around the walls hung framed pictures of trees, branches and leaves presumably there to cheer up the patients but their sequence from new bud through full leaf to brown and crinkly autumn and finally a bare winter twig might have seemed too threateningly symbolic of life's transience had anyone looked. In fact all eyes were on the TV screen slung obliquely across the corner of the room at ceiling height. The sound had been turned so low that no one could hear it. It was a daytime repeat of 'Come Dine with me', 'Deal or no Deal' maybe even 'Cash in the Attic'. It didn't really matter, most people just looked up blankly at the screen. Every few minutes a nurse would pop out of one of the row of doors that ran along the side of the clinic, announce a name and usher a woman in to see the doctor. Diana, trying hard to be somewhere else at least in her head, was so self-consciously engrossed in her copy of The New Statesman that her name had to be called three times before she responded.

The doctor, a woman no older than Lucy was straightforward.

"Your left breast is abnormal on the recent mammograms- different from the images taken two years ago. I'll need to examine your breasts, then we'll send you off for an ultrasound scan." She examined Diana's breasts, felt under her arm, palpated for her liver . Diana watched her face anxiously as she did it trying to divine what she'd found. Good or bad? The doctor was careful to betray nothing.

"You do have a lump on the left – about the size of a grape. If the ultrasound scan shows it's solid not a cyst they'll take some biopsies with a needle. They'll put some local anaesthetic in – you won't feel it. I'll see you back here later this morning. Here are the forms for the test. Nurse will tell you where to go" and with that she was out of the room, just another package moving along an implacable conveyor belt towards one of two outcomes, cancer or no cancer.

Within an hour she was back in front of the doctor supporting a now painful breast with her hand. The doctor swivelled her chair from the computer screen to face Diana.

"You'll have deduced from the biopsies that the lump was not a cyst but is solid and has the appearance of a cancer though we can't be sure about that until we have the biopsy results next week. You'll certainly need to have the lump removed then probably some radiotherapy to the breast and maybe some chemotherapy. If we need to do all those things then the treatment will take six to eight months."

"Will I need to lose my breast?" Diana was struggling to remain objective whilst a little voice in her head wailed "cancer, it's cancer, I'm going to die".

"Probably not. You'd only need that if analysis of the surgical excision specimen showed the cancer to be more widespread than it appears on the scans. And now I think it would be helpful for you to talk all this through with the nurse counsellor; she'll take you next door for that. I'd like to see you again next week to discuss the biopsy results and fix a date for the operation. Okay?" The doctor leaned her head to one side and gave the big consoling smile reserved for this situation. Without waiting for a reply she handed Diana to the nurse who had been sitting at the end of the desk listening. They went into the next door room, bleak, identically uncomforting. There was nothing on the desk except a phone and a box of tissues. The nurse gently pushed the box of tissues towards Diana, inviting her to weep if she wished to. She didn't; she'd do that on her own later at home. The nurse took it all a lot more slowly than the doctor had, repeated it all making sure Diana had a chance to respond. She'd heard every question and every reaction so many times before it was difficult to stay genuine and not descend to formulaic responses. Sometimes it was easier to comfort when the patient let out their emotions. She could see that was not about to happen with Mrs. McCulloch.

"If I have chemotherapy will I lose my hair?"

"It depends on the particular drugs used but you probably will, but it grows back and modern wigs look great" she added brightly. "Next week" she said as the session ended "it might be best to bring your partner with you. They usually have lots of questions of their own and they may remember better what we tell you. Now before you go here are some pamphlets to take home and look at. One on Cancer, one on Radiotherapy and another on Chemotherapy."

'Oh my darling Lucien how badly I need you now' thought Diana to herself reaching for the box of tissues. "Actually my husband and I are living apart at present. I 'll see if my daughter can come with me if that's OK."

October 10th-13th. The Vendange, St Jean

After a wet end to September the first week of October had been hot and sunny and the prospects for the grapes were improving daily, but it was October and everyone was anxiously aware that the good weather might break at any time so the Vendange was soon underway. The most timid picked first and those who gambled on the weather were this year rewarded by riper, sugar laden fruit. At the chateau Franck and Victor planned to get all the grapes picked in one four day sprint over the weekend of 10th to 13th October. Two thirds of the picking at the chateau was mechanical, done by a gangly machine that bestrode the rows of vines and trundled to and fro, the vines shaken and tweaked to knock the ripe grapes onto a chain of trays passing underneath then at the end of the rows disgorged into a trailer to be taken back and emptied onto the sorting trays so the worst of the leaf debris, stalks and rotten grapes could be picked out before the harvest went into the destemming machine. To make the chateau's best wines the grapes were picked by hand, each bunch cut off from the vine with secateurs and dropped into a plastic basket and then the next, and then the next, and then the next. It was back breaking work as the grapes hang low on the vine. Hard, unending work but at least after that they didn't have to tread the grapes though there was still plenty of hard work to do as Lucien quickly discovered.

Victor and Franck wanted him to experience every aspect of the business and by lunch on the first day he was tired, sweaty and dusty, his hands sticky with grape juice. On the second day his legs and shoulders ached so much he wondered if he would ever be normal again and there was little respite. Picking was done early in the morning and in the evening when the grapes were cool. The other work continued late into the night. On the third day one of the two tractors broke down slowing the work. A storm was predicted for the late evening and the picking had to be done by then. Summer storms can be vicious, damaging the fruit so much that it can become unusable so Franck, Anna and Lucien and a half dozen friends and neighbours who'd come to help toiled all day. As night fell the picking machine was still lumbering along the last few rows its headlights flickering crazily up and down as it stumbled over uneven ground. The air was thick, humid and it felt even hotter than it had in the day, so hot that when they stopped briefly no-one felt hungry, just tired and thirsty and keen to get on. By 10pm they were done, the last grapes harvested before the storm broke. Beneath purple clouds and with lightning flickering across the hills to the south the last tractor load came in just as the rain started; huge warm gobbets of rain splashing into the dust. Lucien and Anna stood outside faces up into the rain. Oh the relief of the sudden coolness. In the winery it was still warm and muggy; squashed grapes and spilled grape juice had made the flagstones slippery. The last of the crushed red grapes went into two big stainless steel fermentation tanks, the boxes and trays were washed out and stacked, the floor hosed down. Franck and the pickers went gratefully home. Victor however would sleep on a camp bed as he had for each night of the Vendange, as he had during every Vendange for the last forty years. There was too much as stake to leave unsupervised the fermenting grapes, the precious results of a year's care.

"It's ten o'clock let's go and get something to eat" said Anna leading Lucien through a door in the corner of the winery that led into the main part of the chateau. At the centre of the ground floor of the chateau a large cobbled area at the foot of a stone staircase opened onto the courtyard beyond through a pair of doors three metres high. High enough for a horseman to come in and dismount indoors. The dogs were waiting by the doors jumping up to be scratched behind the ears before racing off into the darkness and rain whilst Anna and Lucien went through into the kitchen. Anna flopped down into an old leather armchair by the fireplace, a fireplace big enough to spit roast a whole boar, the centrepiece of a kitchen the size of a tennis court. She signalled to Lucien to sit in the other.

"It may not seem appropriate when we have been making wine but what I really need is a huge whisky and ice. How about you?"

"Me too, I'll get them." He could see a row of bottles of single malt whisky on a shelf.

"Three fingers please, your fingers are probably bigger than mine so it's best for you to do it." She shook off her sandals stained with grape juice and freed her hair from a scarf that had held it in control all day. She shook her head and her hair cascaded down onto her shoulders. "I love the hurly burly of the Vendange but even more I love it when it's finished. What would you like to eat? Would bread and cheese and a peach do?"

So they sat with their tumblers of whiskey and torn bread and lumps of cheese nursing their aching limbs, silently listening to the rain sluicing noisily down the gutters and gullies outside.

"Christ! Where are the dogs? They'll be soaked." Anna suddenly exclaimed.

They were not in the courtyard and there was no response to whistling or shouting their names from the door. Rain was falling incessantly and lightning flared amongst the clouds. Then between the rumbles of thunder Lucien heard a distant yowl from somewhere beyond the vines.

"Do you have a torch? I'll go and look for them."

"I'm coming too."

Twenty minutes later they found Marguerite the bitch on a bank at the edge of the vineyards beside a scrub choked stand of trees that lay between the vineyard and the river. She led them slipping and sliding down the muddy slope and into the wood, brambles pulling at their clothes until they found her mate lying on his side whimpering, gnawing at his hind leg. His white fur was stained with blood. Lucien crouched down beside him.

"He's caught in a trap, a wire snare."

"The bastards; those things are illegal."

Whilst Anna held the dog's head, whispering pacifying sounds into its ear, Lucien managed to untwist and loosen the loop of rusty wire that was snared around its leg freeing it. The dog stood up unsteadily.

"The skin wounds are actually quite small. He's got a limp but it looks as if he'll get home okay" and so the four of them, Anna and Lucien hand in hand, the two dogs, the bitch stopping from time to time to nuzzle the neck of the limping dog, went back through wet vines and mud and rain to the chateau and in through the still open doors into the dismount hall. The thunder was closer now, almost continuous, accompanied by sheets of lightning every few seconds. Lucien and Anna soaked and muddy and the two wet dogs were lit by the lightning as if on a stage, the whole bedraggled tableau reflected in the full height, gray flecked mirrors that lined the walls.

Lucien and Anna took off their shoes and the dogs slunk off to curl up together on their heap of blankets in the kitchen. Lucien looked at Anna, her clothes heavy with water, her hair wet and dishevelled, plastered to her face and neck.

"This is very Bronte-esque" said Lucien, "Is there a bathroom, hot water, dry towels and a big soft bed at the top of this staircase?"

"There is but I was hoping for less Bronte sisters and more Errol Flynn!"

"I'll do my best!" And he led her up the stairs, their journey marked by wet footprints on each stone step.

The next morning Lucien woke, aching and confused deep under a duvet. Something was licking his hand; it was the dog, its wet muzzle thrust into his palm, big, sad eyes willing him awake. Lucien was lying in the centre of a four-poster bed, Anna had gone. Above him yellow silk hangings drawn up like the apex of a tent. The curtains were open and the shutters latched back, one window ajar. Outside a cloudless, pale blue sky with no trace of the storm of the night before. Pushing the door open with her foot Anna came in carrying a tray, two cups and a pot of coffee. She set them on the bedside table, straightened the duvet and sat on an upholstered damask chair beside the bed, like someone visiting an invalid.

"Did you sleep well?"

"Exquisitely well thank you;" he sat up and took the proffered coffee. "Aching all over though."

"Well you've had a hectic few days with every manual labour a vineyard and Franck can throw at you and now you've done everything, even slept with the chatelaine, which was very enjoyable, thank you!"

"It was." He kissed her hand. There was a pause.

"Maybe I'm getting old" she said "but actually it's the warmth, the cosiness, the nearness that I like. It's almost the same need as a child's. It's what I've missed most since Hector died. Physical contact is a very basic necessity – like food and drink."

"Just ask, any time" said Lucien amazed at how much more at ease he felt with this than with Lily's narcissistic needs for sex and nakedness; a fantasy that for him had been exorcised in Paris.

"How's the dog?" he asked.

"He's fine; they've been out this morning and he doesn't even have a limp today."

And so without any formality Lucien began to spend much of each day and most of his nights with Anna. In love? No, just happy together. Love is after all a collective noun for half a dozen ingredients as well as passion and comfort. Trust, interdependence and more. Their relationship was simply friendship and the comfort of a shared bed. Could he trust her? It never occurred to him to think that he ought not to. There was no ice pick under the bed and they'd talked about Hector's death. He'd stood up from his chair after lunch, dropped his blood pressure, had a stroke and had fallen over backwards. A heavy, tall man he stove in the back of his skull as he hit the ground. The injury wasn't what killed him but the gendarmes were correctly suspicious until the full post-mortem result was known a week after his death. Plenty of time for a small community like St. Jean to spin a spider's web of exciting presumptions to enmesh the beautiful chatelaine for ever.

A few days later Lucien was lying in bed at the Chateau, reading.

"You're very cool Lucien" said Anna. She was standing in front of a mirror wearing a green silk kimono brushing her hair; long generous sweeps from the top of her head to the curling ends on her shoulders.

"What do you mean?"

"You don't seem needy. It would be nice to think you had a really passionate need for me. I'm not sure what to make of you. You're a considerate man, you're keen to be kind and gentle, adaptable to what you think I want. Don't misunderstand me you can be passionate, I've got your thumb prints in my *poignees d'amour,* to prove it! No it's just that you are always so nice! I need someone to have rows with; there's nothing I like more than a flaming row that ends up in bed. I can't handle polite quiet relationships. Since Hector died I've had no one to have rows with except Franck."

"And do those rows end up in bed too?"

"Of course not!" but Lucien sensed she was lying.

"So perhaps you and I are simply not compatible" he said.

"Maybe so dear Lucien but in a place as small as St Jean, at the moment it's the best match either of us is likely to make so let's just enjoy it whilst we can shall we." Slipping out of her kimono she walked over to the bed and taking Lucien's head in her hands bit his ear so hard it could have drawn blood.

It was clear that becoming a wine maker wasn't an option and that was brought to a head when several days later Anna offered to merge his vineyards with the chateau's and share the business. He wouldn't need to know how to make wine, Victor and Franck could do that and a merged business could afford to hire another person to help the ageing Victor. But Lucien, fond as he was of Anna could see potential hazards in this. Suppose they fell out, as they might. She had a fiery temperament and a strong will. One morning he'd found two small scars between the ribs beside her right breast.

"One's a stab wound and the other's where they put a tube in to drain out the blood" she explained.

"A stab wound?"

"Hector did it but I'd started the fight. It was in the kitchen and we'd both picked up knives."

"For God's sake Anna – you could have died – what were you arguing about?"

"Same as usual – his womanizing. He'd been almost bragging about it and I just flipped."

"Why at that moment?" asked Lucien, this was all outside his experience.

"I can't remember. Normally I'd just put up with it, I'd like to be able to say that it was because marriage is about companionship not ownership but in truth I probably tolerated it most of the time because I'd told myself that it was really me that he loved and he'd always come back."

"And he did."

"He did – he was never with any of his conquests for more than a night at a time, occasionally two. Sometimes it was just a couple of hours in the afternoon on some transparent pretext. He'd always come back as if nothing untoward had happened."

"Did you discuss it?"

"Normally no."

"Did you want to?"

"No, not really, it was easiest just to pretend it wasn't happening or was unimportant; it's so middle class to complain about infidelity. He once said it was just a hobby, less time consuming than golf and cheaper than running a yacht."

"Didn't he show any contrition?"

"No, he seemed to think it was his right. He had a saying *'infidelity is an existential obligation'. "*

Lucien felt the shock. Of course! The note signed "H", Diana's solitary trips to St. Jean to 'recuperate'. Not just Henry Lightwood but Hector too, so who else? He didn't discuss this with Anna; he simply added it to the enlarging dossier of things he kept to himself. Lucien had never been a man to keep a stash of secrets, he'd always shared them with Diana but now he was accumulating a whole portfolio of them. It bemused him that he felt it made him stronger , helped him establish his own territory as an individual. Odd that. He'd not told Lucy about Anna and certainly not about the weekend with Lily. Lucy would, of course, guess that there was another woman; if she had not done that already she'd do so when they were in London and face to face over dinner.

Monday October 20th. Decisions

Lucien was sitting at a desk in the library of the Chateau. A fine Louis XV writing bureau of the type where the writing flap folds up and locks away your papers and letters and all the little secrets you have in its tiny drawers and shelves. Hector must have sat here looking sideways out to the open courtyard beyond the row of windows that stretched from ceiling to floor. Lucien wondered whether it was at this desk that the note to Diana had been penned. "*Infidelity is an existential obligation*". Now however Lucien had the future to concentrate on, not the past.

After breakfast a week earlier he'd phoned Julian Scantlebury because apart from confirming his safe arrival in France and thanking him for his advice he had not spoken to Julian for almost a month. He knew that at this hour of the morning Julian would probably still be in his dressing gown and would be sitting with his third or fourth cup of coffee scanning the morning papers in his apartment in the Albany off Picadilly.

"Hello Lucien dear boy. I'd presumed you were dead or gone off to live in China. How are you? Any news on the Diana front?"

Lucien brought him up to date – it didn't take long; he and Diana were now separated. That's all there was to it.

"And the other stuff? I read that your nasty Libyan was assassinated."

"Yes he was. Everything could go back to normal from the end of October, so I've got to decide how to lead my life in the future. Anyway what have you been up to?"

"Oh, dreadful, dreadful. I've spent all morning recovering."

"From what?"

"Last evening. The editor insisted I cover a concert in Portsmouth. Part of his project to show there is a cultural life outside London and I can tell you dear boy there isn't. It was awful .... Not just the music but Portsmouth too, not a sailor to be found anywhere! The recital was abysmal beyond words. Half of it was a specially commissioned piece to celebrate 'Summer by the Sea' a squeaky woodwind ensemble and a caterwauling soprano. Shrill, dissonant crap. The soprano was so out of contact with the players they could have been doing different pieces. And as for the self-justificatory programme notes they were longer than the bloody score. I guarantee there will never be another performance. I hope not anyway. Christ the things I do for art! And after all that the editor refused my piece because it was too rude. Enough of that though I want you to tell me your plans. I can't believe you're thinking of staying where you are....You must be sick of the bloody French countryside by now.... It's so parochial dear, don't you wish you were here in London?"

"No I don't. I like the pace of life here. There's no pressure, no difficult decisions to make. At the moment I'd be happy to stay."

"Oh for God's sake Lucien you'll get bored with the place.... There'll be no-one to challenge you.... Your intellect will shrivel to the size of a raisin.... Simple romantic affection for it all won't sustain you for long.... You're just enjoying an overdue rest.... It'll pass you'll see. What are you going to do? Get some chickens and a goat and grow radishes? For God's sake! Are you going to pretend to be a farmer? Marie Antoinette tried that and look what happened to her! But then I expect you won't notice the wasted days because you'll be joining the other alcohol based life-forms, all those expats living for the next bottle of cheap booze.... Sorry Lucien I've said my piece but I fear for you I really do."

"That's kind of you Julian but you really don't need to. I'm very happy here. I have good friends and I'm making new ones."

"Aha! I take it that means there's a woman! Right? After all that mumping and moaning about Diana you've simply gone and sold your soul to a different woman – that's it isn't it? I know it's your business but for God's sake be sensible. Find someone nice to sleep with by all means but give us all a break Lucien, don't jump into another long term relationship just because the old one's temporarily gone sour. You give yourself up to people too easily."

"You're right Julian but I've not had as many relationships as you have over the years so a new one is exciting in a way I'd forgotten about, but I won't let it cloud my decision about what to do next. In fact I've pretty much decided not to go back to the RUH, there are lots of keen youngsters who can grapple more effectively with that. The UN have offered me a part time job overseeing some projects from their Geneva office. They tend to be awfully bureaucratic so that will offer all the managerial challenges I could want. If I were to do that together with my private work at the Clinic and keep on with my work for the Royal College I guess I'd be busy and content. That's shaping up as my conclusion."

"And the woman?"

"Not sure yet, we'll see how it goes."

And so there it was, he'd made his decision effortlessly in the course of the conversation. The speed and the neatness of it intrigued him. He'd had a long conversation with a poet once, he and the poet were fairly drunk. The poet said that many of the lines which most pleased him seemed to come from no-where, suddenly appearing fully formed on the page. Clearly there was some place deep in the brain where these things were worked on subconsciously by a million little neuronal helpers who only delivered the text when it was polished and ready for use. At which point Lucien remembered the poet falling off the chair and banging his head on the table which apparently happened regularly. Presumably the little neuronal helpers were unfazed by this.

By whatever process Lucien's decision had been made there was now the hard work of arranging it. Lily Harper Smith had confirmed that the GMC had notified her that his suspension from the medical register would end on October 31st so he was free to return to work from November 1st. Not a whisper of an apology though from them or the DPP about their crude and dilatory handling of the matter. Anyway he'd put all that behind him. His laptop was open on the desk and connected to the Chateau's wi-fi network, he had a phone beside him and a list of people he needed to contact.

First there was Pam, dear faithful Pam his secretary at the hospital.

"If I were to resign from the hospital how would you react?"

"I'd say you'd made a good decision."

"And?"

"I'd say that I wanted to get out of full time work too so the timing was perfect."

"And if I asked you to stay on as my part time personal assistant, details to be arranged to suit you, how would you feel about that?"

"Very happy!"

This was a good start. If Lucien was to lead a life of odds and ends here and there he'd need Pam to keep it in order.

Next was the Medical School. He phoned the Secretary, a red faced, red haired Scotsman called Donald McDonald who always wore tweeds and would pace up and down his office shouting at the speaker-phone on his desk. He was much less supportive than Pam.

"But it would not be good for the Medical School Professor. All the papers you publish help our Research Assessment Exercise enormously. Enormously Professor and you know how critical the RAE results are for our funding." Lucien had anticipated this.

"I'm sure I'll keep on publishing and if you'd like to keep me on as Emeritus Professor with just the occasional session at the hospital your well known sleight of hand could probably arrange for all that work to be included in the RAE."

"You're a canny one Professor" retorted McDonald "It'll be yer Scots blood."

So that too was sorted out, after which Lucien sent a coolly worded e-mail to Henry Lightwood, now the stand-in CEO, announcing that he was resigning from his Honorary Consultant post with immediate effect. He copied it to Constance Jefferson Jones the Director of Human Relations and to Harvey Bauerman who had replaced him as Clinical Director. He would talk on the phone one by one to the people in the organization that he valued and cherished to explain what was going on.

Next he spoke to the WHO Office in Geneva about the contract they had offered him and was delighted to discover that his old friend Mohammed El-Hammedi from Tripoli would be on the committee that he'd be chairing.

It was all shaping up well and his enthusiasm for going back to work gathered pace with each call. Later having confirmed with the Brigadier, the CEO of the Clinic for Women and Children, that he'd be welcomed back he had a long conversation with the secretary who dealt with his patients. There was a big backlog of work and she was pleased to be able to start giving the patients dates though there was one particular case with which the Professor was familiar where she thought he might wish first to reconsider whether to keep her on as one of his patients.

By midday he was almost done. All that remained was to talk to Lucy about what he'd decided. He would do that this evening from the privacy of the Vieux Tour.

Anna came into the library and stood behind him looking at the computer screen and the sheaf of written notes on the desk.

"You're going back to London aren't you. I'd guessed you would and I'm happy for you. It's the right decision. I'll get a bottle of wine and we can celebrate. Not celebrate the fact that you'll be leaving but the fact that you've got your life back." She returned with two glasses and a bottle of white wine in an ice bucket. They sat by the open doors, the dogs asleep on the terrace outside, the spray sparkling on the fountain in the centre of the courtyard whilst a bird standing in the shallow pool below fluttered its wings in the falling water. Beyond the courtyard the vines were showing the first glimpses of autumn russet and gold. Beyond the vineyards hills receded into the hazy distance where the sky was lilac, above that Wedgewood blue then cobalt blue just now punctuated by a V shaped skein of cranes migrating south. Lucien began to wonder if he'd made the right decision.

"I feel embarrassed to be leaving."

"Don't be" said Anna refilling his glass, "we're friends, nothing with any more commitment than that. I'll miss your company but that doesn't mean I disagree with your decision. Where will you live in London?"

"I'll have to find a flat somewhere."

"I have a little mews house off Montagu Square that you could use. George used to live there but he's got his own place now. You'd be walking distance from your College and from Harley Street. I could visit you to make sure you were happy!"

Lucien having so recently believed that he'd resolved his dilemmas did not know how to respond. He realized the dangers.

"It's very sweet of you Anna. Can I think about it?"

Friday October 31st . London. King's College Hospital

Lucy was sitting in the visitors' room at the hospital waiting; alone in the room listening to the alien sounds of the ward outside. The clanks and clatters, squeaky wheels going by and the mutter of conversations she couldn't quite make out. She'd forgotten to bring anything to read, expecting her visit to be brief but they weren't ready yet. There were things that still needed doing and forms to be completed, pills to be brought from the Hospital Pharmacy. The TV in the corner of the room was turned off and all there was to read was yesterday's "Daily Mirror" and a copy of the hospital's "Major Incident Procedure Manual" attached to the wall by a length of string but Lucy had plenty to think about as she reflected on the last two months. They'd been filled with unwelcome events, her parents' separation, the cancer diagnosis but during the time she'd developed a new and better relationship with her mother. Had she been asked about it two months earlier she'd have simply said "it's fine, just fine, we get on well together. Much better than when I was younger." When she was young she had hated her mother though not for any specific reason that she could describe, the hate was just a daily fact of life. She always wanted to argue with her mother or shout at her or if not that then be in a different room. It was not that her mother had been cold or distant or overcritical or overbearing. Even now she had no idea what the problem was, or indeed whether there actually was one. She was just unhappy and wanted to blame someone. Fortunately she never became so miserable as to self-harm or stop eating. The real problem was the drugs and that had all started in the dark corners of noisy clubs in dirty cellars and abandoned warehouses that a boy-friend had taken her to. Try this. Try that. Have some more. Until there was no escape. The more her parents attempted to intervene the harder she kicked against them. It was only Robin's death and maybe the simple physiology of getting older that got her free. Even then she felt excluded within the family. Not unloved, just not within the family inner circle for she'd felt her mother's best quality love was reserved for her grandfather, her brother and her father; three men – how could she compete? Even the death of her brother had not broken the circle but a month ago

284

discovering her mother's adultery, talking to her about it, trying to engineer a solution had put her if not in command then at least on a level with her. They'd both sensed it and in the last month she and her mother had at last become close as friends and confidantes. Lucy had been openly angry with her mother that the Paris rapprochement she had so carefully orchestrated had come to naught but her mother had become so fixed on a vision of independence that she seemed hardly to hear.

Then a fortnight ago Lucy had arrived at the house in Dulwich to find some of the windows open, the radio on, the garden door open but no sign of her mother. She'd gone into the garden and found her crouched on the grass almost out of sight behind some bushes. She seemed to have intended to do the weeding for she had her gardening gloves on and a wickerwork trug on the grass beside her but now her head was in her hands. She'd looked up red eyed and had obviously been weeping. Lucy sat on the grass beside her and wrapped an arm around her; she could feel tears of sympathy welling up but managed to hold them back.

"What is it Mum? What's wrong? Is it the cancer thing?"

Her mother shook her head and stabbed the trowel viciously into the soil over and over again, then lapsed into a tense silence. She was wearing jeans and an old grey sweater, her hair was tangled; she looked to Lucy very old.

"No Lucy it's not the cancer, it's me. It's all come to me how horribly I've screwed things up through my own selfishness and pig headedness. I mistook adultery for freedom, worse than that I thought it might cure the anger and the loneliness. actually it's made it worse. Maybe if Robin were still alive none of this would have happened, we never dealt with his death did we? We just pretended that because we were all together as a family we could behave as if the hurt had gone away. But it hadn't had it Lucy ? And I've been so cruel to your father, he didn't deserve that and I don't deserve him."

"But of course you do Mum."

"No I don't. I just hope I die of this cancer quickly and then he can find someone else, someone who can make him happy."

That was a week ago, and then her mother had come into the hospital for her operation.

A ward aide came into the visitors' room. Thin and hunched, her pink floral housecoat many sizes too large for her.

"Would you like a cup of tea love?"

"Thank you, yes I would."

"How many sugars?"

"None, thanks."

"You look anxious love ; are you waiting to be admitted?"

"No, just here waiting to collect my Mum, she's had an operation."

"Oh dear! Well never mind they're very good here. I'm sure she'll be alright. Would you like me to ask the nurses if you can sit with her?

"No thanks, it's not necessary, I'm waiting for someone to join me so I'll stay here; but the cup of tea would be welcome."

When Diana had heard that she had cancer she'd asked Lucy not to tell Lucien about it, or about the impending operation.

" It's me who set this course" she'd said "and I mustn't expect your father to come rushing to support me just because I've got cancer."

"Why not Mum, why not respect his beliefs?"

"What beliefs?"

"Love, unconditional love."

"Don't be daft Lucy. That's so old fashioned."

"You mean it's OK to be a modern, independent woman living the feminist fall out; aggressive driving, public drunkenness, no strings sex but deny what's sustained relationships for centuries." Lucy realized this made her sound hopelessly staid. She didn't care.

"Even if I wanted it there's not much chance of no strings sex after they've taken half my boob out and I'm bald from the chemotherapy. Also there's nothing wrong with my driving and I'm hardly ever drunk in public."

"Don't duck the question Mum."

But Diana was adamant so Lucy had to rely on her own judgment. She'd blurted out the facts to her father when he'd phoned, very animated, to say that all the uncertainties about his future were now resolved and he'd be returning to work and to London. He was obviously happy at that and she felt sick at heart telling him about her mother's cancer. He listened in silence, stunned. He asked her practical medical questions, noted the name of the surgeon treating Diana and said it was fortunate that he'd be returning to London but he was obviously, though silently, distraught. Another pause.

"And how are you Lucy? How are you coping?"

"Yes, OK thanks Dad. I have a very supportive new boyfriend – an old one actually – you'll remember him. George Ponsonby from the Chateau in St Jean. I don't know how he got my number but I'm glad he did. He might even turn out to be 'The One'. The most important person now though is Mum."

That was all a week ago.

Diana had had the two tube drains pulled out, her wounds redressed, had got out of the awful smock nightie the hospital forced her to wear and put on her normal clothes. She'd combed her hair and put on lipstick. She had been given letters for her GP and more pamphlets and a follow up appointment and packets of pills in case she had pain and at last she was free to leave. At the other end of the ward she could see her surgeon and the ward sister talking to a tall distinguished looking man deeply tanned, smartly dressed in a blue linen jacket and a white shirt without a tie, his hair a little long and curling at the ends. It was Lucien, she barely recognised him. Lucy was there too. She hugged Lucy and squeezed Lucien's hand.

"I thought you were in France. What are you doing here?"

"I've come to take you home. Are you ready for that ?"

"Absolutely!"

It was a sunny morning after a rainy night, the streets still mirrored with puddles as he walked up Harley Street to the London Clinic for Women and Children. Seven thirty, a good hour to start the day, a straight forward day. Or at least as straight forward as it ever is. He sprang purposefully up the stone steps of the entrance and paused as the perfectly polished glass doors slid gently apart.

"Good morning, Professor" said the receptionist,

"Good morning Professor McCulloch" said the nurse in the corridor

"Good morning Professor" said the porter in the lift.

He emerged on the 5th floor of the clinic, a floor completely occupied by operating theatres neatly sequenced along the roof line of the clinic, their big glass windows invisible from the street and not spoiling the fine Portland stone facade of the building.

Lucian slipped into the changing room and donned his blue theatre pyjamas, declined a cup of coffee and went through the door on the other side into the clean area of the theatre suite.

"Good morning Professor, nice to have you back" said the theatre Sister

"Good morning Sister, good morning all, lovely day, It's good to be back."

The doors from the anaesthetic room were pushed apart announcing the opening scene of the familiar drama. The anaesthetist, Dr. Gwyn Davies, stood holding the doors open with his outstretched arms; Samson and the pillars of the temple.

"Are you ready?" asked the anaesthetist, rhetorically, as he always did "The Patient is ready."

Behind the anaesthetist in the bright halogen glow of the anaesthetic room a woman lay neatly on the centre of the trolley, an endo-tracheal tube in place, two drips and an oxygen mask..

The anaesthetist and the anaesthetic technician wheeled in the trolley and set the patient onto the operating table.

Lucien McCulloch went to the stainless steel trough in the Scrub Up Room and began to scrub, carefully lathering his hands with pink

Chlorhexidine soap from the wall dispenser. Gwyn Davies, the anaesthetist came to the doorway,

"Well Lucien it's very nice to have you back, my wife has been complaining about my drop in income since I stopped having your Monday morning patients to anaesthetise but why the hell did you take this woman in again? I hadn't realized that the patient they've labelled as Mrs. Noorah bint Mohammed is the same as the lady whose husband wanted to kill us. Anyway I thought he was dead.

"He is, but she's remarried."

"Already?"

"To one of his brothers. It's a tradition."

"So now you are going to attempt to reverse her sterilization so this whole charade can start again! You must be mad and I must be mad to be part of it."

Lucien smiled at him consolingly,

"I don't know what you're worried about Gwyn; all went well before, we're both still alive. Anyway I always try to fit in with women's wishes, maybe that's my problem. Shall we start?"